A SECRET AFFAIR

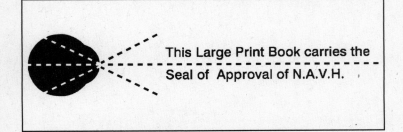

This Large Print Book carries the
Seal of Approval of N.A.V.H.

A Secret Affair

Mary Balogh

THORNDIKE PRESS

A part of Gale, Cengage Learning

GALE
CENGAGE Learning·

Detroit • New York • San Francisco • New Haven, Conn • Waterville, Maine • London

GALE
CENGAGE Learning™

Thorndike Press® Large Print Basic.
The text of this Large Print edition is unabridged.
Other aspects of the book may vary from the original edition.
Set in 16 pt. Plantin.

LIBRARY OF CONGRESS CATALOGING-IN-PUBLICATION DATA

Balogh, Mary.
   A secret affair / by Mary Balogh.
      p. cm. — (Thorndike Press large print basic)
   ISBN-13: 978-1-4104-2762-5
   ISBN-10: 1-4104-2762-5
   1. Large type books. I. Title.
PR6052.A465S426 2010b
823'.914—dc22   2010014863

Published in 2010 by arrangement with Delacorte Press, a division of Random House, Inc.

Printed in the United States of America
1 2 3 4 5 6 7 14 13 12 11 10

A Secret Affair

CHAPTER 1

Hannah Reid, Duchess of Dunbarton, was free at last. Free of the burden of a ten-year marriage, and free of the endlessly tedious year of deep mourning that had succeeded the death of the duke, her husband.

It was a freedom that had been a long time coming. It was a freedom well worth celebrating.

She had married the duke after a five-day acquaintance — his grace, all impatience to be wed, had procured a special license rather than wait for the banns to be read — when she was nineteen and he was somewhere in his seventies. No one seemed certain of exactly where in his seventies that had been, though some said it was perilously close to eighty. At the time of her marriage, the duchess was a breathtakingly lovely girl, with a slender, lithe figure, eyes that rivaled a summer sky for blueness, a bright, eager face made for smiling, and long, wavy tresses that were almost white in their blondness — a shimmering white. The duke, on the other hand, had a body and face and head that showed all the ravages of age that time and years of hard living could possibly have piled upon them. And he suffered from gout. And from a heart that could no longer be relied upon to continue beating with steady regularity.

She married him for his money, of course, expecting to be a very rich widow indeed within a matter of a few short years at most. She *was* a rich widow now, quite fabulously wealthy, in fact, though she had had to wait longer than expected for the freedom to enjoy her riches to the full.

The old duke had worshiped the ground she walked upon, to use the old cliché. He had heaped so many costly clothes upon her person that she would have suffocated beneath their weight if she had ever tried to wear them all at once. A guest room next to her dressing room at Dunbarton House on Hanover Square in London had been converted into a second dressing room merely to accommodate all the silks and satins and furs — among other garments and accessories — that had been worn once, perhaps twice, before being discarded for something newer. And the duke had had not one, not two, not even three, but *four* safes built into the walls of his own bedchamber to safeguard all the jewels with which he gifted his beloved over the years, though she was perfectly free to come and fetch whichever of them she chose to wear at any time.

He had been a doting, indulgent husband.

The duchess was always gorgeously dressed. And she was always bedecked with jewels, ostentatiously large ones, usually diamonds. She wore them in her hair, in the lobes of her ears, at her bosom, on her wrists, on more than one of the fingers of each hand.

The duke showed off his prize wherever he went, beaming with pride and adoration as he looked up at her. In his prime he would have been taller than she, but age had bent him and a cane supported him, and for much of his time he sat. His duchess did not stray far from his side when they were together, even when they were at a ball and prospective partners abounded. She tended him with her characteristic half-smile playing always about her lovely lips. She was always the picture of wifely devotion on such occasions. Nobody could deny that.

When the duke could not go out himself — and it became increasingly difficult for him to do so as the years went on — then other men escorted his duchess to the social events with which the *ton* amused itself whenever it was in town in large numbers. There were three in particular — Lord Hardingraye, Sir Bradley Bentley, and Viscount Zimmer — all handsome, elegant, charming gentlemen. It was common knowledge that they enjoyed her company and that she enjoyed theirs. And no one was ever in any doubt of what was included in that enjoyment. The only detail people wondered about — and wonder they did, of course, without ever reaching a satisfactory conclusion — was whether all that pleasure was enjoyed with the duke's knowledge or without.

There were some who even dared wonder if it was all done with the duke's *blessing.* But deliciously scandalous as it might have been to believe so, most people actually liked the duke — especially as he was now elderly and therefore deserving of pity — and preferred to see him as a poor wronged old man. The same people liked to refer to the duchess as *that diamond-laden gold digger,* often with the addition of *who is no better than she ought to be.* Those people tended to be female.

And then the duchess's dazzling social life

10

and scandalous loves and dreary incarceration in a union with an aged, ailing husband had all ended abruptly with the duke's ultimately sudden demise from a heart seizure early one morning. Though it was not nearly as early in the marriage as the duchess had hoped and expected, of course. She had her fortune at last, but she had paid dearly for it. She had paid with her youth. She was twenty-nine when he died, thirty when she left off her mourning soon after Christmas at Copeland, her country home in Kent that the duke had bought for her so that she would not have to leave when he died and his nephew took over his title and all his entailed properties. Copeland *Manor* was its full name, though the house was more mansion than the name implied and was surrounded by a correspondingly large park.

And so, at the age of thirty, the best years of her youth behind her, the Duchess of Dunbarton was free at last. And wealthy beyond belief. And very ready to celebrate her freedom. As soon as Easter had come and gone, she moved to London and settled in for the Season. It was at Dunbarton House she settled, the new duke being a genial man of middle years who preferred tramping about the country counting his sheep to being in town sitting in the Upper House of Parliament listening to his peers prosing on forever about matters that might be of crucial importance to the country and even the world but were of no interest whatsoever to him. Politicians were all prize bores, he would tell anyone who cared to listen. And being a man without a wife, he had no one to point out to him that sitting in the Upper House was only the most minor of reasons for the spring gathering of the *ton* in London. The duchess might occupy Dunbarton House and have a ball there every night with his blessing. And so he informed her. Provided, that was, she did not send him the bills.

That last was a comment typical of his rather parsimonious nature. The duchess had no need to send her bills to anyone. She was enormously wealthy in her own right. She could pay them herself.

She might be past her youth, and really thirty *was* a quite nasty age for a woman, but she was still incredibly beautiful. No one could deny that, even though there were a few who would have done so if they could. Indeed, she was probably more beautiful now than she had been at the age of nineteen. She had gained just a little weight during the intervening years, and she had gained it in all the right places and none in any of the wrong places. She was still slender, but she was now deliciously curvaceous. Her face, less bright and eager than it had been when she was a girl, had settled pleasingly into its perfect bone structure and complexion. She smiled frequently, though her characteristic smile was half arrogant, half alluring, and altogether mysterious, as though she smiled at something inside herself rather than at the outside world. Her eyes had acquired a certain droop of the eyelids that suggested bedchambers and dreams and more secrets. And her hair, at the hands of experts, was always immaculately styled — but in such a way that it looked as if it might tumble into luxuriant disarray at any moment. The fact that it never did made it only the more intriguing.

Her hair was her best feature, many people said. Except for her eyes, perhaps. Or her figure. Or her teeth, which were very white and perfectly formed and perfectly aligned with one another.

All this was how the *ton* saw the Duchess of Dunbarton and her marriage to the elderly duke and her return to London as a wealthy widow who was free at last.

No one *knew,* of course. No one had been

13

inside that marriage to know how it had worked, or not worked. No one but the duke and duchess themselves, that was. The duke had become more and more reclusive in his final years, and the duchess had had hordes of acquaintances but no close friend that anyone knew of. She had been content to hide in plain sight within the air of luxury and mystery she exuded.

The *ton,* which had never tired of wondering about her during the ten years of her marriage, wondered again now after a one-year interval. She was a favorite topic in drawing rooms and at dinner tables, in fact. The *ton* wondered what she would do with her life now that she was free. She had been Miss Nobody from Nowhere when she reeled in the great prize of the Duke of Dunbarton and persuaded him to marry for the first time in his life.

What would she do next?

Someone else wondered what the duchess would do with her future, but she actually did it in the hearing of the one person who could satisfy her curiosity.

Barbara Leavensworth had been the duchess's friend since they were both children living in the same neighborhood in Lincolnshire, Barbara as the vicar's daughter, Hannah as the daughter of a landowner of respectable birth and moderate means. Barbara still lived in the same village with her parents, though they had moved out of the vicarage a year ago when her father retired. Barbara had recently become betrothed to the new vicar. They were to marry in August.

The two childhood friends had remained close, even if not geographically. The duchess had never gone back to her former home after her marriage, and though Barbara had been frequently invited to stay with her, she had not often accepted, and even when she had, she had not stayed as long as Hannah would have liked. She had been too intimidated by the duke. And so they had kept up their friendship by letter. They had written to each other, usually at great length, at least once a week for eleven years.

Now Barbara had accepted an invitation to spend some time in London with the duchess. They would shop for her bride clothes in the only place in England worth shopping *in,* the duchess had written as an inducement. Which was all very well, Barbara had thought when she read the letter, shaking her head in slight exasperation, when one had pots of money, as Hannah did and she most certainly did *not.* But

Hannah needed the company now that she was alone, and *she* rather fancied a few weeks of exploring churches and museums to her heart's content before finally settling down. The Reverend Newcombe, her betrothed, encouraged her to go and enjoy herself and lend her support to the poor widow, her friend. And then, when she decided that she would go, he insisted that she take an astonishingly large sum of money with which to buy herself some pretty dresses and perhaps a bonnet or two. And her parents, who thought a month or so with Hannah, of whom they had always been inordinately fond, would be a wonderful thing for their daughter before she settled to a sober life as the vicar's wife, pressed a largish sum of spending money on her too.

Barbara felt quite decadently rich when she arrived at Dunbarton House after a journey during which it had felt as though every bone in her body had been jolted into a new, less comfortable position.

Hannah was waiting for her inside the hall, and they hugged and squealed and exclaimed over each other for several minutes, both talking, neither listening, and laughing over nothing at all except the sheer happiness of being together again. The *ton,* if they could have seen Hannah, might have been forgiven if they had not recognized her. Her cheeks were flushed, her eyes wide and bright, her smile broad, her voice almost shrill with excitement and delight. There was not the merest suggestion of mystery about her.

And then she became aware of the silent figure of the housekeeper in the background, and she relinquished Barbara to her competent care. She paced aimlessly in the drawing room while her friend was taken up to her room to wash her hands and face and change her dress and comb her hair and otherwise use up half an hour before being brought down for tea.

She was looking her neat, tranquil self again. Dear, dependable Barbara, whom she loved more than anyone else still living, Hannah thought as she beamed at her and crossed the room to hug her again.

"I am so, *so* happy that you came, Babs," she said. She laughed. "Just in case you did not understand that when you arrived."

"Well, I did think you might have shown just a *little* enthusiasm," Barbara said, and they both laughed again.

Hannah suddenly tried to remember when she had last laughed, and could not recall an occasion. No matter. One was not meant to laugh while one was in mourning. Some-one might call one heartless.

They talked without ceasing for all of an hour, this time both listening and talking, before Barbara asked the question that had been uppermost in her mind since the Duke of Dunbarton's death, though she had not broached it in any of her letters.

"What are you going to *do* now, Hannah?" she asked, leaning forward in her chair. "You must be dreadfully lonely without the duke. You adored each other."

Barbara was probably one of the few people in London, or in all of England for that matter, who truly believed such a startling notion. Perhaps the *only* one, in fact.

"We did," Hannah said with a sigh. She spread one hand on her lap and regarded the rings she wore on three of her well-manicured fingers. She smoothed her hand over the fine white muslin of her dress. "I do miss him. I keep thinking of all sorts of absurdities I simply must rush home to share with him, only to remember that he is not here any longer waiting to hear them."

"But I know," Barbara said, her voice earnest in its sympathy, "that he suffered dreadfully with his gout and that his heart was giving him much pain and trouble in his last years. I daresay it was a blessing that he went quickly in the end."

Hannah felt inappropriately amused. Barbara would make an excellent vicar's wife if her head was full of platitudes like that one.

"We should all be so fortunate when the time comes," she said. "But I daresay his heart seizure was helped along by a too hearty indulgence in beefsteak and claret the night before he died. He had been warned off such extravagances ten years or more before I even met him and every year after that — oh, *at least* once a year. He was forever saying that his headstone ought to have been already gathering moss in the graveyard when I was rocking my dolls to sleep in the nursery. He used to *apologize* to me once in a while for living so long."

"Oh, Hannah," Barbara said, half distressed, half reproachful. And clearly unable to think of anything else to say in response.

"I finally put a stop to it," Hannah said, "when I composed a *very* bad ode entitled 'To the Duke Who Ought to Have Died' and read it aloud to him. He laughed so hard that he brought on a coughing fit and very nearly *did* die. I would have written a companion piece, 'To the Duchess Who Should Be a Widow,' but I could think of nothing to rhyme with *widow,* except perhaps *his toe,* referring to his gout. But it seemed rather lame."

She half smiled as Barbara recognized the pun and exploded into laughter.

"Oh, Hannah," she said, "you *are* bad."

"Yes, aren't I?" Hannah agreed.

And they both laughed.

"But what *are* you going to do?" Barbara came back to the question and looked very directly at Hannah for an answer.

"I am going to do what the *ton* expects me to do, of course," Hannah said, spreading her other hand across the arm of her chair and admiring the rings she wore on her third and little fingers. She tipped her hand slightly forward so that they caught the light from the window and sparkled in a thoroughly satisfying way. "I am going to take a lover, Babs."

It sounded a little . . . *wicked* spoken aloud. It was not wicked. She was free. She owed nothing to anyone any longer. It was quite unexceptionable for a widow to take a lover provided it was a secret affair and she was discreet about it. Well, perhaps not *unexceptionable.* But certainly quite acceptable.

Barbara was, of course, of a different world than her own.

"Hannah!" she exclaimed, color rushing

20

up her neck and over her cheeks and on up across her forehead to disappear beneath her hair. "Oh, you horrid creature. You said it to shock me and succeeded admirably. I almost had a fit of the vapors. *Do* be serious."

Hannah raised her eyebrows. "But I am perfectly serious," she said. "I have had a husband and he is gone. I can never replace him. I have had escorts. They are always good company, but I find them less than completely satisfactory. They feel depressingly like my brothers. I need someone new, someone to add some . . . oh, some *vividness* to my life. I need a lover."

"What you need," Barbara said, her voice far firmer, "is someone to *love.* Romantically, I mean. Someone with whom to *fall* in love. Someone to *marry* and have children with. I know you loved the duke, Hannah, but it was not —"

She stopped and flushed again.

"Romantic love?" Hannah said, completing the sentence for her. "It hurts anyway, Babs. Losing him, I mean. It hurts here." She set her hand over her ribs beneath her bosom. "And romantic love did not serve me well before I met him, did it?"

"You were little more than a *child,*" Barbara said. "And what happened was not

21

your fault. Love will come in time."

"Perhaps so." Hannah shrugged. "But I do not intend waiting around for it to show its face. And I have no intention of going in desperate search of it and perhaps persuading myself that I have found it when I have not and so trapping myself in another marriage so soon after the last. I am *free,* and I intend to remain so until I choose to give up my freedom, which may be a long, long time in the future. Perhaps I will never give it up. There *are* advantages to widowhood, you know."

"Oh, Hannah," Barbara said reproachfully. "*Do* be serious."

"A lover is what I am going to have," Hannah told her. "I have quite decided, Babs, and I am perfectly serious. It will be an arrangement purely for enjoyment with no strings attached. He is going to be someone sinfully handsome. And devilishly attractive. And wickedly skillful and experienced as a lover. Someone with neither a heart to break nor any aspirations whatsoever toward matrimony. *Is* there such a paragon, do you suppose?"

Barbara was smiling again — with what looked like genuine amusement.

"England is said to abound with dashing rakes," she said. "And it is quite obligatory,

I have heard, that they also be outrageously handsome. I do believe, in fact, that it is against the law for them *not* to be. And of course almost all women fall for them — and the eternal conviction that they can reform them."

"Why ever," Hannah asked, "would anyone wish to believe *that?* Why would any woman wish to reduce a perfectly wicked rake and rogue to the dullness of a mere worthy *gentleman?*"

They both doubled over with mirth for a few moments.

"Mr. Newcombe is not a rake, I suppose?" Hannah asked.

"Simon?" Barbara was still laughing. "He is a *clergyman,* Hannah, and very worthy indeed. But he is not — he is definitely not a dull man. I absolutely reject your implication that all men must be either rakes or dullards."

"I did not intend to imply any such thing," Hannah said. "I am quite sure your vicar is a perfectly splendid specimen of romantic gentlemanhood."

Barbara's laugh had become almost a giggle.

"Oh," she said, "I can just picture his face if I were to tell him you had said that, Hannah."

"All I want of a lover," Hannah said, "apart from the aforementioned qualities, of course — *they* are obligatory — is that he will have eyes for no one but me for as long as I choose to allow him to continue looking."

"A lapdog, in other words," her friend said.

"You would put remarkably strange words into my mouth, Babs," Hannah said, getting to her feet to pull on the bell rope and have the tea tray removed. "I want — indeed, I *demand* — just the opposite. I will have a masterful, very masculine man. Someone I will find it a constant challenge to control."

Barbara shook her head, still smiling.

"Handsome, attractive, besotted, devoted," she said, counting the points off on her fingers. "Masterful, very masculine. Have I missed anything?"

"Skilled," Hannah said.

"Experienced," Barbara amended, flushing again. "Goodness, it ought to be quite easy to find a dozen such men, Hannah. Do you have anyone in mind?"

"I do," Hannah said and waited while a maid took the tray away and closed the door behind her. "Though I do not know if he is in town this year. He usually is. It will be inconvenient if he is not, but I have a few others in mind should I need them. I should have no difficulty at all. Is it conceited of me to say that I turn male heads wherever I go?"

"Conceited, perhaps," Barbara said, smiling. "But also true. You always did, even as a girl — male *and* female heads, the former with longing, the latter with envy. No one was at all surprised when the Duke of Dunbarton saw you and had to have you as his duchess even though he had been a confirmed bachelor all his life. And even though it was not really like that at all."

Barbara had come dangerously close to talking of a topic that had been strictly off-limits for eleven years. She had broached it a few times in her letters over the years, but Hannah had never responded.

"*Of course* it was like that," she said now. "Do you think he would have afforded me a second glance if I had *not* been beautiful, Babs? But he was kind. I adored him. Shall we go out? Are you too tired after your travels? Or will you welcome some fresh air and the chance to stretch your legs? At this time of day Hyde Park — the fashionable part of it, at least — will be teeming with people, and one must go along to see and be seen, you know. It is obligatory when one is in town."

"I can recall from a previous occasion," Barbara said, "that there are always more people in the park at the fashionable hour of the afternoon than there are in our whole village on May Day. I will not know a soul, and I will feel like your country cousin, but no matter. Let us go by all means. I am desperate for some exercise."

CHAPTER 2

They went to fetch their bonnets and walked to the park. It was a fine day considering the fact that it was not even officially summer yet. It was partly sunny, partly cloudy, with a light breeze.

Hannah raised a white parasol above her head even though there were actually more cloudy periods than sunny. Why have such a pretty confection, after all, if one was not going to display it to full advantage?

"Hannah," Barbara said almost hesitantly as they passed between the park gates, "you were not *serious* over tea, were you? About what you plan to do, I mean."

"But of course I am serious," Hannah said. "I am no longer either an unmarried girl or a married lady. I am that thoroughly enviable female creature — a widow of wealth and superior social standing. I am even still quite young. And widows of good *ton* are almost expected to take a lover, you know — provided he is also of good *ton,* of course. And preferably unmarried."

Barbara sighed.

"I hoped you were joking with me," she said, "though I feared you were not. You have grown into the manners and morals of this *fast* world you married into, I see. I disapprove of what you intend. I disapprove of the morality of it, Hannah. But more important, I disapprove of your rashness. You are not as heartless or as — oh, what is the word? — as *jaded,* as *blasé* as you believe yourself to be. You are capable of enormous affection and love. An affair can bring you nothing but dissatisfaction at best, heartbreak at worst."

Hannah chuckled. "Do you see the crowds of people up ahead?" she said. "Any one of them would tell you, Babs, that the Duchess of Dunbarton does not have a heart to be broken."

"They do not know you," Barbara said. "I do. Nothing I say will deter you, of course. And so I will say only this. I will love you anyway, Hannah. I will *always* love you. Nothing you can do will make me stop."

"I do wish *you* would stop, though," Hannah said, "or the *ton* will be treated to the interesting spectacle of the Duchess of Dunbarton in tears and wrapped in the arms of her companion."

Barbara snorted inelegantly, and they both laughed yet again.

"I will save my breath, then," Barbara said, "and simply gaze about at this extraordinary scene. Does your masterful man, who may or may not be in London, have a name, by the way?"

"It would be strange if he did not," Hannah said. "It is Huxtable. Constantine Huxtable. *Mister.* It is very lowering, is it not, that fact, when I have consorted with almost no one below the rank of duke and marquess and earl for the past ten years and more. Even the *king.* I have almost forgotten what the word *mister* means. It means, of course, that he is a lowly commoner. Though not so lowly either. His father was the Earl of Merton — and he was the eldest son. His *mother,* lest you should assume otherwise, was the countess. There was marvelous stupidity there, Babs, at least on her part and that of her family. And marvelous resistance, I suppose, on the part of the earl. They married, but they did so a few days *after* their eldest son was born. Can you imagine any worse disaster for him? I believe the actual number of days to have been two. Two days deprived him forever of becoming the Earl of Merton, which he would have been by now, and made him plain Mr. Constantine Huxtable instead."

"How very unfortunate," Barbara agreed.

A little way ahead of them the *ton* had gathered in great force and was affecting to take exercise as carriages of all descriptions and riders on all kinds of mounts and pedestrians in all the latest fashions milled about a ridiculously small piece of land considering the size of the park, trying to see everyone and be seen by everyone in return, trying to tell the gossip they had just heard themselves and listen to any that someone else had to impart.

It was spring, and the *ton* was hard at play again.

Hannah twirled her parasol.

"The Duke of Moreland is his cousin," she said. "They look remarkably alike, though in my estimation the duke is the more purely handsome, while Mr. Huxtable is the more *sinfully* so. The present Earl of Merton is his cousin too, though the contrast between *them* is quite marked. The earl is fair and good-looking to a quite angelic degree. He looks amiable and as far from being dangerous as it is possible to be. Besides, he married Lady Paget last year even though the rumor had still not quite died that she had murdered her first husband with an axe. *That* story reached me even in the country. Perhaps the earl is not quite as meek and mild as he looks. I hope he is not, poor gentleman. He is *so* good-looking."

"Mr. Huxtable is not fair?" Barbara asked.

"Oh, Babs," Hannah said, giving her parasol another twirl. "Do you know those busts of Greek gods and heroes, all white marble? They are beautiful beyond description, but they are also ridiculously deceiving because the Greeks lived in a Mediterranean land and certainly would not have looked as though they were ghosts. Mr. Huxtable's mother was Greek. And he has taken his looks entirely from her. He is a Greek god brought to magnificent life — all black hair and dark complexion and dark eyes. And a physique — Well, you may judge for yourself. There he is."

And there he was indeed, with the Earl of Merton and Baron Montford, the earl's brother-in-law. They were on horseback.

Oh, she had been quite right about him, Hannah decided, looking critically at Mr. Huxtable. Memory had not deceived her even though she had not seen him for two years, having spent last spring in the country for her mourning period. His physique was perfection itself and showed to great advantage on horseback. He was tall and slim, but he was shapely and well muscled in every place where a man ought to be. He had long, powerful-looking legs, always a great advantage in a man. His face was perhaps harsher and more angular than she remembered. And she had forgotten his nose, which must have been broken at some time in his life and not set quite straight afterward. But she did not revise her opinion of his face. It was handsome enough to make her feel quite pleasantly weak at the knees.

Sinfully handsome.

He had the good sense to dress in black — apart from his buff riding breeches and white shirt, that was. His riding coat was black and molded the powerful muscles of his chest and shoulders and upper arms like a second skin. His boots were black too, as was his tall hat. Even his horse was black.

Goodness, he looked downright dangerous, Hannah thought approvingly. He looked unattainable. He looked like an impregnable fortress. He looked as if he would be able to pick her up in one hand — while she was storming the fortress, that was — and crush every bone in her body.

He was very definitely the one. For this year anyway. Next year she would choose someone else. Or perhaps next year she would give some serious consideration to finding someone to love, someone with whom to settle down permanently. But she was not ready for that yet. *This* year she was ready for something quite different.

"Oh, Hannah," Barbara said, doubt in her voice, "he does not look like a very pleasant man. I do wish —"

"But who," Hannah asked as she walked into the crowd with her half-smile firmly in place, "wants a pleasant man for a lover, Babs? He sounds like a dreadful bore, whoever he might be."

So here he was again, Constantine Huxtable thought. Back in London for another Season. Back in Hyde Park, surrounded by half the *ton,* his second cousin Stephen, Earl of Merton, riding on one side of him, Monty — Jasper, Baron Montford, his cousin Katherine's husband — on the other.

It might have been yesterday that he was here last. It was hard to believe another year had gone by. He had thought he might not bother to come at all this year. He thought it every year, of course. But every year he came.

There was just some irresistible lure that brought him back to London in the springtime, he admitted to himself as the three of them tipped their hats to a couple of elderly ladies in big bonnets who were being driven slowly by in an ancient barouche manned by an even more ancient coachman. The ladies acknowledged the greeting with identically raised hands and nodding heads. As if they were royalty.

He loved being home at Ainsley Park in Gloucestershire. He was never so happy as when he was there, immersing himself in the busy life of the farm, in the equally busy activities in the house. There was scarcely a moment to call his own when he was in the country. And he certainly could not complain of loneliness there. His neighbors were always eager to invite him to participate in all their social entertainments, even if they *were* a bit dubious about his activities at Ainsley.

And at Ainsley itself . . . Well, the house was so teeming with people that he had taken up residence in the dower house two years ago in order to preserve some privacy in his life — as well as to make his rooms in the house available for new arrivals. The arrangement had worked perfectly well until a small group of children had discovered the conservatory attached to the dower house this past winter and made a playhouse out of it. And then, of course, they had needed to use the kitchen to find dishes and water for their dolls' tea parties. And . . .

Well, and one day, in the absence of his cook, Constantine had found himself raiding the pantry to find the sweet biscuit jar for them — and then joining their tea party, for the love of God.

It was no wonder he made his escape to London every spring. A man needed some peace and quiet in his life. Not to mention sanity.

"It always feels good to be back in town, does it not?" Monty said cheerfully.

"Even if I *have* just been banished from my own home," Stephen said.

"But the ladies must be allowed to admire the heir without the interference of mere men," Monty said. "You would not *really* wish to be there, would you, Stephen? When your sisters have gone to all the trouble of inviting a dozen other ladies to join them in their admiration and to bring gifts, which Cassandra will have to admire and they will all have to examine and, ah, *coo* over?" He shuddered theatrically.

Stephen grinned. "You have a point, Monty," he said.

His countess had recently borne him a son. Their first. An heir. A future Earl of

35

Merton. It really did not matter to Constantine. After his father there had been his brother Jonathan — Jon — as earl for a few years and now there was Stephen. Eventually there would be Stephen's son. He and Cassandra might proceed to have a whole string of spares over the next number of years if they chose. It would make no difference to Constantine. He would never be the earl himself.

It did not matter. He had always known that he would not. He did not really care.

They stopped to exchange pleasantries with a couple of male acquaintances. The park was full of familiar faces, Constantine saw as he looked idly around. There were almost no new ones at all, and those few there were belonged mostly to very young ladies — the new crop of marriageable hopefuls come to the great marriage mart.

There were a few beauties among them too, by Jove. But Constantine was surprised and not a little alarmed to discover how clinical the inward analysis was. He felt no stirring of real interest in any of them. He might have done so without any fear of seeming presumptuous. His illegitimacy was a mere legal trifle. It prohibited him from inheriting his father's title and entailed property, it was true, but it had no bearing on his status in the *ton* as the son of an earl. He had been brought up at Warren Hall. He had been left comfortably well off on his father's death.

He might shop at the marriage mart if he chose and expect considerable success. But he was thirty-five years old. These new beauties looked uncomfortably like children to him. Most of them would be seventeen or eighteen.

It really was a little alarming. He was never going to get any younger, was he? And he had never intended to go through life as a single man. When, then, was he going to marry? And, more to the point, *whom* would he marry?

He had made his prospects somewhat dimmer, of course, when he acquired Ainsley Park a number of years ago and proceeded to populate it with society's undesirables — vagabonds, thieves, ex-soldiers, the mentally handicapped, prostitutes, unwed mothers and their offspring, and assorted others. Ainsley was a hive of industry and was gratifyingly prosperous after a few years of nothing but expenses — and hard work.

A young wife, however, particularly one of gentle birth, would certainly not appreciate being taken to live among such company and in such a place — and in the dower house to boot. A month or so ago his living room had been commandeered as a nursery for the dolls too tired to keep their eyes open after their tea in the conservatory.

"Let me guess," Monty said, leaning closer to Constantine. "The one in green?"

He had been staring quite fixedly, Constantine realized, at two young ladies with two stern-looking maids a couple of paces behind them — and all four had noticed. The girls were giggling and preening themselves while the maids were closing the gap to one and a half paces.

"She *is* the prettier of the two," Constantine conceded, looking away. "The one in pink has the better figure, though."

"I wonder which one," Monty said, "has the richer papa."

"The Duchess of Dunbarton is back in town," Stephen said as the three of them moved on. "Looking as lovely as ever. She must be just out of mourning. Shall we go and pay our respects?"

"By all means," Monty said, "provided we can get from here to there without being mowed down by the next six carriages in line and without mowing down the next six pedestrians in line. They always *will* stray from the footpath, to their imminent peril."

He proceeded to lead the way, weaving a

skillful path among carriages and horsemen until they reached the pedestrians, most of whom were strolling safely on the path designed for them.

Constantine saw her at last. But how could anyone *not* once he paid the proper attention to his surroundings? She was all willowy, delicate whiteness and pink-tinged complexion and lips and blue, fathomless bedroom eyes.

If the woman had chosen to be a courtesan instead of Dunbarton's wife she would be the most celebrated one in England by now. And she would have made a veritable fortune. Of course, she had made a fortune anyway, had she not, by persuading that old fossil to marry for the first and only time in his life. And then by squeezing him dry of everything that was not nailed down by the entail.

She had a suitably respectable-looking companion with her. And she was holding court, favoring a large number of persons gathered about her — almost exclusively male — with her enigmatic half-smile and occasionally one of her white-gloved hands, on the forefinger of which winked a diamond large enough to bash out the brains of any man incautious enough to be impudent.

"Ah," she said, turning her languid gaze from her court, most of which was forced onward by the crowd, "Lord Merton. Looking as angelically handsome as ever. I do hope Lady Paget appreciates the value of her prize."

She was soft-spoken. Her voice was light and pleasant. Of course, she must never need to speak loudly. When she opened her mouth to speak, all about her fell silent to listen.

She favored Stephen with her hand, and he carried it to his lips and smiled at her.

"She is Lady Merton now, ma'am," he said. "And *I* certainly appreciate the value of *my* prize."

"Good man," she said. "You have made the correct answer. And Lord Montford. Looking really quite . . . tamed. Lady Montford is to be commended."

And she offered him her hand.

"Not at all, ma'am," Monty said, grinning as he kissed the back of it. "I took one look at her and . . . was instantly tame."

"I am glad to hear it," she said, "though that is not quite what a little bird once told me. And Mr. Huxtable. How do you do?"

She looked at him almost with disdain, though she arched the look from beneath her eyelashes and somewhat spoiled the effect — if she had indeed intended disdain, that was. She did not offer him her hand.

"Very well indeed, Duchess, I thank you," he said. "And all the better for having seen that you are back in town this year."

"Flatterer," she said, making a dismissive gesture with her ringed hand. She turned to her silent companion. "Babs, may I have the pleasure of presenting the Earl of Merton, Baron Montford, and Mr. Huxtable? Miss Leavensworth, gentlemen, is my dearest friend in the world. She has been kind enough to come and stay with me for a while before returning home to marry the vicar of the village where we grew up."

Miss Leavensworth was tall and thin with a long, Nordic face, slightly protruding upper teeth, and fair hair. She was not an unhandsome woman.

She curtsied. They all bowed from the saddle.

"I am delighted to make your acquaintance, Miss Leavensworth," Stephen said. "Are the nuptials to be soon?"

"In August, my lord," she said. "But in the meantime I hope to see as many places of interest in London as I can. All the museums and galleries, anyway."

The duchess was looking his horse over, Constantine could see. And then his top-boots. And then his thighs. And then . . . his face. She raised her eyebrows when she found him staring directly back at her.

"We must move on, Babs," she said. "I fear we are blocking the path, and these gentlemen are holding up traffic. They are so very . . . large."

And she turned and processed onward toward the next wave of admirers come to greet her and welcome her back to town.

"Goodness me," Monty murmured. "There goes one very dangerous lady. And she has just been let off the leash."

"Her friend seems very sensible," Stephen said.

"It would seem," Constantine said, "that only titled gentlemen are to be granted the great honor of kissing her hand."

"I would not lose any sleep over that, if I were you, Con," Monty said. "Perhaps it is only *untitled* gentlemen who are favored with a leisurely toe-to-head scrutiny instead of a hand."

"Or maybe one should make that *unmarried* gentlemen, Monty," Stephen said. "Perhaps the lady fancies you, Con."

"But perhaps *I* do not fancy the *lady*," Constantine said. "It has never been my ambition to share a mistress with half the *ton*."

"Hmm," Monty said. "Do you think that is what Dunbarton did, poor devil? Though, speaking of which, he apparently had one devil of a reputation as a dangerous character when he was a young man. He never *looked* like a cuckold after his marriage, did he? He always looked more like the cat who had climbed right into the cream bowl to bask and bathe there while he lapped it up."

"I have just thought of something," Stephen said. "It was just last year, maybe even on this very date, and in just this place that I first set eyes upon Cassandra. You were with me, Con. And if memory does not deceive me, Monty, you rode up with Kate while we were looking at her and remarking upon how uncomfortably hot she must be beneath her heavy widow's weeds."

"And you went on to live happily ever after with her," Monty said. He grinned again. "Are you predicting a like fate for Con with the gorgeous duchess?"

"The sun is not shining," Constantine said, "and it certainly is not hot. And the duchess is not in heavy mourning. Or walking alone with her companion while no one takes any notice. And I am not looking for a leg shackle, thank you kindly, Monty."

"But then, Con," Stephen said, waggling his eyebrows, "neither was I."

They all chuckled — and then noticed
Timothy Hood driving a spanking-new
high-perch phaeton drawn by a pair of
perfectly matched grays. Their attention was
effectively diverted from the widow in white
who had looked at him, Constantine realized now that he had had a minute or two
to think about it, not so much disdainfully
as provocatively.

He really was not interested. He chose his
mistresses — and he took one almost every
year when he was in town — with an eye to
his maximum comfort for the duration of
the Season.

There would be no comfort at all in a
woman whose daily pastime seemed to be
gathering as many adoring men about her
as she could — and her ability in that regard
was considerable.

He did not dance to any woman's tune.

Or at the end of any puppet strings.

Certainly not the notorious Duchess of
Dunbarton's.

CHAPTER 3

Over the next few days Barbara was confirmed in her conviction that Hannah had moved into a puzzlingly and disturbingly different world from the one they had known together in their Lincolnshire village. A less moral world. During those days Hannah told two whoppers of lies, which she would not even admit *were* lies.

Not *real* lies.

The first happened when the two of them were stepping out of a milliner's shop on Bond Street late one morning, a footman behind them more than half hidden beneath four large hatboxes. Their intention was to see the boxes safely deposited in their waiting carriage and then proceed to a bakery a little way along the street for refreshments. But as fate would have it, Mr. Huxtable was approaching alone along the pavement. He was still some distance away and might easily have been avoided, especially as he appeared not to have noticed them among the crowd of shoppers. But Hannah waited for him to draw closer and see them.

He touched the brim of his hat, inclined his head politely, and asked them how they did.

"We have been shopping for *hours,*" Hannah said with a weary sigh.

That part at least seemed like a mere exaggeration to Barbara rather than an out-and-out lie. An hour and a half was longer than just one hour, after all.

"And we are absolutely *parched,*" Hannah continued.

Barbara was a little uncomfortable. Hannah was, of course, trying to attract Mr. Huxtable, but did she have to be so blatant about it?

But the big lie was coming up, and Barbara did not see it coming.

Mr. Huxtable responded with the gallantry almost any true gentleman would have shown under the circumstances.

"There is a bakery or a pastry cook not far from here," he said. "May I have the pleasure of escorting you ladies there and buying you tea?"

And instead of looking grateful or perhaps embarrassed, Hannah looked sorrowful. Barbara observed the expression in surprise.

"That is extraordinarily kind of you, Mr. Huxtable," she said, "but we are expecting visitors and must hurry home."

And the coachman had to gather the ribbons in a hurry, and the footman had to scramble to open the carriage door, and Mr. Huxtable bowed and handed them in.

Hannah nodded graciously to him as they drove off.

"Hannah?" Barbara asked.

"One must never appear too eager," Hannah said.

"But you practically *asked* him to take us for tea," Barbara pointed out.

"I remarked on the fact that I was thirsty," Hannah said. "That was perfectly true."

"*Are* we expecting visitors?" Barbara asked.

"Not to my knowledge," Hannah admitted, "but one never knows."

She had lied, in other words. Barbara disapproved of lies. But she said nothing. Hannah was playing her game, of which Barbara also disapproved, but Hannah was an adult. She could choose her own course in life.

The second lie was told a few evenings later, when they were at a ball hosted by Lord and Lady Merriwether. Barbara had not wanted to attend it. It was a *ton* ball, and she had been to nothing grander than a country assembly her whole life.

"Nonsense," Hannah had said when she voiced her concern. "Show me your feet, Babs."

Barbara had lifted her skirt to just above her ankles, and Hannah had looked down at her feet, a frown between her brows.

"As I suspected," she had said. "You have one right foot and one left. Perfect for dancing. I might have allowed you to remain at home if you had had two left feet, as some people do, poor things. Usually men. But you are coming. There is no point in arguing. You are coming. Tell me that you are."

Barbara was — of course — at the ball, and she was quite sure her eyes might pop right out of her head if she was not careful. She had never even dreamed of such splendor. She was going to be writing *very* long letters home tomorrow.

They were practically mobbed as soon as they set foot in the ballroom. Or rather, Hannah was mobbed and Barbara was caught in the middle of the crowd with her. It amazed and half amused her to watch the transformation of her friend when she was in public. She hardly even *looked* like the person Barbara had known all her life. She looked like a . . . Well, like a duchess.

Mr. Huxtable was in the ballroom. He was with the two gentlemen with whom he had ridden in the park and two ladies. But he did not remain with them for long. He moved about and stopped frequently to converse with different groups.

And Hannah, Barbara observed, was careful to position herself so that she frequently caught his eye. The exchanged glances were usually accompanied by a flutter of Hannah's white feathered fan and a glance that succeeded once or twice in looking almost forlorn. As though she were unhappy in the crowd and needed rescuing.

There were probably a few dozen ladies in the room, Barbara thought, who would have been delighted to be similarly unhappy and in need of rescuing. The power Hannah had over men was truly astounding, especially as she appeared to make no great effort to wield it. Of course, she had always drawn eyes wherever she went, even as a girl. She was one of the purely beautiful creatures of this world.

Finally Mr. Huxtable answered her silent plea and came striding across the floor.

He bowed first to Barbara and wished her a good evening. Then he bowed to Hannah.

"Duchess," he said, "would you be good enough to dance the opening set with me?"

She looked sorrowful again.

"I regret that I cannot," she said. "I have already promised it to someone else."

What? Barbara blinked. Hannah had explained to her when they were on their way here that she never allowed any man to reserve a set in advance with her — not since the days when the duke still danced, anyway. And Barbara had not heard her friend agreeing to dance with anyone since they arrived. There was more to come.

"Perhaps the second, then?" Mr. Huxtable said. "Or the third?"

Hannah closed her fan and set the tip against her lips.

"I am sorry, Mr. Huxtable," she said, sounding truly remorseful. "I have promised *every* dance. Perhaps some other time."

He bowed and went away.

"Hannah?" Barbara said.

"I *will* dance every set," Hannah said. "One must not appear too eager, Babs."

And her court was back, vying for her attention again.

Such blatant and strange lies, Barbara thought. How could inviting a man's attention and then spurning it when he gave it actually *attract* him? How could it convert him from a stranger into a lover?

Barbara hoped it would not. She *truly*

believed that Hannah would be making a grave mistake in taking any man as a lover. And Mr. Huxtable, though he appeared to be a perfect gentleman, also looked very dangerous indeed. The sort of man who would not be content to be toyed with forever.

Barbara could only hope that his final reaction would be to ignore Hannah altogether.

And then Barbara's thoughts were very effectively distracted when one gentleman asked Hannah to present him, and he bowed over Barbara's hand and asked if he might lead her into the opening set.

She could barely restrain herself from looking down to make sure that she really did have one right foot and one left. Suddenly her mouth felt dry and her heart felt like a hammer and she very badly wanted Simon.

"Thank you." She smiled serenely and set her hand on the gentleman's sleeve. She had already forgotten his name.

Hannah meanwhile was displaying one of the most important attributes she had acquired over the past eleven years — patience. One must never appear too eager — or eager at all, in fact — when one wanted something. And she wanted Constantine Huxtable. He was even more attractive than she remembered from other years, and she had no doubt he would be a satisfactory lover. Probably a great deal more than satisfactory, in fact.

But she knew he did not believe that he wanted *her* for a lover. That had been obvious during their meeting in Hyde Park. He had stared rather stonily down at her from his vantage point on horseback, and she had concluded that he despised her. Many people did, of course, without ever really knowing her — which, to be fair, was largely her doing. But they flocked about her, nonetheless. They could not keep their eyes off her.

The duke had taught her how to be not only noticed, but irresistible.

No one admires timidity or modesty, my dearest love, he had told her on one occasion early in their marriage, when she had possessed an overabundance of both. *My dearest love* had been his name for her. He had never called her Hannah. Just as she had never called him anything but *Duke.*

She had learned never to be timid.

And never *ever* to be modest.

And to be patient.

Three evenings after the ball, Hannah and

Barbara were attending a private concert at the home of Lord and Lady Heaton. They were in an oval anteroom with a crowd of other early arrivals, enjoying a glass of wine before taking their places in the music room for the entertainment. As usual they were surrounded by a court of Hannah's friends and admirers. Two of the admirers were vying with each other for the honor of sitting beside her for the evening. She might have reminded them that she had *two* sides, but she did not believe that would settle the argument to the satisfaction of either.

She wafted a fan before her face and noted the arrival of the Earl and Countess of Sheringford, a couple whose marriage had begun amid the most shocking scandal several years ago and then settled into what appeared to be a happy union.

The countess saw Hannah and nodded and smiled at her. The earl smiled too and raised a hand in her direction. Mr. Huxtable was with them. He was related to the countess, of course. She was the Earl of Merton's sister. He inclined his head to Hannah and Barbara without smiling.

All the other inhabitants of the room paled into insignificance beside him. And he was going to be *her* lover.

It *was* going to happen. She refused to

doubt it.

If you want something, my dearest love, the duke had once told her, *you will never get it. Want is a timid, abject word. It implies that you know you will be left wanting, that you know you do not deserve the object of your desire but can only hope for a miracle. You must expect that object instead, and it will be yours. There is no such thing as a miracle.*

"I cannot sit with you, I am afraid, Lord Netherby," Hannah said now to settle the argument between her two contending admirers, "though I do thank you for your kindness." She did not need to raise her voice. All around her hushed to listen to what she said. "Nor will I be able to sit with you, Sir Bertrand. I am sorry. I am going to sit with Mr. Huxtable. I had no time, alas, a week ago to accept his very kind invitation to treat Babs and me to tea and cakes when we met him on Bond Street. And I had no free sets remaining when he asked to dance with me at the Merriwether ball a few evenings ago. I will sit with him tonight instead."

She closed her fan and rested the tip of it against her pursed lips as she gazed at Mr. Huxtable. He showed no reaction — not surprise or disdain or gratification. He certainly did not fawn, as so many men always did, the foolish creatures. Neither did he turn and walk away.

That was a relief.

"Good evening, Duchess," he said, strolling closer to her as her court opened up a path for him. "It is rather crowded in here, is it not? I see it is less so in the music room. Shall we stroll in there for a while?"

"That sounds pleasant," she said, handing her empty glass to a gentleman on her right and slipping her hand through Mr. Huxtable's arm.

Mr. and Mrs. Park, she could see, were talking with Barbara, to whom they had just been introduced. Their second son, Hannah recalled, was a clergyman.

It was a very solid arm she had taken, Hannah realized. And it was all clad in black, except for the crisp white cuff that showed at his wrist. His hand was dark-skinned and long-fingered and well manicured, though there was nothing soft about it. Quite the contrary. It looked as if it had done its fair share of work in its time. It was lightly dusted with dark hair. His shoulder was a few inches above the level of her own. He wore a cologne that wrapped itself very enticingly about her senses. She could not identify it.

The music room was indeed still half

empty. Entertainments of this nature never did begin on time, of course. They began to stroll slowly about the perimeter of the room.

"And so," he said, looking down at her, "I am to be consoled for my disappointments, am I, Duchess, by being granted the seat next to yours this evening?"

"*Were* you disappointed?" she asked.

"Amused," he said.

She turned her head and looked into his very dark eyes. They were quite impossible to read.

"*Amused,* Mr. Huxtable?" She raised her eyebrows.

"It *is* amusing," he said, "to watch a puppeteer manipulate the strings in order to make the puppet dance only to discover that the strings are not attached."

Ah. Someone who knew the game and refused to play by its rules — *her* rules, that was. She liked him the better for it.

"But is it not *intriguing,*" she said, "when the puppet dances anyway? And proves that he is *not* a puppet after all, but that he does love to dance?"

"But you see, Duchess," he said, "he does not like dancing with the chorus. It makes him feel quite . . . ordinary. Indeed, he quite refuses to be an insignificant part of any such group."

Ah. He was setting out his terms, was he?

"But it can be arranged," she said, "that he dance a solo part, Mr. Huxtable. Or perhaps a pas de deux. Very definitely a pas de deux, in fact. And if he proves to be a superior partner, as I am confident he will, then he may be offered the security of exclusive rights to the part for the whole of a Season. There will be no need for any chorus at all. It may be dispensed with."

They turned to walk along the front of the room, between the shallow dais where the orchestra's instruments lay and the front row of gilt, velvet-seated chairs.

"He is to be on trial, then, at the start?" he said. "At a sort of audition?"

"I am not sure that will be necessary," she said. "I have not seen him dance, but I am convinced he performs superlatively well."

"You are too kind and too trusting, Duchess," he said. "He is perhaps more cautious. If he is to dance a pas de deux, after all, he must be given an equal chance to try out *his* prospective partner, to discover if she is as skilled a dancer as he, to discover whether she will suit his style for a whole Season and not very quickly become tedious."

Hannah opened her fan with her free hand and fluttered it before her face. The music room was still not crowded, but it already felt stuffy and overhot.

"*Tedious,* Mr. Huxtable," she said, "is a word not in her vocabulary."

"Ah," he said, "but it is in *his.*"

Hannah might have been offended or outraged or both. Instead, she was feeling very pleased indeed. The word *tedious* figured largely in her vocabulary — which meant she had just told yet another lie. Barbara would be upset with her if she could hear. Though it was very fortunate indeed that she could hear no part of this conversation. She would expire from shock. Most gentlemen of Hannah's acquaintance were tedious. They really ought not to set her on a pedestal and worship her. Pedestals could be lonely, barren places, and worship was just plain ridiculous when one was very mortal indeed.

They had turned to walk up the far side of the room.

"Ah," she said, looking ahead, "there are the Duke and Duchess of Moreland. Shall we go and speak with them?"

The duke was Mr. Huxtable's cousin, the one who looked like him. They might easily have passed for brothers, in fact.

"It seems," he murmured as she drew him in their direction, "that we shall."

The duke and duchess were very polite to her, very chilly to him. Hannah seemed to recall hearing that there was some sort of estrangement between the cousins. But she caught herself in time before censuring them mentally for quarreling when they were family. That would be rather like the pot calling the kettle black, would it not?

She had been right in her earlier assessment. The duke *was* the more handsome of the two men. His features were more classically perfect, and there was the surprise of his blue eyes when one expected dark. But Mr. Huxtable was, nevertheless, the more attractive of the two — to her, anyway, which was just as well given the fact that the duke was a married man.

"Mr. Huxtable and I are going to be seated now," Hannah said before the encounter could become too strained. "I am tired after having been on my feet for so long."

And they all nodded and smiled at one another, and Mr. Huxtable took her to sit in the middle of the fourth row back from the dais.

"It is not a promising sign," he said, "when a dancer's feet ache after she has been on them for a mere hour or so."

"But who," she said, closing her fan and

59

resting it on his sleeve for a moment, "is talking about dancing? Why have you quarreled with the Duke of Moreland?"

"At the risk of sounding quite ill-mannered, Duchess," he said, "I am compelled to inform you that it is none of your business."

She sighed.

"Oh, but it is," she said. "Or will be. I will absolutely insist upon knowing everything there is to know about you."

He turned his very dark eyes upon her.

"Assuming," he said, "that after the audition you will be offered the part?"

She tapped the fan on his sleeve.

"After the audition, Mr. Huxtable," she said, "you will be *begging* me to take the part. But you know that already. Just as I know that in your case an audition is absolutely unnecessary. I hope you are a man of great mystery, with more secrets to be revealed than just the cause of your quarrel with your cousin. Oh, I do hope you are. But I fervently believe I will not be disappointed."

"You, on the other hand, Duchess," he said, "are very much an open book, are you not? You will have to think of other ways to hold my interest than unfolding all your nonexistent secrets."

She half smiled up at him from beneath her lashes.

"The room is starting to fill," she said. "I believe we can expect this concert to begin within the next fifteen minutes or so. Yet we have not talked about *anything* of any significance yet, Mr. Huxtable. What is your opinion of the weather we have been having lately? Too good too early, do you suppose? We will suffer for this later in the summer? That is the accepted wisdom among many, is it not? What do *you* think?"

"I think, Duchess," he said, "that too hot too early is not something that alarms you. You are doubtless of an optimistic nature and expect that there will be more heat to come as the spring turns to summer."

"I really *must* be an open book," she said. "You read me so well. And you must not tell me, Mr. Huxtable, that you are the sort of man who prefers a cool spring in the hope that it will build to a moderate degree of heat during the summer. You are *Greek*."

"Half Greek," he said, "and half not. I will leave you to work out which half is which."

The chairs in front of them and behind and beside them filled up, and conversation became general among the audience until Lord Heaton stepped up onto the dais and a hush fell in anticipation of the concert.

Hannah let her fan fall on her wrist and rested the fingers of one hand lightly on Mr. Huxtable's sleeve.

That had all been very intriguing. Having made her point on Bond Street and at the Merriwether ball, she had intended to take one step forward this evening before taking it back the next time she saw him. She had been in no real hurry. The preliminaries could surely be as exciting as the game itself.

But he had refused to allow her to play the game her way. And instead of one small step, she felt as if they had dashed forward at least a mile tonight. She felt almost breathless.

And quite humming with anticipation.

She could not allow him the last word, though. Not this early in their connection. Not ever, in fact.

"I see that Mr. Minter arrived late," she said when the intermission began an hour later and the audience rose to go in search of wine and conversation. "I must go along and scold him. He begged to sit by me this evening, and I took pity on him and agreed. I suppose I had better sit beside him for the rest of the concert. He is quite alone, poor man."

"Yes," Mr. Huxtable said, speaking low against her ear. "I suppose you had better go, Duchess. I might conclude that you were being too *forward* if you remained."

She tapped his arm one more time with her fan and bore down upon the unsuspecting Mr. Minter, who probably had not even known she was coming here this evening.

CHAPTER 4

Constantine's spring mistresses — Monty had once dubbed them that — were selected almost exclusively from the ranks of society's widows. It was a personal rule of his never to visit a brothel and never to employ either a courtesan or an actress. Or, of course, to choose a married lady, though there was a surprising number of them who indicated their availability. Or an unmarried lady — he was after a mistress, not a wife.

Many widows, he had always found, were in no great hurry to marry again. Though most of them did remarry eventually, they were eager enough to spend a few years enjoying their freedom and the sensual pleasure of a casual amour.

He almost always took a lover for the Season. Rarely more than one, and never more than one at a time. His lovers were usually lovely women and younger than he, though he never thought of beauty or age as a necessary qualification. He favored women who were discreet and poised and elegant and intelligent enough to converse on a wide variety of interesting topics. He looked for a certain degree of companionship as well as sexual satisfaction in a lover.

And *this* year?

He was standing on the wide cobbled terrace behind the Fonteyn mansion in Richmond — though *behind* and *before* were relative terms in this case. The front of the house faced toward the road and any approaching carriages and was really quite unremarkable. The back of the house, on the other hand, overlooked the River Thames, and between it and the river there were the terrace, the wide, flower-bedecked steps, the sloping lawn below them, bordered on one side by a rose arbor and a small orchard and on the other by a row of greenhouses, and another terrace, this one paved, alongside the river. A small jetty stretched into the water for the convenience of anyone desirous of taking out one of the boats that bobbed on either side of it.

And at the moment the back of the house, which might easily claim to be the real front, was bathed in sunshine and a heat that was tempered by an underlying coolness, as one might expect this early in the year. It was all very picturesque and very pleasant indeed.

It had been a bold move on the part of the Fonteyns to host a garden party this early in the Season, long before anyone else was prepared to take such a chance with the weather. Of course, there was a spacious ballroom inside the house as well as a large drawing room and doubtless other rooms large enough to accommodate all the guests in the event of chill weather or rain.

This year there was a new widow in town, and she was quite blatantly and aggressively offering herself to him as this Season's mistress. If one discounted her very obvious ruse of appearing hard to get, that was. He really had been amused by her behavior on Bond Street and at the Merriwether ball.

At the moment she was doing it again. She was standing on the lawn not far from the orchard, her hand on the arm of Lord Hardingraye, one of her old lovers with whom she had arrived half an hour ago. They were surrounded by other guests, both male and female, and she was giving the group her full attention as she twirled a confection of a parasol above her head. Inevitably it was white, as was everything else she wore. She almost always wore white, though she never looked the same on

66

any two occasions. Amazing, that.

She had not once looked Constantine's way. Which might mean one of two things — she had not seen him yet, or she was no longer interested in pursuing any sort of connection with him.

He knew very well that neither possible explanation was the real one.

She was determined to have him. And she had certainly seen him. She would not have so studiously *not* looked at him if she had not.

He was amused again.

He sipped his drink and carried on a conversation with a group of his friends. He was in no hurry to approach her. Indeed, he had no intention of making the first move. If she wished to ignore him all afternoon, he would not leave brokenhearted.

But as he talked and laughed and looked about at all the new arrivals, smiling at some of them, raising a hand in greeting to others, he mulled over the question that had been bothering him for the past three days.

Did he really *want* the Duchess of Dunbarton as a lover?

He had said a very firm no to that question in Hyde Park, and he had meant it.

Most men would have thought the question a ludicrous one, of course. She was, after all, one of the most perfectly beautiful women anyone had ever set eyes upon, and, if it was possible, she had improved with age. She was still relatively young, and she was as sexually desirable as she was lovely. She was much sought after — an understatement. She could have almost any man she chose to take as a lover, and that did not exclude many of the married ones.

But . . .

Something made him hesitate, and he was not quite sure what it was.

Was it that *she* had chosen *him?* But there was no reason why a woman might not go after what she wanted just as boldly as a man could. When he decided upon a woman, after all, he always pursued her with determined persistence until she capitulated — or did not. Besides, was it not flattering to be singled out by a beautiful, desirable woman who could have almost anyone?

Was it that she was *too* available, then? Had her lovers not been legion while the old duke lived? Were they not likely to continue to be numerous now that she was finally free, not only of the duke but also of her obligatory year of mourning? But he had never balked at the prospect of competition. Besides, if it turned out that she expected to keep other lovers as well as him, he could simply walk away. He was not looking for *love,* after all, or anything like a marital commitment. Only for a lover. His heart was not going to be involved.

And she had said in so many words at the Heaton concert that while he was her lover no one else would be.

Was it, then, that she was too much of an open book, as he had told her at the concert? Everyone knew all about her. Despite the bedroom eyes and the half-smile she kept almost always on her lips, there was no real mystery about the woman, nothing to be uncovered a layer at a time, like the petals of a rose.

Except her clothing.

One never knew exactly what a woman was going to look like unclothed, no matter how many times one's eyes roamed over her clad body. One never knew exactly what she would *feel* like, how she would move, what sounds she would make . . .

"Constantine." His aunt, Lady Lyngate, his mother's sister, had come up behind him and laid a hand on his arm. "Do tell me you have not been down by the river yet. Or, if you have, do lie about it and tell me you will be delighted to escort me there."

He covered her hand with his own and grinned at her.

"I would not be lying, Aunt Maria," he said, "even if I had been down there a dozen times already, which I have not. It is always my pleasure to escort you anywhere you wish to go. I did not know you were in town. How are you? You grow lovelier with every passing year and every newly acquired gray hair. More distinguished."

He was not lying about that either. She was probably close to sixty years old and a head-turner.

"Well," she said, laughing, "that is the first time, I believe, I have been complimented on my gray hair."

She was still very dark. But she was graying attractively at the temples. She was Elliott's — the Duke of Moreland's — mother but had never cut their acquaintance just because her son rarely talked to him. Neither had Elliott's sisters.

"How is Cece?" he asked of Cecily, Viscountess Burden, the youngest of them and his favorite, as he led his aunt off the terrace and down the broad steps to the lawn. "Is her confinement to be soon?"

"Soon enough that she and Burden have remained in the country this year," she said, "much to the delight of the other two children, I am sure. What a good idea it was to set up tables on the terrace down there.

One may sit and enjoy refreshments and be right by the water."

They proceeded to do just that and sat for ten minutes or so before being joined by three of his aunt's friends — a lady and two gentlemen.

"You will take pity on me, if you will, Lady Lyngate, and if your nephew can spare you," the single gentleman said after they had all chatted for a while. "We came down here to take out a boat, but I have always had an aversion to being a wallflower. Do say you will make up a fourth."

"Oh, indeed I will," she said. "How delightful! Constantine, will you excuse me?"

"Only with the greatest reluctance," he said, winking at her, and he watched as the four of them climbed into a recently vacated boat and one of the men took the oars and pushed out into the river.

"All alone, Mr. Huxtable?" a familiar voice asked from behind his shoulder. "What a waste of a perfectly available gentleman."

"I have been sitting here waiting for you to take notice and have pity on me," he said, getting to his feet. "Do join me, Duchess."

"I am neither hungry nor thirsty nor in need of rest," she said. "Take me into the greenhouses. I wish to see the orchids."

Did anyone ever say no to her, he wondered as he offered his arm. When she had announced at the Heaton concert that she would sit with *him* in the music room, had she even considered how embarrassed she might have been if he had refused to sit with *her?* But why should she fear rejection when even the crusty, crabby old Duke of Dunbarton had been unable to resist her after resisting every other woman for more than seventy years?

"I have been feeling dreadfully slighted," she said as she took his arm. "You did not come to greet me when you arrived."

"I believe," he said, "I arrived before you did, Duchess. And *you* did not come to greet *me.*"

"Is it the woman's part," she said, "to go out of her way to greet the man?"

"As you have done now?"

He looked down at her. She was not wearing a bonnet today. Instead she was wearing an absurd little hat, which sat at a jaunty angle over her right eyebrow and looked — of course — quite perfect. Her blond curls rioted about it in an artless style that had probably taken her maid an hour or more to create. The white muslin of her dress, he could see now that he was close, was dotted with tiny rosebuds of a very pale pink.

"That is unkind repartee, Mr. Huxtable,"

she said. "What choice did you leave me? It would have been too, too tedious to have gone home without speaking with you."

He led her diagonally up the lawn in the direction of the greenhouses. And he gave in to a feeling of inevitability. She was clearly determined to have him. And for all his misgivings, he could not deny the fact that he was not at all averse to being had. Being in bed with her was going to be something of a wild adventure, he did not doubt. A struggle for mastery, perhaps? And mutual and enormous pleasure while they fought it out?

Sometimes, he thought, the prospect of extraordinary sensual pleasure was enough to ask of a liaison. The mysteries of a character that had some depths worth exploring could wait until another year and another mistress.

He really was capitulating with very little struggle, he thought. Which meant that she was very good at seduction. No surprise there. And he would not begrudge her that since it was beginning to feel rather pleasant to be seduced.

"Where is Miss Leavensworth this afternoon?" he asked.

"Mr. and Mrs. Park invited her to accompany them on a visit to some museum or other," she said, "and she preferred to go there than to come here with me. Can you *imagine* such a thing, Mr. Huxtable? And they are to take her to dinner afterward and then to the *opera*."

She shuddered delicately.

"You have never been to the opera, Duchess?" he asked. "Or to a museum?"

"But of course I have," she said. "One must not appear an utter rustic in the eyes of one's peers, you know. One must show some interest in matters of superior culture."

"But you have never enjoyed either?" he asked.

"I really *did* enjoy looking at Napoleon Bonaparte's carriage at . . . Oh, in *some* museum," she said, waving the hand that held her parasol in a dismissive gesture. "The one in which he rode to the Battle of Waterloo, I mean. He could not ride his horse because he was suffering with piles. Did you know that? The duke told me and explained what piles *are*. They sound like dreadfully painful things. Perhaps the Duke of Wellington won the battle on the strength of Napoleon Bonaparte's piles. I wonder if the history books will reflect that fact."

"Probably not," he said, feeling vastly amused. "History will doubtless prefer to perpetuate the modern eagerness to see Wellington as a grand, invincible hero, who won the battle on the strength of his grandness and invincibility."

"I suppose so," she agreed. "That is what the duke said too. *My* duke, that is. And he took me once to see the Elgin marbles and I was not at all *shocked* to see all those naked figures. I was not even vastly impressed by them. They were pale marble. I would far rather see the real flesh-and-blood man. Greek, that is. With sun-bronzed skin instead of cold stone. Not that a real-life man could ever be quite so perfectly beautiful, of course."

She sighed, and her parasol twirled again.

The minx, Constantine thought.

"And the opera?" he said.

"I never understand the Italian," she said. "It would all be very tedious if it were not for all the *passion* and the tragedy of everyone dying all over the stage. Have you noticed how all those dying characters sing the most glorious music just before they expire? What a waste. I would far prefer to see such passion expended upon *life.*"

"But since opera is written for a living singer and an audience of living persons rather than for a dying character," he said, "then surely that is exactly what is happening. Passion being expended upon life, that is."

"I shall never see opera the same way again," she said, giving her parasol one more twirl before lowering it as they came to the first greenhouse. "Or hear it the same way. Thank you, Mr. Huxtable, for your insight. You must take me one evening so that I may hear it correctly in your presence. I will make up a party."

It was humid and very warm inside the greenhouse. It was filled with large banks of ferns down the center and orange trees around the glass walls. It was also deserted.

"How very lovely," she said, standing still behind the central bank and tipping back her head to breathe in the scent of the foliage. "Do you think it would be eternally lovely to live in a tropical land, Mr. Huxtable?"

"Unrelenting heat," he said. "Bugs. Diseases."

"Ah." She lowered her head to look at him. "The ugliness at the heart of beauty. Is there always ugliness, do you suppose? Even when the object is very, very beautiful?"

Her eyes were suddenly huge and fathomless. And sad.

"Not always," he said. "I prefer to believe the opposite — that there is always an

76

indestructible beauty at the heart of darkness."

"Indestructible," she said softly. "You are an optimist, then."

"There is nothing else to be," he said, "if one's human existence is to be bearable."

"It is," she said, "very easy to despair. We always live on the cliff edge of tragedy, do we not?"

"Yes," he said. "The secret is never to give in to the urge to jump off voluntarily."

She continued to gaze into his eyes. Her eyelids did not droop, he noticed. Her lips did not smile. But they *were* slightly parted.

She looked . . . different.

The purely objective part of his mind informed him that there was no one else in this particular greenhouse, and that they were hidden from view where they stood.

He lowered his head and touched his lips lightly to hers. They were soft and warm, slightly moist, and yielding. He touched his tongue to the opening between them, traced the outline of the upper lip and then the lower, and then slid his tongue into her mouth. Her teeth did not bar the way. He curled his tongue and drew the tip slowly over the roof of her mouth before withdrawing it and lifting his head away from hers.

She tasted of wine and of warm, enticing woman.

He looked deeply into her eyes, and she gazed back for a few moments until there was a very subtle change in her expression. Her eyelids drooped again, her lips turned upward at the corners, and she was herself once more. It had seemed as if she were replacing a mask.

Which was an interesting possibility.

"I hope, Mr. Huxtable," she said, "you can live up to the promise of that kiss. I shall be vastly disappointed if you cannot."

"We will put it to the test tonight," he said.

"Tonight?" She raised her eyebrows.

"You must not be alone," he said, "while Miss Leavensworth is off somewhere dining and attending the opera. You might be lonely and bored. You will dine with me instead."

"And then?" Her eyebrows remained elevated.

"And then," he said, "we will indulge in a decadent dessert in my bedchamber."

"Oh." She seemed to be considering. "But I have another engagement this evening, Mr. Huxtable. How very inconvenient. Perhaps some other time."

"No," he said, "no other time. I play no games, Duchess. If you want me, it will be tonight. Not at some future date, when you deem you have tortured me enough."

"You feel tortured?" she asked.

"You will come tonight," he said, "or not at all."

She regarded him in silence for a few moments.

"Well, goodness me," she said, "I believe you mean it."

"I do," he said.

He did too. He had warned her before that he was no puppet on a string. And while a little dalliance was amusing, it was not to be perpetuated indefinitely.

"Oh," she said, "I *do* like a masterful, impatient man. It is really quite titillating, you know. Not that I intend to be mastered, Mr. Huxtable. Not by any man. And not ever. But I do believe I am going to have to disappoint the gentleman with whom I promised to spend this evening. He has only dinner to offer without the dessert, you see. Or a *decadent* dessert, anyway. It sounds quite irresistibly delicious."

"It is a sweet that can be consumed only by two," he said. "We will consume it tonight. I shall send —"

She interrupted him at the same moment as he heard the door opening.

"But these are only *ferns,*" she said disdainfully. "I can find ferns in any English country lane. I wish to see the orchids. Take me to find them, Mr. Huxtable."

"It will be my pleasure, Duchess," he said as she took his arm.

"And then you may take me for tea on the upper terrace," she said just before they nodded and exchanged pleasantries with the group of guests entering the greenhouse.

"The third greenhouse along for the orchids, Your Grace," Miss Gorman said.

"Ah, thank you. How kind." The duchess smiled at her. "We started at the wrong end."

And so, Constantine thought as they emerged into the spring sunshine and went in search of the orchids, it appeared to be a done deal. He had his mistress for this Season. Which was very satisfying in many ways, especially as the liaison was to be consummated tonight. He had been celibate for quite long enough.

But . . . not in *every* way?

Despite the fact that she was a beautiful, alluring, fascinating creature? Who apparently wanted him as much as he wanted her?

He was not quite sure why this year felt different from any other.

You must always be aware of the power of

the unexpected, my dearest love, the duke had once told Hannah. *You must also be aware that it ought not to be used at all frequently, or it no longer is the unexpected.*

"The emeralds, of course, Adèle," Hannah said now to her maid.

She had clothes and jewels in all sorts of bright colors, though she very rarely wore anything but white. It was what people expected of her — white garments and diamonds. And of course white, which included all colors of the spectrum, was always startlingly more noticeable in a crowd than all the myriad colors with which others bedecked themselves. The duke had taught her that too.

Tonight, though, she would not be in a crowd.

And tonight she would do the unexpected and throw the oh-so-complacent Constantine Huxtable off balance.

Tonight she wore a gown of emerald green satin. It was cut really quite shockingly low at the bosom, and it caught the candlelight with her every movement, shimmering about her person as it did so. And tonight she would wear emeralds instead of diamonds.

And tonight, most unexpected of all, she did not wear her hair up as she almost

81

always did — as most ladies almost always did. She wore it in a sleek, shining cap over her head and held at the nape of her neck with an emerald-studded clasp. All the hair below the clasp billowed in untamed waves and curls halfway to her waist.

"You will not wait up for me, Adèle," she said as she rose from the stool on which she had been seated before the dressing table, all her jewels in place to her satisfaction. "I shall be very late. And you will be sure to deliver my note into the hands of Miss Leavensworth when she returns from the opera."

"I will, Your Grace." Her maid bobbed a curtsy and left the dressing room.

Hannah looked at herself critically in the long pier glass. She straightened her spine, drew her shoulders back, raised her chin, and half smiled at her image.

She had not been quite sure about the hair. But she had made the right decision, she thought now. And if she had not, it did not matter. This was how she *chose* to present herself to her lover. And so it was the right decision.

Her *lover.* Her smile became almost mocking.

He would *not* look at her with his usual dark, inscrutable eyes when he saw her tonight. She would see in them the spark of desire that she knew he felt.

The devil was about to be tamed.

Which was a ghastly thought if she stopped to consider it. If she tamed him, of what further interest would he be to her? A tamed devil would be the most bland and abject and *pathetic* of creatures.

She wanted a *lover.* She wanted it all. Everything that the world of sensual pleasures had to offer even if she had to descend to the underworld with the devil himself to find it.

She was *thirty years old.* Why did that seem so very much older than twenty-nine?

What would Barbara have to say if she were here now, Hannah wondered as she turned from the glass and took up her cloak, which had been set over the back of a chair. She drew it on and clasped it at the neck and settled the wide hood carefully over her head. She picked up her small reticule. No fan tonight. She would have no need of one.

Barbara would probably not say anything. She would not need to. She would *look* with reproachful, slightly wounded eyes. Barbara would think she was about to do something dreadfully immoral. Hannah disagreed with her. She was no longer married. And Barbara would think she was about to set her feet on the road to heartbreak. Hannah disagreed again. She was merely going to sleep with a very, very attractive, experienced man. Almost every part of her body was going to be involved *except* her heart.

Very *happily* involved.

She was not making a mistake. This was all happening faster than she had intended, it was true. She was not quite sure she should have capitulated quite so easily this afternoon. He had probably not *really* meant that he would have nothing more to do with her if she refused to go to him tonight. And if he had meant it, so what? There were other men. But she *had* capitulated. She had wanted a masterful man, after all, one who was not going to be a mere lapdog, as Barbara had phrased it.

No, she was not making a mistake.

She glanced one more time at her image. There. She was all white again.

The carriage he had sent for her had already been waiting at the door when Adèle had been sent in search of the emeralds. It had arrived right on time.

Which meant that she was now about fifteen minutes late.

Just right.

She swept from the room and down the

stairs to the hall, where a smartly liveried footman waited to open the door for her.

CHAPTER 5

Constantine Huxtable did not take bachelor rooms in the area of St. James's and all the gentlemen's clubs, as many gentlemen did when they were in town alone. Instead, he leased a house each year in an area quite respectable enough for his status in society, but not quite fashionable enough to impinge upon his privacy.

Or so Hannah guessed as the coachman handed her down onto the pavement outside his door and she looked curiously up and down the street. It was still daylight. They were to dine relatively early.

A servant had already opened the door of the house. Hannah lifted the hems of her cloak and dress, climbed the steps, and swept past him into a square, spacious hall with a black and white tiled floor and landscapes in heavy gilded frames hanging on the walls.

Constantine Huxtable was standing in the

middle of the hall, all in black, as usual, and looking really very satanic indeed.

"Duchess?" He made her an elegant bow. "Welcome to my home."

"I hope," she said, "your chef has excelled himself this evening. I have not eaten since the garden party, and I am famished."

"He will be dismissed without a reference tomorrow morning if he has not," he said, stepping forward to take her cloak.

"How very ruthless you are," she said and stood where she was, a few steps inside the door.

He pursed his lips slightly and came even closer in order to lower her hood and then undo the clasp that held her cloak closed at the throat. He removed the garment and handed it to the silent servant without taking his eyes off her. They moved very deliberately down her body and back up to her head and down to her eyes.

There was not a flicker of surprise in his eyes. But there was *something* there. Some suggestion of heat, perhaps. He *had* been taken by surprise.

Hannah wished that after all she had brought a fan.

"You are looking particularly lovely this evening, Duchess," he said and offered her his arm.

He led her to a room that was small and square and cozy. Heavy draperies drawn across the window shut out the last vestiges of the daylight. The only light came from the fire crackling in the hearth and two long tapers in crystal holders set on a smallish table in the middle of the room. The table was set for two.

This was not the dining room, Hannah guessed.

He had chosen a more intimate setting.

He crossed to a sideboard and poured two glasses of wine before pulling on a bell rope. He handed one of the glasses to Hannah.

"On an empty stomach, Mr. Huxtable?" she asked. "Do you wish to see me dancing on the table?"

"Not on the *table,* Duchess," he said, clinking his glass against hers in a silent toast.

She sipped her wine.

"But I need no encouragement to dance elsewhere," she told him. "The wine will be wasted on me."

"Then I hope that at least it tastes good," he said.

It did, of course.

The butler and a footman entered with their food, and they took their places at the table.

The chef was excellent, Hannah soon discovered. They ate in near-silence for a while.

"Tell me," she said at last, "about your home, Mr. Huxtable."

"About Warren Hall?" he said.

"That *was* your home," she said. "It is the Earl of Merton's now. Do you have a good relationship with him?"

But they had been riding in the park together.

"An excellent one," he said.

"And where do you live now?" she asked.

He indicated the room with one hand.

"Here," he said.

"But not all year," she said. "Where do you live when you are not in town?"

"I have a home in Gloucestershire," he told her.

She stared at him while their soup bowls were removed and the fish course was set before them.

"You are not going to tell me about it, are you?" she said. "How tiresome of you. Another secret to add to the one concerning your quarrel with the Duke of Moreland. And to add to the mystery of why you have an excellent relationship with the Earl of Merton when he stole the title that should rightfully be yours."

He set his knife and fork down quietly across his plate. He looked into her eyes across the table. His looked very black.

"You have been misinformed, Duchess," he said. "The title was never to be mine. There was never any question that it might be. It was my father's and then my younger brother's, and now it is my cousin's. I have no reason to resent any of them. I loved my father and brother. I am fond of Stephen. They are all family. One is meant to love family."

Ah, she had rubbed him on the raw. His voice and manner were perfectly controlled, but . . .

Too controlled?

"Except the Duke of Moreland," she said.

He continued to look at her and neglect his food.

Their plates were borne away and another course brought on.

"And what about *your* family, Duchess?" he asked.

She shrugged.

"There is the duke," she said. "The current duke, that is. He is blameless and harmless and about as interesting as the corn and the sheep upon which he dotes. And the duke, my husband, had an army of other relatives, with none of whom he was remotely close."

"And *your* family?" he asked.

She picked up her glass, twirled it slowly for the pleasure of seeing the light of the candle refracted off the crystal, and sipped the wine.

"None," she said. "And so there is nothing to say. No secrets to hide or divulge. Let me tell you about *my* home in Kent — Copeland. The duke bought it for me five years ago. He always referred to it as my quaint little country box, but it is neither quaint nor little nor a box. It is a manor, even a mansion. And it has a park that rolls away in all four directions from the house in a rural splendor that is half cultivated, half not. At least, it is *all* well kept, but it is all natural woodland and natural grassland and a natural lake. There are no arbors or parterres or wilderness walks. It really is quite . . . rustic. That is something the duke might have called it without any sacrifice of accuracy."

She cut into her beef, which looked and felt as if it had been cooked to perfection.

"It is all perhaps a little *too* natural for you, Duchess?" he asked.

"Sometimes," she said, "I fear it is. I feel that I *ought* to impose my human will upon it all, that it ought to look *pretty,* as the

91

garden this afternoon looked pretty."

"And yet?" He paused in his eating again.

"And yet," she said, "I confess to liking it as it is. Nature needs to be tamed sometimes. It is only civilized. But ought we to force it to be something it is not meant to be just for the sake of beauty? What *is* beauty?"

"Now there," he said, "is a question for the ages."

"You must come and see for yourself," she said, "and tell me what you think."

"I *must* come?" He raised his eyebrows. "To Kent?"

"I shall arrange a brief house party a little later in the Season when everyone is starting to find the endless round of balls here tedious," she said. "It will all be perfectly respectable, I assure you, though everyone will know by then, of course, that we are lovers. People always *do* know these things, even when they are not true. Which will not be the case with us. You will give me your opinion about the park."

"And you will follow my advice?" he asked.

"Quite possibly not," she said. "But I will listen anyway."

"I am honored," he said.

"And I am full," she announced. "You will

give your chef my compliments, Mr. Huxtable?"

"I will," he said. "He will be vastly relieved to know that he is not to be dismissed tomorrow morning. Do you not want cheese or coffee? Or tea?"

She did not. She had been trying all evening to distract herself with conversation. And she had been trying to pretend to herself that she was hungry — which she ought to be since she really had not eaten since the garden party, when he had filled a plate with dainties for her from the table on the upper terrace.

She rested one elbow on the table, set her chin in her hand, and gazed at him between the two candles.

"Only dessert, Mr. Huxtable," she said and felt all the delicious anticipation of what she had dreamed about through the second half of her year of mourning and planned during the months since Christmas.

Anticipation and trepidation too. She must certainly not show the latter. It would seem quite out of character.

She was so glad it was him. She would have been disappointed if he had not been in town this year. Not devastated. She had had other, perfectly eligible alternatives in mind. But none quite to match Constantine

Huxtable.

She thought he might be an extraordinary lover. In fact, she was quite confident that he would be.

And she was about to find out if she was right. He had stood up, pushing his chair out of the way with the backs of his legs, and he was coming the short distance around the table to offer her his hand.

It was warm and firm, she discovered as she set her own in it. And he seemed somehow taller and broader when she got to her feet. His cologne, the same as she had noticed before, wrapped about her senses again.

"Let us go and have it, then," he said, "without further ado."

She looked up at him through her eyelashes.

"I do hope *this* chef does not disappoint," she said.

"If he does, Duchess," he said, "I shall not only dismiss him in the morning, I shall also take him out to some remote spot and shoot him."

"Drastic measures indeed," she said. "And what a waste it would be of all that Greek beauty. But doubtless it will be quite unnecessary. For he will *not* disappoint. I will not allow it."

He tucked her arm through his and led her from the room.

The English language was sometimes quite inadequate to express one's thoughts, Constantine had been realizing all evening. What words were there to describe something that was more beautiful than beautiful and more perfect than perfect?

He had always thought of the Duchess of Dunbarton as a perfectly beautiful woman even when he had not felt particularly drawn to her.

Tonight she exceeded those superlatives.

He could not remember ever seeing her in any color but white. He had always thought it remarkably clever of her to make that single color her signature, so to speak. But of course, this departure from the norm was equally clever — and stunning.

She looked . . . Well, she looked those words that did not exist. *Stunning* was perhaps the only word that was even remotely adequate.

His cook might have served them leather and gravel for all the attention he had paid to his meal. And all the while he had had to concentrate hard upon not gawking.

The color of her gown and jewels transformed her from an ice queen into some sort of fertility goddess. And her hair, which every male member of the *ton* had probably dreamed of seeing tumble about her shoulders, was in a billow of riotous waves down her back while it hugged her head in shining smoothness.

The décolletage of her gown left little to the imagination and yet teased it nevertheless. Just one inch lower . . .

Monty had called her dangerous that afternoon in Hyde Park.

She was more dangerous than the Sirens of mythology.

And she had carried on a conversation that contained almost none of the innuendo that usually characterized their verbal exchanges. Indeed, when she had got to talking about her home in Kent, she had sounded . . . warm. As if she genuinely liked the place.

She was very, very clever. He was going to have to be very careful, he thought as he led her in silence up the stairs in the direction of his bedchamber. Though he did not know quite over *what* he needed to exercise care. They were about to become lovers, after all. And they would remain lovers, probably, for the whole Season.

Not any longer than that, of course. And if she wished to make it not so long, well then, that was her choice. He was not going to be heartbroken, was he?

There was a single branch of candles burning on the low chest in the corner of his room. The bedcovers had been turned back, the curtains drawn across the window, a wine decanter and glasses left on a tray beside the bed. Everything was ready.

He closed the door behind them.

The Duchess of Dunbarton sighed audibly as she slipped her arm from his and turned toward him. It sounded almost like the purr of a contented cat.

"There is nothing quite like the pleasure of anticipation, is there?" she said. "It has been humming through my blood since this afternoon, I must confess. I am not at all sorry I decided to cancel my earlier appointment and come here instead."

She set the tip of her finger lightly against the point of his chin and moved it slowly back and forth. Her eyes followed her finger.

"I am not altogether sorry either," he admitted.

"You will savor every moment, I trust," she said. "I do hope you are not one of those men who feel they must demonstrate their masculinity by the speed with which they run the race."

Her eyes came up to his though she did

not raise her head.

"Alas, Duchess," he said, "I *do* plan to run a race. A marathon. Do you know your Greek history?"

"Many miles?" she said. "Many hours? Almost superhuman endurance?"

"You do know it," he said.

Her hand slipped downward to rest on his shoulder. Her other hand came up to rest on the other.

"You had better not expend any more energy on talk, then, Mr. Huxtable," she said. "You had better begin this endurance race, this *marathon,* without further delay."

And her glorious blue bedroom eyes gazed dreamily into his.

He lowered his head and set his lips to hers.

He rested his hands on either side of her small waist while she slid her hands about his neck and pressed her lips back against his own.

She was hot, already very much aroused despite her clear warning to him not to forget the importance of foreplay.

He had not expected a passionate woman, and perhaps he would be proved right once they got fully launched into this encounter. Perhaps after all she would be the skilled, experienced, sensual, controlled lover he had thought she would be. And perhaps she was clever enough, confident enough, to throw passion into the mix as well.

He enjoyed passion, though he rarely got it with any of his mistresses, he realized. Passion involved some feeling, some emotion, a little bit of risk. Most of the women he had bedded had been looking for some companionship and a lot of vigorous sex. And that had always suited him too. Better no passion at all than too much of the wrong sort.

Passion could lead to an unwelcome emotional attachment. He did not want any woman attached to him that way. It had never been his wish to hurt any woman.

But the objective thoughts were only fleeting. She had pressed her bosom against his chest, her abdomen and thighs against his, and her mouth had angled and opened over his.

He felt a flaring of intense desire.

At last!

It was many months since he had had a woman. He had not realized quite how famished he was.

He lifted his hands to cup her face, to hold it a few inches from his own. And he slid his hands around the base of her head to the jeweled clasp that kept her hair confined.

He unclasped it and let it fall to the carpet. He took her hair in both hands to rearrange it. It needed no encouragement but spread across her back and over her shoulders in a gleaming cloud of soft waves.

He almost hissed in an audible breath.

She looked ten years younger. She looked . . . innocent. With bedroom eyes that even in the dim candlelight looked very blue. An innocent Siren — an enticing oxymoron.

"I cannot do the like for you," she said, "though some might say your hair is a little overlong for fashion. You must not cut it, though. I forbid it."

"I am to be your love slave and ever obedient?" he asked, dipping his head to kiss her behind one earlobe, holding her hair back with one finger as he did so. He flicked his tongue over the soft flesh there at the last moment, and had the satisfaction of feeling a slight tremor run through her.

"Not at all," she said, "but you will do what pleases me because it pleases *you*. I shall remove your coat since you wear no hair clasp."

It was not easy. His valet had a hard enough time getting him into his coats so that they fit him, as fashion dictated, like a second skin. But her fingers fluttered over his chest beneath it and up over his shoulders and down along his arms, and his coat obediently followed the path her hands took and soon fell to the floor behind him.

It was not, he thought, the first time she had done that.

Her eyes moved over his shirt and cravat, and then her hands moved up to the latter and deftly removed it. She undid the buttons at his throat and opened the top of his shirt.

Constantine watched her as she worked, her eyes on what she was doing, her lips slightly parted.

There was no hurry. Absolutely no hurry at all. They had all night, and there were no prizes for the number of times he would mount her. Once might well be enough on this first occasion.

"You look magnificent in a shirt," she said. "Manly and virile. Take it off."

She was not going to do it for him?

He looked into her face as he pulled his shirt free of his waistband, undid the buttons at his wrists, crossed his arms, and drew the garment off over his head. She watched what he was doing, and then her eyes roamed over his shoulders, his upper arms, his chest and down to the waistband of his pantaloons. She set her fingertips

101

against his chest.

He nudged her hands aside with the backs of his, drew the satin of her gown to the edges of her shoulders, and then slid his thumbs into the décolletage of her gown at the center. He slid them outward, hooking the bodice under her breasts as he did so — something he had wanted to do every moment as they dined.

Her breasts were not particularly large. But they were firm and well shaped and up-tilted — helped by her stays, it was true — and they fit, warm and soft, in his hands. Her skin was fair, almost translucent in comparison to his. Her nipples were rosy and pebbled with sexual desire. He lowered his head and sucked one into his mouth. He rubbed his tongue over the tip.

He felt, rather than heard, her deep inward breath.

He moved his mouth to the other breast.

"Mmm." She made a sound of appreciation deep in her throat, threaded her fingers through his hair, and lifted his head. She tipped her own head back, hair streaming behind her, her eyes closed, and brought her breasts against his chest and then the rest of her body against his. She brought his face to her own, her mouth opening as it touched his.

He wrapped his arms about her, bringing her even closer, and abandoned himself for a long while to a kiss in which tongues thrust and parried and circled and stroked and teased and arms strained and breath quickened.

Then her arms moved down his back, her fingers pressing hard into his flesh. They kept on going when they reached his waist — beneath his pantaloons and his drawers. They spread over his buttocks.

"Take these off," she said into his mouth, pressing the backs of her fingers against the fabric.

Again — she was not going to do it herself? But she had already proved to him tonight that she was mistress of the unexpected. She watched as he removed first his shoes and stockings, and then his pantaloons and drawers. And she held her gown beneath her bosom — until he was finished. Then she released her hold, and the emerald green satin slithered down to the floor, and she stood before him in her stays and her silk stockings and slippers.

He would surely have taken her there and then if he had not had a glimmering of an understanding of how confining stays must be for a woman — and if he had not prom-ised a marathon. He unlaced her instead and dropped the stays on top of her gown.

A strange thing, fashion. She doubtless would not feel dressed without her stays, but she did not need them. She was slender and firm-muscled and shapely. Her breasts were firm and youthful. Her legs were long and slim. Sometimes she gave the illusion of being small in stature, but it *was* an illusion.

She sat on the side of his bed, her arms braced behind her, and lifted one of her legs toward him, her toes pointed. He drew off her stocking and then the other when she offered him that leg.

He leaned over her, bearing her back to the mattress, and kissed her deeply and open-mouthed, covering her breasts with his hands as he did so. He moved between her spread legs. Her arms were stretched out along the bed.

"How long does it *take* to run a marathon?" she asked when he lifted his head some time later. There was color in her cheeks, he could see.

"A whole night if necessary," he said. "Of course, it is always possible to cheat a little, to take shortcuts when no one is looking, to reach the finish line in considerably less than the whole night."

"I am all in favor of doing naughty things

when no one is looking," she said, her fingers tiptoeing over his shoulders.

"Very well, then," he said.

It was a huge relief actually. He was already aroused to the point of discomfort.

He straightened up and slid his hands beneath her, lifting her fully onto the bed, and turning her so that she lay along it instead of across. He peeled back the covers to the foot of the bed and lay down on his side, half over her, his head propped on one hand.

Her hands lay palm-down on the mattress.

He cupped her chin with one hand and kissed her as his hand moved downward, between her breasts, over her flat stomach, over the mound below, and between her legs. She was warm and moist there. He found her opening and pressed two fingers a little way inside her.

"Mmm." That deep sound in her throat again.

He rolled on top of her, spread her legs wide with his own, slid his hands beneath her to hold her firm, found the opening again, and thrust his full length deep into her.

There was the shock of heat, wetness, tight muscles, soft woman.

He imposed control on his breathing, on

his bodily reactions. The time of greatest enjoyment had come — at last — and he would not rush its conclusion, even with the encouragement she had given and his own driving need. He held still and noticed the almost rigid tension of her body only gradually relaxing. He waited for her.

The Duchess of Dunbarton.

Hannah.

He had a sudden mental image of her as he had seen her in the park that afternoon when he had been with Stephen and Monty.

Her arms wrapped loosely about his waist. Her legs lifted from the bed one at a time to twine about his. Heat radiated from her.

He lifted his head and looked down into her face.

Her eyes were in shadow. Her lower lip was caught between her teeth.

"The finish line is in sight," he murmured, "though it is still some distance off."

She had nothing to say. Her eyes closed, and he felt her clench hard about him.

He withdrew from her, heard her wordless murmur of protest, and pressed inward hard and deep again. And he repeated the motion until the rhythm matched his heartbeat and his whole being seemed immersed in the wet heat at the heart of her.

She was exquisite.

It was exquisite.

But it — the sex — could not be enjoyed without the awareness of who was giving him such pleasure. And she was clever to the end. Instead of the skilled moves he had expected — and had thought he wanted — she lay open and receptive and almost passive.

He had steeled himself for long endurance during foreplay and had been reprieved — though he would have enjoyed every moment of it if she had *not* reprieved him. He used the unexpended energy and control on the real play, the intercourse, the sex with the woman who would be his mistress for the next few months.

He played long and hard and deep in her until thought was gone and only the pounding pleasure-pain of thrust and withdrawal remained, and the woman's open receptiveness.

Hannah's receptiveness.

She was hot and slick with sweat and the juices of sex. Her breathing was labored.

And then even endurance went, and the ache of physical need broke the bonds of his control. His hands went beneath her again and held her while he plunged faster and harder and then pressed deeper than deep and held and . . . released into her.

107

Spilled into her.

He felt all the tension drain from his body as he relaxed down onto her. She had her head turned on his shoulder, her face away from him. She held him with her arms and legs — and he felt her gradually relax with him.

He drew free of her, felt the coolness of the air against his damp body, and reached down to pull the bedcovers up over them. He turned his head to look at her. Her hair was damp and in a riot of curls. Her eyes were blue again in the candlelight and were gazing back into his.

"I was quite right about you," she said.

"Is that good?" he asked her. "Or is it bad?"

"To be perfectly honest," she said, "I was *not* right. You are far better than I expected, Mr. Huxtable."

"Constantine," he said. "Con to most people."

"I shall always call you Constantine," she said. "Why shorten a perfectly wonderful name? And you have passed the audition with flying colors. You have the part for a lengthy spell."

Lengthy?

"Until the summer, that is," she said. "Until I go home to Kent to stay and you go to wherever it is you live in Gloucester-shire."

"How do you know," he said, "that *you* have passed the audition?"

She raised her eyebrows.

"Don't be foolish, Constantine," she said.

And it struck him that he was not certain she had climaxed with him. She certainly had not done so before or after him.

Had she? Climaxed, that was?

And what did it mean if she had not? That he had failed her? Her words indicated quite the contrary. That for her even sex was a matter of power and control, then? Oh, and some enjoyment too. She had certainly enjoyed herself.

He would prefer to know, though, that she had enjoyed herself to completion. He would not ask her, however.

"I shall put you to the test again later," he said. "For now you have exhausted me, Duchess, and I need to recoup my strength."

"Hannah," she said. "My name is Hannah."

"Yes, I know," he said, rolling onto his back and setting the back of one hand over his eyes. "Duchess."

He was not going to get too close to her. Which was a somewhat absurd thought under the circumstances.

He was not going to get emotionally close.

She was not going to control him.

That was something that was *not* going to happen.

He really was exhausted. Pleasantly so. He stretched luxuriously beneath the covers. He could feel her body heat along his right side. He could smell her — a mingling of expensive perfume and sweat. An erotically pleasant smell.

He drifted off to sleep.

And woke up an indeterminate amount of time later to find the bed empty beside him, the curtains drawn back from the window, and the Duchess of Dunbarton, clothed only in his white shirt and her white-blond hair, sitting on the wide window ledge, her legs drawn up before her, her arms wrapped about herself, gazing out through the window.

Fortunately — *very* fortunately — the candles had all burned themselves out. She would have made a very interesting window ornament to anyone glancing up from the street below, even clad in his shirt.

The fact that the candles *had* burned out, of course, meant that he must have slept most of the night. Though he could see when he gazed into the corner that the tapers were still fairly long.

She had had the good sense to snuff them, then, before taking up her place in the window.

"Anything interesting going on out there?" he asked, linking his hands behind his head. She turned her head to look at him.

"No, nothing at all," she said. "Just as there is not in here."

Well. He had walked straight into that one.

CHAPTER 6

There was just empty night out there, Hannah saw when she parted the curtains and gazed out. There were no carriages, no pedestrians, no light in the windows of the houses opposite, except perhaps one flickering in a downstairs window about six houses down. She had blown out the candles in this room before looking out.

She closed the curtains and stood for a few moments at the foot of the bed. Constantine was fast asleep, one arm draped over his eyes. He was breathing deeply and evenly. One of his knees was raised and making a small tent of the bedcovers. She could see him quite clearly even in the darkness.

She wondered if he would sleep all night and smiled slightly. He had said she had exhausted him, and she was not surprised. He had run his marathon after all.

She was really very sore indeed. It was not

an altogether unpleasant sensation.

She shivered in the night air and looked around for her gown. She could see it in a dark heap on the floor under her stays, no doubt horribly creased. And she could see the lighter outline of his shirt. She bent and picked it up and held it to her face for a moment. It smelled of his cologne and of him.

She pulled it on over her head, pushed her arms through the sleeves, and hugged it about herself. Goodness, but he was large. She approved of his largeness.

She considered climbing back into bed beneath the covers and curling up beside him, warming herself with his body heat. But she did not want to *sleep* with him. There was a certain loss of control in slumber. One never knew what one might say when asleep or when one first awoke, before one was fully conscious and aware. Or what one might *feel* in those unguarded hours.

She went back to the window, parted the curtains again with the backs of her hands, and looked at the sill. It was not exactly a window seat, but it was wide enough nevertheless. She pulled the curtains right back and sat on the sill, pulling her feet up onto it, wrapping her arms about herself for warmth. She rested the side of her head against the glass.

All was quiet. And dark. And peaceful.

She could still hear his deep breathing. It was a strangely comforting sound. Another human being was close.

She was not sorry. She was *never* sorry for anything she did, especially as she rarely acted out of impulse. All was planned and controlled in her life — as she liked it.

The only thing you can neither plan nor control, my dearest love, the duke had once told her, *is love itself. When you find it, you must yield to it. But only if it is the one and only true passion of your life. Never if it is anything less than that, or life will consume you.*

But how am I to know? she had asked him.

You will know. It was the only answer he had been willing to give.

She was a little afraid that she would never know love. Not *that* kind of love, anyway. Not the all-consuming, once-in-a-lifetime kind of which the duke had spoken — from personal experience. It surely did not happen to everyone. Maybe not to many people at all. Maybe not to her.

She had loved *him.* She shivered and hugged herself more tightly. Sometimes she thought she had never loved anyone else in her life *but* him. But that was surely not true, and there were degrees of love. She loved Barbara.

No, she was not sorry for tonight.

And she was *not* feeling guilty. There was no reason in the world why she should not be here with her lover, in his bedchamber, having just had marital relations with him. Except that they had not been marital, had they? Her vocabulary was really quite puritanical at times. She must do something about that. She was free and unattached, and so was he. They might have relations as often as they chose without feeling *guilt.*

She ought to have noticed that she could no longer hear his breathing. His voice took her by surprise.

"Anything interesting going on out there?" he asked.

She turned her head to look at him, but her eyes had adjusted to the slightly lighter darkness of the outdoors and all she could see for the moment was a dark silhouette.

"No, nothing at all," she said. "Just as there is not in here."

"Are you complaining, Duchess," he asked, "because I used up so much energy that I had to sleep?"

"And are you looking for another compliment, Constantine?" she asked in return. "I believe I have already told you that you far exceeded my expectations."

He had thrown back the covers and was getting out of bed. He bent down to rummage among the heap of their clothing, and pulled on first his drawers, and then his pantaloons. He turned his back to her, and she heard the clink of glass against glass. He came toward her carrying two glasses of wine. He handed her one and stood with one bare shoulder propped against the window frame. He looked long and lean and virile.

All of which attributes Hannah viewed with open approval as she sipped from her glass. She could not possibly have chosen a more perfect male specimen if she had tried. He was even more splendid without his clothes — and even half clothed — than with. With many people clothes disguised a multitude of imperfections.

And he *had* exceeded her expectations.

Foolishly, given the fact of her soreness, she started to throb down there even *thinking* about how large and hard and very satisfactory he had been.

He crossed one leg carelessly over the other and drained his glass before setting it down on the end of the windowsill and crossing his arms over his chest.

"You are terribly beautiful," she said.

"Terribly?" She could see him raise his eyebrows. "I inspire terror in you?"

She drank some more.

"You are often referred to as the devil," she said. "You must know that. It *is* a little terrifying to have run a half marathon with the devil himself."

"And survived," he said.

"Oh, I will always survive," she said. "And I thrive on terror — for I am never terrified, you know."

"No," he said. "I don't suppose you are."

They gazed silently out at the street for a few moments while she finished her wine. He took the empty glass from her and set it down beside his.

"Your brother, the earl," she said. "Was he your only sibling?"

"The only surviving one," he said. "The eldest and the youngest — the only ones tough enough to live through childhood. And then Jon died when he was sixteen."

"Why?" she asked. "What was the cause of his death?"

"He should have died four or five years sooner than he did," he said, "according to the physicians. He always looked different from other people — in facial features and physique, I mean. My father always called him an imbecile. So did most other people. But he was not. His mind moved slowly, it is true, but he was by no means stupid. Quite the opposite. And he was love."

Hannah sat very still, hugging the shirt to herself. He was gazing out the window as if he had forgotten her for the moment.

"Not *loving*," he said, "though he was that too. He was love itself — a love that was free and unconditional and total. And he died. I had him four years longer than I was supposed to have him."

It was the nighttime and the darkness that made him talk so openly, Hannah suspected, and the fact that he had just been sleeping and had not yet fully armored himself with his usual defenses. She had been right not to sleep herself.

"You loved him dearly," she said softly.

His eyes rested on her. They looked very black.

"I also hated him," he said. "He had everything that ought to have been mine."

"Except health," she said.

"Except health," he agreed. "And wisdom. He loved even me. Especially me."

Hannah shivered again, and he reached down with both hands, clasped her upper arms, and lifted her off the sill just as if she weighed nothing at all. He wrapped his arms tightly about her as soon as her feet touched the floor, crushing her to him, and his mouth came down, open and hard, on her own.

Any attempt to struggle would be pointless, Hannah thought in the first startled moment, and it was always best not to indulge in a fight one could not win anyway. Not that she would *not* fight if this were something she really, really did not want, but —

Well, it was easier to stop thinking. And enjoy. For she *did* want it. And him.

She stepped closer until her bare feet touched his, wrapped her arms about him, and kissed him back with hot fervor. There was something different about this kiss. It was not the same game they had played earlier, before lying down on his bed. There was something more . . . *real* about this. More raw.

She stopped thinking.

And then his shirt was off over her head and his lower garments were on the floor again, and they were on the bed once more, tangled together, rolling together, first one on top and then the other, hands and mouths everywhere, even teeth, and this was indeed no game.

This was raw passion.

And she was giving as good as she got. This was . . .

She should put an end to it, Hannah thought. She should say no and he would stop. She knew he would. She was not at all afraid. Not that she needed to be afraid. He was her lover. She had chosen him for just this. But —

He was on top of her, thrusting her legs wide, and she was a moment or two late saying no. Indeed, she never did say it.

He plunged inside her.

It felt like a dagger being stabbed into a raw wound.

She flinched, gasped, tried to relax, and . . .

And he was gone.

At least, he was not *gone* exactly. He was out of her body, but he was still on the bed beside her, propped on one elbow, looming over her. She was very glad she had snuffed the candles. Not that the darkness gave much cover from eyes that had become accustomed to it.

"What?" he asked.

She reached up one hand and ran the tip of her forefinger down the center of his chest.

"What indeed?" she said.

"I *hurt* you?" he asked.

"It was time to stop," she said. "Once is quite enough for one night, Constantine. I must be getting home. You must not expect that I will spend all night with you now that we are lovers. That would be tedious."

"You were not a *virgin,* were you?" he asked.

It was a question asked in jest, of course. But she took just a little too long to answer, and when she did, it was with haughtily raised eyebrows, the full effect of which was probably lost in the darkness.

"You were a *virgin?*" It was not a joke this time. It was not even really a question.

She was thirty years old. There had been no barrier left. There had been no blood. But she had still been a virgin in every way that counted.

"Is there a *law* against virginity?" she asked him. "I have never chosen to take a lover until now, Constantine, when I chose you. I thought you would be superior, and you are. Not that I have anyone with whom to compare you, it is true, but only a fool would wonder if perhaps you are only mediocre."

"You were married," he said, "for *ten years.*"

"To an elderly gentleman who was really not interested in that aspect of our marital relationship," she said. "Which was just as well because I was not interested in it either. I married him for other reasons."

"You became a duchess," he said, supplying the only reasons there could possibly be, "and a wealthy one."

"Positively rolling in riches," she agreed. "And I am unlikely ever to acquire that ghastly title of *dowager* duchess as the current duke will almost certainly never marry. He has a mistress and ten children, ranging in age from eighteen to two, but he took her out of a brothel and will not, of course, marry her."

"That is rather unsavory knowledge for a *lady* to have," he said.

"Fortunately," she said, "the duke — *my* duke — never did withhold the most interesting pieces of information from me. He heard all the most salacious gossip and came home and entertained me with it."

"So," he said, "no marital relations, Duchess. But what about the army of lovers you took during your marriage? *Apparently* took, that is."

"You listen to too much gossip," she said. "Or, rather, since we all *listen,* you believe too much. Do you really believe I would break *marriage* vows?"

"Even when you were getting no satisfaction from your husband?" he asked.

"I may be a merry widow now, Constantine," she said. "Indeed, I intend to make very merry with you for the rest of the spring, though not again tonight. I may be a merry widow, but I was a faithful wife. And not because I was coerced into fidelity, though you may jump to that odious conclusion. It would be odious, you know. My duke was anything but a tyrant — to me, anyway. I *chose* to be faithful, just as I now *choose* to take a lover. I am always in control of my own life."

He stared down at her in silence for a few moments, and for the first time it struck her that it must have taken enormous control on his part to withdraw from her when he was fully aroused, and then lie still and talk with her.

If she had said no in time, he would have stopped sooner, and they would not have had this conversation. That would teach her a lesson about hesitation.

It did not matter, though. Nothing was changed. Not for her. For him, perhaps. He had thought he was getting an experienced mistress.

"Well," he said softly, "an outer petal falls away from the rose. Are there any more within, I wonder?"

He was not expecting an answer. He got none. Whatever was he talking about, anyway?

"I might have run the race with you with somewhat less, ah, *vigor* if I had known," he said. "I might —"

"Constantine," she said, interrupting him, "if you *ever* try to patronize me or be gentle with me or humor me as a delicate *lady*, I shall —"

"Yes?" he said.

"I shall drop you," she said, "as I would a live coal. And by the next day I shall have another lover, twice as handsome and three times as virile as you. I shall not spare you another thought."

"And that is a threat?" he asked, sounding anything but threatened.

"Of course not," she said scornfully. "I never make *threats*. Why ever would I need to? It is *information*. It is what will happen if you should ever try to treat me as anything less than I am."

"I was merely telling you," he said, "that the way a man makes love to a virgin is different from the way he does it with an experienced woman. I would have given you no less pleasure, Duchess. Perhaps I would have given you more."

His free hand, she realized, was stroking

lightly over her abdomen. It was warmer than her own flesh.

"I suppose," she said, "you make love to a virgin at least once a fortnight."

She could see his teeth very white in contrast to the rest of his face. He was smiling. That was a rare enough event — and there was no daylight with which to see it properly.

"One hates to boast," he said, "or exaggerate. Once a *month*."

He bent his head and kissed her softly on the mouth.

"I am sorry," he murmured.

She tapped him sharply on one cheek.

"You must never *ever* say you are sorry," she said. "You must never even *feel* sorry. If you always act with deliberate intent, there is nothing to be sorry about. And if you act in ignorance, there is nothing to apologize for. I do not apologize for having been a virgin until an hour or two ago. It was what I chose to be. And I do not apologize for withholding the information from you. It is something you did not need to know. It was, as you said on the night of the concert when I asked about your quarrel with the Duke of Moreland, none of your business. And while we are on this topic, I will tell you now that for the rest of this spring, while we are having our affair, I will be faithful to you. And I expect that you will be faithful to me. I will go home now."

"There may be no more petals on the bloom," he said, "but there are certainly thorns enough on the stem. I do believe, Duchess, you may be quite confident of my fidelity for the next few months. I would not have the physical stamina to take on another one like you — or even unlike you, for that matter. Lie there for a while, and I will go and rouse my coachman. He will not be delighted. He expects to be called out early in the morning, but I believe this hour qualifies more as middle of the night than morning."

He got out of bed as he spoke and pulled on his clothes.

Hannah lay where she was until he had left the room.

Well, this had been an interesting night. And not an altogether comfortable one. It had not turned out anything like what she had expected.

For one thing, the actual . . . *experience* had been far more carnal than anything she had imagined. Oh, and probably at least twice as pleasurable too, even if it *had* left her annoyingly sore.

But it had also left her with the uneasy

suspicion that having a lover was going to involve a little more than just sprightly innuendo and vigorous bed sport. And she really had not expected or wanted more.

She suspected that this liaison with Constantine Huxtable was going to involve some sort of *relationship,* just as her marriage had.

She did not *want* a relationship. Not this time.

Except that she did. She just wanted it to be one-sided or on her terms. She realized that fact with some surprise. Right from the start she had wanted to know more about him — *everything* about him, in fact. She had told him so. He was such a dark, mysterious man. Certain things were known *about* him. But she did not know anyone who *knew* him. Her duke had not, though he had spoken of him from time to time. He had suspected that Constantine's brooding darkness held hatred, that his often charming social manner held love, and that therefore he was a complex, dangerous, impossibly attractive man. He had actually *said* that.

It was probably in those words that she had found the seed of her decision to take Mr. Constantine Huxtable for a lover.

Tonight he had told her he had hated his young, mentally handicapped brother. And yet *she* could tell *him* with the greatest confidence that he had loved his brother too. Probably to the point of great pain.

What she had *not* realized until tonight, fool that she was, was that a relationship could not be an entirely one-sided thing. He had found out more about her tonight than she had about him.

Good heavens!

Her reputation would be in tatters if he told the *ton* what he had discovered tonight. Not that he would tell, of course.

But *he* knew.

How provoking!

She did not want a relationship. She wanted only . . . well, she must learn to use the word. The duke had always used it in her hearing, and she was not missish. She wanted only *sex* with Constantine Huxtable.

And it really had been glorious tonight, the sex. It had not even been painful until afterward. While it had been happening, it could have gone on all night as far as she was concerned. Poor Constantine. He would be *dead*.

Hannah snorted inelegantly as she swung her legs over the side of the bed and found her stockings.

■ ■ ■ ■

She did not want him to go with her, but Constantine gave her no choice. He handed her into the carriage and climbed in beside her. He took her hand in his and rested it on his thigh.

She looked more her usual self in her white cloak, the wide hood pulled up over her head.

He would never see her the same way again, though. Which was understandable, of course. He had seen her without the clothes and the careful coiffure. He had possessed her body.

But it was not just that.

At least in one respect she was not the woman everyone thought her to be, that everyone *assumed* her to be. The sort of woman she had surely gone out of her way to pretend to be.

Her marriage to the duke had never been consummated. That was not particularly surprising in itself. There had been endless speculation about it, in fact. But all those lovers she had flaunted before society — Zimmer, Bentley, Hardingraye, to name just a few.

Not lovers.

He had been her first.

It was a dizzying thought. He had never before been anyone's first. He had never wanted to be.

Good Lord!

"You will need a few days to recover, Duchess," he said as the carriage neared Hanover Square. "Shall we say next Tuesday, after the Kitteridge ball?"

She would never allow him the last word, of course — though she *had* at the garden party yesterday afternoon, had she not? It was her turn, then.

"Next *Monday* night," she said. "The duke keeps a box at the theater, but there is no one to use it except me. I have promised Barbara that we will go. I shall invite Mr. and Mrs. Park too, and perhaps their son, the clergyman, if he is in town. You will escort me."

"The perfect group," he said. "A clergyman, a clergyman's betrothed — though not to the aforementioned clergyman, the first clergyman's parents, and the Duchess of Dunbarton with her new paramour, sometimes known as the devil."

"One always likes to provide interesting topics for drawing room conversations," she said.

Yes, he could imagine one did if one happened to be the Duchess of Dunbarton.

He lifted her hand to his lips as he felt the carriage turning into the square and then slowing and stopping. He lowered his head and kissed her mouth.

"I shall look forward to Monday night with the greatest impatience," he said.

"But not Monday *evening?*" she asked.

"I will tolerate it," he said. "Dessert is always more appetizing at the end of a meal, after all, as we discovered this evening."

And he rapped on the inside of the carriage door to indicate to his coachman that they were ready to descend.

Someone had already been roused inside the house. The doors opened even as Constantine stepped down to the pavement and turned to hand the duchess down.

A moment later he watched her ascend the steps unhurriedly, her back straight, her head high. The doors closed quietly behind her.

This felt a little different from his usual springtime affair, Constantine thought.

A little less comfortable.

A little more erotic.

What the devil had he meant — *I also hated him.*

He had *never* hated Jon. Not even for the merest moment. He had *loved* him. He still

131

mourned him. Sometimes he thought he would never stop grieving. There was a huge, empty black hole where Jon had been.

I also hated him.

He had spoken those words to *the Duchess of Dunbarton,* of all people.

What the *devil* had he meant?

And what *else* was she hiding apart from the minor, now-revealed fact that she had come to him tonight as a virgin?

The answer was absolutely nothing, of course. She had readily admitted that she married Dunbarton for the title and the money. And now she was using her freedom and power to take a little sensual pleasure for herself.

He could hardly blame her.

He turned and frowned at his coachman, who was waiting for him to climb back inside the carriage.

"Take it home," he said. "I'll walk."

His coachman shook his head slightly and shut the door.

"Right you are, sir," he said.

CHAPTER 7

The clergyman son of Mr. and Mrs. Park was *not* in town. Mrs. Park's younger brother was staying with them for a while, however, and was more than gratified to be invited to join a party in the theater box of the Duchess of Dunbarton on Monday evening with his sister and brother-in-law. Hannah also invited Lord and Lady Montford after she and Barbara met the latter at Hookham's Library on Monday morning and stopped for a brief chat.

Lady Montford was Mr. Huxtable's cousin.

"The opera and the theater both in one week," Barbara said as she and Hannah sat side by side in the carriage on Monday evening. "Not to mention the galleries and museums and the library and the shopping. I find myself writing half a *book* each day to Mama and Papa and to Simon instead of just a letter. I will be running you dry of ink, Hannah."

"You must come to town more often," Hannah said. "Though I do not suppose your vicar will be willing to spare you once you are married, odious man."

"I probably will not want to spare *myself* once we are wed," Barbara said. "I *so* look forward to being the vicar's wife, Hannah, and to living at the vicarage again. I shall persuade Simon to bring me here once in a while, though, and we will see you then. And perhaps you will come —"

But she stopped abruptly and turned her head to look at Hannah in the semidarkness of the carriage interior. She smiled apologetically.

"But no, of course you will not," she said. "Though I do wish you *would.* And it is perhaps time —"

"It is *time,*" Hannah said, "to go to the theater, Babs."

The carriage was drawing to a halt outside the Drury Lane, and they could see crowds of people milling about, many of them no doubt waiting for other arrivals so that they could go inside. Constantine Huxtable was among them, looking both elegant and satanic in his long black evening cloak and hat.

"Oh, there he is," Barbara said. "Hannah,

134

are you perfectly *sure* —"

"I am, silly goose," Hannah said. "We are lovers, Babs, and I am not nearly finished with him yet. I would wager *that* detail has not slipped into your letters to the vicar."

"Nor to Mama and Papa," her friend said. "They would be very distressed. They may not have seen you for eleven years or so, Hannah, but they are still enormously fond of you."

Hannah patted her knee.

"He has seen us," she said.

And indeed it was Constantine who opened the carriage door and set down the steps rather than Hannah's coachman.

"Ladies, good evening," he said. "We are fortunate that this afternoon's rain has stopped, at least for a while. Miss Leavensworth?"

He offered his hand to Barbara, who took it and bade him a civil good evening. Barbara's manners were always impeccable, of course.

Hannah drew a slow breath. It was the first time she had seen him since last week. That night at his house seemed almost like a dream except for the physical aftereffects she had felt for a few days. And except for the alarming rush of sheer physical aware-ness that assailed her as soon as she set eyes

135

on him again. And the *longing* for tonight.

Oh, goodness me, he really was quite, quite gorgeous.

Within minutes, of course, everyone who was at the theater this evening would know, or think they knew, that he was her newest lover. One in a long line of lovers. By this time tomorrow everyone who was *not* here tonight would know too.

Mr. Constantine Huxtable was the Duchess of Dunbarton's newest paramour.

But this time, for the *first* time, they would be right.

Barbara was safely down on the pavement.

"Duchess?" He reached out his hand for hers and their eyes met.

She had never in her life seen such dark eyes. Or such compelling eyes. Or eyes that had such a weakening effect on her knees.

"I do hope," she said, placing her hand in his, "someone has swept the pavement. I would not enjoy getting my hem wet."

Someone obviously had. And someone had done some quick crowd control too. A path had opened up to allow them into the theater. Hannah half smiled about her as she stepped inside, her hand on Constantine's right arm while Barbara's was linked through his left.

The ducal box, which was on the lowest

of three tiers surrounding the theater like a horseshoe, was close to the stage. Entering it was a little like stepping out onto the stage itself. It was doubtful that anyone in the house did *not* turn to watch them enter and greet the duchess's other guests, all of whom had arrived earlier, and stand conversing with them for several minutes before taking their seats. Or to observe the fact that while the duchess's friend eventually took a seat between Mrs. Park and her brother, the duchess herself sat beside Mr. Constantine Huxtable.

Her new favorite. Her first since the demise of the old duke and her return to town. Her new paramour.

It was not hard to interpret the slightly heightened buzz of conversation in the theater.

It was not hard either for Hannah to look around with leisurely unconcern, as she had done on dozens of other similar occasions when the duke was still alive. He had taught her to look about her like that instead of directing her gaze at her lap. The only difference this time was the absence of the slight amusement she had always felt to know how wrong the speculation about her male companion always was.

Tonight it was *not* wrong.

She was very glad of it.

She set one white-gloved hand on Constantine's sleeve and leaned a little toward him.

"Have you seen *A School for Scandal* before?" she asked. "It is really quite an old play. I must have seen it a dozen times, but it is always amusing. You will not find it too dull or too long, I believe."

"On the assumption," he asked her, "that I am all impatience for it to be over so that we may proceed to the main business of the evening, Duchess?"

"Not at all," she said. "But I thought you might have more of an interest in tragedy."

"To suit my satanic looks?" he asked.

"Precisely," she said. "Though you did, of course, explain to me how the dreadful tragedies of the opera are not really tragedies at all. I was reassured. I suppose next you will be telling me that the heroes of tragedy do not really die at the end of a play."

"Reassuring, is it not?" he said. "You are looking dazzlingly lovely tonight in white. Indeed, you *sparkle*."

There was a gleam of something in his eyes — mockery, perhaps.

"With high spirits?" she said. "I *never* sparkle with high spirits. It would be vulgar. I daresay you mean my jewels." She held up her left hand. "The diamond on my third finger was a wedding present. At the time I did not believe it was real. I did not know they came so large. The one on my little finger was a gift for my twentieth birthday." She held out both hands. "There was a ring for each of my birthdays after that, to fit different fingers, until I ran out of fingers and we had to start over again since I thought they would be uncomfortable on my toes. And there was a ring too for each wedding anniversary and for other assorted occasions."

"And for Christmas?" he asked.

"It was always a necklace and earrings for Christmas," she said, "and a bracelet for Valentine's Day, which the duke *would* observe, foolish man. He was very generous."

"As the whole world can see," he said.

She lowered her hands to her lap and turned her head to look fully at him.

"Jewels are *meant* to be seen, Constantine," she said. "So is beauty. I will never apologize for being either rich or beautiful."

"Or vain?" he said.

"Is it vain," she asked him, "to be truthful? I have been beautiful since childhood. I will probably retain some beauty even into old age, if I should live so long. I have been told that I have good bone structure. I claim no credit for my beauty just as a musician or actor can claim no credit for his talent. But we can all claim credit for using the gifts we brought with us into this life."

"Beauty is a *gift?*" he asked.

"It is," she said. "Beauty ought to be cultivated and admired. There is too much ugliness in life. Beauty can bring joy. Why do we decorate our homes with paintings and vases and tapestries? Why do we not hide them away in a dark cupboard so that they will not fade or become damaged?"

"I would hate it, Duchess," he said, "if you hid yourself away in a dark cupboard. Unless, that is, I could hide in there with you."

She almost laughed. But laughter was not a part of her public persona, and she did not doubt that many eyes were still upon her.

"The play is about to begin," he said, and she turned her attention to the stage.

She had not explained that very well, had she? The duke had taught her not to curse her beauty or be wary of it or try to hide it. Or deny it. All of which she had been well on her way to doing when she married him. He had taught her to enhance it and to celebrate it.

And she *had* celebrated. For ten years she had been the light in his eyes, and somehow that had been enough.

Almost enough.

Now she asked herself how much joy her beauty had really given. To him, yes. But to anyone else? Did it matter if it had not? He had been her husband. It had been her duty and her joy to give *him* joy.

When had she last felt *real* joy? The sort that set one to twirling about in a meadow of hay and wildflowers, one's arms outstretched, one's face lifted to the sun? Or that sent one running along a sandy beach, the wind in one's hair?

Was beauty *really* a gift, as musical talent was?

And wherever were these maudlin thoughts coming from when there was a *comedy* in progress on the stage? The audience laughed as one, and Hannah fanned her face.

She had found intense *enjoyment* in Constantine's bedchamber last week. But *joy?*

She would find it there tonight. She might even stay *all* night. It must be a strange feeling actually to sleep with a man in bed. To wake up beside him. To —

"Duchess." His breath was warm on her ear. His voice was almost a whisper. "Woolgathering?"

"Constantine," she murmured in response without taking her eyes off the stage, "watching *me* rather than the play?"

He did not answer.

Constantine had had a brief conversation with Monty in the box before going back down to the lobby to await the arrival of the duchess and Miss Leavensworth. Katherine had been speaking with the Parks and Mrs. Park's brother, who were also of their party.

"Now let me guess, Con," Monty had said. "Miss Leavensworth, is it? She is not a bad looker, but — Well, for shame. She is betrothed, I seem to recall. To a *clergyman.*"

"*Not* Miss Leavensworth, Monty, as you are very well aware," Constantine had said.

Monty had recoiled in mock amazement. "Never tell me it is the *duchess?*" he had said. "After your disclaimer in the park when she looked you over from toe to head but did *not* offer her hand to be kissed?"

"A man may be allowed to change his mind from time to time," Constantine had said.

"So the *duchess* is to be your mistress for this year." Monty had grinned and shaken his head. "Dangerous, Con. Dangerous."

"I do believe," Constantine had said, "I

142

can handle all the danger she cares to throw my way, Monty."

Monty had waggled his eyebrows.

"Ah," he had said, "but can *she* handle everything you throw *her* way, Con? This will be an interesting spring."

Yes, it would, Constantine thought at the end of the evening as his carriage followed the duchess's to Hanover Square — she had insisted, as she ought, upon returning to Dunbarton House with her friend. She would transfer to his carriage once they arrived there.

Yes, it would be an interesting spring. A sensually satisfying one, anyway, he did not doubt. The wait from last week to tonight had seemed interminable, and he guessed that his sexual appetite for the Duchess of Dunbarton would be barely sated before it was time for them both to go to their separate homes for the summer.

Their affair would not resume next year, of course. Neither of them would want that.

But was he making a mistake even this year?

She was beautiful, desirable, and vain. She was rich and arrogant and shallow.

He had not thought himself capable of abandoning all other considerations just for lust. Lust was his only motive for taking the duchess as his mistress, though.

And perhaps a certain fascination too. One he shared with much of the male half of the *ton,* of course, and with a significant proportion of the female half, for different reasons.

But only he knew the one *very* interesting fact about her — that she had lived to the age of thirty without ever once having sex.

It was still hard to believe.

His carriage drew to a halt behind hers, and he watched the two ladies disappear into the house. The doors closed. Her carriage was driven away, and his drew up closer to the front steps.

The front door remained closed for eighteen minutes. Constantine slouched in his seat and wondered how long he would wait and how many persons were standing behind curtains at darkened windows about the square, preparing to make him the laughingstock tomorrow.

He felt more amusement than anger.

She was certainly not going to relinquish any control to him, was she?

He wondered if the old duke had found her a handful. But damn it all, she had never been unfaithful to him.

How long would he wait? he wondered again.

After eighteen minutes the doors of Dunbarton House opened again, and she emerged, dressed in last week's white cloak, the wide hood over her head.

Had she changed clothes?

Constantine got out of the carriage, extended a hand for hers, and helped her in. He climbed in after her and took a seat beside her. His coachman shut the door, and the carriage rocked on its springs as he climbed up to the box and drove the carriage around the square and out onto the street.

Constantine turned to look at her in the darkness. Neither of them had spoken. He reached for the clasp at her neck and undid it before lowering the hood from her head and opening back the cloak.

Her hair was loose again, held back from her face with heavy jeweled clips above her ears. Her dress was dark in color — blue or purple, perhaps. Royal blue, he saw in the shaft of light from a street lamp as they passed. It was low cut, high waisted. The diamonds had gone from her neck and earlobes.

She was a woman ready for her lover.

He lowered his head and kissed her. Her lips were warm, slightly parted, receptive.

He slid one arm behind her back, one

beneath her knees, and swung her over onto his lap.

He kissed her again, and she slid her arms about his neck.

Oh, yes, there was lust right enough.

And something else, perhaps?

It was pure rationalization that made him imagine so. This was not partially about companionship, as his affairs usually were. This was purely about lust.

Sex.

Which they were going to be having with great vigor within the hour. It was enough. The summer and winter had been long. Surely he could be forgiven a little unbridled lust during the spring.

They had not spoken a word to each other since they left the theater.

She was not to be whisked upstairs and tossed onto his bed without further ado, Hannah discovered when they stepped inside his house and he dismissed the butler for the night, saying he would have no further need of him.

Constantine then took her by the elbow and guided her into the room where they had dined last week. The table was set again, with cold meats and cheese and bread and wine this time. A single candle was burning in the center of the table. And a fire crackled in the hearth again.

It was as much a relief as a disappointment, Hannah found. Not that she was particularly hungry. Or in need of wine. And she had certainly been wanting him very badly all evening. She had hardly concentrated at all upon the play, one of her favorites. And desire had all but boiled over in the carriage, especially after he had lifted her onto his lap.

How deliciously strong he was to be able to do that without heaving and hauling her and panting with the exertion. She weighed a mite more than a feather, after all.

She was glad desire had not quite boiled over. Which was a strange thought. She was doing all this purely out of lust, was she not? This spring she was free to take a lover, she had deliberately chosen to take one, and she had very carefully selected Constantine Huxtable.

Only to discover that lust was not quite sufficient in itself.

How very provoking!

One really ought to be able to fix one's mind upon a certain goal — especially when one had chosen it and worked toward it with deliberate care — and move inexorably forward until it was achieved.

Her goal was to enjoy the person of Constantine Huxtable until summer drove her off to Kent and him to wherever in Gloucestershire he had his home.

What was the big secret about that place, she wondered, that he would tell her nothing?

And now she was discovering that perhaps his *person* — gorgeous and perfect as it was — was not enough.

Maybe she was just tired. Oh, but she was still feeling lusty too. She was glad, though, that there was to be some supper first — even if she did not eat anything.

He drew her cloak off her shoulders, standing behind her as he did so. His hands barely touched her.

"Duchess?" he said, indicating the chair on which she had sat last week. "Will you have a seat?"

He poured the wine as she seated herself. She placed a little of everything on her plate.

"Did you enjoy the performance?" she asked.

"I was somewhat distracted through much of it," he said. "But I believe it was entertaining."

"Barbara was ecstatic," she said. "She views the London scene, of course, through eyes that have not become jaded."

"She has never been here before?" he asked.

"She has," she said. "While I was married I occasionally prevailed upon her to spend a couple of weeks or so with me, though most of those visits were in the country rather than in town. And she would never stay long. She was terrified of the duke."

"Did she have reason to be?" he asked.

"He was a *duke*," she said. "He had been since the age of twelve. He had been a duke for longer than sixty years when I married him. Of course she had reason to be terrified even though he always went out of his way to be courteous to her. She is a *vicar's* daughter, Constantine."

"But you were not terrified of him?" he asked.

"I adored him," she said, picking up her glass and twirling the stem in her fingers.

"How did you meet him?" he asked.

How had the conversation swung in this direction? That was the trouble with conversations.

"He had a family which he liked to describe as 'prodigious large and tedious,' " she said. "He ignored them when he could, which was most of the time. But he had a sense of duty too. He attended the wedding of one relative, who was fourteenth in line to his title. He always felt an obligation to anyone who was higher than twentieth in line, he told me. I was at the wedding celebrations too. We met there."

"And married soon after," he said. "It must have been love at first sight."

"If I had not noted the hint of irony in your voice, Constantine," she said, "I would tell you not to be ridiculous."

He gazed at her silently for a few moments.

"Your youth and beauty and his rank and wealth?" he said.

"The reason behind a thousand marriages," she said, biting off a piece of cheese. "You make the duke and me sound quite *ordinary,* Constantine."

"I am quite sure, Duchess," he said, "you do not need my assurance that you were in fact a quite *extraordinary* couple, but I will give it anyway."

"He was quite splendid, was he not?" she said. "Courtly and stately and oh-so-aristocratic to the end. And with a *presence* that drew all eyes but not many persons. Most people dared not approach him. Oh, he must have been a sight to behold when he was a young man. I do believe I would have fallen hopelessly in love with him if I had known him then."

"Hopelessly?" he said.

"Yes." She sighed. "It would have been quite, quite hopeless. He would not have spared me a glance."

"Hard to believe, Duchess," he said. "But I do believe you were a little in love with him anyway."

"I *loved* him," she said. "And he loved me. Would not the *ton* be amazed if they knew that we had a happy marriage? But no, not amazed. They would be *incredulous.* People believe what they choose to believe — just as you do."

"You proved me colossally wrong on one recent occasion," he said.

"You called me vain tonight," she said, "when in reality I am simply honest."

"It *would* be rather foolish," he said, "if you went about calling yourself ugly."

"And massively untruthful," she said.

She drained her glass as he gazed across the table at her.

"And you have called me greedy tonight," she said.

His eyebrows arched upward.

"I hope, Duchess," he said, "I am too much the gentleman to accuse anyone of greed, least of all the lady who is my lover."

"But you have implied it," she said. "At the theater you chose to view my jewels and hear about them with amusement. And here at this table you have presumed to know my motive for marrying the duke."

"And I am wrong?" he asked.

She spread her hands on the table on either side of her plate. She had removed all her jewels at home and returned them to their respective safes. But she had put on other rings. She always felt a little strange without them, truth to tell. They sparkled up at her from every finger except her thumbs.

She drew them off one at a time and set them in the center of the table, beside the candlestick.

"What is their total worth?" she asked when they were all there. "Just the stones."

He looked at the rings, at her, and at the rings again. He reached out a hand and picked up the largest. He held it between his thumb and forefinger and turned it so that it caught the light.

Oh, goodness, Hannah thought, there was something unexpectedly erotic about seeing one of her rings in his dark-skinned, long-fingered hand.

He set the ring down and picked up another.

He spread them apart with the tip of a finger so that they were not all clustered together.

And then he named a sum that showed he knew a thing or two about diamonds.

"No," she said.

He doubled the estimate.

"Not even close," she said.

He shrugged. "I give in."

"One hundred pounds," she said.

He sat back in his chair and held her eyes with his.

"Fake?" he said. "Paste?"

"These, yes," she said. "Some are real — the ones I received for the most precious occasions. All the jewels I wore to the theater this evening were real. About two-thirds of those I own are paste."

"Dunbarton was not as generous as he appeared to be?" he asked.

"He was generosity itself," she told him. "He would have showered me with half his fortune and probably did, though of course most of it was entailed. I had only to admire something and it was mine. I had only *not* to admire it and it was mine."

He had nothing to say this time. He regarded her steadily.

"They were real when they were given to me," she said. "I had the diamonds replaced with paste imitations. They are very good imitations. In fact, I probably underestimated the value of those rings on the table. They are probably worth two hundred pounds. Perhaps even a little more. I did it *with* the duke's knowledge. His consent was reluctantly given, but how could he refuse? He had taught me to be independent, to think for myself, to decide what I wanted and refuse to take no for an answer. I believe he was proud of me."

His elbow was on the table, his chin propped between his thumb and forefinger.

"There are certain . . . *causes* in which I am interested," she said.

"You have given away a minor fortune in the proceeds of your diamonds for *causes,* Duchess?" he asked. "Not so minor either, at a wager."

She shrugged.

"A mere tiny drop in a very large ocean," she said. "There is suffering enough in the world, Constantine, to feed the philanthropic leanings of a thousand rich people who like to believe they have a conscience and that it can be soothed with the giving of a little money."

She stopped herself from saying more. He doubtless would not understand. Or he would think her a bleeding heart. And maybe that was all she was. Why had she felt the need to share even as much as she had with him? He thought her frivolous and rich and spoiled, just as everyone else did. He thought her a gold digger, a woman who would use her beauty to enrich herself.

Which, in a sense, she was.

But that was not the whole story.

She had never before felt the slightest need to justify her existence to anyone. Not for the past eleven years, anyway. She was secure in herself. She rather liked herself. The duke had liked her too. She did not care the snap of two fingers what anyone else thought of her. Indeed, she had always rather enjoyed leading the whole *ton* down the garden path, so to speak.

Was Constantine different because he was her lover?

She had expected only an intimacy of bodies.

She wanted no more.

But she had brought these particular rings deliberately tonight. She had wanted him to know.

He had called her vain and had all but called her greedy.

Did she *care* what he thought? How bothersome that she did.

Was this spring fling to prove less purely enjoyable than she had planned?

He got to his feet and came about the

table. He held out a hand for hers.

"We did not come here, Duchess," he said, "to talk about either philanthropy or consciences."

"I thought," she said, getting to her feet, "you would never remember, Constantine."

And she was being kissed very thoroughly indeed, her body pressed to his from face to knees. She twined her arms about his neck and became a full participant.

Ah, he had such a firm, masculine, *young* body.

And she did not regret a thing. This was what, for this spring anyway, she craved more than anything else in life. There was so much time to make up for, so many pleasures she had never yet experienced.

He lifted his head and looked down at her, and she noticed again how dark his eyes were and could only guess at how much they hid of who he was. She did not need to know. And yet she had always wanted to know. He was not, alas, just a male body to be used for her pleasure. She wished he were. Life would be so much simpler.

And so much less worth living.

She drew one hand forward and set her forefinger along the length of his nose.

"How did this happen?" she asked.

"The broken nose?" he said. "A fight."

"Constantine," she said, "don't be tiresome. Don't make me ask."

"With Moreland," he said, "though he was
not Moreland then. With my cousin. Elliott.
We were just boys."

"And you got the worse of it?" she said.

"He looked like a masked highwayman for
a whole month," he said. "Unfortunately,
black eyes do not have to be set skillfully in
order to heal. Broken noses do, and mine
was not set skillfully at all. The physician
was a dashed country quack."

"You look the more handsome for it," she
said. "Perhaps the quack knew very well
what he was doing for you. What was the
fight about?"

"Lord knows," he said. "We had a few very
satisfactory bouts of fisticuffs when we were
growing up. That was one of the best."

"Does that mean," she said, "that you
were always enemies? Or that you were
friends?"

"We lived only a few miles apart," he said,
"and we were close enough in age. Elliott
was — is — three years older than I. We
were the best of friends, except when we
fought."

"But then you quarreled," she said, "and
did not make up."

"Something like that," he said.

"What happened?" she asked him.

"He was a pompous ass," he said, "and I was a stubborn mule. And I probably ought not to use the past tense. He still *is* a pompous ass."

"And you are still a stubborn mule?"

"He would call me worse," he said.

"Ought you not to talk to each other?" She frowned at him.

"No," he said firmly. "I ought *not* to talk at all, Duchess. Neither ought you. We should be in bed by now, deeply engrossed in pleasure."

"Ah," she said, "but as we are, we can still enjoy all the pleasure of anticipation, Constantine."

"To the devil with anticipation," he said, and he reached down, scooped her up into his arms, and strode from the room with her.

"A masterful man," she said approvingly, twining her arms about his neck again. "Doubtless if I resisted, you would drag me upstairs by my hair."

"A studded club waving from my free hand," he agreed. "Do you *wish* to resist?"

"Not at all," she said. "Is it possible for you to move faster? Take the stairs two at a time, perhaps?"

And, ah, at last she startled a laugh out of him.

"You will be fortunate indeed, Duchess," he said, "if I have any energy left by the time we reach my bedchamber."

"Then save your breath, you foolish man," she said.

He appeared not to be lacking in either energy or breath, though, when he finally set her down inside his bedchamber.

Hannah moved against him and wrapped her arms about him and sighed with contentment — and desire and an anticipation that had her blood pumping almost audibly through her body.

"If you wish," she said, "you can continue masterful, Constantine, and toss me on the bed and have your wicked way with me. Or if you do not wish, for that matter."

He picked her up again and tossed her.

Quite literally. She bounced three inches into the air before sinking into the mattress.

Oh, she had very definitely chosen the right man.

He proceeded to have his wicked way without stopping to unclothe either one of them first, except in strategic places.

It was, Hannah thought when it was over, worth sacrificing her royal blue evening gown for, even if it *was* one of her favorites.

It must be creased beyond redemption.

And she was committed to her spring affair beyond redemption too.

"Mmm," she grumbled when he moved off her and rearranged them so that her head was on his arm and her body was curled against his — the bedcovers had somehow materialized around them.

And she promptly fell asleep.

CHAPTER 8

Hannah was seated on the window seat in her private sitting room at Dunbarton House, her legs drawn up before her. It was one of her favorite poses when she was not on public display, but she was reminded of that first night at Constantine's the week before. This seat was wider, though, and padded with comfortable cushions, and it was daylight and the window looked out on a long green lawn and colorful flower beds rather than on the street. It was a lovely day. Yet here they were, indoors.

"You are quite sure you do not want to go out, Babs?" she asked, turning her head to look at her friend. Typically, while she sat idle, Barbara was sitting very straight-backed on her chair, working diligently at an intricate piece of embroidery. "I feel guilty for keeping you inside."

"I am quite happy," Barbara said. "There has been nothing but a whirlwind of activity

161

since I arrived here, Hannah, and I am feeling almost overwhelmed by it all. It is pleasant to have a quiet day."

"But there *is* the Kitteridge ball tonight," Hannah reminded her. "Are you sure you are up for it?"

"Of course," Barbara said. "If I do not go, then you cannot, Hannah."

"Because I will be unchaperoned?" Hannah asked with a smile.

"Even you would not be brazen enough to attend a ball alone," her friend said, looking up.

"I could dash off a letter to Lord Hardingraye or Mr. Minter or any of a dozen others, and I would have a willing escort in no time at all," Hannah said.

"Not Mr. Huxtable?" Barbara raised her eyebrows.

"After our appearance together last evening at the theater," Hannah said, "even though you and the Parks and Mrs. Park's brother and Lord and Lady Montford were there with us, I do not doubt that drawing room conversations throughout London this afternoon have firmly established us as lovers. Nevertheless, there is still the game called propriety to be played, Babs. Mr. Huxtable will not be my escort tonight even if no one else will be and I am doomed to remain at home."

"Oh, I shall come," Barbara said, picking up her work again. "There is no need to write to any gentleman."

"Only if you are sure," Hannah told her. "You are not my paid companion, Babs. You are my *friend.* And if you would like an evening at home, then so should I."

"I must confess," Barbara said, "that having attended one *ton* ball with you, Hannah, I am quite eager to attend another. Am I becoming quite . . . *decadent,* do you think?"

Hannah smiled at the top of her head.

"You have a long, long way to go before you can legitimately apply *that* epithet to yourself," she said. "Unlike me."

The sunshine beaming through the window was making her feel drowsy. She had woken up at five this morning and had roused Constantine to bring her home, but it had been well after six before they had actually left. She had been quite right about the danger of actually sleeping with a man, especially a man who had somehow got up during the night without waking her and removed all his clothes. They had both been warm and sleepy and amorous, and they had already been tangled together. A whole hour had passed very pleasantly indeed before they got out of bed.

"Was it very difficult," Barbara asked after a few minutes of silence, her head bent over her work, "to change from who you were to who you are, Hannah? After you married, I mean."

Hannah did not answer immediately. Barbara had never asked such a question before.

"Not at all," she said eventually. "I had a very good mentor. The best, in fact. And I did not at all like who I was. I liked who I became. I *like* who I have *become.* The duke taught me to grow up, to value myself as I was created to be. And he taught me how to be a duchess, *his* gift to me. He taught me to be independent and self-reliant. He taught me to *need* no one."

That last point was not strictly true. She had not realized quite how much she needed *him* until he was gone. And he had never told her that she needed no one. Quite the contrary, in fact. He had always told her that she needed love and the precious cluster of persons that would surround that love when she found it — her little community of belonging, he had called it. He had assured her that she *would* find it one day. He had taught her in the meantime not to be needy, but to rely upon her own inner strength to resist grabbing at any pale substitute for love.

Like sex, she thought now, closing her eyes briefly. It was far more intoxicating than she had expected it to be. It would be very easy to come to rely upon it, to live for the hours at Constantine's house when all her needs could be satisfied.

But not *all*. She must never forget that. She must never make the mistake of believing that the needs Constantine satisfied in her were the fundamental needs of her being.

They had nothing to do with *love. He* had nothing to do with love.

"*I* liked you, Hannah," Barbara said. "Indeed, I loved you dearly. I often remember how wonderful it was to have you always close, just a brisk walk away across fields and meadows. And I often wish you were still there."

"I would soon find myself abandoned if I were," Hannah said. "You will be marrying your vicar soon."

"He is not exclusively *my* vicar," her friend said with a smile for her embroidery, "though he *is* exclusively my Simon. I love him dearly, you know. He is bookish and intelligent and quite incapable of holding a frivolous conversation, though he does try, the poor dear. He wears eyeglasses and is losing his hair a little at the forehead and temples even though he has not quite reached his middle thirties yet. He is perhaps an inch shorter than I am, though when he is wearing riding boots we are of a height with each other. And he has the kindest smile in the world — everyone says so. But he has a special smile just for me. It pierces right through to my heart."

Her needle was suspended above her work. Her cheeks were slightly flushed, her eyes shining as they gazed at her embroidery and saw a man who was physically far away.

Hannah felt a twinge of envy.

"I am very happy for you, Babs," she said. "I know you thought you were doomed to spinsterhood even though you had several quite eligible offers over the years. But you waited and found love."

"Hannah," her friend asked, her needle still in the air above her work, "do you ever wish *you* had waited?"

The flush deepened in her cheeks, and she lowered her needle again.

"No," Hannah said softly. "No, never for a single moment."

"But —" Barbara set the cloth down on her knee before she had worked even one more stitch. "But you were in no fit state to make such a momentous decision at that particular time. You were so terribly upset.

Justifiably so."

"I had a guardian angel," Hannah said, "and his name was the Duke of Dunbarton. I told him that once. I thought he would choke on his port."

"But Hannah," Barbara said, "he was so *old*. Oh, I do beg your pardon."

"He was only fifty-four years older than I was," Hannah said with a half-smile. "Only old enough to be my grandfather. Indeed, he once presented me with numbers that proved I could quite reasonably have been his *great*-granddaughter. You might as well give up, Babs. I will never admit that I married him in haste and regretted it ever after. I married in extreme haste and never regretted it for a moment. Why should I have? I was pampered and rich, and I was elevated into this world." She gestured at the room around them with one arm. "And now I am free."

She turned her head rather sharply to look out through the window.

Tears? *Tears?*

"Hannah," Barbara said, "you ought to come back home. You ought —"

"I *am* home," Hannah said, interrupting.

Her friend gazed at her with unhappy eyes.

"Come for my wedding," she said. "You can stay with Mama and Papa. The cottage will be nowhere near up to your usual standards, but I know they would love to have you. And it would make my wedding day complete if my dearest friend was there. I know that Simon wishes to meet you. Oh, *please* come."

"He will not wish it when he knows what I have become," Hannah said. "And I would be dealing deceitfully with the Reverend and Mrs. Leavensworth if I were to stay beneath their roof as I am. Theirs is a different world from the one I inhabit, Babs. *Yours* is a different world. A more innocent, more *moral* world."

"Come anyway," Barbara said. "They will love you for yourself, as I do. I am straitlaced and puritanical, Hannah. I am still a spinster who has grown up very close to the church. If you were to shake me, I daresay I would become invisible within a cloud of old dust. I hate what you have done to yourself in the past week or so because I do not believe you are happy. And I believe you will only grow unhappier as your liaison with Mr. Huxtable progresses. You think you want *pleasure,* when what you really want is love. But I digress, and I promised myself that I would never scold you or reproach you. Come to my wedding anyway. Is it not time to come back? It has been more than ten years."

"That is entirely the point," Hannah said. "I am living in a different lifetime now, Babs, and in a different universe. The old ones no longer exist for me. I do not *want* them to exist."

"What does that make me?" her friend asked. "A ghost?"

"Oh, Babs," Hannah said, and she had to turn her head away again to hide the tears welling in her eyes, "don't ever abandon me."

She heard a rustling behind her, and then she was being enfolded in a tight hug. They clung wordlessly to each other for a while, Hannah feeling very foolish indeed. And, strangely, almost as grief-stricken as she had felt on the day the duke died.

"Silly goose," Barbara said in a voice that was not quite steady. "Why would I drop your friendship when you are so *rich?* And when you take me to *ton* balls and insist upon buying me a perfectly frivolous bonnet every time I wangle an invitation to London from you?"

Hannah swung her legs over the side of the window seat and brushed her hands over the muslin skirt of her dress.

"It was a particularly splendid bonnet, was it not?" she said. "If you had not allowed me to buy it for you yesterday, Babs, I would have bought it for myself, and where would I have put it? I already have a whole dressing room and the guest room adjoining it positively bursting at the seams with clothes — or so rumor has it, and everyone knows how reliable rumor is."

"*I* have the guest room adjoining your dressing room," Barbara said, straightening up and turning to fold her embroidery.

"You are greatly to be pitied," Hannah said. "It must be extremely difficult, Babs, to get through the door, even if you walk sideways."

Barbara laughed.

"*Will* you come to my wedding?" she asked softly.

Hannah sighed inaudibly. She had hoped that matter had been dropped.

"I cannot, Babs," she said. "I will not go back. But perhaps you and your vicar would like to come and spend at least a part of your honeymoon with me in Kent."

A maid came into the room at that point, bringing their tea, and the conversation moved on to other topics.

She was *not* unhappy, Hannah thought. Barbara was quite, quite wrong about that. And she was not going to become unhappier. How could she when she was not unhappy to start with?

She could hardly wait for tonight, after the ball was over. The need she felt might be a superficial one, but it was very powerful nonetheless.

She did not believe she would *ever* tire of Constantine's lovemaking. She would have to, of course, by the time the Season ended. But that was long in the future. She did not have to even start thinking about it yet.

She got up to pour the tea.

A note was delivered to Constantine's house early in the afternoon from Cassandra, Countess of Merton, Stephen's wife, inviting him to dine at Merton House before the Kitteridge ball. He had no other engagement and was pleased to send back an acceptance.

He had tried a number of times over the years to resent, even to hate, Stephen, who had inherited Jon's title and had turned up at Warren Hall at the age of seventeen as the new owner, bringing his sisters with him. They had all been strangers to Constantine, who had not even known of their existence until Elliott and his solicitors had searched the family tree and found a distant heir. Even then it had not been easy to track him down to some remote village in Shropshire.

Constantine had been sick with hatred before he met them. They were coming to invade *his* home, to trample upon *his* memories, to take over what ought by rights to have been his. More important than all that, Jon was buried on land that now belonged to a stranger.

Even afterward he had hated them for a while.

But how could one hate Stephen once one got to know him? It would be like hating angels. And his sisters were equally hard to dislike. They had been so very pleased, all of them, to discover him. They had embraced him as a long-lost member of their family. They had been sensitive to how he must feel about the whole succession.

Margaret and Duncan, Earl of Sheringford, had also been invited to dinner, Constantine discovered when he arrived at Merton House. Margaret was the eldest of the three sisters, the one who had held the family together after the early death of their parents. She had remained stubbornly single until they were all grown up. Only then had she herself married. Her choice of husband had seemed disastrous at the time. But the marriage had survived and apparently flourished.

172

Constantine relaxed and enjoyed dinner. The food was good, the company and conversation congenial. Until they retired to the drawing room afterward with an hour or so to kill before they must leave for the ball, he did not even suspect that there had perhaps been an ulterior motive in inviting him.

"Cassandra and I went to call on Kate this morning," Margaret remarked as Cassandra poured the tea. "Nessie came with us too. Kate is in a delicate way again after all this time. Did you know, Constantine? She is both delighted and queasy in the mornings. She told us about the pleasant evening she and Jasper spent at the theater yesterday."

Ah, Constantine thought.

"I did not know about her condition," he said. "I daresay they are both pleased."

They had got to talking about *him* during the morning visit, he would wager. He waited for them to say it.

"We got to talking about you," Margaret said.

"Me?" he said, all amazement. "Am I to feel flattered?"

"You are in your thirties," Margaret said.

Hmm. What angle were they going to take with this? They could hardly come right out and scold him for taking the Duchess of

173

Dunbarton as a mistress, could they? As genteel ladies, they could not admit to knowing any such thing, or even *suspecting* it.

Margaret was doing the talking, of course. Cassandra was busier than she need have been with the teapot. Stephen and Sherry were trying to look as though they thought this was just another harmless topic of conversation.

"Yes, well," Constantine said with a sigh, "the powers that be will not allow one to remain in one's twenties for longer than ten years, Margaret. It is really quite unobliging of them."

They all laughed, even Margaret, but she was undeterred from her purpose, whatever it might be.

"We all agreed, Constantine," she said, "that you ought to be considering marriage. You are our cousin, and —"

"*Second* cousin," he said. "Second cousin-in-law to Cassandra."

"He is in his charming mood, Meg," Cassandra said. "As opposed to his brooding mood. He is determined to take nothing seriously."

Stephen sipped his tea. Constantine exchanged a blank-eyed stare with Sherry.

"I take the idea of marriage very seriously

indeed," he assured them. "Especially my own. And more especially when it is being suggested to me by a deputation of my female relatives. This *is* a deputation, I gather? Is there any lady you particularly wish me to consider?"

Margaret opened her mouth and shut it again. Cassandra merely smiled. The gentlemen *both* sipped their tea.

"Or anyone you particularly wish me *not* to consider?" he suggested.

Cassandra laughed outright.

"I told you he would instantly know what this was all about, Meg," she said. "But really, Con, all we want is your *happiness.* I have been a member of this family for only a year — less, actually — but I too want to see you happy."

"Beware a happily married woman," he said. "She will scheme and plot to force everyone else to be happy too."

Stephen grinned and Sherry chuckled.

"And there is something wrong with that?" Margaret asked, visibly bristling. She was looking at Sherry.

"Katherine saw the way the wind blew at the theater last evening, did she?" Constantine asked. "And did not approve of what she saw? And you all concurred with her opinion this morning? It would be interest-

175

ing to know if Vanessa did too."

"You have a favorite almost every year, Constantine," Margaret said as she sat back in her chair, her cup and saucer in hand. "They have all been pleasant ladies. I particularly liked Mrs. Hunter the year Duncan and I met and married."

Her cheeks would probably bloom with a thousand roses if he asked her to explain exactly what she meant by *favorite,* Constantine thought.

"I liked her too, Margaret," he said. "That was why she was my *favorite* that year. But I hope you are not about to ask me to consider her as a bride. She married Lord Lund two summers ago."

"And presented him with an heir last year, I believe," Sherry said. "You are wise not to go pining after her, Con."

Margaret gave him an indignant look.

"The Duchess of Dunbarton is beautiful," she said. "No one can dispute that. She draws all eyes wherever she goes, and it is more than just her beauty that does it. She is really quite fascinating."

"I hear a *but* in your voice," Constantine said.

Cassandra took over.

"Kate was of the opinion that the duchess has decided to make *you her* favorite, Con," she said. "And what the duchess wants, apparently, she usually gets. But she is said to be fickle in her preferences. Next week or the week after it is likely to be someone else."

She was looking decidedly uncomfortable and turned her head to frown at Stephen, who was grinning at her.

"She does indeed have a reputation for being somewhat *fast,* Constantine," Margaret said. "And I believe it is well deserved."

What would they say, he wondered, if he told them that the duchess had been a virgin until a little more than a week ago, and that she had lost that virginity courtesy of himself?

"And you are afraid I will end up hurt and brokenhearted if I succumb to her wiles this week and perhaps next?" he asked. "I will be no match at all for someone of the duchess's, ah, *experience?* Even though I am frequently said to be the devil himself? I am touched at your concern."

He was feeling vastly amused.

"Oh, dear," Cassandra said, setting down her cup and saucer with a clatter. "This was not how we planned to approach the subject, was it, Meg? Kate will be quite vexed with us. *Of course* you can cope with her grace if she should become your, er, *favorite*, Con. Indeed, I daresay there are people warning *her* against becoming involved with *you*. What we *intended* to say, or to hint or suggest, purely out of filial fondness for you, you must understand, is that perhaps it is time you turned your attention away from mere flirtation and toward matrimony. You are extremely eligible. And really very handsome indeed, though I am not sure that is quite the correct word to describe you. You draw admiring eyes wherever you go — just as the duchess does."

"We *have* rather made a mess of things, Constantine," Margaret admitted. "We meant to oh-so-subtly nudge your thoughts in the direction of marriage rather than . . . Well."

"Perhaps," Sherry suggested, "we ought to talk about tomorrow's weather, my love. Or last week's. Or next month's."

She smiled and then laughed aloud with what sounded like genuine amusement.

"May we forget about the last five minutes and start again?" she asked.

"Heaven forbid," Sherry and Stephen said in unison.

"What I want to know," Constantine said, "is what *Vanessa* had to say about all this."

Vanessa, the middle sister, had been a

warm friend of his until she married Elliott, now Duke of Moreland. Then, in trying to get at Elliott in the asinine, somewhat childish way in which he had tended to conduct their long-standing quarrel in those days, he had inadvertently — but quite predictably — hurt and humiliated her, and she had been barely civil to him since.

It had *not* been his finest moment. In fact, it had easily been one of his worst. He was dogged by guilt and shame every time he saw or even thought about Vanessa, in fact.

"To be honest, Con," Cassandra said, "we had the discussion while she was up in the nursery taking a gift to Hal and paying homage to Jonathan. Cassandra had brought him with her."

Hal was Katherine and Monty's four-year-old son.

Stephen had actually written to Constantine after the birth of his son to ask if he would mind terribly much if they called the baby Jonathan. Constantine *had* minded very much indeed and had almost written back to say so in no uncertain terms. But he had stopped to think of how delighted his brother Jon would have been. He had been almost able to *hear* the boy's excited, ungainly laughter. So the new heir to the title was Jonathan.

It had even felt strangely comforting to know that when he had made his duty call here to see the baby after his arrival in town.

"We ought not to have said anything," Margaret said. "Duncan and Stephen have been odious enough to laugh behind their hands ever since we came from the dining room, and you are no better, Constantine. You have chosen to be amused."

"Better that than his choosing to be wrathful, Maggie," Sherry said.

"You see, the trouble is, Con," Stephen added, "that my sisters expected to be matchmakers to their hearts' content for years yet with me. But I was disobliging enough to fall in love with Cass last year when I was only twenty-five, a mere babe in arms. You are the only one left, even if you *are* a mere cousin, so you must be prepared to be *cared* about until you marry a worthy woman and settle down to live happily ever after. If you were really wise, you would do it this year and live in *peace* forever after."

"Except," Constantine said, "that I would be married."

"Enough!" Margaret got firmly to her feet. "There is a ball to attend, and I would hate to arrive so late that the receiving line had even been abandoned."

And that, Constantine thought, was the

end of that. For the time being, anyway.

And his family did not approve of this spring's mistress. Or *favorite,* to use the euphemism with which the ladies could be reasonably comfortable.

CHAPTER 9

They were late arriving at the Kitteridge ball, though not by any means the last of the guests. They were there before the Duchess of Dunbarton, though that was no surprise.

Constantine was talking with a group of acquaintances when he was made aware of her arrival by a slight change in the quality of the sound around him. It was certainly true what Margaret had said earlier. The duchess really did draw eyes wherever she went, and this occasion was no exception. All she was doing was passing along the receiving line with her friend, but almost everyone had turned a head to watch.

She was all in gleaming white again — silver-threaded white lace over white silk. Her hair was piled high in intricate curls, though wavy tendrils had been allowed to trail over her temples and along her neck in order to tease the eyes and the imagination.

A small diamond tiara glistened in her hair. Diamonds at her ears and bosom and on her wrists and gloved fingers sparkled and winked in the candlelight. There were even rosettes of diamonds sewn to the outsides of her white dancing slippers.

Or *not* diamonds.

Another petal had been peeled away from the rose last night, leaving Constantine to wonder if there were perhaps more within after all. She had sold two-thirds of her diamonds, doubtless for a colossal sum, because there were certain *causes* in which she was interested.

Charitable causes, he had understood. The lady had a heart, then, and a social conscience.

In its own way it had been as startling a revelation as the fact that she had come to him as a virgin.

He had the rather unsettling suspicion that he had misjudged the duchess, that perhaps she was not shallow after all. But he was certainly not alone in his former opinion of her, as Margaret's words had proved. He had no cause to be indignant with her.

Constantine strode across the ballroom in the duchess's direction, aware that he was being watched with interest. There would not be many people in this room who did not know that she was his new mistress or that he was her new lover — depending upon the perspective of the beholder. There was no such thing as a secret affair between two members of the *ton.*

He bowed to them both, secured a waltz with the duchess for later in the evening, and asked Miss Leavensworth for the opening set. By that time the duchess's usual court was gathering about her.

He led Miss Leavensworth onto the floor, where the lines were already forming. He had asked her to dance because she was the duchess's friend and house guest and because she had been a member of the theater party the evening before and he had conversed with her there for several minutes and liked her. She seemed an intelligent, sensible lady.

He certainly had no ulterior motive in dancing with her — not at first, anyway. He asked about her home only because he guessed that she was probably homesick, especially as her fiancé was back in the village she had left behind.

"The trouble with being in London for the Season," he said to her as they waited for the dancing to begin, "is that no matter how much one enjoys oneself, one invariably misses one's home in the country. I always do. Do you find the same thing?"

"I do indeed, Mr. Huxtable, though it seems quite ungrateful to admit it," she said gravely. "It is wonderful to be here, and I will never forget that I have attended *ton* balls and gone to the theater and opera and visited some of the most famous of the museums and galleries here. And the best thing of all is being with Hannah, whom I see all too rarely. Even the shopping is more exciting than I expected. But you are right, and I must confess to a longing to see my family and my betrothed again."

"And your village?" he said.

"And that too," she said. "London is so . . . *vast.*"

And he saw a way of satisfying some idle curiosity. Or perhaps not so idle. Everyone knew how the duchess had used her beauty to rise out of obscurity and become the bride of a duke who had resisted matrimony until well into his seventies. It would have been the stuff of legend if the huge age gap had deprived the story of all romance and made it merely rather sordid instead. No one seemed to know anything about the obscurity from which the duchess had risen, however. When he had asked her about her family, she had shrugged and said she had none.

But she must have had family at some time.

"What *is* your village?" he asked.

"Markle," she said, "in Lincolnshire. No one except those who live within ten miles of it has even *heard* of it. But it is quiet and pretty, and it is home."

"Your parents are both still living?" he asked.

"Yes," she said. "I am well blessed. My father was the vicar, but he has retired now, and we live together in a cottage at the edge of the village. It is smaller than the vicarage but very cozy. My mother and father are very happy there. So am I, but of course I will be moving back to the vicarage when I marry in August."

"And you will be the lady of the house this time," he said, "instead of the daughter."

"Yes." She smiled. "It will seem strange. I am looking forward to it immensely, though."

"Markle," he said, frowning. "Something sounds familiar about the name. What is the main family living there?"

"Sir Colin Young?" she said, posing the answer as a question. "He lives at Elm Court just beyond the village with Lady

Young and their three children. Lady Young, in fact, is —"

She stopped abruptly. She flushed.

He waited for a moment, eyebrows raised, but she did not continue.

"I do believe the dancing is about to begin," he said.

"Oh, yes," she said with bright enthusiasm. "You are right. Oh, just *look* at all the flowers. And all the candles in the chandeliers. There must be *dozens* of them. And so many guests. I shall be dreaming of this when I leave here."

He guessed that she was not the sort of lady who gushed with enthusiasm a great deal. Something had flustered her. His questions, probably, especially the last. And the answers she had given — and almost given. Did she realize now, he wondered, that he had been deliberately probing for information?

That had not been well done of him.

But who *was* Lady Young? He had never heard of either Markle or Sir Colin Young. The man might be a baronet, but he had never mingled in London society to Constantine's knowledge.

They danced an elegant country dance with intricate, almost stately figures. She was a good dancer.

The duchess must have grown up in Markle too. Was that where she had met Dunbarton at a wedding? *Whose* wedding? Young's?

He had already made Miss Leavensworth uncomfortable. He had already chastised himself for prying. There was no excuse, then, for continuing to do so. But he did.

"Sir Colin Young," he said when the figures brought them together for perhaps a whole minute. "Was he not somehow connected with the Duke of Dunbarton?"

"A very distant cousin, I believe," she said.

Fourteenth or so in line to the dukedom, if Constantine was not very much mistaken.

There was no casual way of asking for the duchess's maiden name. But her family must be lower on the social scale than Young, or Miss Leavensworth would have named *them* as the most prominent family. Unless the duchess was a sister or daughter of Young, that was. It was a distinct possibility. Either way she had done extremely well for herself in snaring a duke for a husband even if he *was* an old man. Or perhaps especially *because* he was an old man. Marrying him had been a brilliant way of gaining instant status and wealth and the prospect of freedom not far distant.

It was the conventional way of seeing the

Duchess of Dunbarton, of course.

But . . .

But she had converted the large bulk of the jewels Dunbarton had given her into cash, which she had given to "causes" in which she was interested. She kept the other jewels because of their sentimental value.

If she was to be believed, that was. But he believed her.

Was the duchess a bit of a mystery after all?

And why was he doing this? Of what possible interest could it be to him to discover just who she was? Or who she had been? He had never felt this compulsion with any of his other mistresses.

And then another thought struck him. Would he like *her* probing into the secret places of *his* life?

He must ask no more questions.

They had worked their way to the head of the lines, and it was their turn to twirl down between them to land at the foot and begin the upward climb all over again. Miss Leavensworth laughed as they twirled, and Constantine smiled at her.

He could not stop his thoughts, though.

They had been friends since childhood, she and the duchess. It had not struck him as strange until now. Miss Leavensworth was a woman of modest birth and aspirations, daughter of a retired vicar and betrothed of a working one. Yet the duchess had remained close to her in the eleven years or so since her marriage had elevated her in status far above the vicar's daughter.

One more question.

"Do you and the Duchess of Dunbarton write to each other when you are not visiting her?" he asked when there was a chance for some verbal exchange again.

"Oh, at least once a week," she said. "Sometimes more often if there is something more than usually interesting to report upon. We are inveterate letter writers, Hannah and I."

"She never comes to visit you?" he asked.

"No," she said.

No explanation.

"Though I am trying to persuade her to come for my wedding in August," she said a few moments later. "It would mean so much to me to have my dearest friend there. She says no, but I have not given up hope yet."

So she would not go back to Markle even for Miss Leavensworth's wedding? The Duchess of Dunbarton he had thought he knew — the one the *ton* thought it knew — would surely have loved nothing better than to return home with a large entourage of servants to flaunt her title and wealth before the rural yokels among whom she had grown up.

Was it *true* that she had no family?

"She has no family with whom to stay?" he asked.

"She could stay with my parents," she said. "They would be delighted to have her."

Which could mean yes or no. But he must leave this. He felt vaguely guilty. Perhaps even a little more than vaguely. He *was* prying.

"Have you visited the Tower of London yet?" he asked.

"I have not," she said. "But I am very much hoping to do so before I return home."

"Perhaps," he said, "you and the duchess will allow me to escort you there one afternoon."

"Oh," she said, "that is very obliging of you, Mr. Huxtable. I am not sure how interested Hannah is, though, in —"

"I shall remind her," he said, "that she will be able to stand on the very spot on which Queen Anne Boleyn, among others over the years, had her head chopped off. I daresay *that* will draw her interest."

She laughed.

"You are quite possibly right," she said.

"It is one spot I will quite studiously avoid, however."

"I shall make arrangements with the duchess," he said.

And he concentrated upon the dancing. It was an activity he had always enjoyed. He looked along the line of ladies opposite and could see his cousins — all of them, including Vanessa, and including Averil and Jessica, Elliott's sisters. Only Cecily was absent, at home in the country awaiting her third confinement. The duchess was there too, looking stunningly beautiful. Next to her was the Countess of Lanting, Monty's younger sister. And of course there were all the young misses who had recently been launched upon society and the marriage mart, some of them bright and eager, some affecting a fashionable ennui, as though this was something they were *so* accustomed to doing that it really was a quite colossal bore.

And on his side of the line, all the gentlemen.

The orchestra was lively. Feet thumped rhythmically on the wooden floor, a sound that always set his toes to tapping even if he was standing on the sidelines merely looking on. The air had become heavy with the scent of flowers and perfume and human exertion.

The Kitteridges must be breathing a sigh of relief. Their young daughter was dancing with Viscount Doran, an eligible young gentleman who had doubtless been hand-picked for the occasion, and they might deem their ball a grand success.

Constantine and Miss Leavensworth were approaching the head of the line again.

Hannah danced the opening set with Lord Netherby, the second with Lord Hardin-graye, a particular friend of hers with whom she could relax and converse at her ease. She was feeling the pleasure of anticipation. She would waltz later with Constantine. She would dance only that once with him, but it would be enough. There was no dance more splendid than the waltz when one was with an attractive partner, and none was more attractive than Constantine Huxtable.

She would waltz with him and then, after the ball was over, he would follow her carriage home, as he had done last evening, and she would go with him to spend the night — or what remained of it.

And this would be the pattern of her days — and her nights — for the rest of the spring. Oh, she wished it would go on forever. For once she was not at all eager for the summer to come. Let it linger. She did not feel guilty about Barbara. She was not going to neglect her friend, after all. They would spend all day every day together.

Oh, this all felt very, very pleasant indeed after the dreariness of the past year. And it *had* been dreary. The duke would not have expected her to pretend that it was not. She had grieved for him — she still did — but grieving in virtual solitude and in *black* for a whole year had been tedious in the extreme. He would have told her to go out and enjoy herself — she knew he would. But she had not done that except to ride and ride about the countryside near Copeland and visit her friends at Land's End every few days. She had been a faithful wife while the duke lived. She had been a faithful widow for the full year of her mourning.

And now — well, now she was enjoying herself enormously. She was not even going to pretend that she was not. She had dreamed of this, planned for it, and it was happening. And the best of it was that the duke would not resent it. She knew he would not.

"One would have to say, Your Grace," Lord Hardingraye said, "that you have been positively *glowing* since your return to town. Indeed, if you were to glow any brighter I should have to don an eye shade, and I would be accused of all sorts of eccentricity."

"You already *are* eccentric," she said, smiling at him. "Everyone says so."

His eyes twinkled back at her.

Constantine was dancing with Lady Fornwald.

Barbara was . . . not in the ballroom. Hannah looked all about the room, but her friend was nowhere to be seen. She was not even lurking in the quietest corner. She had excused herself after the opening set to go to the ladies' withdrawing room. But that had been ages ago.

She still had not reappeared when the set was finished. Hannah looked around again at the milling crowd to be sure and then went to check the withdrawing room. But Barbara could not still be in there, surely.

She was, though.

She was sitting in a corner, facing away from the door, ignoring and ignored by a small knot of twittering young ladies who were giggling over something and talking in high squeals. In another corner a maid sat silently waiting to help anyone who needed a torn hem mended or an errant curl returned to its coiffure.

"Babs?" Hannah went to sit beside her.

"Are you unwell?"

Barbara would not look at her. She was twisting a handkerchief in her lap. There was no sign of tears on her cheeks, but she looked on the verge of weeping.

"You are going to hate me," she said. "You will not trust me ever again."

"Babs?" Hannah said again.

"I betrayed you," Barbara said. "I *know* how much you value your privacy, and I betrayed you."

Extravagant words. Hannah waited for an explanation.

"I told Mr. Huxtable the name of our village," Barbara said. "I told him about S-Sir Colin Young. I almost told him about . . . about *Dawn.* I stopped myself just in time. And I told him Sir Colin was a distant relation of the Duke of Dunbarton."

"And this is *betrayal?*" Hannah said after a brief silence. "Did you pour out all this information uninvited, Babs?"

"No," she said. "He asked me. And I told him. I am so *sorry,* Hannah. I do not know how you will ever forgive me. You will not even allow me to mention those names to *you.* And yet I blurted them out blithely to your — To Mr. Huxtable."

"Were they idle questions?" Hannah asked. "The ones he asked, I mean?"

"I don't believe so," Barbara said, and tears welled in her eyes and spilled over onto her cheeks. "No, I don't believe so. He wanted to know, and so he asked a country bumpkin unwise in the ways of the *ton*. I am so *sorry*."

"Silly goose," Hannah said, setting one hand against the back of Barbara's bowed neck. "You told him nothing but facts he could have discovered some other way with the greatest ease. You did not exactly inform him that I was a murderess or a bigamist or a . . . What else might I have been that would have made for a ghastly revelation indeed?"

"A highwayman?" Barbara suggested through her tears.

"Or a highwaywoman," Hannah said. "You told him almost nothing at all. And really, there is not a great deal to tell anyway, is there? Only a lot of sordid nonsense. There is no grand secret. If I have guarded the details of my past, it is only because I have chosen to do so. I have nothing to *hide*. Or to hide *from*."

"Then why —" Barbara began to ask.

"I am not in hiding, Babs," Hannah said. "It is just that I am living a new life now and like it infinitely better than I liked the old. I choose not to look back, not to listen to any reminders, not to do *anything* to revive that life."

"You are angry," Barbara said, and her tears flowed faster.

"I am," Hannah admitted. "But not with you, Babs." She rubbed her hand harder across her friend's neck. "I am angry on your behalf. I am angry with a certain gentleman who is going to have to find another waltz partner this evening. He certainly will not be waltzing with me."

Barbara dabbed at her eyes and blew her nose.

"I should have left here sooner," she said, "and gone back to the ballroom and *smiled.* You know I do not approve of your liaison with Mr. Huxtable, Hannah, but I would not be the cause of any dissension between you."

"If there is dissension," Hannah said, "*you* are not the one who has caused it, Babs. Oh, goodness, your eyes are red. Even your *nose* is."

"I do *try* never to weep," Barbara said. "This is what always happens when I do, especially the red nose."

Hannah laughed suddenly.

"Do you remember," she said, "how we used that fact to our advantage on more than one occasion when we were children?

When we broke a window of the greenhouse by playing ball too close to it, for example, and the gardener was stalking toward us breathing fire and brimstone?"

"You told me to cry," Barbara said, smiling through her tears.

"Your face turned almost instantly red," Hannah said. "Everyone immediately took pity on you. And how could they punish *me* if they were petting *you* and assuring you that it was an accident and you must not upset yourself."

"Oh, dear," Barbara said, "we were quite shameless."

They both laughed. Indeed, for a few moments they sounded remarkably like those very young ladies who had already returned to the ballroom. Music was playing there. The third set was in progress.

Hannah stood up. She had distracted Barbara's mind slightly, but *she* was still angry. Furiously so, in fact.

"We will go home," she said. "I am tired, and you have a red nose. Those are reasons enough."

"But Hannah —" Barbara looked instantly dismayed.

Hannah was speaking to the maid, though, and the maid was scurrying away to have the duchess's carriage brought up to the doors.

"Let's go home," Hannah said, turning to Barbara with a smile, "and have a cup of tea and a comfortable coze before we go to bed. I will not have you with me for very much longer — unless you want to write to tell your vicar that you have changed your mind about being a vicar's wife and have decided to remain with me forever and ever, that is."

"Oh, Hannah —" Barbara said.

"No," Hannah said with a mock sigh. "I thought you would not. And so I must make the most of your company while I have it."

"Are you going to . . . to end your connection with Mr. Huxtable?" Barbara asked.

"I shall deal with that connection *and* with Constantine Huxtable tomorrow," Hannah said as she swept from the room.

Barbara went after her.

The Duchess of Dunbarton was playing games again, Constantine decided. She disappeared early from the ballroom. When he strolled into the card room after the fourth set — the waltz they had agreed upon was next — she was not in there either.

Miss Leavensworth was missing too.

He stayed until the end of the ball. He danced every set, including the waltz. And he went straight home afterward and slept for what remained of the night.

Let her play her games.

But she would make the next move. He was certainly not going to run after her.

She made the move early. There was a note from her beside his breakfast plate the following morning, along with the lengthy weekly report from Harvey Wexford, his manager at Ainsley.

The duchess had bold, rather large handwriting, he saw. And she wrote very much as she spoke. There was no greeting at the top of the note, only his name on the outside.

"You will join my other guests for tea this afternoon," she had written, "and then you will drive me in the park. H, Duchess of Dunbarton."

He pursed his lips. She did not invite. She commanded. Were the notes to her other guests similar to this one? And would all obey?

Would *he*?

But of course he would. He was not ready to let her go yet. He was enjoying her as a lover despite the shock of that first night's discovery, and there was a great deal more

201

sensual satisfaction to be had from their liaison before he would be content to see her go. But more than that, he was unexpectedly intrigued by her. He wanted to know more of what lay beyond her apparently shallow exterior.

Why would a woman give up ten years of her life solely for the acquisition of position and wealth, only to give away a large portion of that wealth to unnamed "causes"? And why would she remain faithful to a sham of a marriage? And even give the impression now that she might have been *fond* of the old duke? Why would a worthy woman like Miss Leavensworth have remained faithful to their friendship all these years? And why would the duchess write to her weekly, keeping up a friendship that could be of no material value to her?

And *why* was his head so full of such questions?

No, he would not give her up yet. He would answer the summons and go to Dunbarton House for tea this afternoon.

And he would drive her in the park afterward.

And tonight? Well, they would see.

In the meanwhile, he turned his attention to Wexford's report, which he always devoured whole and then went back over to read more slowly and with greater attention to detail.

CHAPTER 10

When Constantine arrived at Dunbarton House, he discovered that there were several guests already in the drawing room, all of whom he knew with varying degrees of familiarity. The only two he really saw, though, were Elliott and Vanessa, Duke and Duchess of Moreland.

Hannah came toward him, right hand extended. Her customary half-smile and slightly drooped eyelids were firmly in place.

"Mr. Huxtable," she said, "how charming of you to come."

"Duchess." He bowed over her hand, which she slid from his grasp before he could carry it to his lips.

"You know everyone, I would imagine," she said. "Do fetch yourself some tea and cakes and mingle."

She gestured vaguely toward a table where a maid was serving tea.

And she was gone to join Elliott and

Vanessa, with whom she sat and talked for a while to the exclusion of everyone else.

This was deliberate? Constantine wondered.

But yes, of course it was.

Elliott, who had pokered up considerably when he walked into the room, was soon engaged in the conversation. He looked relaxed, interested, happy. He surely smiled far more than he had used to do. Although inevitably the two of them found themselves in a room together fairly frequently during the spring Season and were even sometimes forced to come face-to-face and be civil to each other, Constantine rarely *looked* at his former friend these days. But it was true, and he had seen it before without really analyzing it. Elliott was happy. He had been married for nine years, he had three children ranging in age from eight to less than one, and he was contented.

Constantine could remember the time when Elliott had viewed marriage as a leg shackle to be avoided for as long as it was humanly possible to do so. In the meantime he had squeezed enjoyment out of every moment of every day. They both had. The wilder the escapade, the better they had liked it. The death of Elliott's father had changed all that — and him. For suddenly he had been a viscount and a duke's heir — and guardian of Jonathan, Earl of Merton. And suddenly he had become grim and humorless and consumed by an excessive devotion to duty.

Constantine took his plate and his cup of tea and mingled, as he had been instructed to do. He was good at mingling. But what lady or gentleman was not? The ability to engage in social chitchat was an essential attribute of gentility.

One thing about chitchat, though, was that it left the mind largely free to wander and engage in any thoughts or observations it pleased.

Vanessa was aging well. She must be in her thirties now. She had never been as beautiful as her sisters, but she had always been warmhearted, vivacious, and fun-loving, and those qualities transcended mere physical good looks. Constantine had liked her from the start. When she had arrived at Warren Hall with Stephen and her sisters not very long after Jon's death, he had been consumed by hatred and resentment. He had stayed for their arrival only because Elliott had ordered him to leave. But the strange thing about losing Jon was that he had not gone away when his body had been consigned to the ground in the churchyard.

He had taken up residence somewhere in Constantine's being that felt suspiciously close to his heart, and it was impossible to look at certain things and people and not see them as Jon would have done.

Jon would have *adored* discovering new cousins. New people to love.

And Vanessa, even more than the other three, had been very easy to like, impossible to *dis*like.

For years now he had tried not to think about Vanessa at all. He had hurt her. He had deliberately introduced her to Elliott's ex-mistress at the theater one evening soon after her marriage, and then he had escorted the ex-mistress to a ball hosted by Elliott and Vanessa. The whole of the *ton* had seen her there. He had done it to embarrass Elliott, of course. But he had ended up causing Vanessa humiliation and untold suffering. Elliott had told her other unsavory things about him, and in the very direct way with which she seemed to confront all the problems in her life, she had taken him aside at Vauxhall one night and told him exactly what she thought of him and added that she wished she might never see him again and that she would never willingly speak with him in the future. It was a promise she had kept.

The memory of it all still needled at his conscience. And there was no mortal thing he could do about it. He had apologized at the time for deliberately exposing her to such humiliation. She had refused to forgive him. There was nothing else to be said.

Why *had* the duchess invited both him and them here this afternoon when she knew they were estranged? What game was she playing? And for how long would he allow it to go on?

Not long, he decided. He would make that clear to her when he drove her in the park later. Not that there would be much chance for private conversation there. He would just have to make some.

The duchess did not spend all her time with Elliott and Vanessa. She circulated among her guests and proved herself to be a warm and welcoming hostess. Constantine had attended a few of her balls in the past, but he had never before been at any of her more intimate gatherings.

Lord Enderby asked her if she would do him the honor of driving in the park with him later.

"But I must decline," she said, "with regret, Lord Enderby. I have already accepted an invitation from Mr. Huxtable."

All eyes turned his way, Constantine realized. If anyone had discounted the gossip that must have been circulating for the past week or so, then they probably doubted no longer. For he certainly had not invited her here during her tea, had he? It must have been prearranged, then.

"Perhaps some other time," she told Enderby.

Her words acted like a signal to everyone to take their leave. Constantine stood at one of the windows, looking out, his hands clasped at his back while the duchess bade her guests farewell.

"I shall fetch my bonnet and meet you on the pavement," she told him when the two of them were alone.

And she had gone before Constantine turned around.

Was it his imagination that there had been a slight chill in her voice when she addressed him?

What was this all about?

But suddenly he knew. Or was pretty sure he knew. It was dense of him not to have realized it sooner, in fact — as soon as her terse little note arrived this morning. Or when she had disappeared without a word last night.

He had asked some intrusive questions of her friend last evening, and she had somehow found out.

Where was Miss Leavensworth this afternoon, anyway?

He made his way downstairs. His curricle had already been brought up to the door, he could see.

"Where was Miss Leavensworth this afternoon?" Constantine asked as soon as he had handed Hannah up to the high seat of his curricle and come around to the other side to take his seat beside her. He gathered the ribbons in his hands.

Hannah loved riding in curricles. But this afternoon's drive was not for enjoyment. She was feeling out of sorts. She opened her parasol and raised it above her head.

"She had a letter at breakfast time from relatives of the Reverend Newcombe, her betrothed," she said. "They are in town for a few days and invited her to visit Kew Gardens with them and their children today."

"That will be pleasant for them all," he said. "And they have the ideal weather for such an excursion. Not too hot and not too windy."

"One might, I suppose," she said as he turned the curricle out of the square, "converse comfortably about the weather

210

until we reach the park, Mr. Huxtable. I would prefer to inform you that I am extremely displeased with you."

"Yes," he said, turning his head to look at her. "I rather guessed you were."

"I discovered Barbara close to tears in the ladies' withdrawing room partway through last evening," she said.

"Ah," he said and faced front again.

"She believed she had betrayed my trust in her," she said. "She feared I would put an end to our friendship. But, being the incurably moral and upright lady she is, she felt compelled to confess rather than hide what she had done."

He did not ask her what she was talking about. Instead, he skillfully guided his horses around a slow-moving cart.

"I grew up in the village of Markle in Lincolnshire," she said, "the daughter of Mr. Joseph Delmont, a gentleman of no particular social significance or fortune. I had one sister, Dawn. She is now Lady Young, wife of Sir Colin Young, baronet. It was at the wedding of his cousin, now deceased, that I met the Duke of Dunbarton, whom I married five days later. I have not been back to Markle or had any communication with any member of my family since then. Is there *anything else* you wish to know, Mr.

211

Huxtable?"

He gazed steadily ahead. A large and ancient town carriage was lumbering toward them down the very center of the road, despite some rather blistering remarks that were being hurled at its oblivious coachman by other occupiers of the road. Constantine was compelled to move the curricle over to avoid a collision. His lips were pursed.

"About why I have never been back home, perhaps?" she suggested.

She could actually *feel* her heart thumping in her bosom. She could hear it hammering in her ears. And then she realized that the carriage belonged to the Dowager Countess of Blackwell and that lady was nodding regally in her direction from one of the windows. Hannah smiled and raised a hand.

"I will tell you why," she said, answering her own question when he did not. "During that wedding I discovered Colin Young, my *fiancé,* behind the rose arbor with my sister, in a situation that could be described as compromising only if one were trying very hard not to shock one's listener by being more graphic. And after they had . . . *parted* and set themselves to rights, they were both defiantly defensive rather than ashamed or apologetic or horrified to be discovered. She was sick to death of always being in my shadow, Dawn told me, of never being noticed because everyone wanted to look only at *me,* of forever feeling *ugly.* She *loved* Colin, and he loved her, and what was I going to do about it? And she was perfectly right, Colin said. He was relatively new to the neighborhood and had been dazzled by my beauty at first until he got to know Dawn and realized that character was of more importance than anything else. And that *love* was. He was very sorry, but he had decided that he wanted a real woman instead of just a beauty. Not that he meant any offense, of course. I really *was* lovely. He hoped I would understand and free him from an obligation that had become irksome to him.

"As if I were unreal. As if I were incapable of love or companionship. As if I were incapable of being *hurt* just because I was *lovely.*

"And when I drew my father into the library and threw myself into his arms for comfort and support, he sighed and told me how my beauty had been nothing but a trial to him all my life — or ever since my mother died when I was thirteen, anyway. I had always been her favorite, but he was mindful of the fact that he had *two* daughters. All the girls had always admired me and wanted to be my friend and virtually ignored Dawn, and all the young men had always buzzed around me and vied for my attention and taken no notice whatsoever of my sister. Must I begrudge her happiness now when she had found love despite everything? If I had had one ounce of sisterly affection in my body, I would have seen how the wind was blowing weeks earlier. Was I going to be selfish, as usual, and refuse to release Colin Young from a promise he had made hastily and regretted almost immediately? Could I not think of someone else for once in my life? It was not as though I could not find someone else anytime I wished.

"But all my life — or so it seemed to me — I had tried to be like everyone else. And I had loved Dawn and tried to make other people like her. I never understood why she was not generally liked. It was *not* that I pushed her back into my shadow. It was *not*. And she had a way sometimes of taking my friends or my admirers away from me and gloating afterward. We were not always friends. Sometimes we fought quite viciously, and I daresay I was as guilty of nastiness as often as she was. But she was my *sister*. I *loved* her. It had never occurred

to me that she would try to take my betrothed. I was *engaged.* The time for games
was over.

"Perhaps they were right. Perhaps it *was*
all my fault. Perhaps . . ."

She paused for breath. Actually she gasped
for breath. The gate into the park was just
ahead.

"Duchess," Constantine said.

But she held up a staying hand. She had
not finished yet.

"I *loved* him," she said. "It had not occurred to me to withhold any part of my
heart from him. I had eyes for no man but
him. I *knew* that my beauty was often a li-
ability. I *knew* that sometimes other girls
resented me when there were young men
around. I tried *not* to be beautiful. Even as
a child I tried because it embarrassed me
always to have my mother complimented
on my looks in the hearing of Dawn and
other girls, and to have her look at me with
pleasure and rearrange my ringlets to look
just so. I tried wearing plain clothes when I
was old enough to choose for myself and a
plain hairstyle. I tried hanging my head and
staying quiet in company. I tried to show
that I was not conceited. But finally, with
Colin, I felt free to love and to be myself at
last.

"I cannot possibly describe how I felt when my father left me after telling me to buck up and look cheerful — the emptiness, the loneliness, the *terror.* And that was when I discovered that we had not been alone in the library. The Duke of Dunbarton had been there all the time. He had withdrawn there out of boredom with the festivities and was sitting in a wing chair that he had pulled up to a window, his back to the room. I did not know it until I was crying so hard that I thought I would die. Literally die."

Constantine turned the curricle between the park gates, but he had slowed its pace.

"I will always remember the first words he spoke to me," Hannah said, closing her eyes. " 'My dear Miss Delmont,' he said in that bored, sighing voice that was so characteristic of him, 'no woman can possibly ever be too beautiful. I see I am going to have to marry you and teach you that lesson until you believe it beyond any doubt. I shall make it the final project of my life.' And strangely, unbelievably, I was laughing at the same time as I was crying. We had all been terrified all day just *knowing* he was there at the wedding. We had all avoided him as much as we could for fear, I suppose, that he would strike us down with one glance if we presumed to step across his path or raise our eyes to his illustrious person. Yet there he was telling me that he must marry me, that he must make my education the final project of his life. And handing me his fine linen handkerchief with a rather pained expression on his face."

Constantine had drawn the horses almost to a halt.

"*Now* are you satisfied?" she asked.

"Yes," he said with a sigh. "I feel quite suitably chastened, Duchess. You could not have found a more effective way of punishing me, in fact, than answering all the questions delicacy and tact would not allow me to ask last night. And you have made me feel all the impertinence of the questions I did ask. I beg your pardon, though I realize that apologies are almost always inadequate. For would I now be begging your pardon if I had not been discovered? I do not know, though I did feel remorseful even at the time when I understood that Miss Leavensworth was uncomfortable with my questions and that I was being less than honorable in asking them of her instead of you."

It was, she supposed, rather handsome as apologies went.

"I shall call on Miss Leavensworth tomorrow if I may," he said, "and make my apology in person."

Even at the snail's pace at which they were moving they would be among the fashionable afternoon crowd soon.

"What now?" he asked. "Do you wish me to take you back home? Would you prefer that we proceed no further with our liaison?"

The last question jolted her. *Would* she? She would probably have said yes last night or this morning. Even earlier this afternoon. But all he had done, when all was said and done, was ask a few questions about her. Was he so different from her? She wanted to know about him too. Except that she had always planned to drag it all out of him personally.

"Oh," she said with a determined twirl of her parasol, "I need an affair. I do not need marriage. Not yet, anyway, and perhaps never. I cannot yet let go of the conviction that I am still married to the duke, even though he has been dead for longer than a year."

"You loved him," he said.

She turned her head toward him, looking for irony. But she could see none in his face and had heard none in his voice.

"I *did* love him," she said, "with all my heart. He was my rock and my security for ten years. He loved me unconditionally and totally. He adored me, and I adored him. No one will ever believe that, of course, but I really do not care."

She was rather horrified to note that her voice was shaking slightly.

"I believe you," he said quietly.

"Thank you," she said. "I need a *lover*, Constantine. It is too soon for anything else — love, marriage, whatever. And in one way — and one way only — the years of my marriage left me feeling starved. If I let you go, I will have to start all over again to find another lover, and I would find that tiresome."

"I am forgiven then?" he asked. "I will not pry again, Duchess. You may keep your remaining secrets, if there are any. I will not try to uncover them."

"You do not want to *know* me, then?" she asked him. "You do not want to know everything there is to know about me?"

"Like you, Duchess," he said, "it is a *lover* I want, not a wife. Curiosity will not get the better of me again."

"I, on the other hand," she said, "still want to know everything there is to know about you. A lover is not an inanimate object, after all. Or even just a body, even if it *is* a very splendid body and makes love in a very satisfactory way."

He was smiling, she could see when she looked at him — something he did not often do. It was an expression that did strange things to her breathing.

"Forgiveness comes at a price, Constantine," she said. "You are in my debt. You will answer some of my questions tonight after we have made love."

"Come home with me now." He turned his head to look at her.

"Barbara will be home for dinner," she said, "and I have accepted no invitations for tonight. We are to enjoy a blessed evening at home just talking to each other and enjoying each other's company. She is more dear to me than anyone else in the world, you know, now that the duke has gone. You will send a carriage at eleven."

"Does anyone disobey your commands, Duchess?" he asked.

She half smiled at him. "You do not *wish* to see me tonight?" she asked him. "Or to make love to me?"

He actually grinned.

"I shall send a carriage at eleven," he said. "You will be ready. If you are not at my house by a quarter past, I shall personally lock the door."

She laughed.

And they were swallowed up in the crowd.

She felt suddenly and quite breathtakingly *happy*.

Barbara was tired after her day at Kew Gardens, though she had had a wonderful time there and told Hannah all about it, especially about the pagoda, which she thought one of the loveliest structures she had ever seen. And she had been perfectly delighted with Simon's cousins, whom she had not met before. They had treated her as though she were quite one of the family already, and she had made them laugh by trying to see resemblances between them and Simon. She had played a game of hide-and-seek with the children even though they were twelve years old. They were twins, a boy and a girl.

She was eager to hear all about Hannah's tea party, which had been planned and arranged in such a hurry after breakfast. And she listened in some dismay as Hannah informed her that Constantine would be calling in the morning to apologize for last night.

"You must tell him that he is forgiven," she said, "as indeed he is. I daresay he meant no real harm, Hannah. He merely wanted to know more about you, and I must honor him for that as it suggests he values you as a person. Perhaps he is in love with you. Perhaps —"

But Hannah was laughing.

"You may convince yourself that you are a dusty spinster, Babs," she said, "but you will not convince *me*. You are a romantic, as you have always been. Who else would have waited until she was perilously close to her thirtieth birthday before choosing her life's companion? Constantine Huxtable's feelings for me have *nothing* to do with romance, I do assure you. Which is just as well, you know, because neither do my feelings for him."

"Do not let him come here tomorrow to speak with me," Barbara begged. "I would be *so* embarrassed."

"I shall try to deter him," Hannah promised.

Barbara retired to bed soon after ten.

The carriage arrived at five minutes to eleven. Hannah, who had been ready since half past ten, waited fifteen minutes before leaving the house. When the carriage arrived at Constantine's house some time after quarter past eleven, the door was locked. Hannah tried it herself when it did not open as it usually did on her arrival and when the coachman's discreet knock brought no results.

"Well," she said, partly dismayed, partly amused.

And, as if she had spoken the magic word, the door swung open. She swept inside and Constantine shut the door behind her. She turned to face him and could see that he was dangling a large key from one finger.

"Tyrant!" she said.

"Minx!"

They both laughed, and she closed the distance between them, threw her arms about his neck, and kissed him hard. His arms came about her waist like vises, and he kissed her back — harder.

Her toes were barely brushing the floor when they were finished. Or finished with the preliminaries, anyway.

"You made a tactical error," she said. "If you wished to take a firm stand with me, you ought not to have opened the door."

"And if you had wanted to take a firm stand with me," he said, "you would not have got out of the carriage to creep up the steps and try the door handle."

"I did not *creep*," she protested. "I *swept*."

"It still showed how desperate you were to get at me," he said.

"And *why* exactly," she asked, "were you skulking behind the door, the key at the ready? Because you did not want me to get at you? And why did you *open* the door?"

"I took pity on you," he said.

"Ha!"

And even her toes left the floor as they kissed again.

"I have some questions to ask you," she said when she could. "I tried writing them all down, but I could not find a sheet of paper long enough."

"Hmm," he said, setting her feet on the floor. "Ask away, then, Duchess."

His dark eyes had turned slightly wary.

"Not yet," she said. "They will wait until after."

"After?" He raised his eyebrows.

"After you have made love to me," she said. "After I have made love to you. After we have made love to each other."

"*Three* times?" he said. "What am I going to look like tomorrow, Duchess? I need my rest."

"You will look far more rugged and appealing without it," she said.

He set the key down on the hall table and offered his hand. She set hers in it, and his fingers closed about her own as he led her in the direction of the staircase.

And oh, dear, she thought, she was *still* feeling happy. She ought to be glad about that. She had looked forward to this spring affair with such eager anticipation all through the winter. And physically speaking, it was more than living up to her expectations.

Why was she *not* glad, then? Because of the bickering and the teasing and the laughter? Because she had the strange, uneasy feeling that they had somehow crossed a barrier today from being simply lovers to being entangled in some sort of relationship?

Because she was feeling *happy?*

Could she not be happy *and* glad about it?

But she would think later, she decided as she stepped inside his dimly lit bedchamber and he closed the door behind them.

Sometimes there were *far* better things to do than thinking.

CHAPTER 11

They made love with fierce energy the first time, with slow languor the second — if it was possible to be languorous while making love. Either way they were both exhausted by the time they were finished.

Hannah curled onto her side, facing away from him, and he curled around her from behind and slid one arm beneath her head while he wrapped the other about her. She snuggled back against him and raised his hand so that she could rest her cheek against the back of it.

And she slept.

Constantine did not. An uneasy conscience was the perfect recipe for insomnia.

Were other people like him, he wondered. Did everyone make the most ghastly blunders at regular intervals through their life and live to regret them ever afterward? Was everyone's life filled with a confusing and contradictory mix of guilt and innocence, hatred and love, concern and unconcern, and any number of other pairings of polar opposites? Or were most people one thing or the other — good or bad, cheerful or crotchety, generous or miserly, and so on.

As a boy he had hated Jon, his youngest brother — the very person he loved most in the world. He had hated Jon because he was sunny-natured and warmhearted and guileless despite the difficulties of his life, because he was overweight and ungainly and had facial features that made him look more Asian than English, and because he had a brain that worked slowly — *and because he was going to die young.* Constantine had hated him because he could not put things right for him — and because Jon had what Con had never wanted anyway. The heirdom.

How could he hate so fiercely and love with such deep agony all at the same time? He had left home as soon as he was old enough and sowed some pretty wild oats, most of them with Elliott. Constantine had not cared about the way life had treated him or about the people he had left behind. Why should he? But he had known that Jon pined for him, and he had hated him more than ever and had gone back home because he loved him more than life itself and knew he would not have him for long.

Was everyone's life such a mass of contradictions? Surely not. There would be no sanity left in the world.

When their father died and Jon became Earl of Merton at the age of thirteen, Constantine had effectively run the estate and his other affairs for him even though their father, in his questionable wisdom, had appointed his brother-in-law, Elliott's father, as Jon's guardian. And then *he* had died two years later and Elliott had inherited the guardianship. And so Elliott, Constantine's best friend, had become his prime adversary. For he had chosen to take his position seriously and had muscled in where his father had been content to let Con take charge.

And the great enmity had begun — the bitter estrangement that had lasted ever since. For Elliott had refused simply to trust his cousin to run the estate efficiently and to do what was best for Jon. He had intruded, and it had not taken him long to discover that a fortune in jewels was missing, though none of them was technically part of the entail. And he had jumped to all the obvious conclusions, and the accusations had flown.

Constantine had invited him to go to hell. He had not simply explained, taken Elliott into his confidence. Oh, no, that would have been far too easy. Besides, Elliott had not simply *asked,* invited his closest friend to explain. He had *known,* or thought he knew. And he had called Con a thief, the worst kind of thief, one who would steal from his mentally handicapped brother who loved him dearly and trusted him implicitly and knew no better.

And, truth be told, Constantine had resented Elliott even before the discovery and accusation, for his cousin, newly elevated to the title of Viscount Lyngate by the death of his father, was a cruel reminder that Con had *not* become Earl of Merton on the death of his father, though they were both eldest sons.

However it was, he had told Elliott to go to hell.

Unlike the other times during their youth when they had quarreled, they had not been able simply to put up their fists and fight it out before grinning at each other and admitting that that had been *fun* — even as they mopped at bloody noses and pressed fingers gingerly to swelling eyes.

It had not been that sort of quarrel. It had not been fixable.

Instead of turning to fisticuffs, Constantine had set out to make Elliott's life hell —

whenever he came to Warren Hall, anyway. And he came often. Constantine had used Jon to play games with Elliott, games that had annoyed and frustrated and even humiliated him, games Jon had thought enormous fun, games that had widened the rift between the cousins. Sometimes, for example, Constantine would have Jon hide when Elliott came, and precious time would have to be spent hunting for him. Con would usually stand by, watching, one shoulder resting against a doorframe, smiling with contempt.

Quarrels always brought out the worst in people. In *him,* anyway.

Even now he could not feel as sorry as perhaps he ought for the childishness of his behavior. For Elliott, who had known him all his life, had actually believed — and still did — that he was capable of robbing his own brother because Jon was easily exploited. It had hurt, that sudden loss of trust. It still would if he had not converted pain into hatred.

But he was in many ways as bad as Elliott. He did not even try to deny that fact now as he held Hannah's warm, relaxed body against his and stared at the wall on the far side of his bed. Instead of sitting down with him and discussing the guardianship, as two men — two *friends* — in their twenties ought to have been able to do, he had been cold and distant and sarcastic, even before the jewels had been missed. And Elliott had been cold and distant and autocratic.

It had been pretty childish, really. On both their parts. Perhaps they would have got over it if it had not been for the infernal jewels. But they were indisputably missing, so he and Elliott never had got over it.

They were equally to blame.

Which fact did not make Constantine hate Elliott the less.

He buried his nose in Hannah's hair. It was soft and warm and fragrant — just as *she* was. He thought of kissing her awake to distract his mind, but she was sleeping peacefully.

He had upset *her* last night. She had still been upset earlier today.

And he had upset the totally innocent Miss Leavensworth.

Just as he had upset Vanessa soon after she married Elliott.

Did other people do such things? Did everyone have these shameful, damnably uncomfortable skeletons in their closets?

He was a monster. He was the devil incarnate. People were quite right to call him that.

Perhaps one of the worst of his sins, a very recent one, had been his denial of all that he knew to be true of human nature. All people — *all* — were a complex product of their heritage, their environment, their upbringing and education and cumulative experiences of life as well as of a basic character and personality with which they were born. Everyone was a rose but even more complex than a mere flower. Everyone was made up of infinitely layered petals. And everyone had something indescribably precious at the heart of their being.

No one was shallow. Not really.

But he had chosen to believe that the Duchess of Dunbarton was different from every other human being. He had chosen to believe that beneath the surface appearance of beauty and vanity and arrogance there was nothing to know. That she was an empty vessel, not truly human.

It was what people had chosen to believe of her all her life — except, it seemed, the late duke, her husband.

He had been no better than her own family, who perhaps had loved her in their own way, but who also had assumed that her beauty made her less sensitive, less needy than her plainer sister. Her father had sympathized with the sister, assuming that his elder daughter could cope better with the vicissitudes of life. Why did people assume that the beautiful among them needed nothing but their beauty to bring them happiness? That behind the beauty there was nothing but an empty, insensitive shell?

Why had *he* assumed it?

Had he failed to accord her full personhood because she was *beautiful*?

He was starting to get a headache. And he was beginning to get pins and needles in the arm beneath her head. He had an itch on his bare shoulder that he needed to scratch. He was not going to sleep at all. That was obvious. Neither was he going to make love again. Not until he had done a good deal more thinking.

He drew his hand carefully from beneath her cheek and slid his arm slowly from under her head. She grumbled sleepily and burrowed her head into the pillow.

"Constantine," she muttered, but she was not awake.

He got off the bed and went into his dressing room. He got dressed, though he did not pull on a coat over his shirt or tuck the shirt into his pantaloons. He went to stand beside the bed to look down at Hannah. She was half awake and blinking up at him.

"Stay here," he said. "I'll be back."

And he bent over her and set his lips to hers. She kissed him back with lazy warmth.

"Where are you going?" she asked.

"I'll be back," he told her again and made off to the kitchen down two flights of stairs.

He built up a fire from the embers of last night's, half filled the heavy built cast-iron kettle, and set it to boil. He raided the pantry for something to eat and set some sweet biscuits on a plate. Awhile later he was climbing the stairs again with a tray, on which were a large pot of tea covered with a thick cozy to keep the brew hot, a milk jug and sugar bowl, cups and saucers and spoons, and the plate of biscuits. He took the tray into the sitting room next to his bedchamber and then went to fetch Hannah.

She was still hovering between sleeping and waking. He went into his dressing room again and came out with a large woolly dressing gown, which he wore on chilly evenings when he was at home alone and merely wanted to lounge inelegantly with a good book.

"Come," he said.

"Where?"

But she sat up and swung her legs over the side of the bed and stood as he held out the dressing gown. She pushed her arms into the sleeves, and he wrapped it about her before securing it with the sash. She looked half buried.

"Mmm," she said, turning her nose into the collar. "It smells of you."

"Is that good?" he asked.

"Mmm," she said again, and he was smitten with guilt once more.

He picked up the branch of candles and led the way to the sitting room. All the furniture was large in here — deliberately so. Large and soft and comfortable. This was a room in which elegance and posture did not matter. This was a place for slouching and risking irreparable damage to one's spine. This was where he relaxed.

Strangely enough, no one else was ever invited in here. None of his former mistresses had set foot inside here.

She sat in a deep leather chair, curled her legs up under her, set her head back, and snuggled into the dressing gown. She gazed at him from beneath lowered lids as he poured the tea, though not in the way she usually did. This time it was a genuinely sleepy look. A look of contentment, or so it seemed.

"Milk? Sugar?" he asked.

"Both," she said.

He set down a cup and saucer on the table

beside her and offered her the plate. She took a biscuit and nibbled it.

"You make a lovely hostess, Constantine," she said. "Virile. And generous. You have filled my cup to the brim. I will need a steady hand not to spill it."

He never saw the sense in half filling a cup. Cups were usually too small to start with.

He sat facing her, a short distance away, a biscuit in one hand, his cup in the other. He slouched back in his chair and crossed one ankle over the other knee.

A pretense of relaxation.

"Tell me, then, Duchess," he said. "What do you want to know?"

And suddenly a huge, dark, empty hole seemed to open up deep inside him. An enormous vulnerability.

But it was the only way he could atone.

Hannah was impressed. Most men would surely have avoided the issue for as long as they could. And she had been fast asleep when he got out of bed. She would probably have slept all night. But he had chosen to remind her that she had the right to ask him questions about himself and to expect answers.

He was a man full of secrets, she suspected, and she doubted he ever gave up any of them willingly, even to those nearest and dearest to him. He was a private man.

And who *were* his nearest and dearest? His cousins? The ones who had usurped what should surely have been rightfully his?

Was he a *lonely* man? Suddenly she suspected that he was.

He was also, it seemed, a man of honor. He had behaved badly with poor Barbara, and he knew it and was remorseful. Now he would atone in the only way he knew how. He would answer any and all of her questions.

It would be cruel under the circumstances to ask them, to force him to give up the secrets of the life he guarded so carefully.

He was not looking his dark, elegant, dangerous self at the moment. He was sitting quite inelegantly, in fact — as was she. He looked gorgeous.

Something touched her heart — and was denied entrance.

She finished eating her biscuit.

"I might have known," he said, "that you would respond with unpredictable cleverness to my offer to tell all."

She raised her eyebrows.

"With silence," he said.

And she realized that when she had chosen

Constantine Huxtable to be her first lover she had done so not just on the basis of his physical attractions, considerable though they were. She had also been drawn to the closed look of him, hinting at depths of character and meaning that might contain nothing but darkness but might just as well hide universes of light. She had been attracted by the mystery of him, though she had had no evidence that there *was* any mystery at all.

She had known all this from the start, of course. She had told him before they became lovers that she would insist upon knowing everything there was to know about him. But she had not really understood what she was saying. She had still thought that primarily her interest in him was physical.

Was it not, then?

She had no one with whom to compare him as a lover. But surely there could be no one else who could so thoroughly satisfy her — a thought that did not bode well for the coming years. She had started with the best, and what did that leave her?

And was not the physical enough?

This craving to *know* him — ought she to have paid it more attention before it was too late?

Too late for *what?*

"Ainsley Park," he said abruptly, setting down his empty cup in its saucer beside him. "It is the name of my property in Gloucestershire. The house and park are not quite on the scale of Warren Hall, but they are impressive enough. Even the dower house is quite sizable. And the home farm is large. I have enlarged it further by not leasing out two of the tenant farms when they went vacant. It is all very prosperous — a hive of industry."

"Was it your father's?" she asked.

"No." He shook his head. "All my father's properties were entailed. They are Merton's."

"How could you afford to purchase it?" she asked.

He smiled slowly.

"It is the question all my closest acquaintance have wanted answered since it became mine," he said. "Especially Moreland, who knows — or thinks he does."

"So?" she asked, setting her own cup down and sliding her hands into the opposite sleeves of the dressing gown she was wearing.

"I did not purchase it," he said. "I won it."

"Won?"

"I gambled as much as most idle young men do when I first left home," he said. "I always ended up losing everything except the shirt on my back, though I was always wise enough to wager only what I had, which was not a great deal. I had a monthly allowance, but my father kept me on a tight enough rein. But this was after his death, when Jon was earl, and this time I deliberately sought out a game where I knew the stakes were high and no prisoners were taken, so to speak. And I wagered with money that was not strictly mine but was what I had received for the sale of a certain jewel — we have both been up to *that* game, Duchess. The money was not mine to lose, and I do not believe I have ever felt a terror to match what I felt when I sat down to play and made a bet of the type of magnitude my fellow players expected."

Hannah closed her eyes.

"Within ten minutes," he said, "I had won Ainsley Park. It was not the principal seat of the man who lost it, and he did not seem unduly disturbed at losing it with one turn of the card. He and his fellows *did* seem annoyed, however, when I took my winnings and left. They threatened never to allow me into their hallowed midst again. I do not know if they would have carried through on the threat. I believe they probably would have. I have never gambled since — except in a very small way at balls and private parties, I suppose."

"And the money from the sale of the jewel?" she said.

"That went where it was intended to go," he told her.

"And no one knows how you acquired Ainsley Park?" she asked.

"Let them guess," he said.

"And what is the usual guess?" she asked.

"That I bought it with ill-gotten gains, I suppose," he said with a shrug. "They are not far wrong."

"You live there alone?" she asked. How sad that he should have cut himself off in such a way from his relatives and friends.

He laughed softly.

"Not quite," he said. "In fact, the house — the *mansion* — is so crowded with people that there is no room left for me. I live in the dower house. And even that haven of peace is being slowly but very surely invaded."

Hannah moved her legs until her feet were flat on the chair. She hugged her updrawn knees and rested her chin on them.

"You are going to have to tell me now, Constantine," she said, "or I will not sleep for a week wondering. And you *do* owe me. Who are all these people?"

"I started with women," he said. "Women whose character and reputation were in tatters because their employers or social superiors had assumed their God-given rights extended to the very persons of the females they fancied. Women and their bastard children. They were given a home at Ainsley and honest work to do in the house and on the farm. And training as seamstresses or milliners or cooks or whatever else took their interest, if I could find someone willing to teach them in exchange for a home and food and a modest salary. And eventually they were found work with people who were willing to take them, reputation and bastard children and all."

"Why?" she asked. "Why them in particular?"

He looked darkly brooding.

"Let us just say," he said, "that I knew some of those women and the man who took everything from them except life itself. I knew what they lost — employment, family, the respect of all who knew them. I knew what they suffered — ostracism. And I knew that the meager handouts of money I occasionally made to them solved nothing substantial. I knew that I dared not befriend them openly or assumptions would have been made and matters would have been worse for them. *If* that were possible. I knew the man who caused it all and felt not a qualm of guilt as one by one they were cast from his employment and forgotten about while others took their place and as like as not suffered their fate."

Hannah hugged her legs more tightly.

Oh, dear God. His *father?* She opened her mouth to ask, but the question was unaskable.

"Elliott — the Duke of Moreland — would tell you that I was that man," he said.

"Did he actually *accuse* you?" she asked.

"Yes."

"And you did not *deny* it?" she asked.

"No."

Oh, dear, getting information from him was sometimes like trying to squeeze blood from a stone.

"Why *not?*" she asked.

He looked very directly at her. "He had been my *friend,*" he said. "He was my *cousin,* almost my brother. Our mothers were sisters. He ought not to have needed to ask. I would never have asked it of him. I would have *known* the answer to be no. We had been pretty wild together when we were younger, but we never *ever* took any woman against her will."

"But you did not deny it when he *did* ask," she said.

"He did not ask," he said. "He *told* me. He had found out somehow about those wronged women and their children. And so he confronted *me*. Accusations are not always or even usually polite questions, Duchess."

"You foolish man," she said. "And so *this* is what your quarrel is all about?"

"Among other things," he said.

She chose not to ask.

"And it all might have been cleared up," she said, "with a simple denial, which your pride would not allow you to make."

"A denial ought not to have been necessary," he said. "Moreland was, and is, a pompous ass."

"And you are a stubborn mule," she said. "You described yourselves thus on another occasion, and I see that you were quite right."

He got to his feet, took the cozy off the teapot, and refilled both their cups. He sat down again, remembered that she took milk and sugar, and got up to add them to her cup. It was full to the brim again. Fuller than last time. He offered her a biscuit, but she shook her head.

"You said you *started* with women at Ainsley," she reminded him.

"I saw a boy in a butcher shop here in London," he said. "I stopped on the pavement outside and took a closer look because he reminded me remarkably of Jon. He had the same sort of facial features and physique, and I guessed that his parents too had been told when he was born that he would not live much beyond the age of twelve. I would have moved on, but even in the minute or so I stood there I could see two things — that he was eager to please and that he did *not* please at all. Even in that minute he was cuffed twice, once by a customer and once by the butcher for displeasing the customer. I went in and paid the butcher the price of an apprentice — he had taken the boy from an orphanage for next to nothing, I would imagine. I took the boy — Francis — down to Ainsley when I went a few days later. I put him to work in the kitchen and farmyard and he became the adored pet of all the women living there, especially the cook. He died a little more than a year later at the age of thirteen or so — he did not know his exact age. I believe it was a happy year for him."

He stopped speaking in order to drink his tea. He directed his gaze into his cup as he

245

did so. Hannah busied herself with her own cup in order to give him a few moments to collect himself. She knew she had not imagined the brightening of his eyes and the unsteadiness of his voice.

He had grieved for that butcher's boy. Francis. The boy who had reminded him of his brother.

"It was meeting him that made me realize," he said, "that if I wanted the Ainsley project to pay its own way and not be a constant drain on my finite resources, I was going to have to get the farm working at full capacity again. It had been sadly neglected for years. And in order to get it working and earning, I needed workers, many of them men to do the heavy work. And if I was going to hire men anyway, I might as well hire men who were unemployable elsewhere. You would be amazed, Duchess, to discover how many men fit that category — those with physical or mental disabilities, retired or discharged soldiers who have lost limbs or eyes or minds in war and are useless to anyone but themselves in peace, vagabonds, even thieves who steal only because they cannot find employment but *do* find that they need to eat. I could fill twenty Ainsleys any time I chose."

No, she would not be amazed.

"Some men," he said, "are capable of doing more than laboring in the fields, and *want* more. Some are given training as blacksmiths and carpenters and bricklayers, even bookkeepers and secretaries. And then they are found work elsewhere so that there is room at Ainsley for more. And some of the men and women marry and go off to a new life together."

"And you have told no one about this?" she said. "No one but me?"

He shook his head and then grinned.

"Yes, actually," he said. "I told the king."

"The *king?*"

"It was before he was king actually," he said. "He was still the Prince of Wales. Prinny. We were sitting together in that bizarre palace of his in Brighton late one night after everyone else had gone to bed. How it all came about I cannot recall. But we were both deep in our cups and one thing led to another and I told him about Ainsley. I do believe — no, I *know* — that he hugged me almost hard enough and close enough to break bones and smother me against his enormous bulk. He almost drowned me in sentimental tears. He declared me to be saint and martyr — why martyr, he did not explain — and a host of other extravagantly complimentary things.

247

And he promised to aid me and reward me and bring me to the attention of the whole kingdom and other shudderingly awful things. Fortunately, he forgot all about the whole thing and probably me too as soon as he was sober."

"I know him quite well," she said. "The duke was his friend even though the prince — now the king — constantly exasperated him. One cannot help liking the man, ridiculous as he often makes himself. More than anything else in life, he wants to be loved. If the old king and queen had only loved him from the start, he might be a different person today. A far more secure one."

"And a thinner one?" he said. "He would have had less need for food?"

She looked at him and smiled. And then laughed.

He smiled too and waggled his eyebrows.

It was a strange moment.

She had spent eleven years acquiring wisdom and discipline, ten of those years at the hands of a man who had known all about those two attributes from a long life of experience. Wisdom and discipline. Always guarding one's real, precious self in a cocoon of tranquillity within a thousand masks.

Life itself had become a secret affair. No

one knew of the life she lived behind the appearance. The appearance was everything to the people surrounding her. It was all they knew. The reality within was everything to *her*.

But suddenly that cocoon was threatened. She had selected a man purely for the sensual delights he could offer, and she had . . . Oh, *what* was the word for what he had become to her instead? She had *not* fallen in love with him. But —

Well, she was somehow deeply involved with him. As his lover, yes. But lovers could be cast off, forgotten, exchanged. They could be kept at a safe distance from the heart. They were for pleasure, for fun.

He was more than her lover.

She had told herself from the start that this year she would devote to pleasure instead of the search for love and permanent happiness. She had told herself that she would cast him off, forget him after this Season was over. And, of course, she would do it. Indeed, she would have no choice anyway. She knew very well that he took a different mistress each year.

But —

But her emotions had somehow got caught up in what was supposed to be a purely physical experience.

The tranquil cocoon of her heart had been ruffled.

The duke had been right. He had warned her that it would happen one day, that cocoons were meant only to guard the fragility of a new life until it was ready to burst forth into the glory of full life.

She ought to have known better than to choose a man of mystery who intrigued her.

For of course his character was layers and layers deep. Some of it was not so pleasant — his sly, intrusive questioning of Barbara at the Kitteridge ball, for example, or his ridiculous pride that had perpetuated an unnecessary quarrel with his cousin and closest friend for years. And some of it . . . Well, she could love the man whose compassion for those less fortunate than himself ran so deep that he had opened up his home, the heart of his privacy and peace, to them. And all for the simple satisfaction of doing the right thing. Far from looking for accolades, he had told no one about his home or what he was doing with it.

Except the king when they were both drunk.

And now her because he owed it to her.

Oh, she was perilously close to doing something foolish that she would regret for the rest of her life. For Constantine

Huxtable was *not the right man for permanence.* Suddenly she felt the emptiness of the duke's absence as a great void. *If only* she could go home and tease him and be teased by him and put her hand in his elderly, arthritic one and be safe again. And ask for his *advice.* Or his interpretation of what was happening to her.

Yet he had taught her self-reliance, and she had thought the lesson thoroughly learned. He would not want her to be dependent upon him indefinitely. *She* did not want it.

They were gazing at each other, she and Constantine, she realized, the smile dying on both their lips.

"We could probably hang for treason for saying such things," she said.

"Or have our heads chopped off," he said. "Speaking of which — I told Miss Leavensworth that I would arrange to take the two of you to the Tower of London since she has not been there yet. Will you come?"

"I have not been there in an age either," she said. "Will you come to Copeland for a few days if I arrange a brief house party there?"

"*Asking,* Duchess?" he said. "Not *telling?*"

"Well," she said, "you asked about the Tower, and I could hardly allow myself to be outdone in civility."

"You are not planning to invite Moreland and his wife too, are you?" he asked her.

"No." She shook her head. "But ought you not to speak with him sometime soon anyway?"

"Kiss and make up?" he said. "I think not."

"And so you will go through life unhappy," she said, "merely because of a little pride."

"Am I unhappy?" he asked.

She opened her mouth to answer and then closed it again.

"And are you," he asked, "going to go back to Markle, Duchess, perhaps for Miss Leavensworth's wedding, and speak with your father and sister and brother-in-law? Is pride going to keep you away?"

"That is a different matter altogether," she said.

"Is it?"

They stared — or perhaps glared — at each other in a silence neither seemed willing to break. He was the one to do it eventually.

"And so you will go through life unhappy," he said softly, "merely because of a little pride."

Touché.

But he had no idea — *no idea* what he

was suggesting.

"I want to go home to Dunbarton House," she said. "It is late."

Or early.

He got to his feet and closed the distance between them. He set his hands on the arms of her chair, leaned over her, and kissed her openmouthed.

It was a horribly gentle, even tender kiss.

Horrible because it was the middle of the night, she had made love with him and slept with him, she had sat here and talked with him, and she did not know where her defenses were. If she could have located them, she would have wrapped them about herself and been safe again.

But again — safe from *what*?

He lifted his head and gazed into her eyes. His own were shadowed and very dark.

"You had better go and dress, then," he said. "My coachman might be scandalized if he saw you dressed like that, even if you *are* covered from chin to toes."

"If I were to step out like this, Constantine," she said, "he would see nothing but duchess. Believe me. People see what I *choose* to have them see."

"Is that something Dunbarton taught you?" he asked.

"Yes," she said, "and he taught me well."

"I believe," he said, "he did. Whenever I have seen you over the years, I have seen nothing but duchess. Very beautiful, very rich duchess. I am only just learning the error of my perceptions."

"Is that good?" she asked him. "Or bad?"

He straightened up.

"I have not decided," he said. "I have seen you as a rose without the multiplicity of petals. But I have begun to realize my error. You have more layers than the most complex of roses. And the heart of the rose has yet to be revealed. I begin to believe that there *is* a heart. Indeed, I more than believe. Go and get dressed, Duchess. It is time to take you home."

And contrarily, given the fact that she had been the one to say it first, she felt bereft. As if he did not want her to stay. And shaken. He saw her as a rose, and slowly but surely he was finding his way past the petals to the heart. If she allowed it. How could she *stop* it?

Eleven years of learning and discipline were in danger of crumbling within weeks of her setting out on her lone course in life.

It was not going to happen.

For he could not possibly be *the one*. Not the one the duke had promised she would find one day. And she needed to be heart-whole when she finally met that man. Perhaps after all she should not have dabbled in the sensual.

She got to her feet and turned toward the door.

"Like a child who needs her hand held?" she said haughtily. "I came alone in your carriage. I will return alone in it. Be sure it is at the door in ten minutes' time."

Her exit was marred slightly by the sound of a low chuckle.

CHAPTER 12

Since it was raining the next day, Constantine spent most of the morning writing to Harvey Wexford, his manager at Ainsley. There were a few questions he needed to answer and a few minor details he needed to comment upon. More important — and something he did every week — there were all sorts of private little messages to send to various residents at Ainsley. He might leave their management and training and well-being in Wexford's capable and compassionate hands with every confidence that things would run perfectly smoothly, but he did not forget his people when he was away from them, and he was determined that they know it.

There were fifth birthday greetings to send to Megan, young daughter of Phoebe Penn, for example — and the book he went out to buy her before luncheon since the child, together with her mother, was learning to read. And there were congratulations to Winford Jones, the young ex-thief, who was deemed skilled enough as a blacksmith to take a position with someone looking for an assistant in a Dorsetshire smithy. And further congratulations to Jones and Bridget Hinds, who were going to marry before they left — taking young Bernard, Bridget's son, with them. And another book for Bernard since at the age of seven he could already read. And commiserations to Robbie Atkinson, who had fallen from the hay loft and broken his ankle. And get-well wishes to the cook, who had taken the unprecedented step of remaining in her bed for two whole days with a severe head cold, though she had ruled her kitchen with an iron thumb from that bed.

Constantine spent the afternoon at the races with some of his male acquaintances since the weather had cleared up somewhat, and the evening at a soiree given by Lady Carling, Margaret's mother-in-law, on Curzon Street. That was another of those occasions on which he was forced to spend time at the same function as Vanessa and Elliott, but since Lady Carling had opened up more than one room for her guests, they were able to occupy different rooms from one another most of the time and effectively ignore one another's existence.

Constantine thought of Hannah's suggestion last night that he talk to Elliott at last — so that he might be less unhappy. He drew some amusement from imagining how Elliott would react if he were to seek him out and suggest that they sit down and talk out their differences right here and now.

There was nothing to talk *about.* Elliott believed the very worst of him, and Constantine did not care.

Ass and mule.

Two sides of the same coin.

It really was as simple as that.

Hannah was not at the soiree.

Constantine left early, considered going to White's for a while, and went home to bed instead. Having a mistress could do that to a man — it could make him choose sleep over his friends at night when the opportunity presented itself.

He called at Dunbarton House the following morning. He half expected that the ladies would be either still in bed or else out shopping. But they were at home. The duchess's butler, who had gone to see if indeed they were, showed him into the library, which was an unexpected setting in which to find the duchess, though she had a book open on her lap, he noticed, while her friend was seated at the desk, probably writing a letter to her vicar.

The duchess closed her book, set it aside, and got to her feet.

"Constantine," she said, coming toward him, one hand extended.

"Duchess." He bowed over her hand, and for once she allowed him to raise the back of it to his lips. "Miss Leavensworth."

That lady set down her pen and turned toward him, her cheeks unnaturally pink.

"Mr. Huxtable," she said gravely.

"Miss Leavensworth," he said, "I wish you to know that I asked you to dance with me at the Kitteridge ball because I *wished* to dance with you. My ill-mannered probing for information about the duchess's roots was an afterthought and an ignominious one. I do beg your pardon for upsetting you."

"Thank you, Mr. Huxtable," she said. "It was a pleasure to dance with you."

"And I have not forgotten," he said, "that you hope to see the Tower of London before you return home to Markle, and that the duchess has not been there for ages. The weather is much improved today. Indeed, I do believe the sun is about to force its way through the clouds. Would you care to come there with me this afternoon? And perhaps to Gunter's afterward for ices?"

"Ices?" Miss Leavensworth's eyes widened. "Oh, I have never had one, but I have heard that they are simply heavenly."

"Then definitely to Gunter's afterward," he said. He looked at Hannah.

She would say, of course, that they had another engagement this afternoon.

"We will be ready at half past twelve," she said instead.

By which she probably meant a quarter to one.

"I will not keep you any longer, then," he said, "from your reading and your letter writing."

And he inclined his head to both and took his leave without further ado.

She had been wearing a plain dress of pale blue cotton, one shade lighter than her eyes, he remembered as he strode out of the square. No jewelry. And her hair had been caught back in a simple knot at the nape of her neck.

Plain and unadorned.

She had looked achingly lovely.

The duchess, that was.

She looked more her usual self when he arrived outside her door again promptly at half past twelve. He had his carriage with him this time as it would accommodate the three of them in more comfort than his curricle would have done, and it really was quite a distance to the Tower.

Both ladies were ready. Perhaps as a matter of sheer principle the duchess would have kept him waiting if the outing had involved her alone, but it did not, and Miss Leavensworth's face was alive with eager anticipation. And the Duchess of Dunbarton, Constantine thought, loved her friend.

There was much to see at the Tower. Neither lady wished to see the old dungeons or the torture chambers, though, or the place and instruments of execution. The duchess, in fact, shuddered with what looked like very genuine horror when a yeoman of the guard suggested that they might enjoy the displays.

They went to view the menagerie instead and spent a considerable amount of time there gazing at the unfamiliar wild animals, especially the lions.

"How splendid they are," Miss Leavensworth said. "I can see why they are known as the kings of the jungle. Can't you, Hannah?"

But the duchess was not so easily pleased.

"But where is the jungle?" she asked. "Poor things. How can they be kings in a cage? It would be better to be a humble rabbit or tortoise or mole and be free."

"But I daresay they are well fed," Miss Leavensworth said. "And they are sheltered from the worst of the elements here. And they are much admired."

"And of course," the duchess said, "the admiration of others makes up for a multitude of sins."

"I am glad I have seen them," Miss Leavensworth said firmly, refusing to be deterred by the misgivings of her friend. "I have only been able to read about them in books until now and see drawings of them. And books never take account of *smell,* do they? Whew!"

"Shall we go and see the Crown Jewels?" Constantine suggested.

Miss Leavensworth was enthralled by them. And as coincidence would have it, her fiancé's relatives, with their children, came there to look at them less than five minutes after they had arrived there. There were exclamations of surprise and delight and some hugs, and she had to introduce Mr. and Mrs. Newcombe and Pamela and Peter Newcombe to Constantine — the duchess had met them a few mornings ago when they had fetched Miss Leavensworth for the visit to Kew.

"I need fresh air," the duchess announced

after a few more minutes. "Constantine is going to take me up to the battlements of the White Tower, Babs, and now is the perfect time for us to go since you are terrified of heights. We will come back here in a short while."

"We will remain with Barbara for as long as you need to see the view, Your Grace," Mrs. Newcombe assured her. "Do take your time. All we have left to see is the dungeons, at the children's insistence, and there is no hurry."

The duchess took Constantine's arm, and they climbed to the top of the White Tower together — the highest point apart from the four turrets at its corners.

"Tonight?" he asked as they went.

"Yes," she said. "I will need it. I am to attend a dinner and reception at St. James's Palace this evening and it is certain to be a dead bore. But when one receives a royal summons, you know, one does not reply that it does not suit one's purposes to attend, even if one *is* the Duchess of Dunbarton. Barbara is to dine with the Parks. You may send your carriage at eleven."

They stepped out onto the battlements of the Tower to find that all the clouds had moved off, leaving blue sky and sunshine in their place.

The duchess opened her parasol and raised it above her head. She was wearing a bonnet today, tied securely beneath her chin. It was just as well. There was a significant breeze up here.

They walked all around the battlements, admiring the various views over the city and the countryside beyond before coming to a stop when they were facing the River Thames.

She tipped back her parasol and lifted her face to the sky. One of the ravens for which the Tower was famous was flapping about up there.

"Do you ever think," she asked, "that it would be wonderful to fly, Constantine? To be all alone with the vastness and the wind and the sky?"

"The dimension man has not conquered?" he said. "It would be interesting to see the world from a bird's perspective. There are, of course, hot air balloons."

"But one would still be constrained," she said. "I want wings. But never mind. This is quite high enough for now. Is it not *lovely* up here?"

He turned his head to smile at her. One did not often hear such unguarded enthusiasm on the duchess's lips — or see her face so bright with animation. She had leaned her arms on the parapet and was gazing out toward the river. Her parasol was propped against the wall.

"Or perhaps I should sail away to some distant, exotic land," she said. "Egypt, India, China. Have you ever longed to go?"

"To escape from myself?" he said.

"Oh, not *from* yourself," she said. "*With* yourself. You can never leave yourself behind, wherever you go. It was one of the first things the duke taught me after we were married. I could never escape the girl I had been, he told me. I could only make her into a woman in whose body and mind I felt happy to be."

And yet she acted as though she had escaped that girlhood. She would not even go back to the home and people she had left behind when she married Dunbarton.

"I briefly thought of going to sea as a young man," he said. "But I would have been gone for months, even years, at a time. I could not be away from Jon so long."

"The brother you hated?" she said.

"I did not —" he began.

"No," she said. "I know you did not. You loved him more than you have loved anyone else in your life. And you hated him because you could not keep him alive."

He leaned his arms on the parapet beside

her. Some shallow woman she was turning out to be. What had made her so perceptive?

"Even now," he said, "I often feel as though I had abandoned him. I will go a whole day — sometimes more — without thinking about him. I go to Warren Hall occasionally just to visit him. He is buried beside the small chapel in the park. It is a peaceful place. I am glad about that. I go to talk to him."

"And to listen to him?" she said.

"That would be absurd," he told her.

"No more absurd than to talk to him," she pointed out. "I think he is alive in your heart, Constantine, even when you are not consciously thinking about him. I think he will always be there. And he is a *good* part of you."

He leaned farther out to see down, and then looked toward the river again.

"This is foolishness," he said. "I *never* talk about Jon. Why do I do it with you?"

"Did he know," she asked, "about Ainsley?"

What *was* it about her? He never talked about Ainsley either. He heaved a deep sigh.

"Yes," he said. "It was his idea — not the gambling, of course, but the purchase of a safe home for women and children who were not wanted anywhere else, a place where they could work and train for something more permanent in the future. He was so excited by the idea that sometimes he could not get to sleep at night. He wanted to see it all for himself. But he died before there was anything tangible to see."

Her hand, he realized, had moved to cover his on the parapet — and she had removed her glove.

"Was it a hard death?" she asked.

"He fell asleep and did not wake up," he said. "It was the night of his sixteenth birthday. We had played hide-and-seek for a few hours during the evening, and he had laughed so hard that I daresay he weakened his heart. He told me when I went to blow out his candle for the night that he loved me more than anyone else in the whole world. He told me he would love me forever and ever, amen — a little joke that always afforded him considerable amusement. Forever turned out to be a few hours long."

"No," she said. "Forever turned out to be eternal. He loved you forever, as the duke loved me. Love does not die when the person dies. Despite all the pain for the survivor."

How the devil had all this come about,

Constantine wondered. But thank the Lord they were in a public place, even though they appeared to have the battlements all to themselves at the moment. If they had been somewhere private he might have grabbed her and bawled on her shoulder. Which was a mildly alarming thought. Not to mention embarrassing.

He turned his head to look at her. She was gazing back, wide-eyed, unsmiling, minus any of her usual masks.

And he realized that he liked her.

It was not an earth-shattering revelation — or ought not to have been. And yet it was.

He had expected, perhaps, to have all sorts of feelings about the Duchess of Dunbarton when she became his mistress. Simple *liking* was not one of them.

He covered her hand with his own.

"I daresay," he said, "Miss Leavensworth and her fiancé's relatives have exhausted every conversational topic known to man or woman. And I daresay the young people are ready to climb the walls surrounding the crown jewels. We had better go and rescue them — and bear her off for her first ice at Gunter's."

"Yes," she agreed. "How ghastly it would be to arrive there to find it closed for the day. Babs would be inconsolable. She would not admit it, of course. She would assure us both quite cheerfully that she did not mind at all, that the afternoon had been a delight even without her very first ice. She is such a *saint*."

He offered his arm as she pulled her glove back on, settled a large diamond ring — or *not* diamond — on her forefinger, and grasped her parasol.

It was almost midnight when Hannah arrived at Constantine's house. She had not meant to be late — the time for games with him was over, she had decided. But one could not rush away early from St. James's Palace with the excuse that one had promised to be with one's lover soon after eleven. Not especially when one had had a private conversation with the king himself for all of ten minutes just as the hands of the clock were crawling upward to that hour.

Constantine had not locked the door. He did open it himself, though, when his carriage pulled up outside. There was no sign of any servants. He must have dismissed them for the night. Hannah did not offer any explanation for her lateness — she would not go *that* far. She merely wound her arms about his neck and kissed him, and he bore her off to bed without further ado.

A little less than an hour later they were in his sitting room again, he wearing shirt and pantaloons, she in his dressing gown. A tray of tea with plates of bread and butter and cheese stood on the low table between them.

She could grow accustomed to this, she thought — this cozy companionship after the exertion and pleasure of making love.

She could grow accustomed to *him*.

This time next year he would have a different lover, and perhaps she would too, though she was not sure she would wish to repeat the experiment. The thought popped unbidden into her head. There would be a different woman sitting here, perhaps wrapped in this very garment. And he would be there, looking at her with slightly sleepy eyes and relaxed posture and tousled hair.

She frowned — and then smiled.

"The king has not forgotten about Ainsley Park," she said, "or about you."

"Good Lord," he said with a grimace. "You did not remind him, did you?"

"He was complaining about St. James's Palace, which he heartily dislikes," she said, "and wondering if Buckingham House might be made into a more imposing royal residence. I suggested the Tower of London and mentioned the fact that I had been there today with my dearest friend and with you as an escort."

"Prinny as lord of the Tower," he said. "The mind boggles, does it not? He would probably have Traitor's Gate opened for business again, and parade all his enemies inside to the dungeons."

"England would be an empty country," she said. "There would be no one left to run the government, except the king himself. The halls of Parliament would be left to the bats and the ghosts. And the Tower would be bursting at the seams."

They both chuckled at the thought, and Hannah, finished with her buttered bread and cheese and her tea, dug her hands under the cuffs of the opposite sleeves and grasped her arms tightly. None of her dreams and plans over the winter had included them *laughing* together at treasonous absurdities.

He looked purely handsome when he laughed — especially when he was also sleepy.

"And how did the conversation get from the Tower to Ainsley?" he asked.

"He frowned in thought when I mentioned your name," she said, "and then

271

seemed to remember who you were. A dashed shame, he said, that you could not have been Earl of Merton, though he was inordinately fond of the current earl. And there was something about you he ought to remember. He dug *very* deep into his memory, Constantine, and then popped up with the name of Ainsley Park without any prompting at all. He looked just as pleased with himself as if he had pulled a plum out of the Christmas pudding. A wonderful man, he declared — *you,* that is, Constantine — and he fully intends to offer you some assistance in your charitable endeavors and to honor you personally in some suitable way."

He shook his head.

"Was he inebriated?" he asked.

"Not to the point of making an idiot of himself," she said. "But he did drink an alarming amount even when I was looking. I daresay he drank just as much if not more when I was *not* looking."

"One must hope, then," he said, "that he will forget — again."

"He saw a plump and frumpish matron as he finished speaking," she said, "and his eyes lit up and he went in pursuit of her. I was totally forgotten and abandoned. I might not have existed. It was very lowering, Constantine."

"The king's tastes in women were always eccentric," he said, "to put a kind spin on them. Peculiar, to be a little less kind. Bizarre, to be truthful. Did everyone else ignore your existence?"

"Of course not," she said. "I am the Duchess of Dunbarton."

"That is the spirit, Duchess," he said, and his very dark eyes smiled at her.

It was very disconcerting and very knee-weakening. None of the rest of his face smiled. Yet she did not feel mocked. She felt — *teased. Liked. Did* he like her?

And did she like him? *Like,* as opposed to lust after?

"If you had made off with the crown jewels this afternoon and presented them all to Babs," she said, "instead of merely buying her an ice at Gunter's, she would not have been half as delighted."

"She *was* pleased, was she not?" he said. "Have you met her vicar? Is he worthy of her?"

"Among other lesser virtues," she said, "he possesses a special smile, which he saves just for her. And it pierces straight through to her heart."

They gazed at each other across the low table.

"Do you believe in love?" she asked him. "That kind of love, I mean."

"Yes," he said. "I would have said no once upon a time. It is easy to be cynical — life gives one much evidence to suggest that there is nothing else to be and remain honest. But I have four cousins — second cousins — who grew up in the country in genteel poverty and burst upon the social scene with the death of Jon. Country bumpkins, no less, whom I expected to be wild and extravagant and vulgar. I hated them even before I set eyes upon them, especially the new Merton. They turned out to be none of those things, and one by one they all made matches that should have been disastrous. And yet all the evidence points to the conclusion that my cousins have converted their marriages into love matches. All of them. It is unmistakable and extraordinary."

"Even the cousin who married the Duke of Moreland?" she asked.

"Yes," he said, "even Vanessa. And yes, I believe in love."

"But not for yourself?" she asked.

He shrugged.

"Does one have to work at finding and building it?" he asked her. "The experiences of my cousins would seem to suggest that one does. I am not sure I am prepared to put in the effort. How would one know it would not all be in vain? If love arrives in my arms full blown one day, I will be quite happy. But I will not be *un*happy if it does not. I am contented with my life as it is."

And yet it seemed to Hannah that he looked melancholy as he said it. He had, she thought a little wistfully, an enormous amount of love to give to the right woman. A love that would move mountains or universes.

"And you, Duchess," he said. "You loved when you were a girl and were badly hurt. You loved Dunbarton, but not, I think, in any romantic way. Do *you* believe in the sort of love Miss Leavensworth has found?"

"When I was nineteen," she said, "I was in love with being in love, I think. And I was given no chance to discover how deep — or *not* deep — that love would have gone. All things happen for a purpose — or so the duke taught me, and I believe him. Perhaps discovering Colin and Dawn together was the best thing that ever happened to me."

Strange, that. She had never consciously thought it before. What if she had not discovered the truth until too late? What would her life be like now? And what if Colin had never loved Dawn? Would *she* still love him now? Would she be content with her life with him? There was no way of knowing. But she no longer felt the pain of losing him, she realized. She probably had not for a long time. Only the pain of betrayal and rejection. That had lingered.

"Even without the example of Barbara, though," she said, "I would know that real love exists. I mean that real, once-in-a-lifetime, soul-deep love that happens to a few people but never to most. The duke knew it and told me about it."

"Dunbarton flaunted a former *love* before you?" he asked. "If it *was* former."

"He was a year into his mourning when I met and married him," she said. "The worst should have been over and perhaps was. But he never stopped grieving. Never for a moment. It was a love that had endured for more than fifty years, and it was a love that defined his entire life. It enabled him to love *me.*"

He folded his arms and gazed steadily at her for a while.

"And yet," he said, "he never married her. And he kept her such a secret that no whisper of her existence ever seems to have reached the ears of the *ton.*"

"*He* was the duke's secretary," she said, "and remained so all his adult life. And so they were able to be together and live together without anyone remarking upon the fact. They must have been very discreet, though. Even the servants seemed not to know the truth, or else they were so loyal to the duke that they never spoke of what they knew beyond his household. They *were* loyal. They still are."

"Dunbarton *told* you of such things?" he asked her.

"Before we married," she said, "when he was making clear to me that he had no ulterior motive in marrying me but to take me away and teach me to be a duchess and a proud, independent beauty in the short time remaining to him. He had not been able to take his eyes off me during the wedding, he told me, *not* because he felt lasciviously toward me but because I looked so like an angel that I surely could not possibly be human. But angels ought not to have their hearts broken by plodding yokels — his words. I was shocked to the roots of my being by his story. I did not even know such a thing existed as what he described. But I believed in his kindness. Perhaps I was foolish — undoubtedly I was. But sometimes it is a good thing to be foolish. He talked freely about the love of his life during our years together. I think it soothed him to be able to do so at last, after so many years of secrecy and silence. And he promised me that one day I would find such a love for myself — though not with someone of my own sex."

"And you believed him?" he asked.

"I believed in the possibility of it," she said, "even if not the probability. All is artifice in my world, Constantine. Even me. *Especially* me. He taught me to be a duchess, to be an impregnable fortress, to be the guardian of my own heart. But he admitted that he could not teach me how or when to allow the fortress to be breached or my heart to be unlocked. It would simply happen, he said. He *promised* it would, in fact. But how is love to find me, even assuming it is looking?"

She smiled. What a very strange conversation to be having with her lover. She got to her feet and walked around the table.

"But in the meantime," she said, "I am not waiting around for something that may never happen to me. Taking you as a lover is something I wanted to happen — no, something I decided *would* happen as soon as my year of mourning was at an end. And for this spring what you have to offer is quite sufficient."

"You decided even before you returned to

London," he asked her, raising his eyebrows, "that I was to be the one?"

"I did," she said. "Are you not flattered?"

She undid the sash of his dressing gown, opened it back, and climbed onto the large leather chair with him, straddling him as she did so and bending her head to kiss his lips.

"And so Dunbarton taught you, did he," he asked, pushing the dressing gown off her shoulders and down her arms, and tossing it to the floor, "always to get what you want?"

"Yes," she said. "And I have got you."

She looked directly into his eyes and smiled dazzlingly.

"A puppet on a string," he said.

"No." She shook her head. "You had to want it too. And you do. Tell me you do."

"I cannot just show you?" he asked, and there was a smile lurking in his eyes again.

"Tell me," she said.

"Vulnerable, Duchess?" He almost whispered against her mouth, causing her to shiver. "I want it. Badly. I want *you*. Badly."

And he undid the buttons at his waist, opened back the flap of his pantaloons, grasped her by the hips to lift her above him, and brought her down hard onto him.

Hannah had always found their encounters on his bed almost unbearably pleasurable. This time the *almost* was missing. She knelt on the chair, her legs on either side of his body, and she rode him as vigorously and heedlessly as he rode her, feeling him hard and deep inside her, hearing the wetness of their coupling, seeing his harsh, dark-complexioned face, as his head rested against the back of the chair, his eyes closed, his hair disheveled.

And when the pain had reached almost to its limit and he should have held her firm and put a stop to it with his own release, it did not end but hurtled onward until it became all the way unbearable — and then fell away suddenly and instantly into such total glory that there were no words even if she had been searching for them.

Only a wordless cry.

And a shivering, shuddering descent against his body and a shoulder to cradle the side of her head and an irresistible urge to sleep.

He held her close until she had almost completed the descent, and then he disengaged from her and lifted her in his arms, somehow managed to wrap his dressing gown about her like a blanket, and carried her through to his bedchamber.

He kissed her before setting her down.

"Tell me it was as good for you as I think it was," he said.

"You need compliments?" she asked him sleepily. "It was good. Oh, Constantine, it was good."

He chuckled.

She curled up on the bed and was already well on her way back to sleep before he joined her there and covered them both with the blankets.

Jewels, she thought just before she fell over the barrier into sleep.

The crown jewels she had joked about his stealing for Barbara.

Her own jewels, sold for funds with which to finance the dearest wish of her heart.

His half-stolen jewel converted to cash with which he had gambled and won Ainsley Park.

Whose jewel had it been? Jonathan's?

To have been sold for what? For the home for unmarried mothers and their children that had been Jonathan's idea?

Had Jonathan and Constantine between them been up to the same thing as she had? Not just with the one jewel, but perhaps with more?

Was there *that* degree of similarity between her and Constantine?

All things happen for a purpose, the duke

had told her, and she had come to believe for herself.

There are no coincidences, he had also said more than once. She had never quite believed that.

Love would find her one day when she was not looking, he had told her.

She did not expect it. She was afraid to expect it.

But her mind could not cope with so many apparent non sequiturs tumbling about in it.

She slept just as Constantine's arms came about her and drew her close.

CHAPTER 13

Hannah was fully aware that the *ton* had long ago come to the conclusion that the Duchess of Dunbarton's newest lover was Mr. Constantine Huxtable. They would have thought it even if it were not true, as they had thought it of the many men, mostly her friends or the duke's, who had gone before him. She was aware too that it was expected she would tire of him within a week or two and cast him off in favor of someone else.

Her reputation did not bother her. Indeed, she had almost deliberately cultivated it during the years of her marriage. It was part of the cocoon inside which she hid and nurtured her real self.

She did not believe that on the whole the *ton* was actively hostile to her, even the ladies. She was invited everywhere, and her own invitations were almost always accepted. She was taken into any conversational group to which she chose to attach herself at the various entertainments she attended.

It was with some surprise, then, that she greeted the refusal of her invitation to join her brief house party at Copeland Manor first by the Earl and Countess of Merton, then by Lord and Lady Montford, and last by the Earl and Countess of Sheringford. The only members of that family who did *not* refuse were the Duke and Duchess of Moreland, and that perhaps had something to do with the fact that they had not been invited.

Never believe in a coincidence, the duke had always said. Hannah would have had to be an imbecile to believe *this* was a coincidence.

Constantine had confessed to a fondness for his second cousins. They seemed fond of him. That was why she had invited them, though in retrospect it probably had not been a great idea, even if they had accepted. Or perhaps *especially* if they had accepted. He was not courting her, after all. They were *lovers*.

It must be that fact that had caused them all to refuse. She could almost picture them all putting their heads together and deciding that the invitation was in bad taste. Or that *she* was in bad taste. Perhaps they were afraid she would corrupt Constantine. Or hurt him. Or make a fool of him.

Probably that last point.

Hannah had been taught — and had taught herself — not to care what anyone thought of her. Except the duke, of course. He had frowned at her perhaps two or three times in all the ten years of their marriage, though he had never raised his voice against her, and each time she had felt that the world had surely come to an end. And except the servants at Dunbarton House and their other establishments in the country. Servants always knew one for who or what one really was, and it mattered to Hannah that they like her. She believed they did.

And now — annoyingly — she discovered that she did not like being shunned by three families that had meant nothing whatsoever to her until she had taken their second cousin as her lover.

Why she did not like it she did not know, except that they had inconvenienced her and she was going to have to invite other people to take their place.

"The third refusal," she said, holding aloft the note from the Countess of Sheringford at the breakfast table. "And now none of them is coming to Copeland, Babs. It makes me feel a little as though I must have leprosy. Is it because I always wear white, do you suppose? Do I look sickly?"

Barbara looked up with blank eyes from her own letter. It was a long one — it must be from the Reverend Newcombe.

"No one is coming?" she said. "But I thought you had already had several acceptances, Hannah."

"No one from Constantine's family," Hannah explained. "His father's side of the family, anyway. They are the ones to whom he appears to be closest. But they have all refused."

"That is a pity," Barbara said. "Will you invite other people instead? There is still time, is there not?"

"Do they believe it would be distasteful to come to Copeland because Constantine and I are lovers?" Hannah asked, frowning at the offending piece of paper in her hand. "I was *always* rumored to have lovers, even when it was not true, but no one ever shunned me. Even when I was still married."

Barbara set her letter down, resigned to the interruption.

"You are upset?" she asked.

"I am *never* upset," Hannah said. Then

she set down her own letter and smiled ruefully at her friend. "Well, a little, I suppose.
I had looked forward to having them there."

"Why?" Barbara asked. "When one is to
have one's lover at a house party, Hannah,
why would one want his family there too?"

It was a good question and one she had
been asking herself just a few moments ago.

"Is it a little like inviting one's family to
join one on honeymoon?" Hannah asked.

They both laughed.

"But we will, of course, behave with the
utmost discretion," Hannah said. "Good
heavens, the very idea that we might not.
You will be there and all sorts of other
respectable guests."

"Then the cousins will be missing a pleasant few days in the country," Barbara said,
laying a hand on her letter again. "It will be
their loss."

"But I wanted them there," Hannah said,
hearing too late the slight petulance of her
tone. And there was that word again that
she had been warned against — *wanted,* but
could not have.

*Well, you cannot always have what you
want,* she expected Barbara to say before
returning her attention to her vicar's love
letter. But she said something else instead.

"Hannah," she said, "you are not behaving at all like the jaded aristocrat with a new lover you like to see yourself as. You are behaving like a woman in love."

"What?" Hannah half screeched.

"Is it not a little peculiar," Barbara asked — and she looked suddenly every inch a vicar's daughter, "that you should care for the good opinion of your lover's relatives?"

"I do *not* care —" Hannah began, and stopped. "I am not in love, Babs. How ridiculous. Just because *you* are, you think *I* must be too?"

"You said just now," Barbara said, "that you were always rumored to have lovers even when it was not true. Was it *ever* true, Hannah? I never have believed it of you. The Hannah I used to know could never dishonor her marriage vows even if the circumstances of her marriage were . . . unusual."

Hannah sighed. "No, of course there was never any truth in the rumors," she said.

"Then Mr. Huxtable is your first lover," Barbara said. It was a statement, not a question. "I do not believe the Hannah I once knew *or* the Hannah I know now can be simply blasé about that fact. And I saw you together at the Tower and at Gunter's. You are fond of him."

"Well, of course I am *fond* of him," Hannah said crossly — goodness, when had she last allowed herself to be *cross?* "I could not dislike or despise or even be entirely indifferent to any man who was my lover, could I?"

But why not be indifferent, at least? It was what she had expected to be, was it not?

"I know very little of gentlemen of the *ton* and really nothing whatsoever of Mr. Huxtable," Barbara said, "except that I liked him far more than I expected to do when he took us to the Tower. I *thought* he seemed fond of you too, Hannah. But I do not know. And I am afraid for you. I am afraid you will end up hurt. Heartbroken."

"I am never *hurt,* Babs," Hannah said. "And never, *ever* heartbroken."

"I would hate to see you either," Barbara said. "But I would hate even more to believe that neither was possible. It would mean that you had not got the point at all of why the Duke of Dunbarton married you and loved you."

Hannah fixed her eyes upon her friend. She felt suddenly cold. And afraid to move so much as a muscle.

"The point?" The words came out in a whisper.

"So that you could be made whole again," Barbara said. "And ready for love — *real* love — when it came along. The duke did not see just your beauty, Hannah. He called you an *angel,* did he not? He saw all your essential sweetness and your shattered joy on that day when you discovered the truth about Dawn and Colin. Even now you have not seen how very special you are, have you? The *duke* saw it."

Barbara went suddenly out of focus, and Hannah realized that her eyes were swimming in tears. She got abruptly to her feet, almost tipping her chair in her haste to push it back.

"I am going out," she said. "I am going to call upon the Countess of Sheringford. I would rather go alone. Will you mind?"

"I did not have time yesterday to write more than a few lines to either Mama and Papa or Simon," Barbara said. "I need to write longer letters this morning. I am starting to feel selfish and neglectful."

Hannah hurried from the room.

To call upon the Countess of Sheringford? Whatever *for?*

Tobias — Toby — Pennethorne, Sheringford's eight-year-old son and Margaret's too by adoption, had developed an insatiable interest in the geography of the world, and Constantine had spied the perfect gift for him in a shop window on Oxford Street, though his birthday was nowhere on the horizon. No matter. He bought the large globe anyway.

And because he could not show favoritism to one child when there were three, he bought a gaudily painted spinning top for three-year-old Sarah and an impressively loud wooden rattle for one-year-old Alexander.

He bore his offerings off to the home of the Marquess of Claverbrook on Grosvenor Square, where Margaret and Sheringford lived when they were in town — Sherry was the marquess's grandson and heir. And he spent a pleasant hour in the nursery with Margaret and the children, Sherry being from home. He began to have doubts about the rattle, though, when Sarah appropriated it and decided that shattering everyone else's eardrums as well as her own was to be the game of the morning. The baby meanwhile was fascinated by the top, though he spoiled the lovely spinning and humming each time someone set it in motion by grabbing the toy before it stopped. He howled in cross protest every time.

Toby found every continent and country and river and ocean and town in the known world, not to mention poles and elevations and lines of latitude and longitude, and insisted that his mother and Uncle Con come and see each new discovery. The globe began to look like an instrument of torture.

It all made the tea parties in the conservatory at Ainsley seem very tranquil events indeed, Constantine thought cheerfully. And it struck him as an unexpected revelation under the circumstances that he liked children.

But had he not played endless games of hide-and-seek with Jon, that eternal child?

A knock on the nursery door, which they miraculously heard, preceded the appearance of a footman with the announcement that her grace, the Duchess of Dunbarton, had come to call on Lady Sheringford, and that his lordship had had her shown into the drawing room.

The duchess? *Here?*

"Oh, goodness," Margaret said, "Grandpapa never admits visitors. Oh, this is very vexing."

"Vexing?" Constantine raised his eyebrows, and she flushed and did not quite meet his eyes.

"She invited us to spend four days at her home in Kent," Margaret said, "and we sent back a refusal — with regrets."

"Because — ?" Constantine asked as there

was a crescendo from the rattle, accompanied by a beatific look on Sarah's face, a wail of protest from Alex as the top stopped its spinning yet again, and an excited invitation from Toby to come and see Madagascar.

"We do not wish to leave the children for so long," Margaret said, setting the top to spinning again while Sarah went to see Madagascar, the rattle poised at her side.

And the duchess had responded to the refusal by coming here in person? She really did not take well to rejection, did she? And she did not often have to suffer it. Would she win Margaret over after all? Was that why she had come?

Sarah was spinning the globe under Toby's watchful eye, and the baby had spied some other potential toy and was waddling about the furniture toward it, his bad temper — and the top — forgotten.

"Constantine." Margaret met his eyes at last. "We cannot live your life for you — I would not even wish to try. But we can refuse to condone your association with a woman who is an utterly heartless . . . *predator.*"

He clasped his hands behind his back.

"Those are harsh words," he said.

"Yes," she admitted, "they are."

"I can remember a time," he said, "when words of equal harshness were being bandied about over Sherry. But that did not stop you from taking up with him and betrothing yourself to him and ultimately marrying him."

"That was different," she said. "He was not guilty of any of the charges that had been made against him."

"Perhaps," he said, "the Duchess of Dunbarton is not either — guilty of the charges against *her,* I mean."

"Oh, come, now," she said.

He was in danger of losing his temper, he realized. He looked away from her. The baby had hold of one of Toby's books and was about to make a meal of it. Constantine hurried across the room, rescued the book, and prevented the imminent protest by swinging the child up onto one of his shoulders.

"You *must* be besotted if you believe that," Margaret said. "And we are all quite right to be concerned for you."

"*We,*" he said. "Were any of the others invited to Copeland too?"

"Not Nessie and Elliott," she said. "But the others, yes."

"And tell me," he said, "have they all refused their invitations too?"

She had the grace to look away from him again.

"Yes," she said.

Alex was pulling Constantine's hair and shrieking with glee.

"Now let me see," he said, disentangling his hair from the baby's fist and setting him down beside a box of wooden bricks. "Monty was England's most notorious hellion. I could vouch for that — I knew him. Katherine married him. Sherry we have already talked about. You married him. Cassandra was believed to have murdered her first husband — with an axe, even though it was a bullet that was found in Paget, not an axe wound. Stephen married her. And yet you all believe everything you have heard of the Duchess of Dunbarton without any objective proof at all?"

"How do you know we have no proof?" she asked.

"Because there *is* none," he said. "She loved Dunbarton, even if not in a romantic way. She was true to her marriage vows until the day of his death, and she was true to her widowhood throughout the year of her mourning. I *know,* Margaret. I have had proof."

Anger was making him speak quite rashly. She was biting her upper lip.

"Oh, Constantine," she said, "you *do* care for her. It is what we have most feared. But — are you *sure* you have not just come under her spell?"

He did not answer her — or look away from her.

"Proof."

She closed her eyes and then opened them and looked herself again — in charge, as she always had been, the eldest sister who had brought up her siblings almost single-handed and done a really rather splendid job of it too before going in search of some happiness for herself.

"I had better go down and see her," she said. "Oh, goodness, Grandpapa will have eaten her whole by now. She is just the sort of frivolous person to set his teeth on edge. And is *that* too an illusion? Her frivolity?"

"I had better let you make some discoveries for yourself," he said.

She was pulling on the bell rope, and the children's nurse came almost immediately. Toby demanded that she come to see India, Sarah raised the rattle toward her and shook it with a flourish, and Alex banged one wooden brick against another and chuckled.

Constantine left the nursery with Margaret. He half thought of taking his leave altogether, but he could not resist getting a glimpse of Hannah up against one of the gruffest and grimmest old aristocrats in all England. And a near-recluse at that.

He rather hoped she had *not* been eaten alive. But his wager was on her.

Why exactly was she here? Hannah asked herself as she was admitted to Claverbrook House by a footman, and an elderly butler almost elbowed the poor man in the stomach in his haste to move him out of the way when he heard her name. He bowed to her and actually creaked. Foolish man to wear stays at his age, which must be anywhere from seventy to a hundred.

Why *was* she here? To grovel? To demand an explanation? To try to persuade Lady Sheringford to change her mind?

She did not have long to wait. The footman who had narrowly avoided getting elbowed was sent upstairs to see if Lady Sheringford was at home, and he performed his task with nimble speed. He reappeared within moments of disappearing and murmured to the butler that her grace was to be shown up to the drawing room.

Hannah followed the butler up at a speed that was approximately half that of a tortoise by her estimate.

She was glad she had worn the full armor

of a white muslin dress with a white spencer and a white bonnet. She was even wearing some of her real diamonds in her ears and on her fingers. It was all something to hide behind. Though if she wished to impress the countess, perhaps she should have dressed more simply, even more colorfully.

It was too late now for such thoughts.

The drawing room had just one occupant, she saw when she was admitted to the room after the butler had announced her in solemn, ringing tones as though he were addressing thousands. And that occupant was *not* the Countess of Sheringford.

"Yes, yes, Forbes," the old gentleman seated in a wing chair close to the fire said impatiently, "I know who she is. Bindle told me. Where is she?"

Hannah had been gathering as much of her famed dignity about her as she could in preparation for confronting the countess. But she abandoned it at the sound of the voice and hurried across the room to take up her stand before the Marquess of Claverbrook's chair. She extended both gloved hands to him and smiled warmly.

"Here I am," she said. "And there *you* are. It must be years."

He had been one of the duke's friends. Hannah had met him a few times before he shut himself up inside this house after the great scandal involving his grandson and became a virtual recluse, neither going out nor receiving visitors. He had been a gruff, frequently impatient man, but never with her. There had always been a twinkle in his eye when he had looked at her and spoken with her. She had always believed he liked her. And she had liked him.

He took his hands off the silver head of his cane and took hers. His fingers were bent and gnarled, she could see. She curled her own warmly about them but was careful not to squeeze them. She was careful not to touch him with any of her rings.

"Hannah," he said. "There you are indeed. Looking even more lovely than you looked as a girl when old Dunbarton snatched you up from some godforsaken place in the country and married you. The old devil. No other woman would suit him all his life, and then you came along when he was close to doddering."

"Some things," she said, "are meant to be."

"Hmmph," he said, shaking her hands slightly up and down in his own. "And I suppose you married him for his money. Of which he had more than his fair share."

"And because he was a duke and was able

to make me a duchess," she said. "You must not forget that."

"I daresay I would not have stood a chance with you, then," he said, "even if I had seen you first. I was only a marquess."

"And probably not as rich as the duke was," she said.

She smiled at him. His white hair was sparse. His white eyebrows were not. He had a deep vertical temper line between his brows, eyes that tended to glare, and a beak of a nose. He looked like a thoroughly bad-tempered old man.

"I loved him," she said. "And I still grieve for him. If I had ever had a grandfather that I remembered, I would have wanted him to be just like my duke. But since I did not, and since I *did* have the good fortune to meet the duke, I married him."

"Hmmph," he said again. "And you led him a merry dance, I daresay, Hannah?"

"Oh, very merry indeed," she agreed, "though he would not dance after his seventy-eighth birthday, which was very poor-spirited of him. We found something to laugh at every day, though. Laughter is better than medicine, you know."

"Hmmph," he said. "But he died in the end anyway."

"I have heard," she said, "that *your* medicine came in the form of your granddaughter-in-law. I have heard that she takes no nonsense from you and that she is your favorite adult in the world. And I have heard that you dote upon your great-grandchildren, who actually live here with you during the Season. What sort of a recluse is *that?* A rather fraudulent one, I would say."

"You used to be a timid thing when Dunbarton first married you, Hannah," he said. "When did you become so saucy?"

"*After* I married him," she said. "He taught me that people like you are really just pussycats pretending to be lions."

He barked with laughter, and Hannah's eyes twinkled down at him.

"Dunbarton was a devil of a fellow when he was a young man," he said. "Did he ever tell you? There was no pussycat *there,* Hannah. Walsh — he is long gone now — slapped a glove in his face right in the middle of the reading room at White's one morning and challenged him to a duel for cuckolding him with his wife. They met on some barren heath — I can't remember exactly where. That is what age does to the mind. But *I* was there. Walsh's hand was shaking like a leaf in a hurricane, and his shot missed by a mile. Dunbarton lined him

301

up along the barrel of his pistol, taking his time, his hand as steady as a rock, and then at the last possible moment he bent his arm at the elbow and shot into the air. We would all have been vastly disappointed if it had not been so neatly done. Poor Walsh had to retreat to the country for a year or three with his tail between his legs. He would have been happier, I daresay, if Dunbarton had blown a hole in his shoulder or winged the tip of his ear — and he could have done it too, by Jove. He was a deadly shot."

"He was too kindhearted to shoot the man," Hannah said.

"Kindhearted?" The marquess had roused himself into some sort of passion. "He did the most cruel thing any man could have done, Hannah. He showed his contempt for Walsh. Humiliated him. Even suggested that the surgeon lay him out on the grass and administer smelling salts. It was splendidly done. And everyone *knew* that it was Jackman who was making free with Lady Walsh's favors, not Dunbarton. Even Walsh must have known it, but Jackman was a little, weedy fellow, and Walsh would have been the laughingstock if he had slapped a glove in *his* face. So he waited until Dunbarton danced with his wife one evening and made his move at White's next morning. The man

302

must have had a death wish. Or a rock for a brain. Probably the latter."

Hannah continued to smile at him.

"Ah, those were the days," he said with a sigh. "A man's man was Dunbarton, Hannah. The very devil. All the girls wanted him — and not just because he was a duke and indecently rich, let me tell you. But he would have none of them. You ought to have known him then."

"I daresay," she said, "even my father and mother did not know each other then."

He barked with laughter again.

"You got him in the end, though," he said. "You tamed him, Hannah. He was besotted with you."

"Yes," Hannah agreed, "he was. But does one forget manners as well as the location of old duels after one passes the age of eighty? Am I not to be offered a seat and a cup of tea?"

He half shook her hands again.

"You may have any seat you like," he said. "But first you must haul on the bell rope if you want tea. If you were to wait until I got to my feet to pull it, you would probably be ready for your luncheon too."

"I have already given the order for a tray to be brought in, Grandpapa," a voice said from the doorway, and Lady Sheringford came into the room.

Constantine was standing in the doorway. Hannah had no idea how long either of them had been there. She seated herself on a sofa.

"I am sorry to have kept you waiting, Your Grace," Lady Sheringford said, addressing Hannah. "I was busy in the nursery with the children."

"It is about the children I came," Hannah said. "I suspect that I did not make it clear in the invitation I sent you a few days ago that your children were included too. That applies to all the guests I have invited. I would not wish to be responsible for separating any parents from their children for even as long as four days. And Copeland has a long gallery on an upper floor that was surely made for the use of children on a wet day. And rolling parkland and woods and water outside to make for a child's paradise when it is not raining. And several of my neighbors have children of their own who would doubtless go into transports of delight if there were others to play with at Copeland. Indeed, I have been quite busily planning a children's party while I am there. It will be vastly amusing. I am not begging you to reconsider. I daresay you have other engagements on those days that you cannot in all conscience neglect. However, if it was your children that were your main concern, then please do feel free to reconsider."

"Copeland," the marquess said. "I do not remember that property, Hannah."

"It is in Kent," she said. "The duke bought it for me so that I would have a home of my own after his passing."

"You are very kind," Lady Sheringford said. "May I talk it over with my husband?"

"And perhaps with Katherine and Monty and with Stephen and Cassandra too," Constantine said as he came farther into the room. He took a chair some distance from Hannah's. "You were telling me, Margaret, that they too hated to leave the children behind."

"I will," she said just as the tea tray was brought in. "You know Constantine, Grandpapa."

"Huxtable?" he said. "Merton's grandson? I knew your grandfather. A fine man. Didn't much care for his son, though. Your father, I suppose that was. You don't look like him, which is fortunate for you. You must take after your mother. Greek, was she not? Daughter of an ambassador?"

"Yes, sir," Constantine said.

"I went to Greece in my youth," the marquess said. "And Italy and everywhere else a young man was supposed to go in those days before the wars spoiled everything. The Grand Tour, you know. I fancied the Parthenon. Can't remember much else except great expanses of blue sea. And the wine, of course. And the women, though I won't pursue that topic in the ladies' hearing."

They all chatted amicably for half an hour before Hannah rose to take her leave.

"You must come to see me again, Hannah," the marquess said. "It does my heart good to look at your pretty face. And never let that ancient fool of a butler of mine try to tell you I am from home."

"If he should ever attempt anything so foolish," she said, going to take one of his hands in both of hers, "I shall sweep by him and run up the stairs and burst in upon you unannounced. And then when I have left, you may scold him to your heart's content and threaten him with dismissal."

"He would not go," he said. "I have tried retiring him with a hefty pension and a home to go with it. Duncan has tried. Margaret has tried. There would be no point at all in dismissing him. He would refuse to be dismissed."

"Looking after you and guarding your home from invasion is what keeps him active and alive, Grandpapa," Lady Sheringford said. "Your Grace, it has been very good of you to come here this morning. I will send you a definite answer by tomorrow morning, if I may. We all will."

Hannah bent over the old man's chair and kissed him on the cheek before straightening up and releasing his hand.

"Thank you," she said to Lady Sheringford.

"I will escort you home, if I may, Duchess," Constantine said. "Though I am on foot."

What was he doing here? The countess had been in the nursery with her children. Had he been there too? *With the children?*

"Thank you, so am I," she said and swept out of the room ahead of him.

She took his arm when they were out on the pavement, and they walked for a while in silence. What a strange morning, she thought. She was still not quite sure why she had come. But oh, how *lovely* it had been to see the Marquess of Claverbrook again. One of the duke's contemporaries.

"The marquess told me about a duel the duke fought years and years ago," she said, "over the other man's wife, with whom he had been accused of committing adultery. Funny, is it not? The marquess told me he was the very devil in those days."

"But you tamed him," he said. "I heard that much."

"That *is* funny," she said. "When I decided to have you for a lover, Constantine, I told myself then that I would tame the devil. I did not realize that I had already done it — with another man."

She laughed.

"And have you tamed me too?" he asked.

"Oh," she said, "*most* provokingly, Constantine, it has turned out that you are not the devil after all. And I cannot tame what does not exist."

She turned her head to smile at him.

"Disappointed?" he asked.

Was she? Life would be so much easier — so much more as she had planned it to be — if he really were the ruthless, dangerous, sensuous devil she had taken him for. There would have been all the challenge of pitting her wits against his, of conquering him, of enjoying him. And leaving him and forgetting him when summer came would have been the easiest thing in the world.

But was she *disappointed*? Or was she being challenged in other ways? Challenged to conquer him, after all. And challenged to conquer herself and the person she had *thought* she had become.

She was no longer sure who she was. She was not the girl she had been, that was for sure. *She* was long gone. But she was not the person she had thought she had become either — not now that she was alone to live the life of that person.

She was not nearly as hard as that woman was. Or as certain of her destiny or the route she must take to get there. But the duke had never taught her to be either hard or certain. He had taught her to like herself, to take charge of her life, to be immune to the worst of the jealousies and gossip that were certain to follow her about wherever she went, and . . .

And to wait for that someone who would be the center of her life's meaning.

Was *Constantine* that center?

But her mind turned from the thought in some dismay. Heavens, did she have *no* sense of self-preservation even after eleven years?

But he was *not* the devil.

She felt as if she had a whole arsenal of windmills in her head.

"Does that mean yes?" he prompted.

He had asked if she was disappointed.

"Not at all," she said. "I promised myself the best lover in all England, and I have no reason to suppose I have not found him.

For this year, anyway."

"That's the spirit, Duchess," he said. And his eyes laughed into hers again from a face that remained in repose. Not in mockery, she thought, but more in . . .

Affection?

Well.

But . . . *affection?*

The windmills turned in her mind again.

"Now *what,*" he asked her, "is this about a *children's* party at Copeland?"

Ah, yes, and there was *that.* A purely spur-of-the-moment plan that she must now make a reality.

She never spoke impulsively. Nothing with her was spur of the moment.

Except this visit to the Countess of Sheringford.

And the children's party at Copeland.

Constantine laughed softly.

"Duchess," he said, "if you could just see your face now."

"It will be the best party ever," she said haughtily.

He laughed again.

CHAPTER 14

Hannah left for Copeland with Barbara three days before any of the house guests were expected to arrive. Not that their presence there was needed. The housekeeper was an exceptionally competent lady who had complete control over her staff and the running of the household. She also had the advantage of being a likable person, to whom all the servants were devoted.

Hannah was well aware that for those three days, as she prowled restlessly about the house, she was in danger of getting under everyone's feet and possibly on their nerves too. It was somewhat provoking to discover that her household did, in fact, run so smoothly, even under the stress of an imminent house party, that her presence was not needed. She sometimes felt she would be happy if there was a floor somewhere she could get down on her knees to scrub.

How startled and amused the *ton* would

be if they could know that the Duchess of Dunbarton was nervous.

And excited.

The duke had bought Copeland for her when he was a very elderly gentleman indeed. They had come here occasionally and spent a few days at a time. They had even entertained some of their neighbors to tea. Hannah had done some entertaining during her year of mourning here too, but not often and never on any lavish scale. She had been melancholy and quite content to be alone most of the time.

This was to be her first house party here. She wanted everything to be perfect.

She envied — and was somewhat irritated by — Barbara's cheerfully calm demeanor. She strolled outside with Hannah, even inside on the wet third day, the one before the guests were expected. And she sat for hours on end embroidering or reading or writing letters.

"What if it rains *tomorrow?*" Hannah asked as they strolled in the gallery on the last day. Rain pattered against the windows at either end.

"Then everyone will hurry inside from their carriages," Barbara said with great good sense. "It is unlikely to rain hard enough to make the roads impassable."

"But I *do* want everyone to see Copeland at its best," Hannah said.

"Then they will be pleasantly surprised when the sun shines the day after they come," Barbara said. "Or the day after that."

"What if it rains *every* day?" Hannah asked.

Barbara turned her head to look closely at her and linked an arm through hers.

"Hannah," she said. "Copeland is beautiful under *any* conditions. And *you* are beautiful under any conditions — lovely and charming and witty. You must have hosted house parties numerous times before now."

"But never here," Hannah said. "And what will it be like having *children* here, Babs? I have never entertained children."

"They will be delightful," Barbara said. "And they will ultimately be their parents' responsibility, not yours."

"But the *party,*" Hannah said, her voice almost a wail. "I have never in my life given a children's party."

"But you attended any number of them when we were children," Barbara reminded her, not for the first time. "And I was in charge of more than a few when Papa was still vicar and Mama was not up to organizing them herself. You have made more than enough preparations to keep them all busy and entertained for every moment of the party."

"I must have windmills in my head," Hannah said.

Barbara led her to a bench close to one of the windows, sat them both down, and took Hannah's hands in her own.

"I am sorry to see your anxiety, Hannah," she said. "But strangely, you know, I am cheered by it. I do believe that right before my eyes you are becoming the person you were always meant to be. Since I arrived in London, your complexion has started to glow with color and your eyes to sparkle, and your face has become vibrant with life. You are entertaining *families,* not just a select few high-born aristocrats, and you are busy devising ways of amusing them all and keeping them happy. And I think —"

Hannah raised her eyebrows.

Barbara sighed.

"I ought not to say it," she said. "You will be annoyed. I am not even sure I *want* to say it. I think you are falling in love. Or have fallen."

Hannah snatched her hands away.

"Nonsense!" she said briskly. "And see, Babs? While we have been sitting here, the rain has stopped. And look, you can see the sun as a bright circle behind the clouds. It is going to be shining by tomorrow, and the grass and trees and flowers will look all the brighter and fresher for having been rained upon."

She got to her feet and approached the window.

She was very inclined to dismiss what Barbara had said about the changes in her until the thought struck her that the duke had intended from the start that she reach this moment when she could finally unveil her real self. And *be* her real self.

She was finally daring to be the person he had wanted her to be, still a little anxious and uncertain of herself, but ready and eager to meet life and enjoy it instead of protecting herself from it behind the mask of the duchess. She was finally becoming the person *she* chose to be.

"Babs," she said, "what shall I *wear* tomorrow? What color, I mean? White? Or something . . . brighter?"

And why was she asking? It was something she must decide for herself. It was something she had been debating in her mind for three days, perhaps longer. As if the turning of the world depended upon her making the right decision.

She laughed.

"No answer required," she said. "I shall

decide for myself. What are *you* going to wear? One of your new dresses?"

"I want Simon to be the first to see me in those," Barbara said wistfully. "Though I am sure I *ought* to wear them here, Hannah, where there will be so many illustrious guests."

"Your vicar must be the first to see them," Hannah said, turning to look affectionately at her friend. "You have pretty clothes apart from them."

She was *not* going to think about what Barbara had just said, Hannah decided. She was simply not.

But it had been three days, and three nights, since she had seen him last. And she knew that though she wanted everything to be perfect for *all* her guests and that she wanted them *all* to see Copeland at its best when they arrived tomorrow, she wanted it all to be a little more perfect for Constantine.

Something could not be more perfect than perfect.

But it was what she wanted. For him.

She did not care to pursue her reasons.

"I am starved," she said. "Let's go have tea."

Copeland was several miles north of Tun-

316

bridge Wells in Kent. The carriage passed through pretty countryside, past orchards and hop fields and grazing cattle. Constantine kept more than half an eye on the scenery as he traveled with Stephen and Cassandra. They might have left the baby with his nurse, who was coming in another carriage, but he was too new and too precious to be let out of their sight except when strictly necessary, it seemed.

Stephen held him most of the way and spoke to him as if he were a little adult. The baby stared solemnly back, except when his eyelids fluttered and he slept. Cassandra straightened his blanket and rearranged his bonnet and smiled at Stephen.

It was all a trifle disconcerting. *Not* because there were any open and embarrassing displays of affection between husband and wife, but perhaps because there were not. They were so thoroughly *comfortable* with each other, Stephen and Cassandra, and it was very obvious that young Jonathan was their world. It was all so damnably *domestic.* And Stephen, by Constantine's estimation, was twenty-six years old. Nine years younger than he was.

He felt a vague sort of restlessness. And envy.

He really must give serious consideration

to finding a suitable wife. Perhaps next year. This year he was too tied up with the duchess. But if he was going to have children — and this year, for perhaps the first time, he felt the stirring of a desire to have sons and daughters of his own — he would rather start his family before he reached the age of forty. Even now he was older than he ought to be.

He distracted his mind with conversation and a more careful perusal of the latest report from Harvey Wexford at Ainsley than he had been able to give it at breakfast.

One of the lambs had died — but it had been sickly from birth. The others were all flourishing. So were the calves, except for the two that had been stillborn. The crops were coming through nicely, the weather having been warm for a whole month and the rains having come when they were needed — though they could do with another right about now. Roseann Thirgood, the teacher who had once worked at a London brothel, had purchased a dozen new books for the schoolroom since several of her pupils, both children and adults, could read through the primers that had been bought last year with their eyes shut. Kevin Hurdle had had a rotten tooth pulled and had been walking about house and farm ever since with a large, progressively graying handkerchief tied over his head and beneath his jaw. Dotty, Winifred Baker's young daughter, who was well suited to her name, had skipped all the way back to the kitchen from the henhouse one morning, swinging her basket of three eggs in wide arcs, with the result that egg yolk and egg white had dribbled all over the kitchen floor that Betty Ulmer had just scrubbed, and the basket was smeared almost beyond redemption. There was a fox paying the farmyard nocturnal visits, though so far it had gone away hungry each time. One of the plow horses was lame, but the offending thorn beneath its shoe had been found and disposed of, and the horse was on the mend. Winford Jones and his new wife sent their heartfelt thanks for the wedding gift Mr. Huxtable had sent them in a separate package last time he wrote.

He closed his eyes and, like the baby, slept for a while.

And then they were there. The carriage turned sharply between stone gateposts, waking them all, Constantine suspected, except Stephen, who had been holding the baby with steady concentration and keeping his shoulder firm for Cassandra's right cheek to rest against.

The carriage bowled along a very straight driveway, lined with elm trees like soldiers on parade. It ran flat for a while and then sloped upward toward the gray stone house at the crest of the hill. Manor, mansion — it could qualify as either. It was about the same size as Ainsley and square, with a pillared, pedimented portico centered at the front and a flat roof bordered with an ornately carved stone balustrade. Long, narrow windows decreased in size from the first floor to the second to the third. It was a curious and pleasing mix of Jacobean and Georgian in design. The walls were liberally covered with ivy.

The park, Constantine could see, fell away from the house in every direction over lawns, through copses, to denser woods. There was a glimpse of water in the distance. It seemed to him that the elm-lined driveway was the only formal feature in the park.

He liked what he could see of it.

"How perfectly delightful it all is," Cassandra was saying. "It seems very peaceful here."

"A child's paradise," Stephen said. "I can see what the duchess meant when she told Meg that. An adult's paradise too. Much as I love London, it always feels good to escape to the countryside once in a while. This house party was an inspired idea of the duchess's. Would you not agree, Con?"

"Certainly. The air smells clean," Constantine agreed, "even with the carriage windows shut."

The driveway ended at a square, graveled courtyard below the wide steps and the imposing pillars. Miss Leavensworth was standing on the lawn to one side of the courtyard with Mr. and Mrs. Park and Mr. and Mrs. Newcombe, whom Constantine had met at the Tower of London.

Katherine and Monty were standing on the lawn at the other side, young Hal astride Monty's shoulders. Sherry was a short distance away, holding Alex's hands above his head while the child toddled across the grass to destinations unknown. Margaret and a few other unidentified persons — no, one of them was her daughter, Sarah — were strolling up from the direction of the water. Toby, Margaret and Sherry's elder son, was up a tree with a larger boy — one of the Newcombe twins.

His own group was, Constantine guessed, the last to arrive.

Hannah was partway up the steps. She was wearing sunshine yellow. And piled curls that looked as though they might tumble down at any moment — though Constantine would wager they would not. And a wide smile and flushed cheeks and sparkling blue eyes.

He sucked in a breath and then hoped it had been inaudible.

He had not seen her for three days. She had come out here early to make sure everything was ready for her guests. It seemed to Constantine more like three weeks.

She looked like a girl. No, like a very young lady new to the world and full of optimism and hope and joy.

She stepped down into the courtyard when the coachman had opened the carriage door and set down the steps and handed Cassandra down.

"Lady Merton," she said, "*welcome* to Copeland. I positively refused to worry about you after Lady Montford explained to me that you had to stop on the road more often than the rest of my guests because you are nursing the baby. Even so, it is *so* good to see the last of my guests safely arrived."

She offered her right hand, and Cassandra took it.

"I am very happy to be here," she said. "How inspired someone was to build the house just here. One cannot imagine a lovelier spot."

"One cannot," the duchess agreed and turned to Stephen. "And Lord Merton. Welcome. Oh, and the *baby.*"

She took a step closer and peered gingerly at him.

"Oh, he is *beautiful,*" she said, and she was more than just a woman enthusing over another woman's child because it was expected of her.

"He is lovelier to hold," Stephen said, smiling, and he laid the blanket-bound bundle of his son in her arms.

She looked startled, alarmed, and . . .

And suddenly there was a raw, naked look on her face for which Constantine could find no words. She was no longer smiling. She did not need to.

And then she did smile again . . . slowly.

"He is *adorable,*" she said. "I believe I am in love. What is his name?"

"Jonathan," Stephen said.

"Oh." She looked up at him and then at Constantine.

"With Con's permission," he added and took the baby back from her. "My predecessor, Con's brother, was Jonathan too. Has he told you?"

"Yes," she said. And she turned to him at last and held out both her hands. "Constantine. Welcome."

"Duchess," he said. "Thank you."

He grasped her hands and kissed one of her cheeks. And smiled.

She was smiling back.

And Lord. Oh, good Lord.

He withdrew his hands and turned to look about. He drew air slowly into his lungs.

"I can see why you love Copeland and want to show it off," he said. "It is a fine place."

"Yes," she said softly. Wistfully?

Sarah came whizzing up ahead of Margaret and her group, clutching a bunch of daisies in one hand.

"Uncle Con," she yelled. "For you, Your Grace." She thrust the daisies into Hannah's hand. "Uncle Steve. Let me see *the baby*."

Constantine looked at Hannah again. She was smiling down at her daisies. Which became her more than the diamonds she usually wore. Her eyes came up to meet his once more, and they both smiled.

This, he thought, was perhaps *not* a good idea after all.

He did not ask himself what *this* was.

It seemed an age to Hannah, an eternity since she had seen Constantine.

And then, when she *did* see him, she realized how much her perception of him had changed over time. He was no longer the dark, mysterious, possibly dangerous, and very attractive near-stranger she had been half aware of for a number of years, the man she had decided over the winter would be her first lover, the aloof, somewhat mocking man she had seen in Hyde Park earlier this spring, riding with Lord Montford and the Earl of Merton. He was no longer the exciting, difficult challenge he had been when she had toyed with him during a couple of meetings until he took charge of the situation on the third and rushed her into beginning their affair that very night, long before she had expected the consummation.

Seeing him day by day in London, she had not realized how very much he had changed in her perception since that night. Today, she watched the approach of the Earl of Merton's carriage, knowing that he was within, and she could feel her heartbeat quicken. And as she greeted first the countess and then the earl, even as she saw and then held the great wonder of their newborn baby, she could *feel* Constantine's presence like a warm glow inside.

And then, at last, she had been free to turn to him, to look at him, to reach out both hands to him.

And he was simply Constantine.

She was not at liberty to probe that very *un*profound thought. She did not *want* to probe it. But there was a soreness in her chest and throat, as though she held back tears.

She welcomed him and smiled at him and was glad she had *not* probed her feelings or — horror of horrors — shed a few tears when he turned coolly away from her and made some polite remark about Copeland.

Briefly she wished that after all she had worn a white dress and decked herself out with diamonds and been the person who lived safely behind the facade of the Duchess of Dunbarton. But no, she did not *really* wish it. For these four days she had chosen to be herself without the safety of any cocoon. It had become strangely important to her to impress Constantine's relatives. Not as the Duchess of Dunbarton, but as Hannah. As herself.

It was hard to admit that she had been hurt by their initial refusal of her invitation, because she had decided long ago that she would never again allow herself to be hurt by the behavior and opinions — or rejection — of others. But perhaps she had been a little bit hurt this time. She did not know quite why.

They had changed their minds and come. Had it been because of her visit to Claverbrook House? She supposed it must have been. Had her offer to have the children here as well as the adults made the difference? Had the marquess said something after she left? Had *Constantine* said something? Surely not, though. The reason they disliked *her*, Hannah suspected, was that they wanted better for him than someone of her notoriety.

However it was, she had been given her second chance, and she wanted to impress them. To show them that she was . . . human. To show them that she was not the arrogant, ruthless, heartless upstart she knew she was rumored to be. To show them that she could be a warm and welcoming hostess.

And within moments of his arrival the Earl of Merton had let her hold his baby.

And Lord Sheringford's little girl had picked her a bunch of daisies from the unscythed grass down by the lake and shoved them into her hand as she dashed past toward the greater allure of her baby cousin as though Hannah was not anyone so very special.

It felt good indeed to be someone who

was not so very special.

Someone of whom a child need not stand in awe.

She would put the daisies in a glass and place it on the table beside her bed. They seemed more precious than roses — or diamonds.

"I will have you taken up to your rooms," she told the earl and countess and Constantine. "And we will all meet on the west terrace for tea. The weather is warm enough, and the children can eat with us and then play on the grass if they wish instead of being cooped up in the nursery."

She took Constantine's offered arm, and they led the way up the steps to the house. Why had she never thought of having children at any of her other house parties or country entertainments? Not only had she remained childless to the age of thirty, but she had also remained without any connection to children.

She had not even realized until this very moment how much she must have yearned for children all these years without ever admitting it to herself. What would have been the point of admitting it, though? She had been married to an old man who had had only one lover all his life — and that another man.

"I hope," she said to Constantine, "you had a pleasant journey down from London."

"Very pleasant, thank you, Duchess," he said.

As though they were polite strangers.

What was it going to be like meeting him *next* year? But she would think of that when next year came. For now it was *this* year.

"I am glad to hear it," she said.

The duchess looked, Constantine thought, as if she had shed ten years in the three days since he had last seen her.

And at least ten layers of armor and masks.

There was the sunshine yellow of her dress. And the sunshine of her smiles. And the rural setting, in which she looked, quite unexpectedly, far more at home than she looked in London.

She could not possibly be looking more beautiful. And yet she was.

They had all assembled on the terrace outside the drawing room for tea, where she sparkled as a hostess, and then, when they had eaten and drunk their fill, Margaret's Toby and Thomas Finch, the middle son of Hugh Finch and his wife, demanded a game of ball. There *was* a ball apparently — it had come with Margaret and Duncan.

There were several children of the party, ranging in age from Stephen and Cassandra's newborn to the twelve-year-old twins of the Newcombes. But it was not good enough for the children to play with one another, of course. Not when there was a largish gathering of idle, perfectly able-bodied adults sitting outdoors just yearning for some vigorous amusement. The fathers at least must come and play.

And since the fathers did not see why *they* should be victimized just because they had sired children a number of years ago when they knew no better, they demanded that the other men too come and enjoy some exercise — Constantine, Sir Bradley Bentley, and Lawrence Astley. After all, they had all been cooped up inside carriages for most of the day, and here they were idling around in chairs again as if there were nothing better to do.

And then a few of the mothers were offended that *they* were considered incapable of throwing a ball about without making utter cakes of themselves, and Miss Julianna Bentley, Sir Bradley's sister, pointed out to everyone that *she* had been sitting in a carriage today just as long as any of the men. Astley's sister, Miss Marianne Astley, murmured an agreement. Miss Leavensworth reminded the duchess of all the games of cricket they had played on the village green when they were growing up and remembered that she had always been put all the way out on the road when it was her team's turn to field because she could catch a ball and had a good throwing arm. And the duchess remembered that *she* had always had a pretty good arm too because all those odious boys had actually allowed her to bowl the occasional over.

"Yes," Miss Leavensworth agreed, "you had that wicked wobble ball that no one could ever hit, Hannah. All of us found ourselves sawing at the air with the bat, thinking it a sure six because the ball was moving so slowly, and then it would wobble past and shatter the wickets."

"Come, then," the duchess said, getting to her feet, "let us go and play ball."

The Duchess of Dunbarton?

Playing ball?

Constantine caught Katherine and Sherry both looking at her in some surprise, and then looking at *him.*

They all walked down the sloping lawn beyond the terrace until they were on ground flat enough for a game. Toby and Thomas, who had gone to fetch the ball, came dashing after them, and with the exception of a few people who insisted that no game could have any legitimacy if it did not have *some* spectators, they all formed a large circle about an empty center that Toby soon occupied because it was after all *his* ball. They hurled the ball across the circle to one another, trying to hit Toby's lower legs in the process. The one to succeed took Toby's place in the center and the game resumed.

It was probably, Constantine decided, one of the most pointless games ever invented. However, it occasioned a great deal of shouting and jeering and laughing — and a little crying too when Sarah somehow found herself in the middle and was hit with the very first ball. She wailed until Hannah dashed in there with her and scooped her up in her arms.

"That was a *foul*," she cried in a very un-duchesslike voice. "It hit Sarah on the knee instead of *below* the knee. *Now* try."

And she proved remarkably nimble despite the fact that Sarah was shrieking and had taken a death grip about her neck, and despite the fact that she herself was laughing so hard that it was a wonder she could catch her breath. She jumped and dodged until Lawrence Astley clipped her on the ankle with the ball.

Constantine would have lost his wager. One curl had come free of its pins, and one untidy blond ringlet bounced against the duchess's shoulder as she set Sarah down on the outer edge of the circle and Astley pranced about in the middle. She pushed the curl up under some of the others, but it was down again within moments.

Her face was flushed.

So were *all* their faces, actually, except for those of the spectators.

The game came to a natural end when Sir Bradley Bentley, who had just been hit, stretched out on the grass in the center of the circle and declared that if anyone so much as whispered the word *exercise* for the rest of the day, he was going to take to his bed and not leave it until the day after tomorrow. *At the earliest.*

Young Hal, Monty's son, jumped on him. Five-year-old Valerie Finch followed suit, and soon Bentley was lost beneath a writhing, shrieking mass of children.

"I think," the duchess said, "more tea in the drawing room is called for. Or something stronger. *Definitely* something stronger, in fact. Babs, will you see to it for me, if you please? I am going to have to make some repairs to my hair."

They all made their way up the slope to

the house — except for the duchess, who stood where she was, fiddling ineffectually with her hair and watching them go.

And except for Constantine, who stood where he was, watching *her.*

She turned her head to look at him.

"I am a mess," she said.

"You are," he agreed.

She smiled. "That was not very gallant."

"It was a *compliment,*" he told her.

"Oh." She lowered her hands and tipped her head to one side. "That was *very* gallant, then. I do not think I am very much needed in the drawing room. Babs will see to it that everyone has something to drink, and then everyone will want to retire to rest for a while before changing for dinner. Let me show you the lake."

"I have missed you," he said softly.

He was alarmed by how much.

"And I you," she said. "I had no idea that having a lover would be quite so . . . *lovely.* Is it always so?"

He grinned at her.

"You are either fishing for more compliments, Duchess," he said, "or you have just asked me an impossible question."

"Come and see the lake," she said and took his arm even before he could offer it.

Who in his right mind could have guessed

that the Duchess of Dunbarton of all people would turn out to be such an innocent?

I had no idea that having a lover would be quite so lovely. Is it always so?

Was it?

Was it lovely this time? Was it *always* lovely? He was not in the habit of comparing mistresses. Or of analyzing what were really just physical sensations.

"You see what I mean?" she said as they wound their way about the trunks of ancient trees on their way down to the lake. "I have allowed trees to dictate to me. I should have some of them chopped down so that a proper avenue could be constructed here, leading straight down from the house. Lined with rhododendron bushes. Affording a picturesque vista from the house. With a boating jetty straight ahead. And a boat bobbing on the water, of course. And an artfully pretty island in the middle of the lake. And the lake itself redesigned to be kidney-shaped or oval or *something* describable."

"With a temple folly or a small cottage folly on the opposite bank," he said. "Built so that from the house it could be seen perfectly reflected in the water and centered down the avenue."

"Yes," she said.

"But you have not done it."

"I have not," she agreed mournfully. "Constantine, I *like* being dictated to by nature. Why should I take down an oak tree that has been growing for perhaps three or four hundred years merely because it is in the way of a picturesque *prospect* from the house?"

"Why, indeed?" he agreed. "Especially as the house has not been there as long as the tree, I would estimate."

"And why build a folly?" she asked. "What is the point of it? I have never quite understood. It is all so . . ."

"Foolish?" he suggested when her free hand described circles in the air but did not seem able to supply her with the word she wanted.

"Precisely," she said. "Follies are foolish. You are laughing at me, Constantine."

"I am," he agreed as they arrived at the bank of the lake and stopped walking.

She laughed.

"But am I right or am I wrong?" she asked.

"You like Copeland as it is?" he asked.

"I do," she said. "Wild and undisciplined as it is, I *like* it. And though the terrain and scenery are just *perfect* for a wilderness walk, I have stubbornly resisted having one designed and constructed. How can some-

336

thing be both man-made and a wilderness? It is a contradiction in terms."

"And given the choice between wilderness and art," he said, "you choose wilderness."

"I do," she said. "Am I wrong?"

"I am confused," he said. "Is this the *Duchess of Dunbarton* asking someone else — *me,* to be precise — if she is right or wrong?"

She sighed.

"But you see, Constantine," she said, "there is need for *something* wild in my life. Let it be my garden, then. There, I have decided. I am *not* going to have avenues and follies and vistas and wilderness walks at Copeland. Thank you for your opinion and advice."

He turned her to him, wrapped his arms about her, and kissed her hard and open-mouthed. She twined her arms about his neck and kissed him back.

It felt amazingly good to hold her again. To taste her. To smell her.

"You see," he said when he lifted his head, "if there were an avenue from the house, we would be perfectly framed in it, Duchess, and all your guests would be lined up at the drawing room windows to admire the prospect."

"And so they would," she said, and favored

him with one of her wide, full-face smiles. "But since there is not . . ."

He kissed her again, pressing his tongue into her mouth, feeling her fingers twine in his hair, her body arch inward to fit itself to his as his arms tightened about her waist.

He wondered what would happen if he fell in love with Hannah, Duchess of Dunbarton.

He really had no idea. He might introduce chaos into his life.

Or paradise.

Not to mention what it might do to his *heart.*

He would undoubtedly be wise not to put the matter to the test.

CHAPTER 15

Hannah's guests were to be with her for three full days. She had deliberately not overorganized the activities for those days. Everyone, after all, had come from London, where the Season was in full swing and entertainments abounded. Everyone, she felt, would enjoy simply relaxing for a few days in quiet rural surroundings.

Nevertheless, some activities had been arranged for the first day — a morning walk into the village for those who wanted to see the church and get some exercise, a leisurely afternoon picnic down at the lake, an evening of cards with a few neighbors and music provided by various members of their own group. They were fortunate that the weather remained fine and warm.

It had been a successful day, Hannah felt when it was over and the last neighbors had been waved on their way. Sir Bradley Bentley, her friend and frequent escort during her marriage — his grandfather had been the duke's friend — had flirted all day with Marianne Astley, and Julianna Bentley had spent much of her time in company with Lawrence Astley. Just as Hannah had hoped. Not that she had tried to play matchmaker, but she had wanted to invite Sir Bradley after she and Barbara had had tea with him one morning on Bond Street, and he had a sister who had made her come-out last year but still had no steady beau. And her close friend was Marianne Astley, who had a brother in his middle twenties.

Her house party needed some young people, Hannah had decided. Young, unattached adults, that was. And so she had invited all four of them.

All her other guests seemed comfortable with one another, though some of them had been strangers to one another at the start. There were the Parks, the Newcombes, Mr. and Mrs. Finch, who had been the duke's neighbors all their lives and all their parents' lives before them, and the aforementioned young people. And Barbara, of course. And Constantine himself and his cousins and their spouses. And ten children and babies.

The third day was designated for the children's party in the afternoon and would be fairly busy as a consequence, but the second day was left free for whatever the guests wished to do. During the morning Hannah strolled through the flower beds to the east and north of the house with Mrs. Finch, the Countess of Merton, and a rather pale-looking Lady Montford. When Hannah, rather alarmed, inquired into her health, she laughed rather ruefully.

"It is nothing to concern you, Your Grace," she said. "It is not *poor* health that is causing me to feel a little bilious, but *good* health. I am to have another baby."

"Oh," Hannah said, and was assaulted by a great wave of envy.

"We intended to have another within two years of Hal," Lady Montford said. "But the powers that be had other ideas. I am glad they have relented at last."

"You must be my age or even younger," Hannah said. "Yet you lament having to wait so long for your *second* child?"

And she had, she realized in some dismay, spoken aloud.

Mrs. Finch was bent over a rosebud, holding it cupped gently in both hands. Lady Merton and Lady Montford turned to look at Hannah, both with the same expression of . . . compassion?

"I am thirty," Hannah added, and then felt even more foolish.

"I was twenty-eight when I married Stephen last year," the countess said as Lady Montford linked an arm through Hannah's — startling her considerably. "I was a widow too, Your Grace. And I was childless, with four dead babies to mourn. I will forever mourn them, but I have Jonathan now, and we hope to fill our nursery to overflowing before I am forty. There is always hope even in the darkest moments of despair when we can come dangerously close to losing it."

Mrs. Finch straightened up.

"I was seventeen when I married," she said, "and eighteen when I had Michael. Thomas came two years later, Valerie two years after that. I am only twenty-seven now. I love my children dearly, and my husband too, but sometimes I have wicked thoughts about having lost my youth too soon. Perhaps there is no easy road through life. We must each walk our own and make the best of it."

"Wise words indeed," Lady Montford said, patting Hannah's arm.

They strolled onward, enjoying the sight and smell of the flowers, taking a whole hour over it though the gardens were not large.

And Hannah felt . . . Oh, how did she feel? Blessed? She had been drawn into a group of ladies to chat about the pains and joys of marriage and motherhood and the passing of time. It had been a very brief chat, but she had felt included. In all the years of her married life, she thought, she had been part of society, always in the very midst of large groups of admirers, mostly gentlemen. She could not remember another time, though, when she had strolled in a flower garden arm-in-arm with any woman but Barbara.

And two of these ladies had refused her initial invitation.

"Mmm," Lady Merton said, breathing in deeply just before they went back inside the house, "this is perfect. I cannot imagine a better way to spend a few days between one grand ball and another."

"Are you feeling any better?" Hannah asked Lady Montford.

"I am," she said. "It struck me when we first came outside that perhaps it was fool-ish to walk among flowers and breathe in their scent. But the air has done me good. I will be perfectly fine for the rest of the day — until tomorrow morning. It is all in a good cause, though. And soon the morning nausea should be over."

Lady Sheringford was coming downstairs as they stepped inside.

"I have been putting Alex down for a

nap," she explained. "He fell over and scraped his knee and was feeling mightily sorry for himself. The wound has been cleansed and kissed better, his tears have been dried and kissed away, and he is fast asleep. You have a little more color in your cheeks, Kate. Are you feeling better?"

"I am," Lady Montford said. "Her grace has been showing us the flower beds, and I am quite restored."

Lady Sheringford's eyes moved to Hannah, who was thinking how lovely it must be to kiss scraped knees and tear-wet cheeks.

"You really ought to wear colors more often," she said. "Not that you do not look quite stunning in white. But you look more . . . Hmm, what is the word?"

"Approachable?" Mrs. Finch suggested, not perhaps with the greatest of tact. "It is what *I* have been thinking since I saw you in that gorgeous yellow dress yesterday, Your Grace."

"Well," Lady Sheringford said. "You look more *something.* Something *good,* that is. That particular shade of sage green goes well with your blond hair."

"We came inside for coffee," Hannah said, smiling. "Will you join us?"

She was feeling happy, she realized. She

had never had women friends, except Barbara, who was usually far away. She had never thought she wanted or needed any. Today she could live with the illusion that these ladies were her friends.

Clouds moved over late in the morning, and a sudden chill wind drove everyone indoors sooner than they might otherwise have come. A sharp shower kept them indoors after luncheon, but no one seemed unduly unhappy about it. The youngest children were taken to the nursery for a sleep, while most of the others went off to the gallery to play some game devised by Mr. Newcombe and the Earl of Sheringford.

A few of the adults sat in the drawing room conversing or in the library reading or writing letters. One or two had disappeared entirely, probably for a rest in their own rooms, Hannah guessed. The largest group was in the billiard room. That was where Hannah went in search of Constantine.

He was not playing. He was standing just inside the door, his arms folded across his chest, watching.

"It is a pity," she said, "that I have only the one billiard table."

"You must not fret about that, Your Grace," Mr. Park said. "I am a far better billiard player when I watch someone else than when I play myself. I never miss a shot, in fact, and all are perfectly brilliant."

There was general laughter.

"I have come here," Lady Montford said, "so that I will know if the shots Jasper will claim to have made when I ask him later are actually only a figment of his imagination."

"My love!" Lord Montford protested from some distance away — she had not tried to lower her voice. "Do I ever exaggerate? Do I ever *boast?*"

"This is the moment, Kate," the Earl of Merton advised his sister as he chalked the end of his cue before bending over the table to concentrate upon his shot, "when silence is golden."

"Well, *that* was nothing to boast about, Stephen," Lord Montford said a moment later as the earl missed his shot. "If I cannot do better than *that,* I will deserve everything derogatory Katherine will have to say about me."

Hannah touched a hand lightly to Constantine's sleeve.

"Would you care to come out for a ride?" she asked softly.

"Now? Is it not raining?" He raised his eyebrows, but he looked toward the window to see that indeed it was not and then followed her from the room.

"I always keep riding horses in the stables," she said when he had closed the door behind them. "I suppose I should ask if anyone else would like to come too, but everyone seems contented doing what they are doing, and I would like to show you something."

"Just me?" His eyes smiled at her.

"I will ask Barbara to take charge of the tea tray later on," she said without answering him.

"Just me." He answered his own question and dipped his head closer to hers. "Lucky me."

"I will go and change," she said. "I will see you at the stables in fifteen minutes."

And she turned to hurry away.

She changed into one of her oldest, plainest riding habits — her favorite, actually. It had been quite a pale blue when it was new. Now it was even paler. She had Adèle twist her hair into a simple knot at the nape of her neck so that it would not push her hat right off her head. She pulled on her riding gloves and looked with some satisfaction into her dressing room mirror. She wore not a single jewel.

It was important that she look like an

ordinary person this afternoon, that she *not* look like the Duchess of Dunbarton, before whom everyone felt it necessary to bow and scrape. She was beginning to long to be ordinary again, but with all the advantages of confidence and discipline and self-acceptance she had learned from the duke. Or, more accurately, from the duke's *love.*

She hoped Constantine would appreciate what she had to show him, that he would not be bored or uncomfortable. That he would not misunderstand and think she was nothing but a bleeding heart or, worse, nothing but a maker of grand gestures.

She did not believe he would think either thing. She thought that he of all people would understand. But she was horribly nervous. Her stomach fluttered uncomfortably as she strode across the terrace and along the graveled path to the stables, and she wished she had not eaten so much at luncheon.

For this, she admitted to herself, was why she had wanted him to come here, why she had devised the house party so that it would be unexceptionable to invite him.

This was important to her. His reaction was important.

He was in the stables ahead of her, saddling the horse she usually rode herself, while a groom was fitting her side saddle on another. But Jet was the only horse really large enough for him, she conceded. He had changed into buff riding breeches and a black coat with black riding boots and tall hat.

He looked just at he had looked in Hyde Park the first time she saw him this spring. But different too. He was Constantine now. Her lover. Though, alas, they had not been intimate for a week. And would not be for several more days until they returned to London since she would not show disrespect for her house guests by indulging in a continuation of her affair on her own property. It seemed an interminable amount of time to have to wait. However, her courses had been kind enough to put in an appearance on the very day she left London. They were already behind her for another month.

"Duchess?"

He turned and looked her over from head to toe, and she saw open admiration in his eyes and pursed lips. Strange that, when she was really looking almost dowdy. She returned look for look, even to the pursed lips, and he grinned at her.

"Minx," he said.

A few minutes later they rode out of the stable yard and set out behind the house and across country rather than keeping to the driveway and the road beyond it, as they would have had to do if they had traveled by carriage. It was not going to rain anymore — at least for a while. The clouds had broken up, and blue sky was taking over.

"Where are we going?" he asked. "Anywhere specific?"

"To Land's End," she said. "Oh, we are *not* going to be galloping all across southern England and down through Devon and Cornwall, you will be relieved to know. Land's End is the name someone suggested for the dilapidated heap of an old house I bought a few years ago and converted into a very decent home with gardens quite formal enough to satisfy the most exacting of proponents of art over nature. The first suggestion was *Life's* End, but no one would vote for it, and I insisted that all the first tenants of the house must agree upon a name. They liked Land's End, though, when the tenant who suggested it explained that beyond the land was the eternal peace of the eternal deep, though I have not always seen the sea quite that way myself — I never did learn to swim. I did not have a vote, however, and so Land's End it is."

"Is this an elderly persons' home?" he asked.

"Yes," she said.

They rode in silence for a short while.

"This is the *cause* for which you sold your jewels?" he asked.

"It is," she said.

"You love elderly people?" he asked.

She smiled. "I do. I loved one elderly gentleman very dearly. He had everything he needed for his physical comfort at the end of his long days. Thousands do not."

"You are a fraud, Duchess," he said.

"Of course I am not," she said briskly. "What were all those jewels to me except a reminder that I was loved dearly for ten years? I have enough left to remind me more than sufficiently. Not that I need any reminder at all except my memories."

They were coming to open country, she could see, a stretch of flat land that she always looked forward to whenever she rode to Land's End.

His head was turned toward her. She did not return his look. She was *not* a bleeding heart. She *loved* those people. She had come here every few days over the past year, before she went to London after Easter, and so had eased her grief. She had come here five days ago after returning. She had come because she wanted to come, because she *needed* to come, not because she expected applause or adulation. Good heavens, the very idea!

"This particular stretch of the way is tedious if walked across," she said, "and exhilarating when taken at a gallop. Do you see that tall pine tree in the distance?"

She pointed with her whip.

"The one with the crooked top?" he said.

"I'll race you to it," she said and was off before the words were all out of her mouth.

If she had been on Jet's back, she would have had a fighting chance, even hampered as she was by her side saddle. But of course she was on Clover, who liked a respectable gallop but did not have a competitive bone in her body. They lost the race quite ignominiously.

Constantine was grinning at her when she came up to him.

"That will make you think twice before challenging me to another race, Duchess," he said. "We did not even agree upon a prize before you tried to gain an unfair advantage with the element of surprise. That means, I believe, by international law, that I am able to choose my own prize."

"*Is* there such a thing as international law?" she asked, laughing at him. "What would you choose if indeed the law were on your side?"

"Hold still," he said, "while I think about it."

And he rode up alongside her until his knee dug into the side of her thigh, leaned across the gap between them, and kissed her on the lips. Jet snorted and sidled away.

It was perhaps the briefest and least satisfactory of all their kisses. But it was the one that informed Hannah very clearly indeed of what she had known for some time now, though she had avoided admitting it.

She was in love.

Which was very careless and incautious of her. And might well cause some pain at the end of the Season if she had not succeeded in falling *out* of love by then.

But she could not feel as sorry as she knew she ought. She felt as if eleven years of her life had somehow rolled away and left her young again and happy again — and in love again. Not in love with love this time, though, but with a real man, whom she liked and could actually *love* if she let herself. Totally committed, all the way through to the soul love, that was.

She would not be *that* foolish.

But, oh, to have a lover, and to be in love for the whole of a springtime — it made her want to leap from Clover's back and dance in the meadow beneath the pine tree, her face and her arms lifted to the sun.

How wonderful it was to be young.

"You may smile," he said. "That was the sorriest prize ever awarded the victor of a horse race, Duchess. Before this day is over, I am going to demand a *far* more satisfactory kiss than that."

She gave him her best haughty duchess look.

"You have to catch me first, Mr. Huxtable," she said. "But look. You can just see Land's End from here."

She pointed ahead and they moved off together, side by side, at a walk this time. It was visible through a gap in the trees, a solid, quite unremarkable manor that was in many ways as dear to her as Copeland.

"How did you finance Ainsley?" she asked him.

"I am not poverty stricken," he said with a shrug. "I was left well provided for."

"But not well enough, I would be willing to wager," she said. "I know something of what it costs to finance such a project. Did your brother help? You said the whole thing was his idea."

She thought he would not answer. He looked dark and brooding again for some time. And then he laughed softly.

"The truly funny thing is," he said, "that we did it exactly as *you* did, Duchess. Except that you did it with Dunbarton's knowledge and blessing, however grudgingly given. We did not consult Jon's guardian, who would most certainly *not* have given his blessing. That was our uncle before he died, and then Elliott, who had a far sterner sense of duty and a far more eagle eye."

"You say *we,*" she said. "But was it Jonathan's idea or yours to sell his valuables?"

He turned his head to look steadily at her.

"The Huxtable jewels were not mine to sell, Duchess, or even to *suggest* selling," he said. "They were Jon's, and though I was not his official guardian, I felt a great responsibility toward him. He was not by any means stupid, but sometimes he saw things differently from the way other people did. Once he discovered the truth about our fa — Ah, dash it all! But I suppose you had guessed. Once he discovered the truth about someone he had loved during life and mourned after death, he lost all his joy and all his interest in food and sleep for days on end. I had never seen him like it before. And he would not speak to me about his pain. He would only swear me over and over again to secrecy. *No one* must know about our father. And yet the suffering he had caused must not be ignored either. And Jon was very aware that *he* was now Earl of Merton, that putting everything to rights was his *duty.* I could not persuade him otherwise, though I had felt the same way for years, quite impotently, I might add."

"I wish I had known him," Hannah said softly. "Jonathan, I mean."

"And then one morning," Constantine said, "he came bounding into my bedchamber and shook me awake — literally. He was bursting with excitement, bubbling over with it, *giggling* with it. He had concocted his grand idea. And nothing would satisfy him until he had found a way of making his dream a reality. I was the one chosen to do it all for him. There was no point in arguing with Jon when he made up his mind about something important to him, Duchess — and this was more important to him than anything else in his life. He was as stubborn as a —"

"Mule?" she said. "Could he have been like his elder brother by any chance?"

"Ten times worse," he said. "The only way I could have stopped him was to run off and tell tales to my uncle behind his back. But I wanted what Jon wanted too, you see,

and I was too weak to do what was undoubtedly the right thing. For years I had been
sickened by what Jon had just discovered. I
knew about it all my life, it seems. I watched
my mother dwindle with unhappiness and
the repeated loss of children, and my father
debauch everything in skirts. He was not a
pleasant man, Duchess. And he hated Jon,
whom he called an imbecile, sometimes to
his face. I beg your pardon. One ought not
to say anything aloud against one's parents.
Anyway, none of the jewels I sold for Jon
was part of the entailed property. But
several of them had been in the family for a
few generations, and all were costly and
fully documented. A good case could have
been made to say that Jon had no right to
dispose of those pieces without the express
permission of his legal guardian. And even
if he had lived to his majority I daresay the
powers that be would have declared him
incompetent to make his own decisions un-
aided."

"He was stealing from himself, then?" she
said.

"He knew what he was doing," he said.
"Jon was no fool. Sometimes I believe he
was the only truly wise one among us. What
is more important? Those ancient jewels
locked up in a safe at Warren Hall, or those

people at Ainsley?"

She laughed. "You would never be able to guess my answer, would you?"

They were getting close to Land's End. There was just a meadow to cross and then the wide lawn to one side of the house.

"You have told no one all this?" she asked. "No one but me?"

"No," he said. "Not even the king."

"And so everyone thinks you are a villain," she said, "who stole from his helpless brother in order to purchase a home for himself in Gloucestershire, where he lives in the lap of luxury."

He shrugged.

"I believe," he said, "Elliott must have been as closemouthed as I have, except perhaps with Vanessa. If he had not, I do not suppose Stephen or his sisters would still be on speaking terms with me, would they?"

"Or trying to protect you from me," she agreed.

He looked at her and smiled before stooping to open the gate leading from the meadow into the park. They walked their horses through, and he shut the gate behind them.

"Perhaps," she said, "you ought to tell the Earl of Merton what you have told me. He seems to me to be a gentle, honorable soul."

He raised one mocking eyebrow and shot her a glance.

"You believe he would forgive me?" he asked.

"I believe," he said, "he might assure you that forgiveness is not necessary. It is Jonathan he needs to forgive rather than you, anyway, is it not?"

He nudged his horse to a slightly faster pace and moved ahead of her until she made the effort to catch up.

"That is what you fear most?" she asked. "That no one will be able to forgive your brother? Perhaps you need to give them more credit."

He turned to look fully at her again, and his features looked very taut, his eyes very black.

"Have you told anyone about *this?*" he asked her, nodding toward the house. "Anyone except me?"

"No," she said.

"Why not?" he asked. "Why did you not invite all your guests to come here this afternoon?"

"I have a reputation to protect, Constantine," she said.

"Precisely," he told her. "I do too. Devil and duchess. We deserve each other."

In the eyes of the world? Or . . . in truth?

She did not ask the questions.

"If we were not so close to the house," he said, "I might begin on all the reasons you ought to go back home, Duchess. To Markle, that is."

She leaned forward to pat Clover's neck as they stopped outside the stables and a groom hurried out to assist them.

"Point taken," she said.

CHAPTER 16

Watching Hannah over the next hour and a half, Constantine tried to make the connection with the Duchess of Dunbarton as he had always known her, and as he had encountered her earlier in the spring in Hyde Park, at the Merriwether ball, at the Heaton concert, at the Fonteyn garden party. It was rather disorienting to discover that he could not do it. He could not see her as the same person.

It was not just that she wore a faded blue, almost shabby, riding habit. Or that her hair was dressed simply and was even slightly untidy after she removed her hat inside the house. It was not even that she donned a large white apron, which had been hanging on the back of the door in the manager's office. It really had nothing to do with her outer appearance.

It had everything to do with the woman inside the outer shell, the woman he had not seen at all until after they became lovers and had seen only in snatched glimpses since then. At Land's End that woman stood fully revealed, a butterfly free of its cocoon and fluttering about, beautiful, energetic, sparkling with joy and bringing that joy to all around her.

He was, quite simply, dazzled.

He was also quite alarmingly in love.

It was not upon him that her beauty and energy and joy were focused, though she did smile at him every time she looked his way and included him in the aura of her magnetic charm.

She presented him to Mrs. Broome, the manager, a lady of middle years and pleasant appearance and soft-spoken manner, and together they began a tour of the home. But it did not last for very long. An elderly man who was sitting in the residents' drawing room caught hold of the duchess's arm — he called her "Miss Hannah," as they all did — and proceeded to tell her at great length about the latest exploits of his grandchildren. They were a figment of his imagination, Mrs. Broome explained as she walked onward with Constantine, leaving the duchess behind, but they brought him pleasure nonetheless and he loved to have someone willing to listen to his stories. And then two elderly ladies, who were sitting side by side in a wide upper hallway, wanted to know after they had been introduced to him if Mr. Huxtable had come with Miss Hannah — they had heard she was here. When he admitted that he had, they wanted to know if he was going to marry her. She deserved someone young and devilishly handsome like him, they both decided, and they cackled with glee when he grinned and winked at them and told them they would have to ask *her* that. Mrs. Broome meanwhile had been called away to deal with some emergency.

Constantine wandered alone after that, keeping mainly to the lower floor, where it seemed that most of the rooms were open for the communal use of the residents, though Mrs. Broome had explained that all had rooms of their own, where they could be private and no one could enter without first knocking and being given permission to enter. It was one of the few rules of the house.

"It is a *home*," she had added. "It is not an institution, Mr. Huxtable. There are very few rules, and all have to be first suggested and then voted upon by the tenants themselves. It may sound like a recipe for chaos, and I was a little dubious when her grace insisted upon it, I must confess, but for some reason it works like a charm. People, I suppose, are less likely to break rules that have been imposed by themselves and not by some autocratic outsider."

He stopped several times to speak to elderly people as he moved about and to a few of the employees who cared for their needs.

Hannah was still listening to the elderly gentleman with the imaginary grandchildren when he went downstairs. She was holding his hand and giving him her full, bright-eyed attention. The next time Constantine saw her, she was in the plant-filled conservatory, patiently feeding an old woman who was staring blankly ahead of her, and this time *she* was doing the talking, smiling and animated just as if the woman could understand and respond. And who knew? Perhaps she *could* understand. A little later Constantine saw Hannah on the terrace outside the conservatory, a thin old man leaning on her arm as they walked. She had her head turned toward him and was laughing. He stopped walking to look up at her, and *he* was laughing too.

The older one got, Constantine thought, the easier it was to believe that all lives followed their own very definite pattern, that all things happened for a reason. Not fate exactly. That took away free will and made nonsense of life. But some unseen force that drew each person toward the lesson that needed to be learned, the life that needed to be lived, the fulfillment that needed to be achieved. And perhaps ultimate happiness. The disasters of life in retrospect were often its greatest blessings.

Hannah's heart had been broken when she was nineteen in a particularly cruel manner. She had simultaneously lost the man she loved and the future she had planned with him and her trust in her only sister. And her father had let her down, even if he *had* been caught in a nasty situation. And then she had married a man old enough to be her grandfather, and he had lived for ten years, until her youth had gone.

But in the process of all that, she had not only learned how to guard herself against those who would exploit or resent her beauty without ever seeing *her,* how to control her life rather than be at the mercy of those who would do it for her and then blame her for being so beautiful and so vulnerable. She had also discovered what was perhaps the true purpose of her life — a deep love of those weaker than herself, specifically the elderly. And that discovery had released that part of herself that might forever have remained submerged beneath her beauty and its effect upon those around her if Young had married her. It was a self, Constantine was willing to wager, that was far more warm and vibrant than the person she had been when she was betrothed to Sir Colin Young.

The past eleven years of her life had followed a definite pattern, something she could never have predicted or planned twelve years ago. Those years had not been an interval in her life, a lost youth. They had been integral to it, a well-spent youth.

It had been no coincidence that she had discovered the truth about her betrothed and her sister at that particular wedding, or that Dunbarton had attended it and escaped to the very room where she had unburdened herself to her father. It had been cosmic theater in progress. Except that only the scene had been set by the master producer. The script had not been written.

Even now, of course, she was fearful. She hid herself behind the Siren's mask of the Duchess of Dunbarton. But that too was part of the pattern. She was still fragile. Like a person trapped in a burning building and clinging to the sill of an upper floor, she was afraid to take the final drop to the safety of the blanket being held below. She needed to be given time to do it in her own way, when she was ready.

But who was he to judge?

Besides, it would be a pity if the Duchess of Dunbarton were to disappear entirely. She was a magnificent, fascinating creature.

She was coming inside with the elderly man, Constantine could see, and she smiled warmly at *him* when she saw him standing there.

"Are you going to sit in the conservatory and enjoy the sunshine, Mr. Ward?" she asked.

"I am going up to my room to rest for a while," he said. "You have exhausted me, Miss Hannah. I shall sleep and dream of you and of being a young man again like this one here."

"Have you met Mr. Huxtable?" she asked. "He came here with me today. He is my friend."

"Sir." Constantine inclined his head. "May I help you to your room?"

"I can get there on my own, young man," Ward said, "if you will hand me the cane propped against that chair. I thank you for your kindness, but I like to do things for myself while I can. I could have walked outside with my cane, but I was not going to refuse an offer to walk arm in arm with a lady instead, now, was I? And me a mere dock worker all my life."

He chuckled and Constantine smiled.

"We will leave now," the duchess said as the old man walked slowly away. "I hope the time has not been tedious for you."

"It has not," Constantine assured her.

Ten minutes later they were on horseback again and on their way back to Copeland. They did not speak until he had let them into the meadow beyond the lawn and shut the gate behind them and ridden half across the meadow.

"I think, Duchess," he said, "that house is filled with happy people."

She turned her head to smile at him.

"Mrs. Broome is a perfect manager," she said. "And she has a wonderful staff."

And *she* was happy when she was at that house, he thought. It was her marriage to the elderly duke that had brought her there.

The pattern of life.

And the pattern of Jon's life had led to Ainsley, though he had not lived to see it.

And his own? Had he been born two days early — two days before his parents married — so that he would be illegitimate and unable to inherit the title himself? Had he found a better, more meaningful purpose for his life than he would have found as Earl of Merton? Was he better off, *happier,* than he would otherwise have been?

It was a dizzying thought.

Perhaps the circumstances of his birth had *not* blighted the whole of his life after all. Perhaps his secret affair with Jon's dream was what his life was meant to bring him.

Perhaps he had benefited as much from Ainsley as the people who had passed through it.

"You are brooding," she said.

"Not at all," he assured her. "It is just my Mediterranean looks."

"Which of course are quite splendid," she said, sounding more like the old duchess. "No man without them could brood half as well."

He laughed.

They rode onward in companionable silence until they came close to Copeland.

"I'll take you back a different way," she said. "There is something I want you to see."

"Another *cause?*" he asked.

"Not at all," she said. "Quite the opposite. A pure self-indulgence."

And instead of riding into the park and across it on the shortest route to the house, she skirted about its outer wooded edge until by Constantine's estimation they must be quite far behind the house. She drew her horse to a halt.

"It is best to go by foot from here," she said, "and lead the horses."

Before he could dismount and help her down, she had jumped down herself. She patted her horse's nose, looped the reins about one hand, and led the way among the trees. Constantine followed and soon there was the illusion of being deep in a wilderness, far from civilization.

She stopped eventually and lifted her face to the high branches overhead. They had not spoken for five minutes or more.

"Listen," she said, "and tell me what you hear."

"Silence?" he suggested after a few moments.

"Oh, no," she said. "There is almost never true silence, Constantine, and most of us would not welcome it if there were. It would be a little frightening, I believe, like true darkness. There would be only a void. Listen again."

And this time he heard all kind of sounds — the breathing of their horses, birdsong, insect whirrings, the rustle of leaves in the slight breeze, the distant moo of a cow, other unidentified sounds of nature.

"That," she said in a hushed voice sometime later, "is the sound of peace."

"I believe you are right," he said.

"The wilderness walk, if there were one," she said, "would surely pass this way. It is perfect for such a project. There would be benches and follies and colorful plants and vistas and goodness knows what else. It would be easily accessible and wondrously picturesque. But not peaceful. Not as this is peaceful. We are a part of all this as we stand, Constantine. We are not a dominant species. We are not in control of it all. There is enough control in my life. This is where I come to find peace."

He looped the reins of his horse loosely about a low tree branch and then took the reins from her hand and tied them there too. He took her by the arm, turned her so that her back was against the trunk of another tree, and leaned his body against hers. He cupped her face in both hands and kissed her mouth.

Devil take it but he was in love with her.

He had thought he would be safe with her. Safer than with any of his other mistresses. He had thought her vain, shallow. He had expected to enjoy nothing but raw lust with her.

The lust was there right enough.

And it was damnably raw.

But she was not safe at all.

For there was more than lust.

He was afraid to admit to himself that there might be considerably more.

She kissed him back, her arms twined about his neck, and soon she was away from the tree and caught up in his arms, and kisses became urgent and fevered. He glanced down at the forest floor and saw that it would make about as unsuitable a bed as it was possible for a piece of ground to make. He spread his hands over her buttocks and pressed her against his erection. She sighed into his mouth and drew back her head.

"Constantine," she said, "I will not dishonor my other guests by making love with you on Copeland land."

"Making love?" he said, looking pointedly downward. "On *this* mattress? I think not, indeed. I was merely claiming what remained of the prize I won earlier. And a very generous prize it was, I must say. I will race with you any day of the week, Duchess."

"Next time," she said, "*I* will ride Jet, and *you* can ride Clover. And *then* we will see a different winner."

"Never in a million years," he said. "And if you *did* win, if I allowed you to, what prize would *you* claim?"

He grinned lazily.

"If you allowed me to win?" She was suddenly all haughty duchess. "If you *allowed* it, Constantine?"

"Forget I said that," he said. "What prize would you claim?"

"I would have you put a notice in all the London papers," she said, "informing the *ton* that you had been bested in a horse race by the Duchess of Dunbarton, and that *you had not allowed her to win.*"

"You would make me the laughingstock?" he asked.

"Any man who is afraid to be bested by a *woman* once in a while," she said, "is not worthy of her in any capacity whatsoever. Even as her lover."

"Has your cook baked any humble pies today?" he asked her. "If so, I shall eat one whole as soon as we get back to the house. Am I forgiven?"

She laughed and tightened her arms about his neck and kissed him again.

"I am glad we are here," she said. "More and more I discover that I am happier in the country than in London. I am enjoying these few days so very much. Are you?"

"Well," he said, "they are sadly sexless,

you know, Duchess. But enjoyable neverthe-less."

He tightened his arms about her waist, lifted her off the ground and twirled her once, twice about before setting her feet down again and smiling into her eyes.

They *were* sadly sexless days. Why, then, was he feeling so exuberant? So . . . happy?

They stared at each other, and suddenly the air about them pulsed with unspoken words. Words he was afraid to speak aloud lest he discover later tonight that he had been overhasty. Words she might have spoken aloud but did not. Did he imagine that she had words to say?

Could it be that this was more than the simple euphoria of being in love?

He did not know. He had never been in love before.

He certainly did not know that other thing, that love that went beyond the eupho-ria. That forever-after thing.

How *did* one know?

And so the words remained unspoken. On his side, certainly. And perhaps on hers too.

They retrieved their horses and wound their way through the trees until they came out onto open ground at one end of the lake. They walked side by side, easier though it would have been to walk single file. They were hand in hand. Their fingers were laced. It felt more intimate than an embrace.

Hannah had not planned anything specific for the evening. She thought her guests would appreciate a quiet time in which they might do whatever they pleased. Marianne Astley, however, suggested a game of charades soon after the gentlemen joined the ladies in the drawing room following dinner, and everyone seemed happy to join in.

It went on for a couple of hours until some people began to drop out and declared their intention of merely watching.

Hannah found herself drawn to one side by Lady Merton.

"I am going to step outside onto the terrace for some air, if I may," the latter said, indicating the open French windows. "Will you join me?"

Hannah glanced around. No one would need her for a while. Barbara, flushed and animated, was acting out a phrase for her team, which was yelling out responses that elicited laughter and a few jeers from the opposing team.

"It *is* warm in here," Hannah said.

It was cool outside but not unpleasant enough on the bare flesh of their arms to send them scurrying inside for shawls.

Lady Merton linked an arm through hers, and they strolled across the terrace and a little way out onto the lawn, where the light from the drawing room still made it possible for them to see where they were going.

"Miss Leavensworth is a lovely lady," Lady Merton said. "You and she have been friends all your lives, she was telling us earlier."

"Yes," Hannah said. "I have been very fortunate."

"But she lives far away from you most of the time," Lady Merton said. "That is unfortunate. I have a dear friend who was once my governess and was then my companion. But always she was my friend, the one in whom I could confide anything and everything. She married last year, just before Stephen and I did. She is happily wed, I am glad to say, and she lives in London most of the year with Mr. Golding, her husband. I miss her even so. Close friends need to *be* close."

"I am always thankful," Hannah said, "that someone invented paper and ink and pens — and writing."

"Yes," her companion agreed. "But without Alice by my side almost every moment of the day last spring, I would have been dreadfully lonely. I was a widow, I was widely believed to have killed my husband, and I had been abandoned by my husband's family and for a while by my own brother too."

This, Hannah realized, was not just idle chatter.

"Even with Alice I was frequently lonely," the countess said. "Until I met Stephen, that was, and was adopted by his family. They did not take to me easily, as you may imagine. But they are remarkable ladies, his sisters. They grew up in humble surroundings and in near-poverty, and seem far more able to see to the heart of a matter than many other members of the beau monde. And far more capable of compassion and understanding and true friendship."

"You were fortunate indeed, Lady Merton," Hannah said.

"You may call me Cassandra if you wish," the countess said.

"Cassandra," Hannah said. "It is a lovely name. I am Hannah."

They stopped walking and both looked up at the moon, which had just drawn clear of a cloud. It was just off the full and looked lopsided.

"Hannah," Cassandra said, "we made a mistake."

"We?" Hannah asked.

"Stephen and his sisters did not even know of Constantine's existence until they arrived at Warren Hall and met him," Cassandra said. "They loved him immediately, and of course they felt dreadfully sorry for him because he had recently lost his last surviving brother. They understood how difficult it must have been for him to see them take over his home and to see Stephen take the title that had so recently been his brother's. And of course there was all that business of his having been born just a couple of days too early to be able to inherit himself. Constantine is a very private and secretive man, and he has a long-standing quarrel with Elliott and now with Vanessa too, but nevertheless the rest of them are desperately fond of him and want above all to see him happy."

"I have no intention of marrying him," Hannah said, keeping her eyes on the moon. "Or of breaking his heart. We are engaged in an *affair,* Cassandra, as I am sure you are all very well aware, but not of the heart."

She was not at all sure she spoke the truth, but it was probably the truth from his perspective, and that was all that mattered to his family. Though this afternoon . . .

"But that is the whole point," Cassandra said with a sigh. "We *were* concerned, Hannah. Although Constantine is in his thirties and well able to look after his own affairs, nevertheless you are different from other women. We thought it altogether possible that you would toy with his affections, humiliate him, perhaps even hurt him. While we did not believe we needed to *protect* him from you — that would have been absurd — we *did* believe we ought to show our disapproval when we could."

"And so," Hannah said, "you refused my invitation to come here. It was your right. There is never any compulsion to accept invitations that are not to one's liking. I never do. The duke taught me to assert myself in such ways. He taught me not to endure unnecessary boredom or to suffer fools gladly all in the name of obligation where there *is* no obligation. You do not owe me an explanation of why you refused, or why you changed your minds and came."

"Hannah," Cassandra said, "I was horribly misjudged when I arrived in London last year, *and* I was ostracized. There is no worse feeling, much as one may tell oneself that one does not care. You are not ostracized by society. Quite the contrary, in fact. But you *are* misjudged."

"Perhaps," Hannah said, drawing Lady Merton toward a bench beneath an oak tree close by, "I choose to be misjudged. There is a certain comfort in knowing that there is privacy even in the most public situation, in knowing that one can very effectively hide in full sight."

They seated themselves and Cassandra laughed softly.

"I was destitute as well as everything else when I arrived in London last year," she said, "and I had other persons dear to me to support as well as myself. I decided that the only way I could do it was to find a wealthy protector. And so I went to a ball to seduce Stephen, who looked to me like an angel. I made the mistake of believing that angels must also necessarily be *weak* and easily led — but that is another story. I can remember standing in that ballroom, an empty space all about me, everyone shocked that I would have come there uninvited, and wishing that I could curl into a tiny ball and simply disappear. I was sustained by the realization that no one *knew* me, that my real self was safely hidden deep within the brazen red-haired axe-murderer everyone *thought* they saw."

"But the Earl of Merton danced with you," Hannah said.

"That too is another story," Cassandra said. "I of all people ought to have realized when I saw you earlier this spring that what I saw was not the real Duchess of Dunbarton."

"Oh," Hannah said, "she is very real indeed. I *am* the Duchess of Dunbarton. I married the duke when I was nineteen, and though the world will always believe that he married me for my youth and beauty and that I married him for his title and wealth, nevertheless I *was* his wife. And now I am his widow. He taught me how to be a duchess, how to hold my head high, how to control my own life and never let myself be exploited, for my beauty or any other attribute. I *like* the person he helped me to become, Cassandra. I am *comfortable* as the Duchess of Dunbarton."

"I expressed myself poorly," Cassandra said. "What I meant was that looking at you, I ought not to have believed that I was looking at the complete you. Even yet I do not presume to believe that I *know* you. But Margaret told us about how kind you were to Duncan's grandfather when you called on her at Claverbrook House and how you kissed his cheek before you left. And about how you came to invite our children to this house party even though we had all rejected your invitation. And for the last two days I have seen a side of you that no one is allowed even to glimpse when you are in town. You are a warm, hospitable, generous, fun-loving person, Hannah, and I wanted you to know that I misjudged you. We *all* want you to know that."

"You were the one chosen to have this word with me, then?" Hannah asked, not knowing whether to be amused or somehow hurt.

"Not at all," Cassandra said. "But we did talk at length this afternoon while you were gone somewhere with Constantine and the children were either sleeping or playing elsewhere. And we agreed that we really must find a way of telling you how sorry we are that we rejected you on so little evidence."

"You owe me nothing," Hannah said.

"Of course we do not," Cassandra agreed. "But we all want to offer our friendship, if you will accept it after such a shaky start."

"On condition that I do not hurt Constantine?" Hannah asked.

"He has nothing to do with it," Cassandra said. "He is well able to take care of himself. And we now know that you are not the sort of person who would willfully lead him a dance and humiliate him. If he ends the affair at the end of the Season, or if you do, or if you part by mutual consent, that is entirely a matter between the two of you. But I think I would like you as a friend, Hannah, and Margaret and Katherine feel the same way. If it means anything to you, Vanessa told us just last week that she has always liked you and admired you, that you were altogether too good for Constantine."

She laughed softly again.

That was going to have to end, that silly quarrel, Hannah thought. The Duke of Moreland had certainly been at fault in the way he had jumped to conclusions about his cousin and best friend and accused him of really quite heinous crimes. But Constantine had been equally at fault in choosing to take offense to such a degree that he did not even try to explain how much he had been misjudged.

Misjudged. That word again.

She had been offered the friendship of three ladies whom she believed she could like very well if given the chance. Perhaps four. The Duchess of Moreland claimed to like and admire her.

And it was, apparently, an unconditional friendship she was being offered.

"We have been discovered," Cassandra said, and Hannah looked up to see the Earl of Merton and Constantine crossing the lawn toward them. "Angel and devil. It was how I saw them the very first time I set eyes upon them in Hyde Park one afternoon last year. And Stephen really *is* an angel."

Hannah's heart turned over — even though she had seen Constantine in the drawing room just fifteen minutes or so ago. This celibacy was proving to be very hard on the emotions. Not just because she longed to make love with him — though she did — but because the abstinence made her *think* about their relationship. And she did not like the direction her thoughts were taking.

At least, she *did,* but . . .

But what had he been about to say out in the woods this afternoon when he had chosen to remain silent instead? Words had been fairly bursting from him.

As they had from her.

She was going to get dreadfully hurt after all. She should never have believed she could play with fire and not get burned.

Or perhaps she would *not* get hurt. Perhaps . . .

"We have come to be congratulated on our win," the earl called when the men were within earshot. "Which you did not remain to witness."

"Of course," Constantine said, "we have been accused by the other side of winning only because we had Miss Leavensworth on our team. But that sounds like sour grapes to me."

"The other side was *my* side," Cassandra said. "I cannot think of any one of my former teammates who is capable of *sour grapes,* Constantine. And any team that had Miss Leavensworth on it would have an unfair advantage."

"Well, there you are, Cass," the earl said. "You are biased. We might as well change the subject before we come to blows."

He propped one foot on the bench at his wife's side and draped an arm over his leg. Constantine leaned one shoulder against the trunk beside Hannah and crossed his arms over his chest.

"It is so beautifully silent out here," the earl said after a few moments.

"Not so," Constantine said. "If you really listen, Stephen, you will hear wind in the trees, a nightingale singing, laughter from the drawing room, among other sounds. All contributing to a sense of quiet well-being. Hannah taught me that this afternoon when we were strolling in the woods."

They all listened.

Except Hannah.

He had just called her by name. For the first time.

And here she was, part of a relaxed group, feeling the warmth and acceptance of it. She was not at the center of it, holding court as she usually was in groups. She was *part* of it.

If she were to let go of the last vestiges of her defenses, she could believe that she was part of a group of two couples.

She clasped her hands rather tightly in her lap. She would not let go. The looming heartache, not to mention heart*break,* would be just too much to bear. The other couple was married. They had a young baby sleeping up in the nursery. When this house party was at an end, they would return to London together. At the end of the spring, they would go *home* together. Even tonight they would lie in each other's arms.

"You are perfectly right, Con," the earl said after several minutes, sounding surprised.

Constantine's hand came to rest lightly on Hannah's shoulder.

She felt like weeping.

Or leaping to her feet and dancing in the moonlight.

CHAPTER 17

Everyone seemed excited next morning at the prospect of the children's party during the afternoon, even those guests who had no children. After breakfast a few of the men, led by Mr. Park, went out to mark out a cricket pitch not far from the lake. Julianna Bentley and Marianne Astley went with Katherine, who was looking only very slightly pale, to stake their claim to a piece of level land upon which various races would be run. Barbara Leavensworth headed a self-proclaimed committee to plan a treasure hunt. Lawrence Astley and Sir Bradley Bentley offered to test out the boat, which had been repaired and painted last year but never actually rowed out onto the water. Jasper, Lord Montford, took the older children riding to get them out from underfoot. A few of the mothers as well as Stephen and Mr. Finch stayed in the nursery to amuse the younger children.

A total of twenty-two children of various ages from the neighborhood were expected to arrive soon after luncheon. Their parents had been invited too for a picnic tea out on the grass beside the lake.

Hannah was in the kitchen consulting the cook, unnecessarily in Constantine's estimation. But she was more excited than anyone else. She had positively glowed at breakfast. Her cheeks had been flushed, her eyes bright.

He had been on his way out to look at the boat with Bentley and Astley, but he had been delayed by the arrival of a letter from Harvey Wexford at Ainsley. It had been sent on from London. He might have ignored it until later except for the fact that he had received a report just a few days ago and had not expected another so soon. Curiosity got the better of him and he stayed on the terrace to read it.

Hannah found him there when she came through the drawing room and out through the French windows on her way to check on the others at the lake.

Constantine smiled at her and folded the letter.

"Your cook has everything under control?" he asked.

"Of course," she said. "I was made to feel

very welcome as a guest provided I did not step too far into her domain and get in the way."

She laughed and looked at him, and from him to the bustle of activity farther from the house. She glanced at his letter.

"Is anything wrong?" she asked.

"No, nothing." He smiled again.

She sat on the seat beside his.

"Constantine," she said, "what is wrong? I absolutely insist upon knowing."

"Do you, Duchess?" he said, narrowing his eyes upon her.

She sat there waiting.

"There can be no relationship like this," she said at last.

"*Is* there a relationship?" he asked. "We sleep together, Duchess. We take pleasure of each other. That hardly qualifies as a *relationship*."

She stared blankly at him for a long moment.

"We *slept* together," she said at last. "We *took* pleasure of each other. Past tense, Constantine."

And she got to her feet and walked away in the direction of the lake without another word or a backward glance.

It was ingrained in him, was it not? This deep need to protect himself from harm by turning deeply inward. The knowledge had been there for as far back as he could remember that he was inadequate. He had left his mother's womb too soon, two weeks earlier than expected, two days before his father could both acquire a special license and marry her. His mother had complained to him, perhaps believing that he was too young to understand, that her yearly pregnancies and her yearly miscarriages or stillbirths would have been unnecessary if he had only waited to be born at the right time. His father had complained to him, even when it must have been perfectly obvious to him that his son was old enough to understand, that his wife's failures would not have been so tiresome if *he* had waited a few days to be born legitimate. Even his good health had been an inadequacy. It had accused his parents in their efforts to produce another, healthy, legitimate son and heir.

And Jon, whom Constantine had hated because *he* could have done so much better a job of it had *he* become Earl of Merton on the death of their father. And his agonized love for Jon. The guilt of feeling hatred when he had wanted only to love. When he *had* only loved.

And then the need to protect Jon's grand

scheme for Ainsley, to make sure that *nothing* and *no one* stopped him just because he was an imbecile in the eyes of the world. And the refusal to let even Elliott in on the secret because Elliott, surprised by the suddenness with which he had succeeded to his own title and responsibilities, would surely have chosen to protect Jon from himself.

And Elliott's terrible betrayal, lashing out with accusations instead of simply asking questions.

Would Constantine have answered the questions truthfully even if they had been asked, though? Perhaps not. *Probably* not, for Elliott would still have felt it his duty to put a stop to what Jon wanted done. Elliott would have felt it necessary to protect the estate intact. It was what guardians *did*. It was not that Elliott did not have a heart, but after his father's sudden death, that heart had become subordinate to duty. At least at that time it had. He seemed to have rediscovered his heart since marrying Vanessa, but the damage had been done by then. Jon was dead, and a lifelong friendship had been ruined beyond repair.

And so secretiveness, hiding within himself, had become part of Constantine's nature. And now he had been cruel to someone who did not deserve his cruelty.

Good God, he *loved* her!

A fine way he had of showing it. Was cruelty, coldness, part of his nature too? Was he *that* much like his father?

He got to his feet to go after her. But he had not noticed that she had doubled back. She came and stood in front of him.

"I'm sorry," he said.

"We do not *just* sleep together," she said. "We do not *just* take pleasure from each other. There is more than that, whether you admit it or not. I will not put a name to it. I am not sure I can. But there *is* more, Constantine, and I cannot bear to be shut out of your deepest pain. You know mine. Or, if I have never been quite specific about it, this is it. I grew up hating my beauty because it set me at a distance from people I wanted simply to love. My sister was jealous of me, though I tried and tried not to give her cause, and finally she hurt me terribly perhaps because *I* had hurt *her.* Perhaps she had always loved Colin. Or perhaps she loved him only because I did and I got him. My father was caught in the middle and did not know how to cope after my mother died, and he ended up letting me down dreadfully, taking Dawn's side when it ought to have been obvious to him that she had behaved badly, that my heart was breaking. Oh, very well, maybe not one of them, even Colin, was an out-and-out villain. Maybe they all felt justified in what they did and said. Who knows? But they *ought* to have known that I had feelings, that I could be hurt as deeply as the ugliest girl on earth, that beauty is no buffer against pain and loss. Thank God — and I do not blaspheme — thank *God* for Barbara, who knew me and loved me all my life, and for the duke, who saw through my outer looks to the broken, frightened child who was disturbing his peace in that room by weeping noisily and without dignity."

"Duchess," he said.

"He taught me to rescue and nurture and strengthen that broken person within," she said, "so that she could be strong again. He enabled me to love myself again, without vanity, but with acceptance of who I was behind the appearance that has always attracted so many in such a very superficial way. He taught me that I could love again — I loved him — and that I could trust love — I trusted his. He left me still a little fragile but ready to test my wings. That was *my* pain, Constantine. It still *is* my pain. I hover a little uncertainly behind the invulnerable armor of the Duchess of Dunbarton."

He swallowed against a gurgle in his throat.

"Jon's dream is threatening to turn to nightmare," he said. He held up the letter, which was still in his hand. "Jess Barnes, one of the mentally handicapped workers at Ainsley, left the door of the chicken coop unlatched one night and a fox got in and made off with a dozen or so chickens. My manager claims not to have scolded him too severely — Jess tries so very hard to please and he is one of the hardest workers on the farm. But Wexford told him that I would be disappointed in him. Jess went out the next night and helped himself to fourteen chickens from my closest neighbor's coop. And now he is languishing in jail even though the chickens have been returned unharmed *and* paid for, and Jess has made a tearful apology. That particular neighbor has disapproved of me and my project ever since it began. He never loses a chance to complain. Now he has all the evidence he needs that it is a reckless project, doomed to failure."

She took the letter from his hand and set it down on the table before taking both his hands in hers. He had not realized how cold his were until he felt the warmth of hers.

"What will happen to the poor boy?" she asked.

"The *poor boy* is forty years old or there-abouts," he said. "Wexford will sort it out. It is clear that Jess did not intend to *steal* but only to please me by putting right his mistake. And Kincaid has been more than adequately recompensed, though I cannot blame him for being angry. It has always been the worst fear of my neighbors that they are not safe with so many unsavory characters living close to them. I just hate the thought of poor Jess in jail, though, and not quite understanding why he is there. I had better go down to Ainsley next week, after we go back to London."

"Do you want to go today?" she asked.

He looked into her eyes. "There would be too many questions to answer here," he said. "And I want to spend the rest of today here with you even if you *do* insist that we abstain from . . . pleasure."

He grinned at her.

She did not smile back.

"Thank you, Constantine," she said. "Thank you for telling me."

And good God, devil take it, he felt tears welling into his eyes. He drew his hands from hers hastily and turned to pick up Wexford's letter. He hoped she had not seen. That was what happened when one let go a little and confided in someone else.

He ought not to have burdened her with his problems. She was preparing for a party.

"I love you," she said.

He turned his head sharply, tears notwithstanding, and gazed at her, startled.

"I do," she said softly. "You need not feel threatened by it. Love does not deck the beloved in chains. It just *is*."

And she turned about and strode across the lawn again. This time she did not turn back.

Devil take it!

Idiot that he was, he felt frightened. Now wouldn't the *ton* be fascinated to know that the devil himself was frightened by love? Though perhaps it made theological sense, he thought with wry humor.

I love you, Con. I love you more than anyone else in the whole wide world. I love you forever and ever. Amen.

That had been Jon, on the night of his sixteenth birthday.

The following morning he had been dead.

I love you, Hannah had just told him.

He closed his eyes. Pray God Wexford had got Jess safely out of jail by now. And it *was* a prayer. The first one in a long, long while.

The children's party was long and chaotic and excruciatingly noisy. The children all enjoyed themselves enormously, with the possible exception of Cassandra's baby and another babe in arms, who both slept through most of the proceedings as though nothing very special was happening at all.

The adults were looking a little the worse for wear by the time all the neighbors had rounded up their offspring and herded them off back home and the house guests had picked up all the play equipment and debris and trudged back to the house with the remaining children.

"One always knows a children's party has been a vast success," Mrs. Finch said, "when one is so exhausted afterward that even putting one foot before the other takes a conscious effort. Your party has been one of the best, Your Grace."

Everyone laughed — rather wearily — and agreed.

Hannah was feeling happy and proud of herself as she dressed for dinner an hour or so later. She had involved herself with the children all afternoon rather than standing back, as she might have done, playing the part of gracious hostess. She had even run a three-legged race with a ten-year-old girl who had shrieked the whole length of the course, leaving Hannah feeling slightly deaf in one ear as well as sore in all sorts of places from their numerous falls.

She was feeling happy.

She had told Constantine that she loved him, and she was not sorry. She did love him, and it had needed to be said. She expected nothing in return — at least, so she persuaded herself. But too many things were left unsaid in life, and their unsaying could make the whole difference to the rest of life.

She had told him she loved him.

They had scarcely spoken to each other all afternoon. It was not that they had avoided each other. But they had both been involved in playing with the children and conversing with the neighbors, and their paths had hardly crossed.

Of course, she had made no great effort to see to it that they *did* cross. She felt embarrassed, truth be told. She knew he would not laugh at her for telling him such a thing, but . . .

What if he did?

She was not going to brood. There was one whole evening of her house party left, and though everyone would undoubtedly be tired, they would also enjoy relaxing together in the drawing room, she believed. She was looking forward to relaxing with them.

And she believed she had female friends who would *remain* friends after they had all returned to London. Friends in addition to Barbara, that was. She had felt the friendships this afternoon — Cassandra and her two sisters-in-law, even Mrs. Park and Mrs. Finch. Both Lady Montford and the Countess of Sheringford had found a moment in which to invite her to call them by their given names. Katherine and Margaret.

If only she could find the courage to be her inner self as well as the Duchess of Dunbarton in London.

Life was complicated. And exciting. And uncertain. And . . .

Well, and definitely worth living.

"That will do nicely, Adèle," she said, turning her head from side to side so that she could see her hair in the mirror. It was prettily piled and curled without being over-elaborate.

She wore a gown of deep rose pink. She had intended to wear no jewelry, but the low neckline was too bare without anything. A single diamond pendant — a real diamond — hung from a silver chain. And on her left hand she wore the most precious of her rings, her wedding present, along with her wedding ring.

"That will be all, thank you," she said, and she gazed at her image for a while after her maid had left the room. She tried, as she occasionally did, to see herself as others saw her. In London, of course, she always made sure that other people saw her a certain way. But here? She had felt friendship here during the past few days. Apart from the fact that she was the hostess, she had felt as if no one viewed her as being any more special than any of the other ladies.

Was it her clothing? She had not worn white even once. Or her hair? It was more formally dressed tonight than at any time since she had come into the country, but even now it was not as elaborate as she wore it in town. Or her relative lack of jewelry?

Or was it something else? Had her guests seen during the past few days what she was seeing now? Simply herself?

Was she able to inspire love, or at least liking and respect, as herself?

She was not the *only* beautiful woman in the world, after all. Even here. Cassandra and her sisters-in-law were all strikingly good-looking. Mrs. Finch was pretty. So were Marianne Astley and Julianna Bentley. Barbara was lovely.

Hannah sighed and got to her feet. She

was *so* glad there had been this house party. She had enjoyed it more than she could remember enjoying anything for a long while. And there was this evening left. Tomorrow she would be back in London. She and Constantine would be able to spend the night together. Unless, that was, he felt it necessary to hurry down to Ainsley Park to see that all was well with his farm hand.

She hoped for the sake of both him and Constantine that that situation would resolve itself soon.

"Tomorrow night," he said, gazing up at stars too numerous to count. "My carriage at eleven o'clock. At my house by quarter past — not one second later. And in my bed at twenty past. *Not* to sleep. Be prepared for an orgy to end orgies."

She laughed softly, her head on his arm.

They were lying on the bank of the lake. Everyone was pleasantly weary after the children's party and picnic and quite content to sit about the drawing room after dinner, conversing or listening to whoever had the ambition to play the pianoforte or sing. Four people were playing cards. The duchess had clearly felt no qualms about leaving her guests to their own devices when Constantine invited her to step outside with him. Indeed some of his cousins had actually smiled indulgently from one to the other of them.

His *female* cousins and Cassandra were actually calling her *Hannah,* he had noticed during the day.

"You must not expect to hear any argument from me," she said now. "But having made such a boast, Constantine, you must live up to expectations. I insist upon it."

"I'll be going down to Ainsley the next morning," he said. "I must go. Everything is probably settled happily by now, but I must go in person to smooth things over with Kincaid and the other neighbors. And to thank Wexford for handling the matter on my behalf. And to assure Jess that I am certainly *not* disappointed in him. I may not see you for a week or more."

"That will be tiresome," she said. "But I daresay I shall survive, you know. And I daresay you will too. You must go."

Suddenly the end of the Season seemed not very far off at all. Indeed, if it were not for his affair with the duchess, he would probably decide that it was not worth coming back to London this year. But he could not contemplate putting an end to their affair quite yet. And perhaps . . .

Well, he would think of that some other time.

She had told him this morning that she loved him. What *exactly* had she meant by that? It was not a question he could ask aloud, though he would dearly like to know the answer.

"In the meantime . . ." He slid his arm from beneath her head, raised himself onto one elbow, and looked down at her. "Tomorrow night seems a long way away."

He bent his head and kissed her — a lazy exploration, first with his lips, then with his tongue deep inside her mouth.

"It does," she agreed with a sigh when he raised his head again.

He rubbed his nose back and forth across hers.

"I will respect your wishes, Duchess," he said, "even though your guests probably have their own idea of what is going on between us out here. Let me love you without dishonoring those wishes."

"How?" She reached up one hand and set her forefinger along his slightly crooked nose.

"No penetration," he said. "I promise."

"And so respectability will be preserved," she said. "Everything *but* penetration, and our guests believing the worst. It is the story of my life."

He rose up onto his knees and straddled her body. He slid her gown off her shoulders and beneath her breasts and smoothed his hands over her, fondled her, rolled her nipples between his thumbs and forefingers, lowered his head to suckle them one at a time, and kissed her mouth again, his fingers tangling in her hair, his tongue sucked deep and then luring hers into his mouth to be suckled in its turn.

Her hands pressed over his back, under his shirt, down inside his drawers.

She was hot with passion.

He was throbbing with need.

Not a good idea after all. And what the devil difference would it make if he entered her and rode to completion with her? It was what they both wanted. It was what they had both lived without for far too many days and nights.

He moved to one side of her, his mouth still on hers, and slid a hand beneath her skirt, up over the smoothness of her silk stockings, along the heated flesh of her inner thighs and up . . .

"No."

Surprisingly, the voice was his own.

He withdrew his hand, lowered her skirt, and raised his head.

"Damn you, Constantine," she half shocked him by saying. "And thank you."

And she wrapped her arms about his neck and drew his head back to her own. She kissed him softly and warmly. He could feel her heart thudding in her bosom, the heat of her arousal, the determined effort she was making to return their embrace within the bounds of decorum.

"Thank you," she said again a minute or two later, hugging him close. "Thank you, Constantine. I am not sure I would have been able to resist. You are *so* gorgeous. I was perfectly right about you from the start."

Did that mean he might have . . . ?

He was glad he had not.

But dash it all, he deserved some sort of medal of honor.

There was probably not a person in the drawing room who did not believe he was enjoying everything there was to enjoy with her.

She had a strange — and touchingly wonderful — sense of honor.

They strolled arm in arm back to the house, and he remembered again the words she had spoken this morning — and not since. Because he had not said them back to her? *Could* he? *Would* he?

They were the most dangerous words in the English language when strung together. They were so completely irrevocable.

He would have to think about saying them.

Perhaps tomorrow night.

Or when he returned from Ainsley.

Or never.

Coward.

Or wise man.

"I will have to go up to my bedchamber before returning to the drawing room and ordering the tea tray brought up," she said. "I probably have grass clinging to my person from head to toe. My hair surely looks like a bird's nest. I must look thoroughly tumbled."

"I wish you were," he said with a loud sigh.

She laughed.

"Tomorrow night," she said. "And the promised orgy."

He escorted her upstairs to her room and went along to his to comb his hair and make sure that *he* did not look as if he had been rolling in a haystack somewhere.

Hannah shook out her dress, adjusted it at the bosom, washed her hands, and repaired her hair as well as she could without taking it all down, and peered dubiously into the mirror above her dressing table. Were her cheeks as flushed as she thought they were? And her eyes as bright?

Ignominiously, she wished he had not kept his promise outside. That way she could have enjoyed all the pleasure without assuming any of the guilt. She could even have scolded him afterward.

But really that *was* an ignominious way to think. She was very glad — very glad indeed — that he *had* kept the promise.

Oh, how she loved him!

She hurried across her dressing room and reached out a hand to open the door. Someone rapped on the other side before she could do so and opened it without waiting.

Ah, impatient man!

She smiled before two things registered on her mind. Constantine was as pale as a ghost. And he had changed during the minutes since he had left her outside the door. He was dressed for travel in a long cloak and top-boots. He held a tall hat in one hand.

"I must ask a favor of you, Duchess," he said, stepping into the room and closing the door behind him. "I did not bring my own carriage. I came here with Stephen and Cassandra. I must beg the loan of a horse —

Jet, if I may, to get me back to London. I'll get my own carriage there and proceed on my way."

"To Gloucestershire?" she said. "Already? *Now?*"

Foolishly, all she could think of was that he did not want the promised orgy of love-making after all.

"There was another letter waiting in my room," he said. "They are going to *hang* him."

"Wh-a-a-t?" She gaped at him.

"For theft. As an example to other would-be thieves," he said. "I have to go."

"What are you going to *do?*" she asked him.

"Save him," he said. "Talk sanity into *someone.* Good God, Hannah, I do not know *what* I am going to do. I have to go. *May* I take Jet?"

His eyes were black and wild as he raked the fingers of one hand through his hair.

"I'll go with you," she said.

"You most certainly will not," he said. "A horse?"

"The carriage," she said, and she opened the door again and swept out of the room ahead of him. "I'll give the orders. Take my carriage and go directly to Ainsley Park. It will save you at least half a day."

She went out to the stable and carriage house herself, as if her physical presence could hasten him on his way. Horses and carriage were readied with great speed, though it seemed agonizingly slow to Hannah, and to Constantine, who paced, like a caged animal.

She took his hands in hers again when she saw that the carriage was almost ready, and the coachman was hurrying up, dressed in his livery.

But she could not think of anything to say. What *did* one say under such circumstances?

Have a safe journey?

I hope you get there in time?

But in time for what?

I hope you can talk them out of hanging poor Jess.

You probably will not be able to.

She drew his hands to her face and held them to her cheeks. She turned her head and kissed his palms one at a time. Her throat was sore, but she would not shed tears.

She looked up at him. He stared blankly back. She was not even sure he saw her.

"I love you," she whispered.

His eyes focused on her.

"Hannah," he said.

Her name again. It was almost like a

declaration of love. Not that she was consciously thinking of such trivialities.

He turned and climbed into the carriage and shut the door behind him, and within moments the carriage was on its way.

Hannah raised a hand, but he did not look out.

His presence at Ainsley would achieve nothing, Hannah thought with a great sinking of the heart as she watched her carriage disappear at some speed down the straight driveway.

That poor man was going to hang for theft. And Constantine would never forgive himself for taking him in to live at Ainsley and then somehow failing to keep him safe from harm. This was something from which he would never ever recover even though, of course, it was all *none of his fault.*

There must *be* a way of saving Jess Barnes. He had taken fourteen chickens from the coop of a neighbor and then returned them and apologized. Constantine's manager had paid the value of the chickens even though they had been returned. And for all that a man was to lose his life — as an example to others.

The judicial system was sometimes capable of asinine and terrifying madness.

An old adage leapt to her mind: "One might as well hang for a sheep as a lamb." But one *could* hang for either. Or for a few chickens.

Someone must be able to help. Someone with influence. Constantine, despite his lineage, was a mere commoner. There must be . . .

She looked toward the house and then hurried toward it, holding her skirt up out of the way, half running. And it would have been quicker, she thought as she ran up the steps beneath the pillared portico and through the front doors, to have gone around to the side and into the drawing room through the French windows.

Good heavens, it must be very late indeed. Everyone would wonder where she was, where the tea tray was. Everyone was *tired.*

Everyone was still in the drawing room, she saw when she hurried into it after a footman had darted ahead of her to open the doors. They all turned to look inquiringly at her. Belatedly she realized that she must look flushed and disheveled — again. A few of those who were seated got to their feet. Barbara came hurrying toward her.

"Hannah?" she said. "Is something wrong? We heard a carriage."

She took Hannah's hands, and Hannah

squeezed them tightly. Her eyes found the Earl of Merton.

"Lord Merton," she said. "A private word with you, please. Oh, please. And please *hurry.*"

It was fortunate that there was a chair directly behind her. She collapsed onto it, her hands sliding from Barbara's as she did so. She was shaking uncontrollably. Her teeth were chattering. Her thoughts were racing about inside her head. She was, she realized in some dismay, going all to pieces.

And then the Earl of Merton was on one knee before her, and her hands were in his very steady ones.

"Your Grace," he said, "tell me what it is. Is it Con? Has he met with some accident?"

"He has g-g-gone," she said. She closed her eyes briefly, imposing some control over herself. "I am so sorry you have not all had tea yet. Will you order the tray, Babs, please? But may I talk to *you* outside, Lord Merton?" She tightened her hands about the earl's.

No one moved.

"Hannah," Barbara said, "tell us what has happened. We are all concerned. Did you quarrel with Mr. Huxtable? But no, it is more than that."

The earl's hands were still warm and

steady. Hannah looked into his blue eyes.

"How may I be of service to you?" he asked her.

He did not know. None of them did. Oh, foolish Constantine, to have been so secretive all these years.

It was not her secret to divulge.

But the time for secrets had passed.

"He has gone to Ainsley Park," she said, "his home in Gloucestershire. And home to a large number of unwed mothers and handicapped persons and reformed criminals and others rejected by society. One of the handicapped — I think he must be a little like Constantine's brother — let the fox in with the chickens and tried to compensate for the loss so that Constantine would not be disappointed in him, by taking chickens from a neighbor to replace them. He returned the chickens and apologized, and the manager of the project paid for the chickens in addition, but even so poor Jess has been sentenced to hang."

She gasped for breath. She was not sure she had paused for one during her explanation.

There were other gasps in the room. A few of the ladies clapped hands to their mouths and closed their eyes. Hannah was not aware of much, though, beyond the intent eyes of the Earl of Merton.

"So *that* is what Constantine has been doing in Gloucestershire," Lady Sheringford half whispered.

Hannah leaned a little closer to the earl.

"He took my carriage," she said. "He thinks he can save that poor man, but he probably will not be able to. Will you let me take *your* carriage? And will you escort me to London?"

"I'll go myself to Ainsley Park if I can discover where in Gloucestershire it is," he said. "I'll do all in my power —"

"I thought the Duke of Moreland . . ." she said.

"Elliott?" He searched her eyes with his own.

"Oh," she said, and the sound came out as a near wail. "I *wish* my duke were still alive. He would save Jess with one look in the right direction. But he is dead. The Duke of Moreland's word will count for a great deal."

"Elliott and Con have been bitter enemies since before I knew either," he said.

"That is because Constantine was selling the Merton jewels to finance the project at his brother's behest," she said. "It was all his brother's idea, though he embraced it wholeheartedly himself. But the Duke of

414

Moreland accused *him* of robbing his own brother and even of debauching the poor unwed mothers in the neighborhood, and Constantine would not contradict him, partly because he feared the duke would put an end to his brother's dream, and largely because of pride. The duke accused instead of asking."

She watched him draw in a deep breath, hold it, and then release it slowly.

"I am not sure Elliott will be willing to help, Your Grace," he said. "Let me —"

But Lady Sheringford was on her feet and approaching across the room.

"Of course he will help, Stephen," she said briskly. "*Of course* he will. He would not have remained angry with Constantine all these years if he did not care deeply for him. And if he even hesitates, *Nessie* will talk him into helping. She will be easy to persuade. She always likes to think the best of people. I have suspected for years that she would forgive Constantine in a heartbeat if he would only ask her forgiveness for whatever it was he did to hurt her."

"I must *go*," Hannah said, getting to her feet and withdrawing her hands from the earl's clasp. "Even now it may be too late." She slapped her hands to her cheeks. "But I have a houseful of *guests*."

Suddenly everything was taken out of her hands. The guests would *all* go, both to London and to Ainsley Park, if they followed mere inclination, someone declared — perhaps Lord Montford. But they could do nothing but get in the way. They would remain, then, and Stephen would go with her grace. Everything at Copeland ran so smoothly because of the duchess's careful planning, the Countess of Sheringford said, that her presence was not strictly necessary until they all left tomorrow morning. And Miss Leavensworth had been a perfect substitute hostess at tea yesterday and would be again at breakfast tomorrow. It would be a delight to have Miss Leavensworth return to town tomorrow in *their* carriage, Lady Montford said. Which was an extremely generous offer, Mrs. Newcombe declared, as of course *they* would gladly have taken Barbara with them, but she would have been severely cramped, poor dear, in the carriage with them and the twins. *Of course* Hannah could leave without any worries at all, Barbara added. She must *go.*

And Mr. Newcombe knew just where Ainsley Park was situated. Although he had never been there, it was no farther than twenty miles from his own home. He had even heard some good things about the training school there. He had not realized that the owner and Mr. Huxtable, his fellow guest here, were one and the same. If he had, he would have enjoyed a good heart-to-heart chat with him on the subject.

Cassandra had hurried from the room. She was going to come too and had gone to prepare the nurse and the baby for an imminent departure.

"Come, Hannah," Barbara said, quiet and efficient in her usual way. "You must change your clothes and have a bag packed. I will see to everything else."

Lord Sheringford had gone to order up the Merton carriage.

An hour later Hannah was on the way to London. The Earl of Merton sat opposite her with Cassandra. He was holding the baby, who was fast asleep. Apparently Cassandra had fed him before leaving.

Where was Constantine now? How far had he gone?

Would he be in time?

Would it matter even if he were?

Would the Duke of Moreland go?

Would *he* be in time?

Would his influence be powerful enough to stop the madness of hanging a mentally handicapped man whose only crime was trying to put right a wrong that had happened because of his carelessness?

If only her duke were still alive. No one would have stood against him. She had never known anyone with more power than the elderly Duke of Dunbarton. Except the king, perhaps.

The king.

The king.

Hannah pressed herself back into the corner of her seat and closed her eyes tightly.

Could she?

Could she? She was the Duchess of Dunbarton, was she not?

CHAPTER 18

The Duke of Moreland was at breakfast in his London home on Cavendish Square when he was informed that her grace, the Duchess of Dunbarton, and the Earl of Merton were in the visitors' parlor, requesting a moment of his time on a matter of some urgency. His duchess had joined him only a few moments before.

It was early. The duke was due at the House of Lords later and always liked to spend an hour with his secretary, discussing the business of the day, before he went. The duchess was still being dragged from her bed at an unholy hour each morning by a ravenous eight-month-old son, who had not yet learned that there were far more civilized hours at which to demand his breakfast.

They both appeared in the visitors' parlor long before Hannah could establish a satisfactory route to pace. She had changed her clothes since arriving in London a few hours ago, but she had not slept. She would have come and banged on the duke's door long ago if decency had not prevailed. The Earl of Merton had been good enough to arrive back at Dunbarton House a good ten minutes earlier than he had promised.

"Stephen," the duchess said, hugging her brother warmly, though she did look at him and then glance at Hannah with some curiosity.

"Duchess? Stephen? Good morning." The duke looked keenly from one to the other of them.

Hannah did not wait for any further preliminaries.

"You must help Constantine," she said, taking a few steps closer to the duke. "Please. You must."

"Con?" The duke's eyes came fully to rest on her — blue eyes in a narrow, dark-complexioned face with an austere, autocratic expression. So like Constantine and yet so unlike. "Must I, ma'am?"

"Constantine?" the duchess said at the same time. "Is he in some trouble?"

"A man is going to be hanged in Gloucestershire," Hannah said, feeling out of breath, as if she must have run all the way here instead of riding in the earl's carriage. "And Constantine has gone to save

420

him. But he will not be able to do it. He has no authority. You do. You are the *Duke of Moreland.* You must go there too *without delay* and help him. Oh, please."

It all seemed perfectly clear to her.

"Elliott," the Earl of Merton began, but the duke held up a staying hand.

"Vanessa," he said without taking his eyes off Hannah, "would you be so good as to have coffee brought in for the duchess? And for Stephen too, my love. They both look as if they must have just arrived back from Kent and have not breakfasted."

"I will have some toast fetched too," his duchess said as she left the room.

The duke took Hannah by one elbow and indicated a chair close by. She sat down heavily.

"Tell me about the man who is to be hanged, ma'am," he said. "And his connection to Con."

What had she said already? Probably not nearly enough. She had wanted to be as brief as possible so that he could be on his way to Ainsley Park without delay.

"He stole some chickens," she said, "because he was afraid Constantine would be disappointed in him for leaving the door of the coop unlatched and letting the fox in, but he did not really understand that he was stealing until it was explained to him, and then he apologized and took the chickens back, and they were paid for too, but some *stupid* judge thought he should be made an example of and sentenced him to hang. Oh, *will* you go and stop it?"

And where was the controlled, articulate Duchess of Dunbarton just when she was most needed?

The duke's eyes moved to the earl at the same moment as he surprised Hannah by taking one of her hands in his own and squeezing it.

"Stephen?" he said.

The duchess came back into the room.

"The property Con purchased in Gloucestershire," the earl said, "was apparently bought at Jonathan's urging, Elliott, to house unwed mothers and their children. Since it began, it has expanded to include handicapped people — both physically and mentally — and other people who find themselves rejected by society. I gather they are trained to find meaningful work elsewhere. The man in question is mentally handicapped and is inordinately fond of Con by the sound of it. He was responsible for losing some chickens to a fox, so he went and took some other chickens from a neighbor to replace them. It probably seemed logical to him. But he was arrested, and even the return of the chickens and a money payment in addition and an abject apology have been unable to save him from being sentenced to death."

"Is it *possible?*" the Duchess of Moreland asked, her eyes wide with shock. "Can a man hang for something so trivial?"

"The law is not often applied as strictly as it might be," the duke said. "But sometimes it is, and the judge is quite within his rights."

Why were they all wasting time *talking?*

Hannah dragged the dregs of her dignity about her and wished she were not so *tired* or her mind so addled.

"Constantine *loves* those people," she said. "He has devoted much of his adult life to them. If this man should be hanged, he would surely be destroyed. He would find a way of blaming himself. I *know* he would. Though I am sure he would tell you that *he* does not matter at the moment but only this poor condemned man. You have a quarrel with Constantine, Duke, and he with you. But quarrels are petty things at such a time. A man's life is at stake. Your influence can save him. I am convinced it can. I know *my* duke's influence would have saved him, and in many ways you remind me of him. You have a *presence,* as he had. Will you please,

please go to Ainsley Park?"

He looked steadily at her.

"I cannot make or change the law of the land, ma'am," he said.

"But the sentence for such a crime is discretionary," she said. "You said so yourself a few moments ago in so many words. The sentence could change. He does not have to *die* for taking a few chickens, especially when he did not even fully realize that he was stealing."

"I would imagine any judge's argument might be," he said, "that a man who can steal without even realizing it is a dangerous man who is very likely to reoffend, perhaps even to hurt someone in the process."

"He did it because he loves Constantine," she said, "because he could not bear to disappoint him over the incident with the fox. Can you tell me he deserves to *die?*"

"I am quite sure he does not, ma'am," he said. "But —"

"Will you not go for *Constantine's* sake?" she asked him. "He is your cousin. He was your *friend* until, as he put it, you behaved like a pompous ass and he behaved like a stubborn mule."

He raised his eyebrows.

"I should be thankful," he said, "that he paints himself in as unflattering a light as he paints me."

"Elliott," his wife said, coming across the room to lay a hand on his arm, "you must go. You know you must. If *you* do not, then I *will,* and you know very well that if I go I will have to take Richard with me so that he does not starve to death, poor baby, and Belle and Sam will need to come too so that they will not feel abandoned by their own mother. Besides, my influence would be of no more account than the Duchess of Dunbarton's. Less, indeed. She has a far more forceful character than I have."

"My love," the duke said, taking her hand and raising it to his lips, "you are being absurd. But you have made your point. Con needs me at last, and I will go to him. Doubtless he will punch me in the nose for my pains and we will end up looking even more alike."

"I'll go with you, Elliott," the Earl of Merton said.

Hannah looked at him in surprise.

"Cass insisted even before I had a chance to ask if she would mind terribly much if I went," he explained.

Hannah jumped to her feet as a footman stepped into the room bearing a large tray.

Oh, *please* let them not all sit down now to breakfast.

"I'll go home directly," the earl said, "and pack a bag."

"I'll come for you in one hour's time," the duke told him.

And they both left the room.

"Food is probably the very last thing in the world you feel like," the Duchess of Moreland said. "But have some toast anyway. I am going to have some. I had scarcely sat down for breakfast when you arrived."

She was pouring two cups of coffee as she spoke.

"I am so sorry," Hannah said, "to cause all this trouble."

"I am unaware that *you* have caused it," the duchess said, setting a cup and saucer down beside Hannah and going back to the tray to fetch a plate upon which she had set one slice of buttered toast, cut down the middle. "Do you love Constantine?"

"I —" Hannah began.

"That was an ill-mannered question," the duchess said with a smile. "Let me rephrase it as a statement. You love Constantine. I have seen it coming all Season. I have even felt a little sorry for you."

Hannah stared at her as she bit into her toast.

"I love him," she admitted at last. "I am sorry you do not. He said he did something to hurt you soon after he got to know you."

"He did," the duchess said. "And it was pretty nasty. It was meant to embarrass Elliott and humiliated me instead. It was really very childish, but men *can* be childish sometimes. Oh, and women too, I suppose. I refused to accept his apology. I judged him unforgivable, and I have lived with the guilt of that ever since. But by the time he apologized, I believed him guilty of far worse than the mischief in which I had been caught up. Elliott has been wrong about that, has he?"

"Yes," Hannah said. "But only because Constantine was too proud and too stubborn to *explain*."

"Men rarely take the easy way out," the duchess said. "Though sometimes they do when they raise their fists and go at each other's noses and eyes instead of talking like civilized beings. I sometimes think the power of speech was wasted on men. Oh, dear, I do not always have such a low opinion of them, I promise you. May I refill your coffee cup?"

It was empty, Hannah realized. She could taste coffee, though she had no memory of drinking it.

"No," she said, getting to her feet. "Thank you, but I must go. I have other urgent business this morning, and I must not hold you back from being with your husband for a short while before he leaves. Oh, how I *wish* I could go with him and the Earl of Merton. But I would merely delay them."

"Yes." The duchess smiled. "And it would not be at all the thing, even for the *Duchess of Dunbarton*. Elliott can be very autocratic when he chooses to be, Duchess. He will not easily take no for an answer in Gloucestershire. Neither will Stephen. He is sometimes mistaken for a meek, even perhaps a *weak* man because he is so amiable and looks so much like an angel, but he can be an *avenging* angel when he chooses to be. He will do it for Constantine's sake."

"Thank you," Hannah said.

The duchess walked to the door with her and then realized that her brother had taken the carriage. But Hannah would not allow her to call out another conveyance.

"I will walk," she said. "The fresh air will do me good, and there is a pleasant breeze."

The duchess surprised her by hugging her tightly before she left.

"You must come and have tea with me one afternoon," she said. "I will send an invitation. Will you come? I have always wished I knew you better."

"Thank you," Hannah said. "I would like that."

Where was he *now,* she wondered as she hurried away toward home. She did not doubt he had traveled through the night, stopping only for toll gates and a change of horses. She had warned her coachman to expect a nonstop journey. Would they be there by now? Or was he still on the road, wondering if he would be there in time, wondering if he could save his protégé?

And how soon could she decently present herself at St. James's Palace, requesting an audience with the king himself?

Would he see her?

Would he even be allowed to know she was there?

But *of course* he would grant her an audience. She was the Duchess of Dunbarton, widow of the *Duke* of Dunbarton.

Expect something, he had taught her, *and it is yours.*

She expected to see the king within the next few hours. But she needed to hurry home first in order to garb herself in all her finest armor.

Not a fake diamond was to be in sight this morning. And not the merest hint of any color except white.

■ ■ ■ ■

Constantine arrived at Ainsley Park in the middle of a wet afternoon, weary to the bone and unshaven. He found everyone there pale and disconsolate, from Harvey Wexford on down to Millie Carver, the twelve-year-old kitchen maid whom he had rescued from a London brothel almost two years ago just before she was to be offered to the highest bidder for deflowering.

Jess Barnes had one week of life left.

Constantine bathed and shaved and changed his clothes — he did not sleep — before riding to the jail in a town four miles away. Jess looked unwashed but otherwise well cared for. He dissolved in tears when he saw Constantine, not because he was going to die, but because he had let his benefactor down and expected to be scolded.

Constantine took him in his arms, dirt and lice and all, and told him that he loved him no matter what, no matter where or when.

And then Jess smiled sunnily at him and was reassured.

"Everyone sends their love," Constantine told him. "And cook has sent so much of your favorite foods that you will be fat if you eat them all. I am going to get you out of here, Jess, and take you back home. But not today. You will have to be patient. Can you do that?"

Jess could, it seemed, if Mr. Huxtable said he ought.

Not that he had any choice.

Constantine spent the following day in a futile attempt to get the charges against Jess dropped, to get the judge's decision reversed, to get the sentence commuted, to get the defense of insanity admitted, to do *anything* to save Jess's life and preferably to bring him back home to Ainsley.

Kincaid, his aggrieved neighbor, who had ended up with his chickens *and* their value in cash, would not look Constantine in the eye but was quite firm in his opinion that the harshness of the penalty was necessary both to remove a vicious evil from the neighborhood and to deter all the other potential threats to their peace and safety that were residing at Ainsley Park. If there was some way he could sue Huxtable himself for reckless endangerment to his neighbors or something else similar, then he would do it. He was still consulting lawyers on the matter.

Most of the other neighbors received Constantine with courtesy, even with sym-

431

pathy, but none of them was willing to stand up against Kincaid. A few of them, Constantine suspected, were secretly cheering the man on.

A lawyer gave as his professional opinion that the plea of insanity would not accomplish anything since Jess Barnes showed no signs of madness, only of feeblemindedness. He had never denied stealing. He had never denied knowing that it was wrong to steal. There really *was* no defense, only a plea for mercy.

The judge himself received Constantine politely, even with some hearty good humor. But he would not budge on the Jess Barnes case. The man was a menace to society. The county — indeed the whole country — would be well rid of him when he hanged. The judge might have sentenced him to a few years of hard labor if he had been of sound mind, but under the circumstances . . .

Well, Mr. Huxtable had been clever in choosing to man his farms and his house with cheap labor and loose women to keep the men and himself happy, but he had to expect that things like this would happen from time to time. They were both men of the world and understood these things, after all.

At home, Wexford was incapable of doing any productive work. If he could change places with Jess, he told Constantine, he would do it gladly. It was all his fault. He had told Jess that Mr. Huxtable would be disappointed in him, thinking that of all things would teach Jess not to be careless in the future. But it had caused all this — *and it was not even true.* Mr. Huxtable had never been disappointed in anyone at Ainsley except the very few who had left of their own accord, unwilling to work for their keep or observe the few rules that were necessary for the community to exist happily and productively.

Constantine had squeezed his shoulder, but he could give no other comfort.

Everyone else was almost equally upset. Jess was something of a favorite with them all.

By the next morning Constantine was in despair. He could not recall when he had last slept — or eaten. He had ridden in to see Jess again and then ridden home. He did not know what else he could do. He could not remember feeling this helpless ever before.

There must be *something.*

He remained in the stable yard to brush down his own horse. He heard the approach of a carriage before he saw it. A painful hope caused his stomach to lurch. Was it Kincaid, perhaps? Had he had a change of heart? And would it do anything to change the judge's mind?

He walked to the gateway and looked out when the carriage was close. He tried not to hope.

It was not a carriage that could be mistaken for any other. There was a ducal coat of arms emblazoned on the sides. The coachman and the footman beside him up on the box were in ducal livery. The whole conveyance must have caused a stir as it crossed the country — and as it passed through the village on the way here.

It was the carriage of the Duke of Moreland.

Elliott's carriage.

Constantine was too weary to feel any great surprise. He felt only a dull anger.

Elliott had come to gloat.

Though why he should come all this way just to do that he did not try to analyze.

He strode toward the house, just behind the carriage as its wheels crunched over gravel and came to a stop outside the front doors.

The footman jumped down smartly from the box and made off in the direction of the steps leading up to the doors.

"There is no need," Constantine told him. "I am here."

The footman turned, bowed, and returned to the carriage to open the door and set down the steps.

Elliott descended to the terrace, and Constantine's anger was full blown.

"You are lost," he said curtly. "Your coachman took a wrong turn somewhere. He should ask at the village inn for directions."

Elliott turned to him, and they stared at each other.

"It is Con Huxtable I am looking for," Elliott said. "You look like an unkempt, haggard version of him."

Someone else descended from the carriage.

Stephen.

Constantine turned his eyes on him.

"She could not keep her mouth shut, then?" he asked bitterly.

"*She* being the Duchess of Dunbarton?" Stephen said. "She was beside herself with anxiety, Con, not just for you but also for that poor condemned man. She begged me to escort her to London so that she could appeal to Elliott. She believed he could help. Are we still needed? Have you been able to clear up the madness without us?"

"I have not," Constantine said. "But I do not need help, Stephen. Neither yours nor Moreland's. The house is full. There are no rooms to spare. May I suggest *not* staying at the village inn but driving on to a more respectable coaching inn?"

He was behaving badly. He knew it and was powerless to stop it. He was so dashed *tired*. And angry. And *terrified*.

"A stubborn mule," Elliott said. "He named himself well, Stephen, would you not agree? But this *pompous ass* has not come all the way from London only to be sent on to the nearest coaching inn. He is going to throw his weight around — for what it may be worth."

Stubborn mule. Pompous ass. She really had been talking.

"I don't need you, Moreland," Constantine said. "And this is my property. Get off it."

"I *know* you don't need me, Con," Elliott said. "But perhaps Jess Barnes does. Not that I can promise to be any help. But I have come to try, and I am staying until I have done so even if I have to sleep in the carriage just beyond the gates of *your property.*"

"Con," Stephen said, "we care. A whole lot of people care. And why the devil did you not tell us about this place when I first

436

came to Warren Hall? Why make such a secret affair of it?"

"It was upon *your* jewels, or what were potentially yours," Constantine said, "that this place came into existence, Stephen. If you are as rich as a monarch now, you would have been as rich as *Croesus* if those jewels had not been put to another use."

"Do you think I would have cared?" Stephen asked. "Do you honestly think it, Con? Or that Meg would have cared? Or Nessie or Kate? Did you not owe it to your brother's memory to tell us?"

"No," Constantine said. "Jon did not do this to impress anyone. He did it because he wanted to, because it was *right.* And if I had told *you,* then Elliott would have known, and he would have done all in his power to reverse what had been done. This project was in its fragile early stages at the time."

"Surely he would not if you had explained," Stephen said. "*Would* you, Elliott?"

They both looked at him. He was staring at the ground, his features hard. There was a lengthy silence.

His cousin, Constantine thought. His best friend most of his life. His partner in crime when they had both gone to London as very young men to sow some wild oats.

And then Elliott's father had died suddenly, not long after Jon had made his ghastly discovery about their own late father's activities and dreamed his dream of Ainsley and made Constantine promise to tell no one about it. Jewels had been sold, Elliott had noticed they were missing and almost at the same time had found out about all those women and their children in the neighborhood. And the whole mess had blown up in the faces of Elliott and Con.

Ass and mule.

There was a soreness in Constantine's chest as he waited for Elliott to answer Stephen's question.

"I loved Jonathan," he said at last, without lifting his eyes. "It was a painful thing, that love. And then my father died, and I was responsible for him. I knew you were quite capable of looking after both him and his affairs, Con. But I was young and almost overwhelmed by all my new duties, and I felt obliged to do all that was proper and fully understand his business before bowing out and leaving all to you as my father did before me. But then I found that a large number of the jewels were missing, and you refused to explain but merely told me to go to hell when I asked, and —"

"You did not ask," Constantine said, his

voice flat.

His cousin looked up with an impatient frown.

"Of course I asked," he said. "I could not simply let something like that *go,* Con."

"You did not ask," Constantine said again. "You *told* me I was a thief."

"I did *not,*" Elliott said.

"Did." Constantine grinned without humor. "Did, didn't, did, didn't. Sound familiar, Elliott? We must have spent half our boyhood saying one or other of those words to each other. Often it ended in fisticuffs and then laughter. But not this time. It does not matter anyway. Even if you had asked and I had answered and you had believed me, you would not have allowed it to go on. You would have stopped Jon and ruined what turned out to be his life's work. His legacy."

"Surely not —" Stephen began.

But Elliott was staring at Constantine with unfathomable eyes.

"I probably would have," he admitted. "My instinct was to protect Jonathan, even from himself. I always marveled at the way you treated him like a regular person, Con, but one who needed to be met at his own level. I always marveled that you could *play* with him for hours on end even when he

439

had passed childhood. I thought my duty to him needed to be taken *seriously.* But you used to make a game even out of that and infuriate me. And you did it deliberately. You can have no idea how —"

He stopped abruptly and shook his head, his hands clenching and unclenching at his sides.

"You are quite right," he said. "I *would* have stopped him. I would have assumed that he could not possibly know just what he was doing. But he *did* know, didn't he? You always used to say, Con, that Jonathan was love. Not just loving, but *love.* You were right about that too. And you were right not to answer my questions — if indeed I asked them as I am convinced I must have. You were right to keep your secrets. You were right to be a stubborn mule."

"Don't send us away, Con," Stephen said. "Perhaps Elliott can help. Perhaps I can. Perhaps not. But don't send us away. We are your relatives, and you *need* us even if you do not realize it. Besides, the Duchess of Dunbarton sent us, and I believe she may well be brokenhearted if you turn us away without allowing us even to try."

Constantine stared broodingly at him.

Hannah had sent them.

Hannah.

The soreness in his chest deepened.

"There are spare rooms at the dower house," he said, pointing off to the east to where the house could just be seen nestled among the trees not far from the artificial lake that a previous owner had had constructed. "It is where I live. If it is not too humble for your tastes, you may stay there."

It was a grudging enough invitation. He was not sure if he was glad to see them or not. Perhaps it did not matter how he felt, though. He was not the issue here. Jess was. *Could* Elliott help? Elliott with his damned dukedom and his aristocratic air of consequence?

And his honesty?

"Please come to stay with me," he said before either man could answer. "You need baths and rest and a good meal before anything else. Come."

"When —" Elliott began.

"Four days," Constantine said abruptly. "There is all the time in the world."

And he went striding off ahead of them down the gravel path that led to the dower house.

Four days.

He could hear them coming behind him.

CHAPTER 19

Elliott and Stephen went off to call on the judge the following morning, both dressed with immaculate elegance. Elliott would not allow Constantine to accompany them. Not that either he or Stephen could have stopped him if he had chosen to go anyway, but he reluctantly conceded that it was probably for the best that he remain behind.

Elliott sought him out alone before they left.

"I have been having a look around, Con," he said, "and talking with some of your people. You are doing well here. You have been doing well for some time."

Constantine looked at him, tight-lipped.

"Did that sound condescending?" Elliott asked with a sigh. "It was not meant to be. I am brimful of admiration. And contrition. And shame. It was not you with all those women, was it? It was — my uncle? Your father?"

Constantine said nothing.

"Mine was no better," Elliott said. "I grew up believing him to be a paragon and devoted to my mother and my sisters and me. It was only after his death that I learned about his long-term mistress and the rather large family he had had with her. Did you know about them? The whole of the rest of the world seemed to, including my mother."

"No," Constantine said.

"I had been living a pretty wild existence for the previous few years," Elliott continued. "I was suddenly terrified that I would turn out like him, that I would be a wastrel, that I would let down my mother and sisters as he had done. And so I lost all my humor, Con, all my sense of proportion. And when you resented my interference, as you saw it, in Jon's affairs and did all in your power to annoy me, I only grew more irritable. Especially when I realized that things were not as they ought to be at Warren Hall, that my father had neglected his duty in yet another area of his life."

It was, Constantine supposed, some attempt at an apology.

"Jonathan discovered the truth about your father?" Elliott asked.

"Yes. Two of the women — two sisters — came to talk to him when I was away one day," Constantine said. "I had never seen him so upset, so disillusioned. Or so excited as on the day he concocted his grand scheme. I doubt I could have denied him my help in bringing that to pass even if I had disagreed with him. Which I did not. I had known for years. It had sickened me for years. But the little help I had been able to provide had been akin to wrapping a small bandage about a belly rip."

"Con," Elliott said after a short silence. "You were not innocent in what happened between us. I am almost certain that I *asked*. But even if I did not, you could have denied the charges, forced me to listen to the truth. I would have believed you. Good God, you were my *friend*. We were almost like brothers. But you did not *want* me to know. You did not *want* me to believe. You admitted it yesterday. For of course, as Jonathan's new guardian, I would not have permitted him to continue to denude his own estate for the sake of what would at the time have seemed a mad project. And I would have been right. He ought not to have been allowed to be so reckless. I would also have been wrong. Colossally wrong. But none of us could have predicted that at the time. It would not have been easy for me, Con. By withholding the truth, you enabled both

Jonathan and yourself to do what was right. But you forfeited our friendship in the process and made me into the sole villain. The pompous ass."

"You were," Constantine said.

"And you were the stubborn mule."

They stared at each other. The stare threatened to become a glare until Elliott spoiled it all by allowing his lips to twitch.

"Someone should paint us," he said. "We would make a marvelous caricature."

"You are doing all this just for Jess?" Constantine asked.

"And for the Duchess of Dunbarton," Elliott said. "And for Vanessa. She longs to forgive and be forgiven, Con."

"To be forgiven?" Constantine said with a frown. "I am the one who wronged her. Horribly."

"But you apologized," Elliott said, "and she would not forgive you. I know she has felt bad about that ever since. When the duchess called on us with Stephen, Vanessa saw a chance for some redemption. Perhaps for all of us. If I came for any one person, I came for her. I love her."

"I know," Constantine said.

"And I came for you too," Elliott said, looking sharply away. "You are, despite everything, someone I once loved. Perhaps

445

someone I still love. Good God, Con, I have missed you. Can you fathom that? I believed all those things about you, and I *missed* you?"

"This is getting almost embarrassing," Constantine said.

"It is," Elliott agreed. "And Stephen is probably waiting for me. Before I join him, Con, will you shake my hand?"

"Kiss and forgive?" Constantine said.

"I will forego the kissing if it is all the same to you," Elliott said, holding out his right hand.

Constantine looked at it and set his own in it.

"As I remember it," he said, "you did not ask, Elliott. You *assumed.* But as you remember it, you asked, and I told you to go to hell. We can never know who is right. Maybe it is just as well. But you had just lost your trust in your own father, and I was desperate to preserve Jon's dream. We never were good at talking to each other about *pain,* were we?"

"A gentleman never admits to feeling any," Elliott said as they clasped each other's hand tightly. "I have to put on all the full force of my pomposity now. I'll try not to be an ass, though, Con. I'll try my best to get Barnes reprieved. I hope my best

446

is good enough."

"So do I," Constantine said fervently.

He still felt sore that he was going to have to remain behind at Ainsley, idle and helpless. But for the moment the best he could do was let his cousins go and do what he could not. Or at least try.

And if they failed?

He would grapple with that when the time came.

When? Not *if?*

He headed off for the farm, hoping there was some hard manual labor in which he could immerse himself.

For the next three and a half hours he was, Constantine soon became aware, the focus of attention at Ainsley. He was chopping wood beside the stable block. He had stripped to the waist and was giving the task his full attention and every ounce of strength and energy he could muster. Nothing in the world mattered except piling up enough wood to last through next winter — and perhaps even the winter beyond that.

The grooms and stable hands were all at work in the stables. None of them took a break, even when midday came and went. But every single one of them found some plausible reason for appearing at the stable yard gate with strange regularity. No fewer than three of the women were weeding the kitchen garden even though Constantine had observed just two days ago that there was not a weed in sight. Perhaps it was the hunt for new ones that was taking them so long. Two of the boys were handing him logs to chop when one would have been quite sufficient. Millie carried out a tray of drinks and oatmeal biscuits twice and stayed to help one of the boys stack the wood against the outer wall of the stables the second time. The cook came to the side door, presumably to see what had happened to Millie. But instead of calling her to come back or returning to the kitchen after seeing that she was busy, she stayed where she was for some time, drying her hands on her apron. They must have ended up being the driest hands in England. Roseann Thirgood was giving her group of reading pupils a lesson outdoors, perhaps because the weather was warm and the wind gentle enough that it took only two hands to hold open the pages of each book. Another of the women felt it necessary to shake her duster out of a side window of the house every few minutes and to lean out to see where the dust landed.

They all knew, of course, that Elliott and

Stephen had gone to talk to the judge, though Constantine had not told anyone. And they all knew why he was chopping wood so ferociously. None of them spoke to him. Or to one another, for that matter. Except Roseann to her pupils, he assumed, though he did not hear any of them.

And then everyone who had disappeared for a few moments reappeared, and everyone who was busy — or pretending to be — stopped work, and the weeders straightened up, and Millie dropped the two pieces of wood she was carrying. The cook dropped her apron. Constantine paused, the axe poised above his shoulder.

Horses.

And carriage wheels.

He lowered the axe slowly and turned.

The same ducal carriage as yesterday. The same coachman and footman, their livery brushed to a new smartness since yesterday.

Constantine even forgot to breathe for a moment. If he had thought about it, he would have been willing to wager that everyone else forgot too.

The carriage did not proceed all the way to the front doors. It stopped outside the stables. Perhaps the men inside had seen the scattered crowd and Constantine in their midst.

Stephen jumped out first, without waiting for the steps to be put down. He looked about him and then at Constantine, who felt rooted to the spot. He had not moved closer to the carriage.

"It hangs in the balance," Stephen called for all to hear.

An unfortunate turn of phrase.

Elliott also descended without benefit of steps.

"The judge is to consider the matter," he said, also loudly enough for everyone to hear. "His final verdict is by no means sure, but if he *does* reprieve Jess Barnes, it will be into my keeping and on condition that I take him far away from here and never allow him to return to any part of Gloucestershire."

Constantine was almost convinced he heard a collective exhaling of breath. Or perhaps it was only his own he heard.

He set down the axe against a stack of unchopped wood and walked closer to his cousins, who were walking closer to *him.*

"Elliott was absolutely magnificent, Con," Stephen said. "I almost quaked in my boots myself."

"No, you did not," Elliott said. "You were too busy oozing your legendary charm, Stephen. I was almost dazzled myself."

"But the judge was not quite convinced," Constantine said.

"To give the man his due," Elliott told him, "he has backbone, Con. I had the impression that as the day draws closer, he is beginning to regret the harshness of the sentence but has been unable to see a dignified way out. You must have softened him up. He wants to give us what we ask, but he does not want to give the impression that he has been overawed by a couple of men with titles but really no authority over him."

"You think he will let Jess go, then?" Constantine asked.

"Do I *think* he will?" Elliott said. "Yes. Am I *certain* he will? No."

"Has he said when he will make his decision?" Constantine asked.

"Tomorrow," Stephen said.

"But either way, Con," Elliott said, "Jess will not be returning here. I am sorry. Promising to take him with me was the best I could do."

Constantine nodded. And his eyes went past Elliott's shoulder, past the carriage to the driveway beyond. A single horse and rider were approaching at a canter.

Everyone else had heard it too. They all turned.

The judge had made his decision?

It was a chance visitor?

But they could all see as the horse drew closer that the rider was wearing bright livery and that it was looking slightly the worse for wear. He had clearly ridden a long way, probably without stopping except for a change of horse and a quick bite to eat.

"By God," Stephen said, "that is *royal* livery."

There was no doubt about it. The rider was a king's messenger.

He reined in his horse behind the carriage and looked about rather haughtily before focusing his attention on Elliott.

"I am commanded to deliver a message to Mr. Constantine Huxtable," he said.

"I am he." Constantine raised one arm — one *bare* arm dotted with wood shavings — and stepped forward.

The messenger looked haughtier.

"I can vouch for his identity," Stephen said, sounding amused. "I am Merton."

The fellow reached into his saddlebag and withdrew two scrolls affixed with the royal seal.

"I was to hand this to you first, sir," he said, "on the express orders of His Majesty the King."

And he handed one of the scrolls to Constantine, who looked at it as if merely doing so would disclose its secrets. He exchanged glances with Elliott and Stephen, broke the seal, and unrolled the scroll.

He felt the blood drain from his head. He licked his lips. The parchment shook in his hands. He looked up.

"A pardon," he said in a near whisper. And then he raised his head, looked about him, and raised his voice. He held the parchment aloft. "A pardon. A *royal* pardon for Jess. The *king* has repealed the sentence."

"If you will direct me to the judge concerned, sir," the messenger said, "I will deliver a duplicate of that document into his hands without further delay."

No one heard him. There was cheering and laughter and the clapping of hands. And everyone spoke at once, the volume of voices increasing as everyone realized that no one was listening because everyone was talking. Almost everyone. Two of the weeders were dancing with each other in a circle, shrieking as they did so. The cook had thrown her apron over her face. Millie was wailing openly, tears pursuing each other in rivulets down her cheeks.

Constantine shut his eyes tightly and lifted his face to the sky.

"The minx," he said fondly.

"Well," Elliott said, "so much for my being needed, Con."

But he was grinning when Constantine looked at him and stepped up to him and caught him up in a bear hug.

"You were needed," he said. "You were needed, Elliott. You are *always* needed."

And then he embarrassed himself horribly by sobbing, his forehead against Elliott's shoulder.

He felt Elliott's free hand against the back of his head.

"Devil take it," Constantine said, taking a step back and swiping the back of his hand across his wet face. "*Devil* take it."

Elliott pressed a white linen handkerchief into his hand.

"Love is allowed, Con," he said.

Stephen was blowing his nose into his own handkerchief.

The king's messenger was clearing his throat.

"I was commanded to hand this to you next, sir," he said and handed Constantine the second scroll.

Constantine stared up at the rider as he took it. But the man was a messenger, not the message.

What more was there for the king to say? *Ha, ha, I did not mean it — Jess Barnes dies after all?*

454

Constantine broke the seal and unrolled the parchment and read.

And then read it again.

And then chuckled. And then laughed aloud as he handed it to Elliott. Elliott read it — twice — and then handed it off to Stephen before looking at Constantine and laughing with him.

"I say," Stephen said after a few moments. "Oh, I say."

And all three of them were laughing while everyone else looked on, wondering what the joke was.

"What *is* it about time, Babs?" Hannah asked from her favorite perch on the window seat of her private sitting room. "When one is enjoying oneself, it flies by like a bird frantic to reach its nesting ground after a long winter, and just as with that bird there is no stopping it. At other times, it crawls by like a tortoise dosed with laudanum."

Barbara worked at her embroidery.

"There is no such thing as time," she said. "There is only our reaction to the inexorable progress of life."

Hannah stared at the top of her head.

"If I pretended to *enjoy* not knowing what is happening, then," she said, "I would have news of it in a flash, Babs? Could the answer be *that* simple? Please say yes."

Barbara looked up and smiled.

"I am afraid not," she said. "Because the illusion of time creates time itself. Our reactions are too strong to halt it altogether. We are lamentably human. And wonderfully human too."

"You did not learn all this from your vicar, by any chance, did you?" Hannah asked suspiciously.

"From discussions with him, yes," Barbara admitted. "And from my private reflections and some reading that Simon suggested."

"If I cannot halt the illusion any more than I can reality," Hannah said, "then there really is no point in knowing that it *is* illusion, is there? Or in deciding that it is, in fact, reality. And is my head spinning on my shoulders, or is *that* only illusion too?"

Barbara merely laughed and lowered her head to her work again.

"The king promised to help, Hannah," she said.

"But the king's memory is notoriously unreliable," Hannah said. "He means well, but he is easily distracted. I was not the only petitioner to see him that morning, or the last. The fact that he *wept* over my story means little. He weeps over *everything* that contains even one speck of sentiment."

"You must trust him," Barbara said. "And the Duke of Moreland and the Earl of Merton. And Mr. Huxtable himself."

Hannah sighed and picked up a cushion to hug to her bosom.

"It is so hard to trust anyone but oneself," she said.

"You have done all you can," Barbara said. "*More* than all."

Hannah regarded the top of her head again for a while. She considered getting up from her perch and prowling about the room — again. She considered going outside for a brisker walk, but it was raining and the wind was blowing, and Barbara would insist upon going with her. And she would probably contract a chill and have to be dragged back from death's door over the next week or so.

Sometimes Barbara could be a severe annoyance.

"You were supposed to go home as soon as we returned from Kent," she said. "You were *longing* to go home even though you were too polite to say so. And yet here you sit, quietly patient, Babs. I would be *raging* if it were me."

"No, you would not." Barbara looked up at her once more. "You are a far better person than you would have others believe, Hannah. If it were you, you would stay with me for as long as I needed you. We are friends. We *love* each other."

Hannah heard a gurgle in her throat and swallowed. She widened her eyes so that they would not fill with tears. She was dangerously close to becoming a watering pot these days. She had also been a virtual recluse since her visit to St. James's Palace. Though her new friends had been obliging enough to call yesterday afternoon. They had come all together — the *three* Huxtable sisters and their sister-in-law — and had stayed for an hour and a half, far longer than a mere polite afternoon call required. They had been almost as anxious for news as she was.

"You love your vicar," she said. "You should be with *him,* Babs."

"I will be," Barbara said. "We will be married for the rest of our lives after August. When I hear from him, I am as sure as I can be that he will tell me I have done the right thing in staying with you. I thought I would hear today. There will surely be a letter tomorrow."

She returned to work, and Hannah heaved a deep sigh.

And then she held her breath, and Barbara sat with her needle suspended above her cloth.

From a distance below them they had both heard the knocker being rapped against the street door.

"Visitors," Hannah said with an attempt at nonchalance. "They will be told I am not at home."

But she listened for the sound of footsteps outside the door, and when it came, she tensed and pressed the pillow against herself as though she must guard it with her life.

"A gentleman for Miss Leavensworth, Your Grace," her butler said when he opened the door.

"Tell him — For *Barbara?*" Hannah said.

"A Reverend Newcombe, Your Grace," he said, glancing at Barbara. "Shall I inform him that you are from home?"

"Simon?" Barbara spoke softly. Her needle was still suspended above her work. Suddenly, Hannah thought, she looked quite incredibly beautiful.

"Show him up here, if you please," Hannah said.

She never entertained visitors in her private parlor.

She swung her legs to the floor as the butler withdrew, and cast aside the cushion. Her first instinct was to hurry from the room, to leave the field clear for the reunion of the lovers. But she could not resist seeing it for herself and meeting Barbara's betrothed.

Barbara was calmly and methodically putting away her embroidery and then checking to see that her hair was tidy and that no crumbs of her tea remained on her dress. She looked up at Hannah.

"This is why there was no letter from him today," she said. "He has come in person."

She was still radiating beauty. Her eyes were huge and luminous.

It was the look of love, Hannah thought. She had seen it in her own looking glass lately. And much good it would do her.

The door opened again after a token tap.

"The Reverend Newcombe for Miss Leavensworth," the butler said.

And in stepped the most ordinary young gentleman Hannah could possibly have imagined. He was just as Barbara had described him, in fact. He was neither tall nor sturdily built nor handsome. He was dressed soberly and decently and quite without flair. But as soon as his eyes lit upon Barbara, he smiled — and Hannah knew why her friend, who had routinely rejected a number of perfectly eligible suitors throughout the years of her youth, had finally lost her heart to this man.

She was beaming back at him.

Goodness, Hannah thought, if it had been *her,* she would have hurtled across the room by now with a bloodcurdling shriek and launched herself at him.

"Barb," he said.

"Simon."

After which loverlike outburst they both recovered their manners and turned their attention to Hannah.

"Hannah," Barbara said, "may I have the honor of presenting the Reverend Newcombe? The Duchess of Dunbarton, Simon."

The vicar bowed. Hannah inclined her head.

"You have come in person to bear Barbara off homeward," she said. "I do not blame you, Mr. Newcombe. I have been very selfish."

"I have come, Your Grace," he said, "because my future father-in-law very kindly offered to take my Sunday services for me and allow me a short holiday in London, even though I will be having another after my nuptials. I came because it seems years rather than merely weeks since I last saw Barbara. And I came because you are in distress and I thought perhaps I could offer

461

you some spiritual comfort."

Hannah bit her lower lip. Laughter would be inappropriate. And indeed, though part of her wanted to dissolve into giggles, a nobler part of her was deeply touched.

"I thank you, sir," she said. "It *is* an anxious time. A man's life is at stake, and I care even though I have never met him and probably never will. Someone I *have* met has a deep emotional involvement in the matter, and I have a deep emotional involvement with *him.*"

She had not meant to put it quite like that. But the words were out now, and they were the truth. One ought to tell the truth to a clergyman.

"I understand, Your Grace," he said, and it seemed to Hannah that indeed he did.

"I have urgent business elsewhere in the house," she said, "and must be an imperfect hostess, I am afraid, Mr. Newcombe, and quit this room. I will leave you Barbara, however. I daresay she will do her best to entertain you in my absence."

"I daresay she will, Your Grace," he agreed.

Hannah smiled at him, and he smiled back with such sweet good humor that she might have fallen in love with him herself if there had been a vacancy in her heart.

She smiled and winked at Barbara with

the eye that was farthest from the Reverend Simon Newcombe and hurried from the room just as if she really did have a thousand and one tasks awaiting her.

What was *happening* in Gloucestershire? And why did no one think *to write to her?*

CHAPTER 20

The Reverend Newcombe had come all the way to London, and the most entertaining thing he could find to do on his first full day there was visit a bookshop on Oxford Street that he remembered from his student days.

He had come to Dunbarton House to invite Barbara and Hannah to accompany him. And Barbara was glowing with enthusiasm at the prospect.

Hannah gazed from one to the other of them as they all sat in the drawing room drinking coffee. It really was quite extraordinary. It was not even a shop for *new* books. It was probably filled with dust. It was undoubtedly filled too with old tomes so dry that they were crumbling away to create more dust.

"You must come with us, Hannah," Barbara pleaded. "You have scarcely been over the doorstep for several days, and the sun is shining again today. You must not fear that you will be in the way." She blushed.

"I fear no such thing," Hannah said. "You are both too polite to admit even to yourselves that my presence would be de trop. I shall go walking in Hyde Park this afternoon and receive my court and learn all the newest gossip with which to regale you both at dinner. You *will* dine here, Mr. Newcombe?"

"Thank you, Your Grace," he said, inclining his head. "I —"

He was interrupted by a tap on the drawing room door.

"The Earl and Countess of Merton wish to know if you are at home, Your Grace," the butler said when he had opened it.

Hannah shot to her feet. Cassandra? And *the earl* too?

"Show them up," she said.

It was as much as she could do not to run after him and overtake him on the stairs so that she could arrive in the hall ahead of him and discover *what had happened.*

"The Earl of Merton," Barbara was explaining to her vicar, "went to Ainsley Park with the Duke of Moreland to see what they could do to intercede for the condemned man."

"Yes," the Reverend Newcombe said, "I remember the names from your letter, Barb.

And now the earl has returned, perhaps with news. Let us hope it is *good* news. Your concern for a poor misguided man, Your Grace, does you great credit. But it does not surprise me. Barbara has told me —"

Hannah stopped listening. Not because she was being deliberately impolite, but because her thoughts were whirling out of control. She stepped as close to the door as she could and not be bowled over by it when it opened again. She clasped her hands at her waist. She tried to gather her dignity about her.

The Duke of Moreland had not come with the earl? *Constantine* had not?

There was a tap on the door and it opened again.

"The Earl and Countess of Merton, Your Grace," the butler announced.

The earl looked travel worn. Although his clothes did not look unduly rumpled or his face unshaven, there were signs of weariness about his eyes, and it seemed to Hannah that he must have returned home to Merton House only long enough to see his wife. And Cassandra was — beaming.

"All is well," she said and hurried forward to catch Hannah up in her arms. "All is well, Hannah."

Hannah sagged with relief as she submitted to the hug.

"I daresay you knew as much, Your Grace," the earl said. "It is you who must have persuaded the king to intervene. But I suppose you have been anxious anyway to hear that the pardon arrived in time. It did. With three days to spare, in fact."

Only three days?

"It was a complete pardon," he added. "Jess Barnes is free. I promised Con when I left that I would let you know within an hour of my return to London. And I took the liberty of traveling here in your carriage, Your Grace. Con will come with Elliott later."

"With the Duke of Moreland?" Hannah raised her eyebrows. "The two of them together in one carriage?"

He grinned.

"And they will probably not even come to blows," he said. "Or preserve a stony silence either."

"They have settled that foolish quarrel?" Hannah asked.

"They have," he said. "For the first time I have seen them together as they must have been most of their lives before I met them both. They talk incessantly and joke — and even argue. And lest you need more assurance, I will add that it was upon Elliott's shoulder Con chose to weep when he read the king's pardon even though mine was just as close and just as available."

"Oh." Hannah pressed her hands together and brought her mouth down to the tips of her fingers. She closed her eyes and pictured Constantine weeping. How embarrassed he must have been. And how furious he would be if he knew that his cousin was telling her about it.

Men could be very foolish about such things.

How strange that one could be so wrong about another person. She had always called him the devil to herself. He *looked* dark and dangerous enough to justify the name. He was quite the opposite. He was all light and love and compassion. Oh, and perhaps a little dark and dangerous too. He was a dizzying mix of human qualities, in fact — as most people were.

She positively *ached* with love for him, foolish woman that she was.

All of which was quite inappropriate to the moment anyway. She lifted her head, smiled, and turned to introduce her visitors to the Reverend Newcombe.

He and Barbara were both on their feet. Barbara's eyes were glistening with unshed tears. She hurried forward to hug Hannah.

"I *knew* the king would not forget," she said.

Would this now be the end, Hannah wondered. The earl had just said that Constantine would travel back to town with the Duke of Moreland. But would he change his mind and stay at Ainsley since the Season was already more than half over? Would he *need* to stay, as he had intended anyway, to help console poor Jess and soothe some ruffled feathers among his neighbors? Now that he was away from her, would he decide that this was a convenient time to end their affair?

She had told him she loved him. *That* might persuade him to keep his distance from her for the next year or two.

Or would he come back? Would he resume their affair as though there had been no interruption?

Would *she?*

She had not thought about it before now. And now was not an appropriate time. She had two sets of visitors to entertain, though Cassandra was in the process of explaining that they would not stay, that they must go and let Vanessa know what had happened and how soon she could expect the duke's return home.

Would she continue living here by day,

going to Constantine's house by night so that they could make love?

She ached to make love. To be made love to.

She was his mistress.

He was her lover.

Was it enough?

It was what they had agreed upon. It was what she had *wanted* for this, her first year of freedom. Indeed, she was the one who had initiated the whole thing.

Had she changed her mind so soon?

She could not *bear* for them not to be lovers any longer.

She could not bear for them to *be* lovers either.

She really did love him. She had told him the truth about that — which may, of course, not have been a wise thing to do.

Why did *loving* him and being his lover seem like two mutually exclusive things?

Ah, she thought as she bade the earl and Cassandra a good day and thanked them for coming, she was no more calm and in control of her emotions now than she had been at the age of nineteen. The eleven intervening years might never have been.

Except that now she could see that she had a clear choice before her and that it was she alone who must make it. Calmly and rationally. Provided Constantine himself did not make it for her, that was, by staying at Ainsley.

Would they remain lovers for the rest of the Season?

Or would they not?

The choice could not be simpler.

Making it was another matter, of course.

"*Will* you come with us, Hannah?" Barbara asked when the three of them were alone with one another in the drawing room once more. "You no longer have to wait at home for news, do you? It has come, and it is the very best news possible."

"Why not?" Hannah said, looking from one to the other of them. "Let us celebrate by going to look at some old books."

The Reverend Newcombe beamed.

Constantine remained at Ainsley Park for four days after Jess had been freed and Stephen had taken the duchess's carriage and returned to London.

He felt the need to be with his people for a while as they all recovered from their terrible anxiety and settled back to their normal everyday life. He felt the need to call upon all his neighbors and talk openly with them about the situation at Ainsley. He could not promise them that awkward situations like this one would never arise again, but he could and did remind them that the incident with Jess was the first of its kind in all the years he had been here. And he explained that all his people appreciated the new chance in life they were being given here and were doing all in their power to become respectable and productive individuals again. He was not running a thieves' den — or a brothel. Even Jess was not a thief by nature, but a man who had tried to put right a wrong without thinking through what he was doing. And Jess was leaving. He would not be at Ainsley ever again.

Most of his neighbors received him with courtesy. A few received him with warm kindness. A few others reserved their judgment. Kincaid was openly skeptical though not unduly hostile. Time would bring him around, Constantine believed and hoped.

He stayed at Ainsley for four days so that Jess could recover somewhat from his ordeal and accustom himself to the idea that his training at Ainsley Park was over and that he was to be promoted to a position he had always dreamed of, that of stable hand. The Duke of Moreland was offering him such a position at Rigby Abbey, his own country estate. It was going to be hard on them all to see him go, Constantine explained, but the duke was his cousin, and if he *must* let Jess move on to a better position, then he would rather it be with a relative than with a stranger. And he would be able to see Jess from time to time when he visited the duke. He would be able to bring him news of all his friends at Ainsley.

He had never been to Rigby Abbey himself.

One thing that surprised him was that Elliott chose to remain at Ainsley too, though it was obvious he hated being away from his wife and children. He stayed to renew their friendship. There could be no other reason. And renew it they did, tentatively at first, with growing ease as the days passed.

It felt like a gift, a balm to the soul, to have Elliott back. Constantine had not realized just how much he had missed him. Losing him and then losing Jon had all been mixed up together in one massively lonely emptiness.

Now he had Elliott back. And they talked about Jon. They shared memories of him — not the painful last ones, but those encompassing the previous fifteen years or so.

Constantine found those four days healing and relaxing, though a part of him fretted to be back in London. Even so, he tried to keep his mind off Hannah as much as he could. He was not ready yet to think.

She had told him she loved him.

By the time he returned to London in Elliott's luxurious carriage, Jess up on the box with the coachman while the footman rode behind, Constantine had been gone from London for almost two weeks.

He had to go and call upon the duchess to thank her for her intervention on behalf of Jess — he could hardly call it *interference,* could he? — and for the use of her carriage.

He found himself strangely reluctant to go, though. What would happen now? A return to the status quo? She would be his mistress again? He would be her lover again?

He longed for her. It was almost three weeks since he had last had her.

They were having an *affair.* A sexual fling. A temporary one, until the Season's end, for their mutual pleasure.

Good God, was that what they were having?

It sounded damnably . . . what was the word his mind sought? *Cheap? Sordid? Unsatisfactory?* Definitely that last. Probably those first two as well. But that was strange. His previous affairs had never seemed any of the three. He had enjoyed them for what they were worth, ended them when the time came, and put them behind him.

An affair with Hannah, of course, was not enough.

He *loved* her.

He had scarcely thought of her in the past week and a half. Not consciously anyway. And yet she had been there at every moment of every day. A part of him.

It was dashed alarming.

Or was it?

She had told him she loved him before he left Copeland. Did she mean it? In *that* way? Devil take it, but he had so little experience with love. With that kind of love anyway. But perhaps everyone did until love came and punched them between the eyes. What did her actions say? Did they bear out her words?

What had she done after he had left — in *her* carriage?

She had dragged Stephen back to London with her, bearded Elliott in his den, packed the two of them off to Gloucestershire, and then dashed off to rouse the king.

All for a mentally handicapped stranger?

Hardly, compassionate as she undoubtedly was.

Elliott, on the seat opposite him in the

carriage, yawned.

"You were staring fixedly into space when I dozed off, Con," he said, "and you are still doing it when I wake up again. Worried about Jess, are you? You did a fine job of convincing him he has graduated with honors from Ainsley and has been promoted to Rigby. And I can be kind enough to my employees when I forget to be the autocratic duke."

Constantine looked at him.

"I am deeply in your debt," he said. "For everything."

Elliott grinned.

"Do you imagine for one moment," he said, "that I am going to let you forget it?"

Constantine chuckled.

"No," he said. "I know you from of old."

"Are you going to marry her?" Elliott asked.

And there it was. The idea his mind had been skirting about for days.

He wanted to marry. He wanted to have children. He wanted all those things he had avoided for years. He wanted to settle down.

But — with the Duchess of Dunbarton?

With Hannah?

It was like thinking of two different persons. But she was one and the same. She was both the duchess as he had always known her and Hannah as she had revealed herself since they became lovers. She could not be summed up in one word or one sentence. Even in one paragraph. Even in one book or one *library.* She was a vibrant, complex individual, and he loved her.

"The idea had not crossed my mind," he said.

"Liar!" Elliott was still grinning.

"What made you know beyond a shadow of a doubt that you wanted to marry Vanessa?" Constantine asked.

"I didn't," Elliott said. "*She* proposed to *me,* and I was so shocked that I said yes before I knew what I was doing and was stuck with the decision forever after."

"If you don't want to tell me," Constantine said, "you can just say so, you know."

Elliott held up his right hand.

"Honest truth," he said. "By the time I loved her more than life, I was already married to her and didn't have to go through all the agony of deciding how and where and when and *whether* to make my offer."

"She might laugh at me," Constantine said.

"It is a distinct possibility," Elliott conceded after thinking about it for a moment. "She is a formidable lady, is she not? Not to mention *beautiful.* She could probably have any unmarried man in the realm she chose to set her sights upon. She *might* laugh at your suit, Con. She might also weep. That would be more promising."

"The *Duchess of Dunbarton,* Elliott," Constantine said. "I would have to be mad."

"Why?" Elliott said. "You have much to offer, Con, and you are considerably more eligible today than you were a week ago." He grinned again.

Constantine shrugged.

"Vanessa swears," Elliott said, "that there is passion beneath all that sparkling white ice, Con, and that when the duchess finds an object upon which to focus it, she will be as constant as the north star. Vanessa tends to know these things. I would not dream of arguing with her upon such matters. I would turn out to be wrong, and she would gallantly refrain from saying *I told you so,* and I would feel like an idiot."

"Hmm," Constantine said.

"For your edification," Elliott added, "she says that you have become that object, Con. You had better come with me to Moreland House as soon as we get back to town, by the way, and make your peace with Vanessa before you go off to Dunbarton House."

"Right," Constantine said before setting his head back and pretending to sleep so that there would be no more such talk.

He dozed off while wondering if she would laugh or weep if he offered her marriage.

Or whether he would give her the opportunity to do either.

CHAPTER 21

Hannah thought she must have been right to fear that Constantine would stay at Ainsley and so avoid the issue of their affair and the words she had so incautiously spoken to him when they were at Copeland. He did not return to London the day after the Earl of Merton or even the day after that.

But, she discovered after three days, neither did the Duke of Moreland. They were both still out of town. Hannah found that out when she met the duchess during the afternoon when they were both calling upon Katherine to see if she was still suffering morning sickness.

So perhaps he would return after all. The *duke* certainly would.

In the meantime, it did not take Hannah long to discover that she had tired of her new favorite almost as quickly as everyone had predicted. She had cast him off without pity, and he had gone off into the country to lick his wounds. She was looking about her for a new lover, who would have his moment in the sun before being cast off in his turn. Everyone wondered who he would be. There was no lack of eager candidates.

This, at least, was the gossip that was doing the rounds of London clubs and drawing rooms. It would have been amusing had she not been so consumed with anxiety lest *she* be the one abandoned.

There was nothing to be done, however, but to live up to expectations while she waited. She was certainly not going to stay at home like a recluse any longer. On one brilliantly sunny afternoon she donned her most dazzling white muslin dress and bonnet, added ostentatiously large diamonds to her earlobes and gloved fingers and one wrist, raised a white lacy parasol over her head, and sallied forth for a walk in Hyde Park at the fashionable hour.

Barbara and the Reverend Newcombe accompanied her. It was their last day in London. Tomorrow they would return to Markle, Babs in a carriage with her maid, the vicar on horseback beside it so that all the proprieties might be observed. Hannah had wanted them to spend their last afternoon in town alone somewhere together — she had suggested Richmond Park — but they had insisted upon remaining with her.

They were soon surrounded by people, most of them male, though not all. Margaret and Katherine were together in an open barouche and stopped to talk for a while. Katherine, upon learning that Barbara was to leave the next day, insisted that Hannah come to dine in the evening. And Margaret invited her to attend the opera with them the evening after.

"We have almost but not quite persuaded Duncan's grandpapa to come with us," she said. "If he knows *you* are to be of our party, Hannah, he will surely come."

"Then tell him I have accepted *only* on condition that he does too," Hannah said. "Tell him that if he fails to come, I shall be at Claverbrook House the following morning to demand an explanation from him."

Barbara and the Reverend Newcombe were talking with Mr. and Mrs. Park and another couple.

The barouche drove on, and Hannah was swallowed up in a circle of her old male friends, some of whom were also would-be suitors, and a few new admirers. It felt very comfortable, she thought after a few minutes, to be back within the old armor, playing the part of the Duchess of Dunbarton while guarding the more fragile person of

Hannah Reid safely within.

And yet it was a part that could not be played indefinitely. She had not realized that until now. She certainly had not realized it at the start of the Season. Playing the part had been easy and even enjoyable while the duke had lived. There had been his company, his companionship, and — yes — his *love* in which to bask when she was not on public display. But now? There was only loneliness to look forward to after she went home. And Babs was leaving tomorrow.

Would new friends and old be enough in the coming days and months — and years?

Oh, Constantine, where are you? And are you going to avoid me if and when you return?

She was laughing at something Lord Moodie had just said and tapping him sharply on the sleeve of his coat when her court parted down the middle to let a horse through. A queer sort of hush descended too.

It was an all-black horse.

Constantine's.

Hannah looked up and gave her parasol a violent enough twirl to create a slight breeze about her head.

Constantine. All in black except for his shirt. Narrow-faced. Dark-eyed. Unsmiling. Almost sinister. Almost satanic.

Her dearly beloved.

Goodness, where had *those* fanciful words sprung from? The marriage service?

"Mr. Huxtable?" Her eyebrows arched upward.

"Duchess."

Her court hung upon their words as though they had delivered a lengthy monologue apiece.

"You have deigned to favor London with your presence again, then?" she asked.

Her court sighed with almost inaudible approval of her disdain for a man who had come back after she had rejected him. His time was over, that near-silent sigh informed him. The sooner he rode on and bore his heartbreak with some dignity, the better for all concerned.

For answer, he held out one hand, clad in skin-tight black leather. His eyes held Hannah's with an intensity that made it impossible for her to look away.

"Set your foot on my boot," he said.

What?

"Oh, I say," one unidentified gentleman protested. "Can you not see, Huxtable, that her grace . . ."

Hannah was not listening. Her eyes were fighting a battle of wills with Constantine's. She was dressed as unsuitably for riding as she could possibly be. If he wanted to speak with her, it would be far easier and infinitely more gallant for him to descend from his horse's back. But he wanted to see her — and he wanted the *ton* to see her — make a spectacle of herself. He wanted to provide the *ton* with talk of scandal to last a month. He wanted to show the world that he was master, that he had merely to snap his fingers for her to come running.

She gave her parasol one more twirl and looked mockingly up at him.

There was another near-inaudible sigh of approval. If Hannah had looked about her, she would have seen that her court had grown in number and that its members were no longer all male. There was already fodder enough here for drawing room conversation to last a fortnight.

Hannah slowly and deliberately lowered and furled her parasol before handing it without a word or a glance to Lord Harding-graye beside her. She took two steps forward, lifted her skirt with one hand to set her very delicate white slipper on the high gloss of Constantine's hard black riding boot, and reached up her other hand to set in his — white silk on black leather.

The next moment, without any further effort on her part, she was seated sideways on the horse in front of his saddle, and his black-clad arms and hands bracketed her front and back so that even if she had been inclined to fear for her safety she could not possibly have done so.

She was not inclined to fear.

She turned her head and looked into the very dark eyes, now almost on a level with her own.

He was turning the horse, and the crowd was moving back out of his way. The crowd also had a great deal to say and was saying it — to her, to him, to one another. Hannah did not even try to listen. She did not care what they were saying.

He had come.

And he had come to claim her.

Had he?

"That," she said, "was very dramatic."

"Yes, wasn't it?" he said. "I understood upon my return, which was a mere couple of hours ago, by the way, that I was your scorned, rejected swain. For very pride's sake I had to make some extravagant gesture."

"It certainly was extravagant," she said as he weaved his horse skillfully among the horses and carriages that half clogged the path ahead.

"*Am* I?" he asked.

"Scorned?" she said.

"Rejected."

"And a swain," she said. "I like the image of you as a swain. My dress is going to be ruined, Constantine. It will smell of horse for the rest of its life."

They were not quite clear of the crowd. They were fully visible to every part of it. And there were probably very few people among it who were not taking full advantage of that fact.

He kissed her anyway — full on the lips, with open mouth. And it was no token peck. It must have lasted a full fifteen or twenty seconds, which under the circumstances was an *eternity.*

And since she must endure it anyway as she was definitely *not* in any physical condition to fight him off, Hannah kissed him back, prolonging the embrace by at least another ten seconds.

"There," he said when he raised his head. His eyes were looking very deeply into hers. There was no escaping them. Her very soul was invaded and captured. She invaded his in return. "You have been thoroughly compromised, Duchess."

"I have," she admitted with a sigh. "And what do you intend to do about it, sir?"

She wished she had not spoken those

words once they were out of her mouth. They were too much like an ultimatum.

"I *am* a gentleman, Duchess," he said. "I intend to marry you."

She responded with a huge and awkward swallow that almost choked her. She looked away from him, noted that the crowd had been left behind and they were almost alone on the path, rural parkland all about them, and attempted to put back the armor in which she had been so comfortably encased just a few minutes ago.

"Do you?" she said coolly. "And were you planning to consult me, Constantine? Or, since it appears you have literally swept me off my feet, were you assuming that it would be unnecessary to do so?"

"I was *hoping* it might be," he said. "I suppose every man dreads the actual proposal scene of his own love story. But I see you are not to be fooled or deprived of it, Duchess. It is going to have to be a down-on-one-knee thing, then, is it, something I can hardly do at this precise moment. I do not doubt that though we have left the crowds behind, they would come running from all corners of the park if I were to get down off my horse and lift *you* down and proceed to business right here. It is going to have to wait for another occasion, then."

Despite herself Hannah was laughing.

"You seem very confident of success," she said.

"That is as much as you know about me," he said. "If you knew me better, you would understand that I am babbling, Duchess, and that my heart is thumping quite erratically. We will change the subject. Jess is free and happy and puffed up with pride, all thanks to you, I believe. I do not suppose the king heard about his plight in the natural course of events."

He was *changing the subject?* After informing her that he was going to marry her, he was now going to talk about *Jess Barnes and the king?*

Well.

She looked nonchalantly about her.

"I happened to see him," she said, "and happened to mention the case to him. He wept. He would have wept if I had told him I had torn my favorite lace handkerchief."

He laughed.

"Happened to see him," he said. "Strolling on Bond Street, I suppose."

"Constantine," she said, closing her eyes briefly, "is Jess Barnes *really* safe? Will not your neighbors be out to exact some justice of their own against him?"

"He is on his way to Rigby Abbey," he

said. "Elliott's country estate. He has been promoted from a farm hand to a stable hand. He is the happiest and proudest man in England."

"Elliott," she said. "The duke. You are reconciled with him, then?"

"I think we have mutually agreed that we behaved like prize asses," he said. "And we have both admitted that perhaps it had to be that way so that Jon's dream could come true. Our friendship had to be sacrificed for a while for that end — and I would do it all again if I had to. So would Elliott — try to protect Jon from himself, that is, and Stephen's inheritance from his rashness. But we are friends again. Cousins again."

"And almost brothers?" she said.

"And that too," he said. "Yes. And that too."

She smiled at him, and he smiled back.

Her heart melted.

He opened his mouth to speak again.

And a trio of young horsemen who were riding toward them whistled as they came and called out to them with good-natured ribaldry as they passed. Hannah lifted her chin and wished she had her parasol to twirl.

Constantine grinned back at the young men, all of whom Hannah recognized.

"I had better take you home, Duchess,"

he said. "I need to call upon Vanessa and see if she is willing to make peace with me. Elliott wanted me to go there first, but I happened to hear the popular interpretation of my quitting London in the middle of the Season and felt compelled to set the record straight, especially when I discovered from your butler that you were walking in the park."

"You must not keep her waiting any longer, then," she said. "She has become my friend during the past two weeks."

And they rode back to Dunbarton House to the astonishment and delight of everyone they passed in the streets — and to not a few pointed comments. Constantine lifted her down outside her door, waited while she ascended the steps, watched her disappear inside, and rode off.

Without another word.

If she had still had her parasol with her, Hannah thought as she climbed the stairs to her room, she would have bashed him over the head with it before leaving him.

One did not *tell* a woman that one was going to marry her and then fail to *ask*.

Not, presumably, unless one was Constantine Huxtable.

I suppose every man dreads the actual proposal scene of his own love story.

491

She heard the echo of those words of his and *ran* up the last few stairs.

His own love story.

And then she stopped abruptly. That scene he had enacted in the park was surely the most shockingly *romantic* thing that had ever happened to her. He could not *possibly* have done it simply to assert his masterdom over her.

He *loved* her.

She laughed aloud.

The romantic gestures had not ended. The following morning, less than an hour after Barbara's departure, when Hannah was feeling somewhat down in spirits, a single white rose was delivered to Dunbarton House. There was no card with it. At the same time a gigantic bouquet of multicolored flowers of all kinds arrived, done up with glossy yellow ribbons, complete with Hannah's parasol and a flowery, amusing note from Lord Hardingraye, who could be as outrageously flirtatious as he wished without danger of being taken seriously because she knew — and he *knew* she knew — that in one essential respect he was of the same persuasion as her duke had been.

The bouquet was set on a table in the middle of the drawing room, to be enjoyed by all comers for days to come. The rose found its way to her bedchamber, where she alone would enjoy it.

An hour later the butler brought her a note on his silver salver. It had a brief message and no signature.

I lust after you.

Not so very romantic, perhaps, but Hannah smiled as she read it for perhaps the dozenth time — after ascertaining that its author had not delivered it in person and was not waiting in the hall below.

She recognized the beginning of a game.

She dined during the evening with the Montfords and enjoyed their company and conversation along with that of Mr. and Mrs. Gooding and the Earl and Countess of Lanting — the ladies were Lord Montford's sisters.

The next morning a dozen white roses were delivered to Dunbarton House, again with no accompanying card. They were taken up to Hannah's sitting room.

An hour later the butler came with a note atop his salver.

Again it was unsigned.

I am in love with you, it read.

Hannah held it to her lips, closed her eyes, and smiled.

The wretch. The absolute *wretch.* Did he

have no respect for her nerves? Why did he not simply *come?*

But she knew the answer. He had been speaking the truth in Hyde Park — *if you knew me better, you would understand that I am babbling, Duchess, and that my heart is thumping quite erratically.*

The foolish man was nervous.

And long may it last even though the wait seemed interminable. Nervousness was making him quite the romantic.

She went to the opera during the evening with the Sheringfords and the Marquess of Claverbrook and sat with her hand on the sleeve of the latter for most of the evening while they exchanged remarks. The tenor brought tears to her eyes just with the beauty of his voice. The soprano brought tears to the marquess's eyes just with her beauty. He chuckled low as Hannah laughed.

"But not with her voice?" she asked.

"That," he said, "just gives me the headache, Hannah."

Much of the attention of the audience was focused upon their box, and Hannah wondered idly if tomorrow's gossip would be that she was digging her claws into yet another elderly, wealthy aristocrat. The thought amused her.

The following morning it was two dozen roses that arrived — blood-red roses. No note, of course. That came an hour later.

I LOVE YOU, it read, *my multipetaled rose.* No signature.

Hannah wept and thoroughly enjoyed every tear.

She was supposed to go to Lord and Lady Carpenter's Venetian breakfast during the afternoon. Contrary to the name of such entertainments, they were *not* morning affairs. It did not matter either way. She did not go.

She donned a dress she had worn only once about three years ago. She had not worn it again because it made her feel like a scarlet woman inside as well as out, and that was too blatant a disguise even for her. She loved it nevertheless, and today it matched her roses. She wore a single diamond on a silver chain about her neck — a teardrop that would not dry or lose its luster — and no other jewelry.

She waited.

There was no improving upon two dozen red roses.

There was no more to be said on paper either. He had even written the first three words of the last note in capital letters. The rest had to be spoken aloud, face-to-face.

If he could muster the courage.

Ah, her poor, dear devil. Tamed by love.

He would, of course, find the courage. And he would be quite splendid — when he came.

She waited.

CHAPTER 22

This love business, Constantine had discovered over the past several days, could quite unman a person. He had a new respect for married men, all of whom had presumably gone through the ordeal he was currently going through. With the exception of Elliott, of course, who had been proposed *to,* lucky man.

Reconciling with Vanessa had been easy.

"Don't say a word," she had said, hurrying across the drawing room of Moreland House toward him as soon as he had set foot inside it, while Elliott had stood by the fireplace, one elbow propped on the mantel, one eyebrow cocked in amusement. "Not a word. Let us forgive and forget and start making up for lost time. Tell me about your prostitutes."

Elliott had chuckled aloud.

"*Ex*-prostitutes," she had added. "And don't you dare laugh at me, Constantine,

497

just when we are newly friends again. Tell me about them, and the thieves and vagabonds and unwed mothers."

She had linked her arm through his and drawn him to sit beside her on a sofa while Elliott had looked on with laughter in his eyes and on his lips.

"If you have an hour or six, Vanessa," Constantine had said.

"Seven if necessary. You are staying for dinner," she had told him. "*That* is already settled. Unless, that is, you have an engagement with Hannah."

An unfortunate choice of words. And *Hannah,* was it?

"No," he had said. "I have to work myself up to falling on one knee and delivering a passionate speech, and it is going to take some time. Not to mention courage."

Elliott had chuckled again.

"Oh, but it will be worth every moment," Vanessa had told him, her eyes shining, her cheeks flushed. "Elliott looked very splendid indeed when *he* did it. On *wet grass,* no less."

Constantine had looked up reproachfully at his grinning cousin.

"It was *after* Vanessa had proposed to me," he had said, raising his right hand. "I could not allow her to have the final word, now, could I? She said yes before I did."

Theirs might be a story worth knowing, Constantine had thought.

In going impulsively to Dunbarton House within two hours of his return to town, he had hoped to settle the matter with Hannah. And then, when he had found her from home but had learned she was in Hyde Park, he had gone in pursuit of her and had seen — without having to stop and think — the perfect way of declaring himself.

It had not struck him that she might refuse to mount his horse with him. And indeed she had not done so.

It had not occurred to him that after she had done so and after he had kissed her quite lasciviously and *in public,* and she had kissed him back, she might then refuse to marry him.

Not that she had refused.

It was just that he had not asked.

And he had not even realized that until she had pointed it out. Dash it, there was all the difference in the world between asking and telling, and he had *told.*

Just like a gauche schoolboy.

Why was there not a university degree course in proposing marriage to the woman of one's choice? Did everyone mess it up as thoroughly as he had done?

And so he had had to spend three days making amends. Or three days procrastinating. It depended upon whether one was being honest with oneself or not.

But once he had started, he had to allow the three days to proceed on their way. He could hardly rush in with his proposal after sending just one rose and the declaration that he *lusted* after her, could he?

If she intended to refuse him, he really had been making a prize ass of himself during the three days.

But there was no point in thinking about that, he realized as he dressed to make his afternoon call at Dunbarton House on the third day. He could not possibly *not* go now to see this wretched ordeal to its conclusion either way.

What if she was not at home? There must be a thousand and one reasons for her to be out — picnics, garden parties, excursions to Kew Gardens or Richmond Park, shopping, strolling early in the park, to name but a few of the myriad possibilities. Indeed, he thought as he rapped on the door, it would be surprising if she *were* at home.

The baser part of his nature hoped she was out.

Except that he could *never* go through this again.

The butler, as usual, did not know the contents of his own domain. He had to make his way upstairs as if there were no hurry at all to discover if the Duchess of Dunbarton was at home or not.

She was at home. And willing to receive him, it seemed. He was invited to follow the butler upstairs.

Would she have Miss Leavensworth with her?

They passed the doors of the drawing room and climbed another staircase. They stopped outside a single door, and the butler tapped discreetly on it before opening it and announcing him.

It was a parlor or sitting room, not a bedchamber. She was alone there.

On a table beside the door were a dozen white roses in a crystal vase. On a low table in the middle of the room were two dozen red roses in a silver urn. Their combined scent hung sweetly on the air.

The duchess sat sideways on a window seat, her legs drawn up before her, her arms crossed over her waist. She looked startlingly, vividly beautiful in scarlet red, which matched the roses almost exactly. Her hair lay smooth and shining over her head and was dressed in soft curls at her neck, with wispy tendrils of ringlets at her temples and ears. Her head was turned into the room, and she regarded him with dreamy blue eyes.

He was reminded of the scene in his own bedchamber the night they became lovers. Except that then she had been wearing only his shirt, and her hair had been loose down her back.

The butler closed the door and went on his way.

"Duchess," he said.

"Constantine."

She smiled — also dreamily — when he did not immediately continue.

"I need your protection," she said. "I have been receiving anonymous notes."

"Have you?" he said.

"Someone," she said, "*lusts* after me."

"I'll challenge him to pistols at dawn," he said.

"He also claims to be in love with me," she said.

"Easily said," he told her. "It does not go very deep, does it, that euphoric, romantic feeling?"

"But it is one of the most lovely feelings in the world," she said. "Perhaps *the* most lovely. I am quite in love with him in return."

"Lucky fellow," he said. "I am *definitely*

going to call him out."

"He says he *loves* me," she said, and her eyes made the almost imperceptible but quite remarkable change from dreamy to luminous.

"What is *that* supposed to mean?" he asked.

"Mind to mind," she said. "Heart to heart. Soul to soul."

"And body to body?" he asked.

"Oh, yes," she said, her voice a murmur of sound. "And that too."

"No barriers," he said. "No masks or disguises. No fears."

"None." She shook her head. "No secrets. Two become one and indivisible."

"And this," he said, "is what your anonymous penman is saying to you?"

"In capital letters," she told him.

"Ostentatious fellow," he said.

"Absolutely," she agreed. "Just look at all the roses he has sent me."

"Hannah," he said.

"Yes."

He was still standing just inside the door. He strode toward her, and she held out her right hand. He took it in both his own and raised it to his lips.

"I *do* love you," he said. "In capital letters and in every other way I can think of. And in every way I *cannot* think of for that matter."

He heard her inhale slowly.

It was time. And he was no longer nervous. He dropped to one knee, her hand still in his. His face was on a level with her own. The color was high in her cheeks, he could see. Her lips were slightly parted. Her eyes were still luminous and very blue — like the sky beyond the window.

"Hannah," he said, "will you marry me?"

He had been rehearsing a speech for three long days. He could not remember a word of it.

"Yes," she said.

He had been convinced that she would tease him, that she would play the part of Duchess of Dunbarton at least for a while before capitulating — *if* she capitulated at all. He had been so convinced, in fact, that he almost missed her response.

With his *ears* he almost missed it.

But with his heart?

"Yes," she had said, and there really was nothing else to say.

They gazed at each other, and he raised her hand to press against his lips again.

"He used to tell me about it," she said. "About love. And he used to promise me that I would know it for myself one day. I trusted him and believed him for every moment of my life from our first meeting to his final breath, Constantine, but I did not fully believe him in that. I believed that *he* had loved an extraordinary love for more than fifty years. But I was afraid to believe *I* ever would. I was wrong to fear, and he was right to be confident for me. I love *you*."

"And will for more than fifty years?" he said.

"He used to say it was for eternity," she said. "I believe him."

He smiled at her, and she smiled back until he moved his head closer to hers and kissed her.

It had been almost three weeks since they had last made love, and it had seemed to him that he had been hungry for her every moment of every intervening day. Nevertheless, it was not with sexual hunger that they kissed. It was with . . .

Well, he had only ever kissed with sexual appetite and did not have words for this.

Affection? Far too tame.

Love?

A much overused word.

But whatever it was, they kissed with it.

And then, as their arms closed about each other and he lifted her from the sill and got to his feet with her so that he could turn and sit on the window seat with her on his lap, he knew the word. Or the best one available, anyway.

They kissed with *joy.*

And then they smiled into each other's eyes as though they were the ones who had discovered it. Joy, that was. Love ever after.

"Are you quite sure," he asked her, "that you are willing to sacrifice your title simply for the pleasure of marrying me, Duchess?"

"To be simply Mrs. Huxtable?" she said. "At least you will have to call me *Hannah* all the time, and I like that."

"Or *Countess,*" he said.

She looked blankly at him.

"That would be a little absurd," she said.

"Not really," he told her. "The king sent *two* royal proclamations after your visit to him, you know. Or perhaps you do *not* know. The one was Jess's pardon."

She sat upright on his lap when he did not continue and frowned down at him.

"And the other?" she asked.

"You have just agreed to marry Constantine Huxtable, first Earl of Ainsley," he said. "The title was awarded for extraordinary service to the poorest and dearest of His Majesty's loyal subjects. I believe I have quoted him more or less accurately."

Her jaw dropped.

And then she threw back her head and laughed.

The new Earl of Ainsley laughed with her.

The Earl and Countess of Merton were hosting a ball at Merton House the following evening on the occasion of the anniversary of their betrothal ball there the year before.

They had invited family members to dine with them before the ball — Stephen's three sisters and their spouses, and Cassandra's brother, Sir Wesley Young, and his fiancée, Miss Julia Winsmore. They had also invited Constantine since he was Stephen's cousin. And the Duchess of Dunbarton, who was no relative at all.

"I really hoped," Cassandra said as she and Stephen awaited the arrival of their dinner guests in the drawing room, "that by today it would not seem at all odd that we have invited her, Stephen. Con has been back in London for the better part of a week, and Hannah has been here since we brought her with us from Copeland. And she is the one who persuaded Elliott to go to Ainsley Park and then talked to the king himself. She saved the day almost single-handed. But nothing has *happened* yet. Will this dinner be an embarrassment, do you think?"

"Why should it?" he asked. "The duchess has become your friend, and it is perfectly acceptable to invite one's friend to dine. We intend to announce Con's new title at the ball tonight, and she was definitely instrumental in bringing that about. She will surely realize that Con is to be one of our dinner guests and will simply stay away if coming will be embarrassing for her. I do not believe the duchess embarrasses easily, however."

"That scene in the park," she said. "Meg described it so amusingly and Kate so romantically. And everyone has talked about it ad nauseam ever since. And yet — nothing has *happened.*"

"We don't know that," he said. "Nothing has been *announced.* We do not know that nothing has *happened.* They are entitled to some privacy in their own affairs, Cass."

She sighed.

"We were all so horrified," she said, "when Con began his affair with her. Not that we were supposed to know about it, of course. Such affairs are always supposed to be secret. She seemed so unsuitable for him. So . . ."

"Arrogant?" he suggested.

She frowned.

"Well, she did," she said. "But people are not always what they seem to be, are they? I ought to know that better than most. Perhaps she has always been . . . well, someone warm and full of fun, someone I very much want as a friend. Someone *good*. *Why* are she and Con not affianced?"

Stephen stepped up close to her and kissed her on the mouth.

"Perhaps," he said, "you can ask each of them as soon as they arrive. Perhaps you can make it a topic of conversation at the dinner table. I am sure my sisters will have something to say on the matter. They seem to have taken the duchess to their collective bosom, just as you have. Even Nessie."

She laughed and punched him lightly on the arm.

"It would be a lovely opening line," she said, "as soon as each walks in — *why are you not betrothed?* I am not a matchmaker, Stephen, but Con is such a lonely man, and Hannah is a lonely woman."

"And therefore," he said, "they must belong together."

"Therefore nothing," she said tartly. "They *do* belong together. Anyone who was at Copeland with the two of them would have had to be both blind and stupid not to see it."

They were saved from further conversation on the subject by the arrival of Vanessa and Elliott and Wesley and Julia almost simultaneously, and then by the appearance of Katherine and Jasper and Margaret and Duncan soon after.

"Is Con coming?" Elliott asked while they were all sipping their drinks.

"He said he was," Stephen said.

"And Hannah?" Margaret asked.

And they were at it again.

"Mama says they have no choice but to marry," Julia Winsmore said, "after the way he kissed her in the park. I saw it with my own eyes. It was really quite shocking."

She blushed.

"And very romantic too, Jule," Sir Wesley said. "That is what you told me at the time, anyway."

"I do not believe," Elliott said, "the duchess would ever be moved by the argument that she has no choice but to do a particular thing."

"She clearly loves Constantine," Katherine said. "She will torture him before saying yes."

Her husband exchanged a pained glance with Duncan over this blatant example of feminine logic.

"Or no," Margaret said.

"Con is no one's fool," Stephen said. "He dances to no one's tune."

"But he is in love," Cassandra pointed out.

And that stifled the conversation. There was silence for a few moments.

The butler appeared and murmured to Cassandra that dinner was ready. It must wait a little longer, she murmured back. She could imagine the consternation her reply would arouse in the kitchen.

And then the remaining two guests arrived — together and a little more than five minutes late.

Both were looking quite radiant enough to send expectations soaring — at least among the ladies gathered in the drawing room. And to cause Cassandra to forgive them instantly for putting her on the outs with her cook.

The Duchess of Dunbarton was looking resplendent in soft turquoise with very little jewelry. None was necessary. She was going to be drawing all eyes her way all evening without them. The sparkle and luster that was usually on the outside of her person was glowing from the *inside* of her person tonight.

"If we are late," she said before any greetings could be exchanged, "the fault is entirely mine. I was all ready *long* before I expected Constantine, but just as I heard his knock at the door I decided that I did not want to wear my favorite white ball gown after all — or all the diamonds that went with it. So I changed while he kicked his heels and ground his teeth down in the hall."

She smiled dazzlingly about her.

"I never grind my teeth," Constantine said mildly. "I would have them ground down to stumps if I did it every time you are late, Hannah. I am going to cultivate the virtue of patience. I am going to learn to *enjoy* waiting around. You had better not be late for our wedding, though. It is said to be bad luck."

And so all questions were answered without any having to be asked.

And dinner had to wait another quarter of an hour as hugs and kisses and back slaps and handshakes were exchanged and Hannah declared that it was all very lowering but she had agreed to be demoted all the way down from duchess to *countess.*

"Though plain Mrs. Constantine Huxtable would have suited me admirably too," she added with another of her radiant smiles.

And her eyes sparkled with unshed tears, and she bit her lower lip, and Constantine set one arm about her shoulders — and Cassandra suggested that they proceed to the dining room before her cook resigned on the spot.

CHAPTER 23

They had argued since yesterday about where they would marry. Though *argued* was perhaps not quite the right word since both were fully intent upon being unselfish in the matter.

Constantine thought they should marry at Copeland as it was Hannah's home and she clearly loved it. A bride ought to marry from her own home.

He was wise enough not to mention Markle.

Hannah thought they should marry at Ainsley as it was Constantine's home and he clearly loved it. Besides, it seemed fitting that the new Earl of Ainsley should marry at Ainsley Park.

They agreed that St. George's was the best and most convenient compromise. It was on Hanover Square, a mere stone's throw from Dunbarton House. The bride could walk there. The whole *ton* could be expected to attend. Perhaps even the king would come. It was the fashionable place to marry.

Neither of them wanted to marry there, though neither was willing to admit it to the other.

It was going to have to be Copeland.

Or Ainsley.

Or perhaps St. George's.

"Tell us about your nuptials, Your Grace," Miss Winsmore said as soon as they were all seated about the dinner table at Merton House. "When and where are they to be?"

"As soon as possible to answer your first question," Hannah said. "We still have not decided the answer to your second."

She drew breath to give her vote for Ainsley Park, expecting that Constantine's family would back her up, but the Earl of Merton spoke first.

"But you must marry at Warren Hall, Con," he said. "It is still and always your home. It is where you were born, where you grew up. The private chapel has always been used for family weddings and christenings and . . . burials," he added more softly.

"Oh, that would be *so* lovely," Cassandra said as footmen served the first course. "But Hannah may have other ideas, Stephen. It is her wedding as well as Con's."

But she gazed at Hannah with wistful eyes.

"Elliott and I married there," Vanessa said, "as did Cassandra and Stephen last year. It is the loveliest place for a wedding. The chapel is in a quiet corner of the park, among the trees, and it is full to overflowing with just a few guests. There is a wonderful sense of history there too with the churchyard surrounding the chapel. *Family* history."

It must be where Jonathan was buried, Hannah thought. And suddenly she knew that that was where they *must* marry. She felt a sense of rightness about it even before she looked across the table at Constantine and noted the intense, drawn look on his face.

"It is good of you to be willing to lend us the chapel, Stephen," he said. "But I think Hannah must be allowed to —"

"Choose for herself?" she said, interrupting him. "I will, then. Thank you. *I* will choose."

She knew that his smile came at a great cost.

"I choose Warren Hall," she said, her eyes on his.

And she felt almost as though she were falling into them as his smile faded.

"Are you sure?" he asked.

"I am absolutely sure," she told him, and

she was. "Warren Hall it will be. Thank you, Lord Merton. You are very kind."

"I think I had better be Stephen," he said, "if you are going to marry Con. I think we had better *all* be on a first-name basis."

And suddenly everyone was talking at once, and the dinner was being consumed with great appetite. Margaret, Vanessa, and Katherine had the grand ballroom at Warren Hall and the private chapel decorated for the wedding festivities before the main course was removed, and Cassandra had the menu for the wedding breakfast drawn up before dessert was served.

"You might as well relax and let things happen, Con," Elliott advised. "You have done your job. You have offered Hannah marriage and been accepted. The rest is in the hands of the ladies."

For a day or two before her wedding, Hannah was informed, she would stay at Finchley Park, one of the Duke of Moreland's estates adjoining Warren Hall, the place where he had grown up. So would several other people, including Vanessa and Elliott and their children and Elliott's mother and sisters and any personal guests Hannah chose to invite. But she must not worry, Vanessa assured her. There was a picturesque and secluded dower house by the lake at Finchley, where she and Elliott had spent their honeymoon. It was where Hannah and Constantine must spend *theirs*. And if there were a more romantic setting in which to begin a marriage, Vanessa did not know where it might be.

"Do you remember the *daffodils?*" she asked Elliott.

And the rather austere Duke of Moreland was observed to wink back at her.

Hannah caught Constantine's eye across the table, and they exchanged a smile that might well have been imperceptible to anyone else. He had warned her on the way here that his female cousins on his father's side were a formidable trio, and that Cassandra was proving to be a worthy addition to their number. If Hannah was not careful, he had told her, her wedding would be taken right out of her hands and caught up in their very capable ones.

And that was before he had known the wedding would be in their domain — at Warren Hall.

"Oh, dear," Katherine said suddenly, and the tone of her voice caused a general hush about the table. "We are at it again. We grew up in a small country village, Hannah, as children of the vicar. There were always things to be done and things to be organized. And we were the ones who tended to step forward to do them and organize them. Unless *someone* does it, you know, nothing gets done at all and country life becomes unutterably dull. But though we have left that life behind, we have never got out of the habit of *organizing*."

"We have not indeed," Margaret said with a sigh. "You have never been known as a helpless, indecisive lady, Hannah. I daresay you have been sitting there laughing at us. You probably have your wedding all planned without any help from us."

All eyes were on her, Hannah was aware, the ladies' rather wistful, the gentlemen's more amused.

"I am not laughing," she said. "Quite the opposite." And, sure enough, she had to blink away tears. "And I have never planned a wedding — or had one planned for me. I agreed yesterday to marry Constantine, but I can see today that I will be marrying into his family too, and I am happier about that than I can possibly say."

The duke had *told* her that when she found love she would find the community of belonging that went with it.

It was almost time for the ball to begin. The gentlemen did not linger in the dining room after the ladies left. They all adjourned together to the ballroom to await the arrival of the first guests.

Constantine's new title was to be announced at supper, Hannah knew. And so was their betrothal. It was the beginning of a new era. She glanced down at the lovely turquoise of her gown and was glad she had changed out of her white dress even though doing so had made her late. She did not have to hide any longer. She did not have to fortify herself with any armor of ice and diamonds.

She was the Duchess of Dunbarton, soon to be the Countess of Ainsley. But most important of all, she was Hannah. She was herself as life and her own character and experiences had made her. She liked herself. And she was in love.

She was *happy*.

Guests began to arrive, and Constantine took her hand and set it on his sleeve. They strolled together about the ballroom, stopping briefly to talk to acquaintances as they went. They were both smiling.

"Have you noticed," Constantine asked, "that everyone who enters the ballroom looks at you twice, once with a simple appreciation for your beauty, and once with sudden, shocked recognition?"

"I think it is you they are looking at," she

said. "You look quite dazzling when you smile."

"You are happy about Warren Hall?" he asked.

"I am," she said. "You will have *all* your family close by, Constantine. Including Jonathan."

"Yes," he said. "And you, Hannah?"

She looked at him and her smile faded.

"Will you have *your* family close by?" he asked.

"I will invite Barbara and Mr. Newcombe," she said. "Perhaps they will be willing to travel again for my wedding."

"When you are not going to theirs?" he said. "Is that real friendship?"

Why was he talking about this now? The ballroom was filling. The air was growing warm. The level of conversation was rising. The orchestra members were tuning their instruments.

"Very well," she said, lifting both her chin and her fan and becoming for the moment the Duchess of Dunbarton. "I will invite my father and my sister and brother-in-law and my nephews and nieces. I will even invite the Reverend and Mrs. Leavensworth. *And* I will go to Barbara's wedding. We will *both* go. Are you satisfied?"

"I am," he said. "My love."

And very briefly and very scandalously, especially in light of an announcement that had not yet been made, he touched his lips to hers.

"You are going to have to marry me after that, sir," she said.

"Dash it all," he said, grinning, "and so I am."

"None of them will come," she warned him. "Except perhaps Barbara. Even she will probably not."

"The reaching out is everything, my love," he said. "It is all you can do. It is all any of us can ever do. Come and dance with me. And then I will with the greatest reluctance obey all the rules and dance with you only once more — after supper and the announcements. It is to be a waltz. I wrestled Stephen to the floor and held him there until he agreed that a waltz it would be."

She laughed.

"And if my card is full?" she asked.

"Then I will wrestle your waltz partner to the floor and hold him there until he remembers that he is wearing new dancing shoes and they are pinching and blistering his toes horribly," he said.

"Absurd," she said, still laughing.

Something else they had discussed both

yesterday and today was where they would live after their marriage. It had been an easier matter to settle.

At Ainsley Park, Constantine had already moved out of the house in order to accommodate more residents. The dower house had been perfectly satisfactory for his bachelor needs, but it would be less so for a wife and — it was to be hoped — a family. And if he spent less time there, he explained to Hannah, then some of the rooms at the dower house could be opened up too — perhaps for his manager and the instructors. All they themselves would need was one suite of rooms for their use when they went there for visits.

He would go a few times a year, of course. Those people were precious to him, and he dared believe that he was precious to them too.

At Copeland Hannah would be close to Land's End and the elderly people there of whom she was so fond. But Copeland itself would be their own private domain. And it was lovely indeed with its unspoiled park and house on a rise with breathtaking views in every direction. It would be a child's paradise in the years to come. It was close to London.

And London would, of course, be their

home during the spring. Next year he would have to take his place in the Upper House of Parliament. They would live at his house there even though it was not in the most fashionable part of town. They did not need anything ostentatious.

Copeland, then, was to be their primary home.

He was happy about that, Constantine thought as he danced and watched Hannah dance. He would be happy actually to live in a hovel with her — though perhaps it would be as well if no one ever put that theory to the test.

And then it was suppertime and Stephen announced to the gathered *ton* that his cousin, Constantine Huxtable, was to be honored by His Majesty the King with the title Earl of Ainsley before the Season ended. And that the Earl of Ainsley would take the Duchess of Dunbarton as his countess soon afterward in a private ceremony at Warren Hall.

How many weeks was it, Constantine wondered, since he had ridden in Hyde Park with Monty and Stephen and seen Hannah for the first time in two years — and looked upon her with disapproval? It was not very many, but it was hard to remember quite how she had looked to him then. It was strange how very different a person looked when one knew her inside as well as out.

He had been starting to think about marrying even then. Little had he realized, though, as he looked upon her in the park, that she was the one.

The *one.*

His only love.

The dancing was late resuming. Everyone wanted to congratulate them and wish them well. A large number of men swore they would wear black armbands for a whole year, starting tomorrow. Hannah tapped them all sharply on the sleeve with her fan.

And then it was time to waltz.

It was a dance Constantine had always enjoyed, provided he was allowed to choose his own partners. Fortunately, men had more control of such matters than women did. But Hannah did not look as if she was complaining when he led her onto the floor.

"Happy?" he asked her as he circled her waist with his right arm and took her right hand in his left.

"Oh, I am," she said with a sigh. "But I am not at all sure I am going to enjoy all the fuss of these wedding preparations. Perhaps we ought to have eloped."

"My cousins would never forgive us," he

said, grinning at her.

"I know," she said. "But I just want to be with *you*."

He had been trying valiantly to ignore similar feelings.

"You want to come tonight," he asked her, "after the ball?"

She gazed into his eyes for several moments before sighing again.

"No," she said at last. "I am no longer your lover, Constantine. I am your *betrothed.* There *is* a difference."

He was disappointed — and relieved. There *was* a difference.

"We will be good, then," he said, "and look forward to our wedding night."

"Yes," she agreed. "But it is not *just* that. I want . . . Oh, I do not know what I want. I want to be your *wife*."

He smiled at her.

"And I have just remembered something," she said, brightening visibly. "The duke taught me that I should never say *I want,* that it implies a lack in myself and leads to abjectness. I do not *want* to be your wife. I *will be* your wife, and I shall throw myself into preparations for my wedding with Margaret and the others so that the time may go faster. And oh, Constantine, it is wonderful indeed to have *family* to fuss over my wedding, even if part of me *would* prefer to elope."

The music began.

They waltzed beneath chandeliers bright with candlelight and among banks of flowers and ferns and about other dancers with their swirling satins and silks of many colors and their gleaming jewels, and they had eyes only for each other.

He had always felt that he lived on the edges of life, Constantine realized, watching everyone else living, sometimes helping them do it. He had been hurt so deeply by Jon's death because he had tried to live his brother's life and discovered at the end that it could not be done. Jon had had to do his own dying. Which was only right and proper, he knew now. Jon had lived his own life, and he had lived it richly and then died when his time came.

And now it was his, Constantine's, turn. Suddenly, and for the first time, he was at the center of his own life, living it and loving it.

Loving the woman who was at the center of it with him.

Loving Hannah.

She was smiling at him.

He twirled them about one corner of the ballroom and smiled back.

CHAPTER 24

The wedding of Hannah Reid, Duchess of Dunbarton, to Constantine Huxtable, Earl of Ainsley, was a small affair by *ton* standards. More surprising, to Hannah at least, it was a family affair, overrun by children, all of whom attended both the ceremony in the small chapel in the park of Warren Hall and the wedding breakfast at the house afterward.

Most surprisingly, it was not only Constantine's family that was in attendance. Her father came. So did Dawn and Colin, her sister and brother-in-law, and their five children — Louisa, aged ten, Mary, eight, Andrew, seven, Frederick, five, and Thomas, three. And Barbara came with her parents — the Reverend Newcombe was unable to get away so soon after the last time and before his own wedding and honeymoon.

Her father had scarcely changed, Hannah discovered when he arrived at Finchley Park the day before her wedding. The same could not be said for either Colin or Dawn. Both had expanded in girth and looked noticeably older. Colin had lost some of his hair and his youthful good looks. Dawn, in contrast, looked rosy-cheeked and placidly contented — though not at the moment of her arrival.

It had taken some courage for them to come, Hannah guessed.

She had decided ahead of time to behave as though there had been no estrangement, and they had made the same decision, it seemed. They hugged one another, greeted one another, and smiled. And they hid the embarrassment they must all be feeling by turning to the children, who were spilling out of another carriage.

She had two nieces and three nephews she knew virtually nothing about, Hannah thought as she gazed at each of them in turn as they made their curtsy or bow. She had never allowed Barbara to speak of her family.

Under slightly altered circumstances, Colin could now have been *her* husband for ten years or more. He looked like a stranger she had once met long ago.

"Do come inside," she said. "There are tea and cakes awaiting everyone."

"Aunt Hannah," Frederick said, slipping a hand into hers as she turned toward the house, "I have new *shoes* for the wedding. They are a size bigger than the last ones."

"And mine," Thomas said, trotting beside them as they entered the house.

"Then I am very glad I am having a wedding," Hannah said. "We all need a good reason to have new shoes from time to time."

Her heart constricted.

It was not until later that she had a chance to talk privately with her father. He was walking alone on the lawn beside the house after tea, when Hannah expected that he would be resting in his room as almost everyone else was.

She hesitated before going out to join him. But she had come this far toward reconciliation. Why stop now?

He looked up as she came to meet him and stopped walking. He clasped his hands behind his back.

"You are looking well, Hannah," he said.

"I am *feeling* wonderful," she said.

"And so you are to marry another aristocrat," he said. "But a younger man this time. Is this one someone who is likely to bring you at least *some* happiness?"

Had he misunderstood all these years?

"I love him," she said, "and he loves me. I expect a great deal of happiness from my marriage to Constantine. You will meet him later. He is coming for dinner. But, Papa, I knew a great deal of happiness in my first marriage. The duke was kind to me — more than kind. And I adored him in return."

"He was *old*," her father said. "He might have been *my* father. I have never forgiven myself for the part I played in causing you to act so impulsively as to marry him, Hannah. And I did nothing to stop you. I suppose at the time it seemed an easy answer to a nasty problem. Both my daughters loved the same man, and I wanted both to be happy. I thought *you* would more easily recover and find happiness with someone else since all the young men had an eye for you, and so I sided with Dawn. That was shortsighted of me, was it not? You married an old man you did not even know and went away and never came back and never wrote, and — Well. And I never had the courage to write either, did I?"

"Marrying the duke was the best thing I ever did," she said. "And if I judged correctly at tea, marrying Colin was the best thing *Dawn* ever did."

"They seem happy enough," he said. "And

my grandchildren are the light of my life. Perhaps —"

He stopped.

"Yes, perhaps," she agreed. "I am only thirty, Papa. And a child is all I need to complete my happiness."

"Thank you," he said awkwardly, "for inviting us to your wedding, Hannah."

"Constantine has no brothers or sisters," she said, "but he has cousins on both sides of his family. And they are all very close. More than that, they are affectionate and welcoming. They have opened their hearts and their lives to include me. You could see that at tea, could you not, with Elliott and Vanessa, the Duke and Duchess of More-land, and his mother and sisters? They have made me understand the importance of family. And Constantine persuaded me to reach out to my own again at last. I did not know if you would come. I believe I expected that you would not."

He sighed deeply and audibly.

"I wept when your letter came," he said. "There. I did not expect ever to admit *that* to a living soul. I felt — forgiven."

She stepped forward and set her forehead on his shoulder. His hands came to her waist and held her.

■ ■ ■ ■

Her chance with Dawn did not come until the following morning — her wedding day. She was in her dressing room, holding her head still while Adèle curled a stubborn tendril of hair over her right temple more to her satisfaction.

She was wearing pale pink, a color she would not have expected to choose for her wedding. But when she had been shopping for fabrics, she had fallen in love with this shade. She had a new straw bonnet to wear with it, trimmed with pink rosebuds and greenery and pink silk ribbons a shade darker than the dress.

The sky, she could see through the window, was a clear blue. There was not a cloud in sight.

And then everyone, on their way to church, came to see her first. Vanessa and Averil and Jessica, Elliott's sisters, exclaimed over her and smiled at her and declared they would not hug her and risk crushing either her dress or her hair. All agreed that Cecily, Elliott's youngest sister, who was in imminent expectation of a happy event, would be very vexed indeed to be missing all this excitement. Mrs. Leavensworth clasped her hands to her bosom and declared that she had not been happier in her life — though she supposed she would be happier yet in three weeks' time when it was Barbara's turn.

Barbara did not care whether she crushed anything or not. She hugged Hannah tightly and wordlessly for a whole minute. Then she stood back and looked her over.

"This is what I have hoped and hoped would happen, Hannah," she said. "I have even *prayed* about it. Laugh if you will. You have far too much love to give to squander it on mere flirtation. And Mr. Huxtable, or, rather, the Earl of Ainsley, *is* the right man. I thought so when we were at Copeland. I was almost sure when he scooped you up onto his horse in the park. And when I saw the two of you together at dinner last evening, well, there was no doubt left in my mind. And now that I have delivered that little sermon, I had better get off to church with Mama and Papa before the bride races us there." She laughed.

"Babs." Hannah hugged her again. "How would I have done without you all these years?"

"No better than I would have done without you, I suppose," Barbara said. "Oh, there you are, Dawn. Mama and I are on our way out and will leave you with more room."

And they were gone and only Dawn remained, standing uncertainly just inside the door.

"I am ready, Adèle," Hannah said. "I can put on my own bonnet before I leave."

Her maid slipped from the room.

"I don't know how you do it, Hannah," Dawn said, sounding almost aggrieved, "but you are more beautiful now than you were eleven years ago."

"I am in love," Hannah said, smiling, "and this is my wedding day. It is easy to be beautiful under such circumstances."

"It is not just that," Dawn said. "I used to think it was just your looks. But it was always what was inside you too. And now there is even more of that. The Earl of Ainsley is very handsome, is he not, though it is a pity about his nose. I should call him Constantine, I suppose, as he invited me to do last evening, but it seems presumptuous. You *have* done well for yourself, though it must have seemed that the old duke was going to live forever. That must have been a severe trial to you."

"I suppose the whole world believes that," Hannah said. "It is not the truth, but it does not matter if no one knows that but me —

and Constantine. And now I am about to marry a man I love with all my heart. If you ever look back and feel a twinge of guilt, Dawn, let it go. All things happen for a purpose — sometimes a larger purpose than we can possibly see at the time. What happened led me to the duke and ten years of surprising happiness. And marrying the duke led me by slow degrees to today."

"I don't feel *guilt*," Dawn said. "You could have had *anyone* if you had set your mind to it. You chose Colin, and he was dazzled for a while as all men are when they see you. But he really loved *me*, and I loved *him*. We have a good marriage, and we have good, healthy children — which is more than *you* have. I do not feel *guilt*."

Hannah smiled.

"I am glad you are happy," she said, taking a step closer to her sister. "And your children really are a delight, Dawn. I look forward to getting better acquainted with them as time goes on. I'll be in Markle for Barbara's wedding. We will be staying with Papa."

"Barbara *will* be grand," Dawn said, "having an earl and countess on her guest list. No one will talk of anything else for a month or more."

Hannah took another step forward and

hugged her sister. It was a reconciliation of sorts, she thought as Dawn's arms came about her. They would probably never be as close as sisters ought to be. Perhaps Dawn would always resent her even though she had got Colin, of whom she seemed genuinely fond. And she had their five children, who really were good-natured and prettily behaved.

But at least now they had been restored to each other. At least now they could begin to build a new relationship with each other. There was the whole of the future ahead of them. There was always hope.

"I had better go," Dawn said. "Colin and the children will be waiting for me."

Hannah watched her go before closing the dressing room door. There was one more thing she needed to do before putting on her bonnet and going downstairs to join her father.

She reached down one side of her portmanteau and drew out a small square box. She opened it and set it on the dressing table while she looked down at her wedding ring and then slid it slowly off her finger. She held it for a moment and raised it to her lips.

"Good-bye, my dearest duke," she whispered. "You would be happy for me today, would you not? You predicted it would happen. And you would be a little sad too, perhaps? *I* am happy. And a little sad. But you are with your love, and I will be with mine. And always a little part of us will belong to each other."

She set the ring down carefully inside the box, hesitated a moment, and then closed the lid resolutely and set the box back in the portmanteau.

She reached for her bonnet.

And suddenly there was such a welling of excitement within her that her fingers all felt like thumbs as she tied the ribbons into a bow beneath her right ear.

The chapel was crowded to capacity, as Constantine had known it would be even though there were very few guests apart from family. There was the slight buzz of hushed conversation behind him and the fidgetings and louder, higher-pitched voices of all the children.

So many of them. The family was growing. And it had not stopped yet. Katherine and Monty were in the process of doubling the size of their family. Cecily was expecting to give birth any day now.

And it was not just family. Phillip Grainger's wife was large with child and had two others in the pew beside her. Phillip, one of Constantine's oldest friends, was his best man.

It all felt very comforting, somehow. Family. And this morning he was to become a married man himself. A family man. Oh, he *hoped* he was to be a family man.

But he was not even married yet.

Would Hannah be *late?* It would be strange if she were not.

There were five interminable minutes to wait even before she was late. What had he said about cultivating patience?

He wished he had eaten some breakfast.

He was thankful he had not.

And he was, dash it all, getting *nervous.*

What if she was having second thoughts?

What if an old duke had popped up out of a deep chair somewhere in Finchley and eloped with her?

And then there was the sound of carriage wheels — after all of the guests had surely arrived. It was only *three minutes* to eleven.

The carriage stopped. *Of course.* There was nowhere else to go along this trail except the chapel.

There was a greater hush within. Everyone had heard what he had heard.

And then the vicar appeared in the doorway and instructed the congregation to stand. And he walked down the aisle toward the altar and left the doorway clear for Delmont, Hannah's father, and for Hannah herself.

A vision of all that was beautiful in soft pink.

His bride.

Oh, Lord. His *bride.*

He took half a step toward her and stopped. He was supposed to stay where he was. *She* was supposed to come to *him.*

And she did so until she stood beside him, her arm still drawn through her father's though she was smiling at *him* through the froth of a pink veil that was draped over the brim of her straw bonnet.

He smiled back at her.

And why they had spent so much time discussing where they would marry and how many people they wanted as their guests he really did not know. It did not *matter* where they were. And for the moment it did not matter who was there to witness them exchanging vows that would bind them in law and in love for the rest of their days.

It did not matter.

"I do," he said when the vicar had asked him what he was prepared to do in order to make Hannah his wife forever.

"I do," she said in return.

And then he was reciting vows, prompted by the vicar, and she was reciting them in her turn. And Phillip was handing him the shiny gold band of her wedding ring and he was slipping it onto her bare ring finger. And suddenly —

Ah, suddenly it was all over, the anticipation and the excitement, the baseless fears.

They were man and wife.

And what God had joined together, no power on earth could put asunder.

"Hannah." He lifted the veil back from her face and gazed into her eyes.

They gazed back into his own, wide and guileless and trusting.

His *wife.*

And suddenly he was aware of shufflings and murmurings, a child's piping voice, a single cough. And he was aware again of where they were and who was here with them. And he was glad that family and friends were here to celebrate with them.

He felt a warm rush of pure happiness.

Hannah — his wife — smiled at him, and when he went to smile back, he realized that he was already doing it.

There were no carriages outside the chapel. They would all walk back to Warren Hall, the bride and groom leading the way.

But not immediately.

When they had stepped outside the church, Hannah looked at her new husband, her hand slipping from his arm so that she could clasp his hand instead.

"Yes," she said softly as if he had said something.

Her husband. Oh, he was her *husband.*

And they turned together, as if they had discussed it beforehand, and made their way into the churchyard. They stopped at the foot of one small and simple mound of grass. A headstone bore the five-line inscription, *Jonathan Huxtable, Earl of Merton, Died November 8, 1812, Aged Sixteen Years, Rest in Peace.*

They stood side by side, looking down at it, their hands clasped tightly.

"Jonathan," Hannah said softly, "thank you for living a life so rich with love. Thank you for living on in Constantine's heart and in your dream at Ainsley Park."

Constantine's clasp on her hand was almost painful.

"Jon," he said, his voice a whisper of sound, "you would be happy today. But you were *always* happy. Go in peace now, brother. I have kept you too long. I always was selfish. Go in peace."

A tear dripped from Hannah's chin to the

neckline of her wedding dress. She dried her eyes with the gloved fingers of her free hand.

"I love you, Hannah," Constantine said almost as softly.

"I love you too," she said.

And they turned toward their wedding guests, who were crowded about the path outside the chapel doors, talking and laughing. Children darted about, their voices raised in high-pitched chatter.

Constantine laced his fingers with Hannah's and they walked toward their family and friends, smiling with exuberant joy.

And the air rained rose petals.

EPILOGUE

It was a perfect autumn day. Not perfect enough for the baby's nurse, perhaps. But then her anxieties would have denied him any outing at all until he had attained at least his first birthday. She would have made a hothouse plant of him if she had her way — which she had on all sorts of other issues since she had experience at her job and clearly loved the baby with all her grandmotherly heart.

Hannah had found her when her former "family" had outgrown its need for her and she had applied for a position at Land's End, though she had admitted during an interview that she dealt better with infants than with the elderly. Beggars could not be choosers, however.

The day really was perfect. The heat of summer had gone, but the chill of winter had not yet arrived. There was not a sign of a rain cloud, or any other cloud for that matter. And the wind had taken a holiday. So had yesterday's light breeze. The sky was a riot of color. Not the sky itself, of course, which was a uniform blue, but the tree branches against it. Reds mingled with yellows and oranges and browns of all shades, as well as a few hardy greens. And very few leaves had yet fallen to the ground.

It would have been a lovely day for a ride — for a gallop across country and yet another challenge to a race. Hannah still held out hope of beating Constantine one of these days. Not that she had done much riding for several months, of course, even at a sedate walk. He would not have allowed it even if she had been inclined to take a risk. She had *not* been so inclined.

They rode sedately in the carriage — the *closed* carriage. Nurse might be overridden, but she could not be entirely defied. She had experience and they did not.

It was a journey they usually made with the dogs. A sizable and cozy corner of the stable block had been given over to dogs not long after their wedding when Constantine had the idea that the elderly at Land's End needed more stimulus than just their own company and that of a few human visitors. And sure enough, the visits of the dogs were the highlight of their days. Sometimes

Hannah and Constantine took them. More often, Cyril Williams did. He was a ten-year-old who had picked Constantine's pocket in London when they were there briefly after Barbara's wedding to the Reverend New-combe, a ragged, shivering bundle of filth and rags who had lost his mother, his last remaining relative, a few months before and had descended from a life of desperation to one of animal survival.

Cyril and dogs had been made for one another. He fed them and groomed them, exercised and trained them, and loved them — and sometimes sneaked them into his room in the house while all the servants and his master and mistress became inexplicably blind and deaf. They doted upon him and followed him like shadows. They were gentle with him and for him and moped about the stables whenever he was away — under protest — at the village school.

Today it was not the dogs that were being taken to cheer the elderly.

Today it was four-month-old Matthew Huxtable, who in his parents' admittedly biased estimation was the most beautiful child in the world. He had inherited his father's dark hair and skin tone and his mother's blue eyes and bright smile.

And today the elderly residents of Land's

End were indeed marvelously entertained as Matthew was placed in their arms one at a time by his papa and cooed up at them and occasionally, with some coaxing from his father's finger wiggling over his stomach, favored them with a toothless smile.

Hannah meanwhile was talking to those few who could not hold the baby or even talk or respond to what went on about them. She talked to them anyway, telling them about the three weeks her two nieces and one of her nephews had spent at Copeland during the summer after their mother returned home to Lincolnshire with the youngest two — she had come to give Hannah some support and help with her confinement — and about Lord and Lady Montford's daughter, whom they hoped to see no later than Christmas, before her first birthday anyway, and about the new litter of puppies, for whom Cyril was attempting to find homes.

And then the visit was over, and Hannah settled herself beside Constantine in the carriage and watched him as he held Matthew on his lap facing him, both hands behind the baby's head, and made faces at him and spoke nonsense to him.

The baby's eyelids drooped. He was not in the mood to be amused.

Whoever would have expected, Hannah thought, that Constantine Huxtable of all men would turn into such a tender, doting father?

The devil, tamed.

Except that he had never been a devil. Not even close.

He had been a man full of secrets. A man full of love.

She rested her cheek against his shoulder, and he turned his head to look down at her.

"I have just been trying to picture the Duchess of Dunbarton in my mind," he said. "But the face of Hannah keeps getting in the way."

"The duchess served me well," she said.

"I am glad," he said, "you do not need her any longer."

She sighed with contentment.

"I am glad too," she said. "Matthew is sleeping. Let me hold him."

He turned and set the baby in her arms without waking him, and stayed turned to gaze first at his son, and then at his wife.

"Have I told you that I love you?" he asked.

"Yes," she said.

He smoothed one gentle hand over the baby's head and sat back in his seat.

"You can tell me again, though," she said.

"In fact, I absolutely insist that you do."
He laughed softly.

ABOUT THE AUTHOR

Mary Balogh is the *New York Times* best-selling author of the acclaimed Slightly series and Simply quartet of novels set at Miss Martin's School for Girls, as well as many other beloved novels. She is also the author of *First Comes Marriage, Then Comes Seduction, At Last Comes Love,* and *Seducing an Angel,* all featuring the Huxtable family. A former teacher, she grew up in Wales and now lives in Canada. To learn more, visit the author's website at www.Mary Balogh.com.